Part I

Some days went by, Stanley returned to the ring. He lost his second pro fight and complained his managers Larry and Sammy had put him in with a fighter who had too much experience again, to which they both replied it was Stanley's fault because he wasn't using his left hook enough, which is a punch he didn't need much as an amateur and had neglected to work on. He trained more with it, developed it, and after three months of that had his third pro fight, which he won on points.

They shifted him to five round fights and he lost again. That meant he had a despicable pro record of 1 and 3.

Stanley went on a drinking binge and didn't return to the gym for a half a year. He had dated Rosy more than he fought in the ring, and she told him to quit, that he could get a job in another field. But boxing was his life.

He had sex with her, he proposed to her, he promised to have one more fight and if he lost, he'd find other work.

Fortunately he won, using his left hook to some advantage, and Rosy agreed to marry – only if he gave boxing up "sooner than later."

Okay, he thought, because if a child came, he'd be hard-pressed to provide, right then.

Yet Stanley kept fighting. He won again. He reclaimed a little of the admiration that had flowed to him as an amateur around the gym. Even a few kind words were written in the newspaper about him.

Then disaster struck, in the form of a powerful head butt and a knock out, after a follow up punch, and… Rosy refused to marry if he didn't quit. Three wins and four losses was not terrific, by anyone's calculation, even his.

So Stanley told himself he'd try it a couple of times more, and give up. The head butt had stunned him – it was directly to his mouth – and he retained a vague memory of sore teeth. Unfortunately, as can happen, the ref was behind him at that precise moment and didn't spot it. Perhaps his opponent timed it that way – some fighters do. A follow-up punch floored Stanley, and being stunned, he failed to respond clearly to the ref's question, as he lay on his back, and the fight was called. Stanley got on his feet to protest, and his trainer Larry entered the ring complaining, but the ref just shook his head and the opponent jumped up and down with glee. Some people cheered, and a few booed, but since the ref hadn't seen it, it didn't matter.

That wasn't the glory of life Stanley had hoped for, not in the least. It was the opposite.

Well, you're supposed to shrug those misfortunes off, and keep going. He tried, losing a close one, but a certain guardedness had entered his style, even during sparring. It was subconscious guardedness.

Additionally, Stanley "fell back" after his eighth professional fight, because even prior to that head butt he'd hurt his hands in the gym, sparring against Lonnie. Lonnie, the rugged, tough middleweight who always gave him a good work-out, was moving in close, and Stanley brought up his right, directly to his chin. It had the effect of halting Lonnie's progress, but bringing incredible pain to Stanley's fist, partly due to the fact that the gloves Stanley wore were old, and the padding gave weak protection, both to Lonnie *and* to Stanley. Right afterwards he felt distress in his fist and declined to do any work on the heavy bag.

That night, Stanley soaked his hands in warm Epsom salts, but the next day they were swollen and bruised. A few days of rest saw the swelling diminish and the pain subside, but when he returned to the gym it was obvious a difficulty still existed. His punches were less powerful, and his right wrist hurt. He didn't tell Larry or Sammy, for some reason. Shyness about it, afraid they would accuse him of being at fault, or something, kept him quiet.

Finally, as a new bout was arranged, another five rounder, Larry complained Stanley was holding back with his uppercuts. Stanley admitted it didn't feel like it should. Larry examined his hand as best he knew, and since it wasn't painful, told

Stanley not to "worry about it," to go ahead and "throw" it like before. But he didn't.

Such occurrences were not uncommon in boxing, he told him. An injury that heals

can still negatively affect a fighter's performance. "Psychological," he told him. "You

just have to get past it." But then, he'd experienced that head butt. In spite of it he had

another fight, and fortunately his good reliable jab worked so effectively that by the fifth

round Stanley was sure he was winning, and the crowd yelled his name and cheered him

onward. Many boxers are able to "slip" jabs, or quickly block them, so a jab is only

infrequently of "telling" influence. But this opponent had small defense against

Stanley's repeated lefts to the face and chin, relying instead on a strong right hand

which, while landing now and again, didn't often land in the proper area (of Stanley's

left side). Stanley blocked and moved, so the opponent's powerful right missed often

enough to keep the point tally in Stanley's favor.

Yet he didn't throw his own right often, and was wary of getting in too close, his

subconscious sending a warning, a "fear," of another head butt like the one that had

knocked him half-senseless, months earlier. Nevertheless thanks to his jabbing, his hand

was raised in victory by the referee, after the judges' votes were counted, and Stanley

felt that incomparable joyousness boxers know when winning.

The old adage he had heard at the gym was proved correct: "you can sometimes win with only your jab."

A certain knuckle in his right hand continued to bother him, and Stanley virtually gave up throwing right uppercuts, even in the gym. The problem with that – in addition to diminishing his over-all punching effectiveness – was a subtle lessening in Stanley's workouts. He didn't notice it at first but gradually his weight increased, and making Junior Middleweight was so difficult, he moved up in weight for his next two – and last – fights, without knowing why that extra weight had appeared, seemingly out of nowhere. It was many years later when he finally understood.

That second to last fight was rough. The middleweight was experienced, although once again Stanley's jab kept him in the contest until he tired by the third round. Sammy in his corner told him to use his uppercut, but, without exactly knowing why, Stanley failed to keep "turning it under," as Sammy advised, and his opponent, a mean-looking Chicano, pressed forward repeatedly, until a bad blow to Stanley's eye stunned him. He believed it was a head butt, and yet the referee apparently didn't care and a solid left to Stanley's stomach dropped him to his knees.

He had trouble seeing, during the 8-count, and when the fight resumed the Mexican swarmed over him "like white on rice," as they said.

It didn't last long, and the ref stepped in to stop it.

5

Stanley protested, as did Sammy, but naturally to no avail. The opponent approached and said ungraciously "I thought you were supposed to be good, man," and walked away. This insult the referee noticed, and, following the winner to his corner, yelled "Raul! What's that? You're better than that." Raul ignored him.

Stanley heard that, and while the comment felt out of place for a referee, Stanley believed it was an appropriate reprimand. Not that it helped alter the result.

It wasn't such a bad fight, in some respects. He made enough money to keep his car running to take Rosy out – as long as that lasted – and eat well enough, and drive to the beach to run occasionally. The beautiful beach. The idea of living there appealed to Stanley, except it would make Main Street Gym too far away. Not to mention the Olympic Auditorium downtown.

Stanley had strongly resisted any attempt to have him fight in other venues because of the unfortunate experience of his first pro bout when he'd been cheated by the out-of-town promoters. He'd felt more secure climbing into the ring at the Olympic. Who knew if he was right, though? Tricks can be played anywhere, and he wasn't adept at sussing them out. Never had been.

But during his short career, in the late 1970s, Stanley felt "heroic." Each time he walked down that seemingly endless aisle to the bright ring, and each time he made his way up the aisle for the after-fight return, he felt like he was doing heroic things.

But later, walking *other* boxers down to the ring and back up those long steps, Stanley sensed a loss he was ashamed of. A loss that penetrated his whole being, darkened his life, masked even his natural joyfulness and determination.

When his father died in 1980, Stanley didn't feel much pain. They'd not been very close. His mother didn't come to the funeral. She hadn't cared to, since she'd moved and remarried. Stanley and she didn't get along, anyway, so her absence meant little to him.

But before that, in the very late seventies, training off-and-on, not being quite able to get into proper shape (and feeling stressed due to that fact), was Stanley's state for long months. His trainers were disgusted and he couldn't provide any good explanation. He knew he had to fight again, if merely for the money, but frankly, Stanley felt without "drive" (but unconscious of the cause).

Later, many years later, he figured it out, but not then. The lack of his old punching power, the listless "road work," the irregular training schedule – all due to the head butt he'd received, and the injury to his hand. The mind is a funny thing. At the time he agonized, puzzled over his lack of ability to get in fighting shape. Finally, his trainers told him to either fight or quit.

"Forget it," they both advised. "If you can't get ready, just do the best you can. Let's find a bum to match you with." They actually used that word, "bum."

And they did. Stanley panted his way to victory.

Rosy slowly took herself out of the picture, since he still steadfastly insisted he wanted to fight. *He just didn't understand why he couldn't.*

When the money ran out he took another gas station job. What else could he do?

As he looked back over those years, the struggle, the distress, he wished a doctor – a psychologist – had been recommended. But none was. Maybe a little therapy would have freed him from his subconscious fear of head butts, of hand pain. But...that was all past. He hadn't even thought of clinical therapy himself, so how could he blame others for not advising it? The closest he came to it was to acknowledge he truly wanted to fight again but *somehow* was unable to get into condition to do it properly.

After months, he let Sammy set up a new bout, but the week before it was scheduled to take place Stanley told him he had hurt his foot, running, and wanted out. He *had* hurt his foot, that was true, but he exaggerated the extent of it. He limped in front of Sammy, he winced, he complained. The fight was cancelled. Well, not exactly. *Stanley* was out of it, at any rate, but the opponent fought a replacement, who lost. He watched it on TV, drinking beer and feeling sorry for himself.

The job at the gas station was boring, incredibly boring. In years past at such work he'd enjoyed the interchange with people; it was interesting. But since having a pro career, enjoying the yells from the crowd – even when losing – and the pats on the back at the gym, he just lost interest in what customers had to say. And sure there were a few women who drove in but most of them had rings on their fingers, or were so young he was embarrassed to say anything remotely flirtatious.

Rosy continued to be disenchanted. They spoke by phone sometimes, and she was nice about it, but he grew disgusted at her harping against boxing, her gentle nagging about finding more lucrative employment.

He knew women thought of their future, their comfort, etc., more than men did, generally, but regardless, he sensed the division between them had greatly expanded – irrevocably so.

While he was still fighting, the ring doctor had told Stanley to "throw more punches." The doctor had been around the sport a long time, most often at ringside, and knew what he was talking about. He'd given Stanley that simple advice even while he was an amateur. But Stanley could just never follow it. Why not, was a question he pondered, and one day – after his last fight was years in the past – Stanley guessed at the answer: that he had a fear of actually killing a fighter. It seemed paradoxical because Stanley had often in his early career, feared *he* would die in there. But still, he also feared for his opponent, didn't want to beat him up so much as to risk killing him.

So Stanley at last grasped the source of *that* reluctance: having fired at the enemy in Vietnam, and wondered if he'd killed anyone. From the seaplane it was impossible to determine.

Later when he'd turned in his mind against the war, he stressed out regarding that possibility.

He wasn't sure how others who had served in Vietnam felt, or dealt with it, especially the ones on the ground who *knew* they'd killed. Hopefully they could understand they were just doing what was demanded at the time, what was done in service to the USA.

But, haunted by his dread he'd killed in a war he later thought was unnecessary, Stanley internally shied away from such an event in the ring. This too, as in his subconscious shyness about getting butted again, and believing his hands were hurt when they *weren't*, anymore, was an issue that called for therapy – psychological work – which Stanley hadn't recognized. But time heals, to some extent, and he was able to sort it out, only partly, until in his fifties he was led to Primal Therapy, a technique a friend recommended.

But until then he continued to sort it out as his own. He still remembered that head butt to the teeth, and the quick follow-up left hook that dropped him. That seemed in a strange way, the end of his career as a boxer. If it hadn't been for that sharp left *after* the butt, Stanley would have been more inclined to believe, to accept, it as an accident. But he knew fighters and fighting. When you plan a strategy, you tend to complete it more rapidly. Had that fighter been as shocked by the head butt as Stanley, he'd have paused, or moved away in some fashion, instead of proceeding as though the butt was part of his plan.

Some fighters are dirty. It's always been like that. They want to win at all cost. But the sore hands – well, not sore anymore, just a repressed vague memory somewhere in Stanley's mind – had reduced his punching enough to permit the man access inside, close enough to butt him like that. Stanley, usually taller than those he faced, had always found it easy to keep an opponent at a distance, usually with his strong jab. But not so after the session with the old lumpy gloves had made his hands sore. Even after that, in the shower, he had difficulty turning the faucet on. *That* he recalled clearly, but thought nothing of, as time went by. Yet in the recesses of his brain it lurked, it caused him to hold back. This too Stanley realized many years later.

Reflection is a wonderful thing, if it doesn't overwhelm one's life. It can teach, can guide, can provide wisdom. Not that finally learning why he'd held back helped Stanley any, really. He wasn't fighting anymore – it was "yesterday's news."

Certainly he kept his faith the whole time, over the years, and would not relinquish the belief God had some "plan" for him, a plan that didn't appear to include further boxing glory. It saddened him too, but he strove to deal with it, to keep going forward somehow.

Rosy of course had kept singing, and eventually married a drummer, as good-looking female pop artists will. Stanley felt that, too, was acceptable, since he wasn't very forceful regarding sex, and found himself willing to forego Rosy's companionship – mainly because he in fact didn't feel a great deal of pleasure, due to the unfortunate damage to his groin area (at the age of 12).

An older bully had kicked Stanley repeatedly between the legs, smashing and cutting his penis. The doctor who stitched him up said all would be fine, and functioning – which was true to a degree – "but for a little nerve damage."

But the nerve damage interfered with Stanley's sensitivity in that important area. He judged he felt only a half portion of what uninjured men felt, in regard to sexual enjoyment. And so, it was partial, like a finger cut accidentally by a knife, which after healing has some numbness.

Anyway, Stanley had learned to deal with the condition, and while that older boy – teenager – who had hurt him went free with a police reprimand, he'd later suffered a close call in a motorcycle accident which left the older boy mentally deficient. Stanley wondered if God had caused this as a form of punishment, as the older boy was unable to continue in school after that accident.

But neither Stanley, nor anyone he asked, could give a definite answer to the question of whether God brings punishment on transgressions in this life on Earth.

Surely He does in the Biblical record, but is it still the case? It would seem for some transgressors that judgment is not forthcoming – people appear to commit crimes against others and yet escape punishment. But Stanley gave up on that speculation. He let go the grudge and carried on, seeking to live as Christians ought, with forgiveness in his heart.

Yet he couldn't help wondering, did that attack lead him into the ring, and fighting, or was it unconnected? Probably it did have something to do with his willingness to strike another, albeit under such controlled circumstances as the ring.

Doctors were unable to repair (short of surgery) what damage had been sustained; so Stanley lived with a diminished sexual life. No doubt Rosy had wondered at his understated performances, and, slightly embarrassed, Stanley never told her the reason. He never told anyone except his friend George.

Now the goal to be Jr. Middleweight State Champion, as his stable-made Lonnie had been the Middleweight State Champion, was blown away like a dust cloud in the Mojave Desert.

Perhaps it was too much to reach for anyway, even with what skill Stanley possessed. Yet...in his heart he'd believed there was a substantial, actual chance. Oh well, he told himself, he'd made an effort. Why he couldn't get back into shape and reach for his dream was a mysterious problem Stanley fought at the time but couldn't overcome. It was little comfort to know in his heart that if God had so planned, the goal would have been attained.

He had faith enough to know we couldn't do things only on our own power, and God leads us if we open ourselves to His leading, a process Stanley willed himself to do, as much as a person can. After that, it's God's will to bring about the results, not ours.

Nothing was foreseeable in those many years following his last bout. He'd continued a futile effort to reach proper conditioning, to allow himself to climb through the ropes in an arena, but no, even when Larry and Sammy had arranged for one more bout, Stanley failed miserably to attend – he called and pulled out, citing a stomach ailment. And as before, the ailment was partly true, his stomach had been churning as the day (night) approached, but not with the pain he claimed.

The following day, he was shuddering to think he had been cowardly. But always Stanley knew it was more than that, and at last confessed such to Larry, who commiserated, and Sammy, who just shook his head in disgust, and even Duke, the old, wise trainer, said he'd "seen this before" and not to fret: "Some jus' can't cope with the pressure, is all. I was like that myself – jus' a 'ham-and-egger' whenever I got to the ring. Was better in the gym. There's no pressure in the gym," he'd chuckled, patting Stanley on the back. But Duke was only being nice, Stanley knew.

Of course it was partly true, except there *was* even pressure in the gym, sparring, though much less. But such pressure was not what Stanley felt! He felt a decided antipathy, a strange reluctance, which barred him from continuing even as his will urged him forward.

So one particular day many years after, he pondered things, as usual, alone in his apartment. He drank beer, he had some ice cream. Not much – Stanley didn't want to get fat – he was well aware of how it might creep up on ex-sports figures. Yet he liked beer, and ice cream.

He liked music, too, and played a Van Morrison CD. One of his favorites was "Brand New Day."

This day was gloomy, however, outside (and inside)…

Stanley was not working anymore. He had retired as a boxing trainer, gym assistant, co-manager of a handful of mediocre fighters, and actor.

It was funny when you thought about it: he had been a better fighter than these fellows, in general, but his ring record was worse than theirs.

Nearing seventy now, having tried various places, he was in the San Fernando Valley. He had lost some teeth, he felt tired during the day, his back wasn't so good, and his feet had odd callouses on then. Not big, not sizable, but just enough to slow his walking up a little.

He was on Facebook. He shared old photos with other old boxers.

His mind was good, though. He hadn't fought long enough to suffer ill-effects of hard punches, like a few of the boxers he'd known (and admired) from the early days.

He used email sparingly, preferring the phone like others of his generation.

A couple of his friends had died. Not many. Well, the older ones of course – those who had been retired when he started out.

He thought of Howie once in awhile. Howie had run the gym and been murdered in 1977 – before he could see Stanley turn pro. Just as well, since he'd not lived up to his potential. Howie's own fighters had gone on to great pugilistic glory. But maybe he *could* see them win, after he was dead. And Stanley's career, too. Stanley had no idea what Howie's soul had encountered after 1977. Nor did he know who had killed him, or why. Maybe some powerful criminals in the background had arranged it, to take over those fighters. Howie'd been a real tough guy, and wouldn't have agreed to any big shots owning him or his fighters. So…?

He was more of a recluse and loner in his older age. He still listened to Linda Ronstadt, but she had grown away from her folk-pop music foundations and developed into a style of singing older "standards" and Mexican songs. Stanley spoke little Spanish and had never liked the Sinatra music, so he just replayed "Heat Wave" and "Blue Bayou," etc., and a few of her 1980s songs, before her big shift had taken place.

He continued to try to stay in fair shape by working out at a nearby gym, punching bags and shadow boxing. Sit-ups were hard for him, and running had become walking.

In spite of acting in a few films, and a "Western" series, he never felt compelled to pursue that vocation strenuously. But the residuals, and Social Security, were a blessing. He'd never made much money training fighters, although that was his favorite occupation after his pro career.

When the big, strange adventure happened, he was sometimes hanging out at Cherry's and, more frequently, the local coffee shop within walking distance.

He'd call a friend, or a friend would call him, and they'd meet for breakfast. Sometimes he'd go to a movie. Mostly he watched DVDs he'd order, used, from Amazon. They didn't cost much and Stanley could re-watch them at leisure.

Sometimes he'd sit at the gym after his workout, thinking of the old Main Street Gym, the rings, the bags, rope-jumping, glad to see in his mind the familiar activity, scrutinizing the past without being scrutinized himself. But before too long the old pain of lost dreams, of lost pursuits, touched him, as it were – upon the shoulder, with repeated tapping, a significant silent signal disrupting the pleasure of his relaxation, and

Stanley was forced to find his way to the outside, to the street, bag in hand, casting aside memories as best he could.

The adventure took him by surprise, and throughout its mad danger, its twisting advance into dark events, its seeming hopeless and fateful conclusion, he never lost sight of spiritual assistance, invisible as it was.

So that day he'd sat in his apartment, reflecting, since precipitously a sore knee had kept him from the gym. He dozed once or twice. Meanwhile, he noticed an uncharacteristic rainfall. The next a.m. the alley outside his apartment window was wet, and, looking, he saw a woman walk rapidly, without any apparent concern she might slip and fall.

A loud shout, loud enough to overcome the sounds of traffic on the street, and Stanley's closed window, penetrated unpleasantly to his ears.

"Bitch! I'll make you pay, you bitch!"

Stanley noticed too the woman increased her pace, not quite running, but nearly so. She didn't glance behind her toward the sound of the holler, but rather stiffened her neck against it.

Stanley opened his window and looked down the alley, but he saw no one else. When he turned his head to see the woman, she was just disappearing at the end of the alley, to the left, onto the sidewalk of the street.

He heard nothing more, aside from traffic, and within five minutes he was hurriedly dressed and down the stairs to the alley, but still saw nothing. He didn't want to be killed, which he construed as a possibility if the altercation, whatever it was, had evil qualities – which from the sound of the voice hollering, it well might.

In addition, being a normal male mentally and emotionally (if not altogether physically) Stanley had noticed from what he saw of her, a basic attractiveness that compounded his interest.

He was smart enough to know that in this day and age of drugs and gang violence, forcing yourself into an unfamiliar situation such as he'd witnessed might be risky.

He only looked up the alley toward where the voice had come and wandered out to the street where the girl, the woman, had gone.

Not seeing her, he proceeded to the coffee shop three blocks away for breakfast. He soon forgot about the incident and indulged in fried eggs, potatoes, and sourdough toast, his usual.

One week later the second stage of the adventure began, when Stanley saw what he thought was the same woman, in the parking lot of the supermarket a mile from his apartment. She entered the store and he followed her. On impulse he spoke to her in an aisle. Maybe the Spirit of God told him to do it, although he couldn't be sure.

"Excuse me. Did I see you running down the alley a week ago, running from someone?"

She jerked her head up and stared at him in surprise, if not in utter shock.

"Sorry to bother you, miss, but do you need my help?"

He smiled, hoping she'd take him for a nice person. Her face was immobile, but still looked surprised. What she replied was very much not what he expected.

"You did, and I do."

If this woman's words weren't enough to bring his blood up, the little tremble he saw in her body most assuredly spurred him to a chivalry, of an honorable call to aid. Stanley dared to lay a hand on her arm, and nod his head, and say, "Tell me what you'd like me to do, miss."

"I don't hope – I don't – think – there's anything you can do."

"Must be. Tell me what's wrong."

"All right. What's your name?"

"Stanley. Stanley Larson."

"I'm Karen, but – you saw me from your window, or what?"

"Yes. I live right there above the alley."

"Oh. It's a pretty long story," she laughed for the first time. By now Stanley had released her arm, she was more composed. Her eyes shifted around the store and returned to his face. He said:

"Look, can you check out now? And we'll sit outside – you can tell me what's wrong. Okay?"

"Why not? I'll just grab some more things."

That's how it was. Stanley bought a few items, keeping his eye on her, and they went to the cashier, paid, took bags outside, and sat in the front where a number of chairs and tables were. Only a couple of other people were there, drinking cold drinks, looking out at the parking lot.

But Stanley didn't look out, he looked at her. She was pretty but not beautiful. She had a large nose and wide mouth, blue eyes that due to being full of anguish seemed a shade darker than they normally appeared. Her hair was dark but not quite black. Her tiny hands were innocent and childlike, even when clasped one inside the other, tightly.

"Is it that man? The one who –?"

"Yes," she said. "But not only him. A group, a gang if you will."

"Bad?"

"Very. But I can't – I can't go to the police. I can't do –"

"Why not?" Stanley interrupted.

"I was told even the police are afraid, or, most likely, bribed."

"Aww, come on. That's just in the movies."

"Could be," she affirmed. "But it's what I was told."

"By who? Really, I can't help you if you won't tell me about it."

"Okay," she sighed and smiled, briefly. Her teeth were white, her lips curved up, and Stanley felt warmed toward her.

"It's my brother. He's in with them, this gang, on a...a..." she didn't finish her statement, only looked down at her taut hands.

"Is it a crime?" Stanley was getting the idea, he supposed, and didn't like it.

She nodded.

"You want him to refuse to go along with it, and...?"

"He can't refuse. That's the thing. He's, you know, being blackmailed."

"Okay," Stanley sighed. "What can I do?"

"You can get him away from them."

"What? He would go?"

"He would if – look. That about blackmail is true, and I'm the reason for it. I did a bad thing, he doesn't want it exposed, he wants me to, you know, have a good life and all that. Not end up in prison."

"Wow. Prison? What for?"

"Selling drugs. Heroin."

"Oh," was all he could say.

So they became friends that day, yet not without concern, on Stanley's part, for the safety of them both. They ate dinner at Hamburger Hamlet in Van Nuys, and parted company. She drove her car – a Prius – away without looking at him again after they shook hands goodbye.

He had her phone number and more information. She'd been an addict but escaped the addiction. Selling drugs had been a way to make extra money when she was a user, and she'd continued doing that later. Stanley made sure Karen saw him shaking his head in disapproval as she told the story.

She said her brother was mixed up in the heroin traffic, and yet did so against his will. She wanted to get them out of it.

"You're much more well-served by going to the police, Karen. By ceasing this selling of drugs, and – whatever it's called   informing on those people. Let the cops assure your brother if he's –"

"No! They'll kill him. You just wouldn't suggest the cops if you knew how bad these people were."

Stanley laughed. "Getting the cops involved is what you do in such a situation. What would you do, take your brother away at gunpoint?"

"No, but, you know, I could say you were a buyer and then you could ask that someone could go with you to pick up the cash – him – and then you guys would get away *clean*. See?"

"What do you do then?"

"Me? I can leave after you do. They trust me."

That was the last of the first evening's conversation in regard to Karen's plan, except she'd informed him the shouting man in the alley was Jerry, a second-in-control dealer who had come on to her in his car, whereupon she hit him and escaped.

Certainly there was big money in the illegal drug trafficking trade, but not so much "big" as "considerable," when it came to smaller dealers. Nonetheless, violence and even murder were a breath away at all times.

Stanley knew that. Yet, he became infatuated with this girl with the sweet smile and the quick moving eyes. To pretend to be a buyer, to spirit away her brother from criminals, as daunting as the task appeared, found root in Stanley's mind, Stanley's basically moral and law-abiding psyche, and pushed him into this "favor."

Firstly, though, and lastly, he was careless of his own life. His hopes and dreams were behind him. He'd faced danger often, was in fact used to it, and actually didn't care if he died now or many years hence. Wouldn't he go to be with Jesus in Heaven, anyway?

So some days later, Karen took a sip of her rum and Coke while watching Stanley carefully. She wasn't sure of him, obviously. But he was the best she could do. The other friends she had were drug addicts – not to be depended upon, even to speak two sentences clearly, let alone fake being a person with money to spend on heroin.

The waitress swung by, shirt gently flapping, smile fixed in place. "Everything good?"

"Uh-hmm, yes," Stanley replied. He was wearing a suit and tie, unusual for him, particularly in this restaurant he frequented. No one besides businessmen wore suits in there, unless it was a successful business *woman* who was fashionably attired in a gently feminine black outfit, complete with tie.

Mostly Maria's was a casual eatery, with a menu full of Mexican food, rice and beans galore, except for an obligatory hamburger. Even that was offered with guacamole, if desired.

Karen remained cool and collected, seemingly unaware they were facing a dangerous situation with undoubtedly armed dealers.

Stanley gulped his Pacifico Clara, nervously. He stuffed a chip into his mouth. Should he pull out of this deal, he wondered? It had been one thing to agree to it all from a distance, another to face the event looming presently, a half hour away. He was tempted to tell her he wasn't going to go through with it, but the thought of her shock and disappointment held back the words in his throat.

It wasn't so much getting shot (or stabbed?) that he feared, it was the potential failure of it all. He hated failure.

He followed her in his own car up the hills of Tarzana to the hangout. It was that, to his mind. A rather large house, wood mostly, it appeared. Two sharp foreign jobs sat in a short driveway. Stanley couldn't recognize the makes, but it hardly mattered anyway. He felt fearful but yet not in the grip of it – boxing had cooled the fear of death, particularly once he turned pro. He had feared death more as an amateur, that way, in the ring.

Now he couldn't care less. He sure didn't want to end up in a hospital with a bullet in him, though, and he didn't want this strange girl to be harmed in any way.

They both parked on the street, a task, considering the shortage of legal spaces. He smiled on purpose in case they were being watched, then as they approached, stopped smiling in case they would think he was too confident. In fact, he didn't know *how* to behave, but luckily the film work he'd done gave him a kind of ease, or a kind of "equilibrium," to push him along. He was looking serious and calm as she rang the bell.

Years before, he'd done what his friend Andrew "Don't call me Andy" had told him *he'd* done – Primal Therapy. You scream, you cry like a child, you moan with pain. Big pain. That was the idea, the big theory. And he'd found it worked. You escaped the clutches of deep-seated anguish which held you back, repressed your life.

Andrew had issues – pain – with his father and mother. They'd been good parents except for their heavy drinking, and he'd been mistreated due to that. So past unpleasant events meant Andrew, during therapy sessions, had to cry and scream in fear, reliving them over and over until all the deep repressed trauma was brought to the surface of his consciousness and released. It simply vanished.

He told Stanley that the dark sinister skepticism (toward others) he had felt all his life (especially toward others in authority) had left like so much dust in the wind, after primaling. Andrew also said it helped his acting career, because he now could get along with many people that he'd had uneasy, even hostile, relations with, fearing subconsciously they would lash out, as his parents.

Agents had been the easiest for Andrew to deal with, because they had the least power. He would steamroll over their ideas and objections to Andrew's ideas and wishes. It was fairly easy since Andrew was a fine actor who was almost always in demand.

But the others – directors and producers especially – had to be placated and in fact catered to, which Andrew forced himself to do (before). Otherwise conflicts arose and he opposed them tooth and nail about seemingly incidental issues, like wardrobe choices, salary adjustments, hair cuts, dialogue changes. He'd feel under attack if a director insisted the words be exactly the ones in the script. Arguments broke out because Andrew refused to comply when he wanted a word changed and the director didn't.

But that was ended. His life was easier. He could discuss any script changes more rationally and with tact, and if he didn't get his way he more willingly settled for it than he'd been capable of doing in the past. He could now see it wasn't his parents ordering him around viciously, in a sate of drunkenness, it wasn't five or ten-year-old Andrew suffering verbal abuse when they'd come into his room.

In fact, the shortened version of his first name gradually became easier for him to tolerate, and he was free of the pain of when they had been drinking, when they'd used that name in a pejorative manner, for instance: "Andy, Andy, we know you disobeyed us, we know you stayed up! Don't lie, don't say you haven't!" and a slap to his face would always be connected, in his subconscious memories, many years later, with the use of the name "Andy."

When they weren't drinking they called him Andrew, they treated him with more respect.

His distaste in later life for the name "Andy" had disappeared (mostly) like dust in the wind.

Andrew "Don't Call Me Andy" still wanted to be called Andrew but wasn't so quick to correct anyone who used "Andy." He had never seemed to realize that when a person called him Andy they were only being warm and friendly, not disparaging! Even Stanley had attempted to call him by that nickname, and been sternly corrected, years ago (even when he said "You can call me Stan!"). But the primaling, the freedom from childhood hurts, allowed Andrew a comfort with that nickname, comfort he'd never known previously.

He even got along better with his parents, before they had died (as people do) by the turn of the century. And Andrew had more friends now. For years he'd only had Stanley and a couple of other actors close to him, due to his cold manner. Stanley had grown to like him through his association (with Andrew), due to Stanley's boxing. Andrew had wanted to manage him after they'd met at the gym (while Andrew was working out for an upcoming role as a fighter). At that time Stanley had given him a few pointers.

The film had flopped but the friendship survived.

While there was no place for Andrew in the plans of Sammy and Larry, that didn't prevent Andrew from following his short-lived pro career, and getting Stanley a few small parts in movies, and the Western series.

The series had lasted two years, although it wasn't a hit (it was always in the lower half of the ratings). But the network kept it on the air, for reasons not too clear – probably because it didn't cost a great deal to produce and there were several loyal advertisers who liked Westerns.

Stanley had played the deputy Sheriff, a good part, he thought, keeping to the background mostly, but engaging in action often enough to keep him happy. Usually the Sheriff and the two leads, "husband and wife" (who mostly loved and argued and got mixed up in the weekly dramas) carried the majority of the show, story-wise.

He didn't make a whole lot of money, but then again he didn't have that many lines, which was a blessing because it was a struggle to learn new ones for each episode.

He was glad when it was over, though. The riding was tough on his body and the hours were ridiculous. Not that he worked but a few days a week, so it was easier that way, but they were long days.

Still, Stanley would rather be at the gym in town, watching boxers and training them, and collecting a little money to live on.

Andrew tried to get him to audition for more movies, but the whole business just wasn't in his heart.

When Andrew, in his excitement caused by the remarkable results of Primal Therapy, took Stanley to the Institute and pressured him, partly against his will, to begin treatments, a brave new world opened.

Stanley paid the cost of the first few introductory classes, or sessions, and once he broke through to the deep pain, called Primal Pain, with the help of a kind but firm therapist, he began to see those benefits himself.

He'd been told to stay in a nearby motel, to avoid drugs (which he didn't do anyway), to keep a daily journal, to keep (temporarily) from contact with his friends, and oddly enough, not to have sex or to masturbate.

The Pain flooded up in rapid fashion, after the early sessions. It wracked him, it shook him, it wore him out! He would lie on the floor of a room in the Institute, and cry, and scream, involuntarily, and after the seventh session he was allowed into group sessions with other patients.

They all were delving into past trauma, hurts and awful experiences, to free their minds of the hold such suppressed pain had. A hold hard to shake.

Particularly he felt the repressed Pain of those head butts, of hurting his hands, of even a few low blows he'd received but completely forgotten about.

Some of the patients in his group cried about their births, their struggles to be born, and some screamed about beatings and other punishments they'd received, and the Pain of fears and resentments. All felt refreshed, later, some within minutes, some within days, some within weeks.

As the time passed, Stanley wondered why this type of therapy hadn't become more popular, because it appeared to work so well. It remained a mystery. Once, as he saw the founder, Dr. Janov, outside the Institute, climbing into a car, Stanley said "Thank you" to him, and walked away, shyly. Janov watched him, a bit puzzled (he didn't know Stanley, had never met him) and said "Okay!"

Stanley's shyness was a bad thing, mostly, and he hoped a little more primaling would uncover the reason for it, and lead to a solution. But he didn't keep at it.

He quit going to sessions after 6 months, concerned about the cost, but planning to resume in the future. He never did. It was so hard, he told himself.

Maybe that was the reason it never caught on in a larger way. People didn't like to face pain, and they sure didn't like to feel it intensely.

Stanley wandered aimlessly for awhile, a month or so, noting the new ideas that popped into his head as a result of escaping old hurts and the unconscious methods of dealing with them. While feeling the old repressed, "unfelt" pain of the injury to his genitals was a relief, he still didn't have full sensitivity there, maybe because the nerves had suffered damage.

But he realized now he'd had a subconscious fear of being hurt badly, again, and now *that* fear was gone. Gone like dust in the wind.

To test it he had a massage by a "friendly" masseuse who took his member in her hand to play with it gently. He always shied away from "friendly" masseuses in the past, but not understood why. Now he had no fear, no reluctance, and allowed her to do as she pleased.

Although he had saved money from his salary for the series, Stanley spent it over the years and now lived on the fixed income which Social Security and the SAG pension provided him, meager as it was.

Both amounts being dependent on the income he'd achieved during working years, the result was little more than subsistence living. But Stanley didn't care. He saw now how fortunate he'd been to deposit and declare so much of the fees, often in cash, he'd gained from training and co-managing fighters. While not much, it added to his Social Security payments. Had he pocketed that money (as many did) and not declared it, it would be gone instead of having contributed to his retirement. Even the checks he so strenuously earned as a professional contributed now to his retirement comfort.

He did regret, nevertheless, not continuing as an actor after the Western was cancelled. But he knew the major reason. It wasn't only his lack of enthusiasm for the acting profession, it was his careless decision, one night on the set, to agree to a shot – a "B-12 vitamin" shot, offered to "pick him up." He ought to have known better, but it was an injection several crew members got, also, from a non-doctor. A "nurse," he'd been told. It had seemed reasonable.

And while that shot in his rear *did* in fact perk him up, give him energy, it might have been more than merely vitamin B-12.

That evening he saw what appeared to him to be multiple, vivid colors, with a feeling of joy. He thought "Wow, was I low on vitamins! Look how much energy that dose is giving me!" Later, in telling that story to a friend, the friend laughed and informed him, "Why, you fool. That must certainly have been amphetamines. Speed."

Of course, and contaminated also, since it was illegal and of suspicious origin.

"Did you feel weak for a long time after that?" his friend asked, knowingly.

"Uh, as a matter of fact..."

"See? Crappy stuff, crappy. It stays in your system for years, haven't you heard?"

"No, I never played around with drugs, I didn't know."

But for years he'd not felt much like working, had not felt much like doing what he'd always done, jumping rope and punching the bags, and sparring. He had done it, but far less than before that infamous injection of "vitamin B-12." It wore off, eventually, but he seldom returned to acting. Only once or twice. He couldn't recall, exactly.

And then, during that period of time, he noticed the psychological results of primaling were bewildering to him. There was a feeling of freedom, of peace, but also a vast "relaxation" which seemed out of place. He'd figured there would be an excess of energy to complement the freedom from old restrictions, but no. Stanley felt so relaxed he didn't want to do much. That changed after many months but never quite left him. Instead of charging into life, he wanted to sit and just listen to music and read poetry.

The Janov book about Primal Therapy, he never finished. Seemed unnecessary. Andrew agreed, under questioning, that rather than being so engaged in "attack mode," he was himself pleasantly adjusted to life, not as impatient and aggressive as before.

Whether this new mental state was good or bad, Stanley couldn't figure. Perhaps it was the way human beings were intended to be, in a healthy condition. Perhaps neuroses drove most people to strive and push, to grasp for acquisitions and property and activities in an unhealthy way, in order to alleviate the pain they felt deep down inside themselves.

At any rate, Andrew told him he felt "good," in a frank and elevated way, as if feeling "good" was the most valuable and important thing in his life.

Stanley didn't quite feel the immense significance of that word, but then again he hadn't pursued primaling as intensely, or thoroughly, as Andrew had.

Not yet, that was. He still planned on returning to it someday. But now he was standing at a door, and Karen was ringing the bell, and whatever lay ahead he had no idea.

It could be good, it could be bad. He might get his nose broken (again) or he might break a nose (for the first time, as far as he knew). He might help Karen extract her brother from a path of crime, or he might help her make a misstep which would threaten both their lives. Or all three of their lives.

The plan was simple. Meet the guys, agree to a buy somewhere in the range of 5-10 thousand, say he would go for the money while their men hold onto the package of dope. She would advise her brother to accompany him so he wouldn't pull any funny stuff like go to the cops (and bring them there).

The flickering memory of his nose being broken didn't last long, but it was a hot memory because it had been refreshed during his primaling. The bout had gone the distance, and at the time Stanley had no detailed memory of the blow that hit him, in the third round. Only at the Institute did the grisly facts emerge. The other guy had pulled a fast one, had jammed his open glove upturned into Stanley's nose – a short punch with the heel of his hand. Clever. It got past the ref because the fighters were in close and punching furiously. You aren't supposed to hit with the heel of your hand, but...it does happen. It hurt but in the heat of combat it was like so many other blows – painful but ignored.

Later that night, the tenderness appeared, the blackness around both eyes (a tell-tale sign), and the realization that damage had been done. How much that blow had reduced Stanley's performance for the rest of the bout was anyone's guess, but after the primaling revealed the facts, Stanley saw he'd kept back, unconsciously trying to avoid another such blow, and had not performed aggressively enough to win those last two rounds. He'd lost the decision.

Feeling the past suppressed Pain of that illegal punch and broken nose had restored some of Stanley's spirit, which had become undermined, for without realizing it he'd become less of a man, less forceful, even more shy.

So he began to laugh at things more, as he had prior to that spirit-crushing heel-thrust. He was slightly happier now, more benign in his personal aspect, as *before* that broken nose. It was like a miracle, he felt. Andrew had been right, the intense suffering now produced what he'd meant by feeling "good." It wasn't over, however. Stanley knew instinctively he wasn't feeling as "good" as Andrew expressed it. There was more to do, more hurts to recall and be rid of. What they were Stanley couldn't say – they were buried inside him somewhere. Maybe they came from a traumatic birth. Many of the group therapy sessions had led to other patients claiming powerful, tough "birth Primals."

But birth Primals seemed to be the most difficult and sometimes the most painful for patients, and harder to access emotionally. That they were real he didn't doubt after hearing the stories of them and seeing one or two happen right there in the group sessions, before his eyes.

Mainly those Primals involved the "waiting to get out," to be born, to struggle free of the confines of the mother. And that struggle usually hurt because of the narrowness of the escape route.

Stanley was intrigued to know his own birth travail, but unlike most things, it scared him. One patient had stopped breathing and then shrieked loudly a moment or two later. The results were all the same, though – relief, exhaustion, sobbing in the aftermath of the torment. Stanley was not at all positive he was willing to undergo it, no matter how much benefit was to accrue.

The three men in the house (none of whom was her brother) behaved quite friendly until Stanley told them he didn't have the cash on him, but would get it after he saw the "goods," as he called it. They acted suspicious, and Karen tried to calm their nervousness by vouching for him, but the leader, a cold-eyed Mexican-looking short man with a thick head of dark hair, said he shows no one anything before he sees the money. And Stanley stammered a bit. Not much, but still, the leader pulled out a black Beretta and pointed it in Stanley's direction.

They were all sitting on various chairs and couches, Karen on the floor, and when Stanley didn't flinch, didn't bat an eye, at the weapon, the leader smiled.

"You get the cash and you come again. Otherwise no deal, amigo." He glanced with disapproval at Karen who briefly lifted her shoulders and said:

"I told him. I told him to bring it."

"Jerry," the leader said softly, "check our visitor for a wire."

The man, Anglo-looking and very thin, rose from his chair and nodded.

"Mind, amigo?" The leader smiled again.

Stanley said, "Hell no, I don't mind," and stood for the rough pat down Jerry gave him: his shoulders, his back, his front, his legs. Jerry looked at the leader with a face blank and waiting.

In spite of himself Stanley was sweating. Karen laughed for no apparent reason and asked "Where's Marco? He can go with him."

The leader nodded, and Stanley felt a moment of relief, but the leader then said, "He could, couldn't he? But he's not here."

"What?" Karen shot out, fast.

"He's busy. He's with – but never mind. You go. You brought this guy. Marco's doing something else. You go, Karen. Kill him if he tries to escape."

She was more composed now, and replied, "Thanks, boss," rather sarcastically.

Now it was time for the boss to laugh, and the other two did, almost, but held it in.

Karen bravely asked, "Where is Marco? He ought to go with us."

The boss glanced at the other two henchmen. "Yeah, he probably should. Call him," he told the third man, a black man who grimly pulled out his phone from his front jeans pocket and began to make the call.

"Go outside, amigo. You too, honey," the boss ordered. Karen led the way to the front door; Stanley followed, putting a slight swagger in his walk, and they left the house.

Outside he stopped sweating and regained the composure he'd felt prior to sitting inside, and standing for the hands-on search.

Karen was relaxed-looking but she just couldn't be, he thought. Fine little actress. They didn't speak.

It was a normal upper-middle class area, not high enough in the hills to cost an arm and a leg to own houses.

So they waited. The black man came out the door after five minutes to say Marco was on his way, that "Angel" (could that actually be the leader's name?) would make the deal if the money was shortly produced. "Things are tough these days,' he said, rather obtusely.

"Sure, I know," Stanley replied, not knowing anything about it.

The man had his grim look still, and Stanley decided he wasn't unfamiliar with prison, and the bulk of shoulders showed he was not unfamiliar with lifting weights, either. A man not to cross, a heavyweight, a badass.

They all waited. The man was watching Karen, the road, and Stanley, who smiled at him. The strangest thought crossed Stanley's mind, which was: this guy might be an undercover policeman and they were spoiling his long-developed plan to bust this ring. But it was so far-fetched even Stanley couldn't believe that.

They stood outside for at least ten minutes, and the man's phone rang. He answered with a "Yeah?" but watched them all the same. He listened, and looked down the street, and said "yeah," again, and then hung up. "Marco's coming," he told Karen.

A short while later, Marco drove up and stopped at the foot of the driveway. Stanley started off and the grim man asked, "Where are you going?"

"To my car, what's your problem?"

A little aggression can go a long way sometimes, as Stanley had learned in the gym The man just shrugged and Karen said "I'll go with him and Marco can follow us in his car." The man said nothing. Karen waved at Marco to wait, and followed Stanley.

"See you later, Tony." She stopped at Marco's car window and said, "You need to follow. We're picking up a bunch of cash. Where's your pistol?"

"Uh, okay. In the trunk." He stared at Tony and then at Stanley, who was approaching his own car. Karen went in that direction.

"I'll be with him," she said.

So they all drove off. Stanley was to pull to the side of a street somewhere, after it appeared they weren't followed (except by Marco). Karen would be the one determining that, since she knew the others' cars.

She said she'd tell her brother "this was it," his chance to get away, and give him extra money from her pocket. He was to go to their father's old cabin near Big Bear Lake and stay there, keeping a low profile, only buying what he needed when he needed it, trying to avoid attracting much attention. She'd contact him when it felt safe to her.

They did this off Ventura Blvd. In a restaurant parking lot. Marco was all for it, smiling and gratefully thanking them both.

When he drove off, Stanley asked a question, "So I go to my apartment, put my car in the carport, and leave it for...how many years?

She laughed. "Months. I told you, two, three months. Those dummies won't do anything, they'll be on to other deals, when they see nobody has ratted them out."

"All right. As you say."

"Goodbye. You were fantastic."

This part of the plan he didn't like. She would walk in the direction of the house (more than ten miles away), calling Angel to explain that Marco had simply sped away, that Stanley had been extremely nervous and called the whole deal off, leaving her there on Ventura Blvd. Of course she'd repeat she'd only met him in a bar in Studio City, and didn't know where he lived.

It all went according to plan.

Stanley's only concern, or more precisely his *main* concern, was the gas station where Karen and Angel had had their dispute, and she had been chased by him and yelled at in the alley under his window. If Jerry ever went to that gas station again or even drove by the neighborhood, he could perchance spot Stanley walking around. But that was a remote possibility, according to Karen. And anyway it was one of those things Stanley put into God's hands, believing in the Lord's promise to protect the faithful.

He settled down to a routine. Giving his housekeeper two months off, he took laundry to a place a block and a half away, a sort of Chinese laundry but with Thai owners, who washed and folded his clothes expertly. He could reach the market on foot and the coffee shop on foot, and what else did he need? Books he had, cable he had, friends he had who could pick him up to go anywhere distant, like the gym or the movie theaters or the bookstore in Van Nuys where he went occasionally.

Currently Stanley was reading various stories about Sherlock Holmes and Dr. Watson – stories written by writers other than Arthur Conan Doyle, the original creator of the Sherlock Holmes mysteries. He had read the originals, sixty in all, and found there were many more in the tradition, by several accomplished writers. Fun they were.

He didn't worry much about the current state of the "adventure" as he thought of it, since Karen hadn't contacted him with any news. No news is good news, in this situation. While he was fond of her, he just chalked it up as another "appealing woman he couldn't have" – standard characteristic of his unusual life – and carried on.

There was an Asian massage parlor he could get to by bus (not wanting any of his friends to know) if the need arose, so to speak. But that was only half-enjoyable, he knew.

Dark clouds paused overhead, perhaps with moisture in them, and Stanley wore his raincoat outside; but not as it turned out, for any reason – the rain didn't come. The drought persisted. Water shortage persisted. Mandatory restrictions on water use persisted. Lawns were dry, landscapes on the big houses browning, parching.

Stanley sat in the coffee shop, he joked with the waitress, knowing of course she was out of reach, was only humoring him. As usual he ordered a dinner to go, ate his breakfast, drank his coffee, thought about Karen, stared out the big window. This was Sunday, and tomorrow his friend Bill would join him at the coffee shop, Monday being

Bill's day off. He was a mechanic, an older guy like Stanley, but who refused to retire, even though he didn't have to pay alimony anymore, or child support, since his ex-wife was remarried and his two daughters grown up.

Bill was easygoing, outgoing, rather formal for an auto mechanic. He'd also been in Vietnam, as had Stanley. But unlike Stanley, he'd fought on the ground, in the jungle, and didn't care to talk about it too much.

Stanley met Bill on the set of a film he made, in 1992. They both had roles which worked a day here and a day there, and being minor parts both men shared a dressing room. Bill was of average height, built stocky, and had a wry sense of humor. When he found out Stanley had served briefly in Vietnam he became more talkative, although he never spoke at length of anything.

That suited Stanley, who felt he could ramble on about almost any subject and be guaranteed of Bill's attention. He told him of his fights, of Primal Therapy, of Rosy, of college classes he'd taken, of fighters he'd helped, of regrets and dreams. Bill had a few dreams himself, one of which was to become rich, even though he was now in his middle sixties.

At breakfast on Monday they spoke of the movies, the weather, the waiters, the stock market. Bill was dating a slightly overweight Latina named Jovana who worked as a live-in maid and had two children in El Salvador who were taken care of by Jovana's mother. Bill said he might marry the woman and bring the children up here to Los Angeles, but not yet. It was quite a big step, one he wasn't completely sure about. Stanley met her sometimes when she got a day off, and Bill had a day off, and they all ate together. Once Jovana brought a friend to meet Stanley, another slightly overweight Latina, but Stanley was not excited by her, nice as she was.

He told Bill of his injuries and blamed his lack of interest on that. But it was more than that. He just wasn't excited by her. Surely not like Rosy had excited him. Of course Stanley knew he had to let go of his attachment to Rosy, but it was not easy.

Most men, it appeared to him, had longings and regrets, love or otherwise, which they carried with them for years, if not for all time. Letting go was so hard most people could not do it, and quit trying.

But he was trying, as he realized he should, and had had some slight success over the past decades. It was easier for him because he knew the cards were stacked against him anyway, due to his inhibited sexual feelings.

Still, emotional connections are lingering. Just like his emotional attachment to boxing.

Of course the need within him to tell his friend the details of the recent drama was battling his common sense, and both "need" and "common sense" partly won – Stanley's tale of a woman in the alley, and meeting her later for coffee, and even drinks, was told. But that was all.

"I hope I see her again," he told his friend, slightly enigmatically.

"You've got her phone number?"

"Yes…"

"Well, call. Don't be shy. She acted like she liked you, didn't she?"

"Yes," Stanley acknowledged.

The waitress came by with the check, so no further conversation about Karen ensued. The men looked at the check and took the appropriate cash from their pockets. They always split the costs.

They spoke outside by Bill's car, halfheartedly discussing their respective plans. A little thought occurred to Stanley: if he's spotted by the drug dealers now, here, Bill could be an unintended victim, should mayhem follow.

But it wasn't a major thought. He didn't think he'd be spotted, and didn't think those guys would start shooting. Still…it was smart to be careful, so he waved a hand nonchalantly, saying:

"Guess I'll take off. I felt like walking again, you know…"

Bill nodded and went to his car. Just a normal day, Stanley assured himself. No problems, no sweat. He headed along the sidewalk as Bill drove away out the back of the parking lot. No Jerry, no Angel, no Tony.

He stopped at the 7-11 market. The clerk recognized him, said hello. Stanley got beer and cereal and milk and a bag of chips, Mexican-style tortilla chips. Outside he saw a man, in a car, staring at him.

Suspicious, Stanley walked a couple of blocks out of his way but the man in the car didn't follow.

He stopped at a store window and wondered what to do. If he just headed home, they would know where he lived, because maybe he was being tailed and didn't know. Good shadowing can be done with two "operatives": if one thinks the subject of the shadowing has spotted him, the other takes over. Anyway, that's what Stanley learned from detective novels and Perry Mason mysteries.

He went further away from his apartment but didn't notice anyone following him in any sort of car. He just went back around and decided to skip it. The milk was getting warm anyway. So he went up the stairs and into his place. Once inside he placed his items in the fridge and promptly drank a glass of water.

Boxers are trained to drink water whenever they can, if they have smart trainers. Not much can lessen a fighter's condition more than being dehydrated. And old habits stay, once established.

He sat in a chair and heard the traffic outside. Could an enemy be watching, waiting? But for what? Those drug dealers can't be much concerned one of them had run away. Must happen often, as a matter of fact. Stanley closed his eyes and listened. No stealthy footsteps in the street, or on the stairs, as far as he could tell.

He needed to go into the bathroom, and he needed to check his phone for messages. Well, maybe not. He'd had his phone with him the whole time that morning, so it was unlikely he had not heard or felt a text or a call.

He dozed a bit, but did go to the bathroom before long. He did a few stretches, a few sit-ups, a few minutes shadow boxing, and took a shower. He wanted to call Duke, his old trainer and friend, but Duke was dead. He looked up at the ceiling and smiled.

"Are you watching, man?"

It felt like it, sometimes, to Stanley. Who knew?

He popped open a beer and turned on the TV news. After awhile he heated up the food from the café, and sat and ate and watched more news, but it was thick with death stories, so he switched to *Two and a Half Men* reruns. For an hour at least, he didn't feel oppressed by the idea criminals were watching his every move.

When he went to bed, though, Stanley made sure the door was locked and his revolver was loaded.

In the morning he had coffee and a toasted croissant after some stretches and warm-ups – shaking his arms, flexing his hands, turning his head back and forth to limber up his neck. Those serious neck exercises on the workout table at the gym were a thing of the past. Unless...someday Stanley could get to a good gym and try to get his body into shape, real shape, and even spar. Now, how many times has he thought of that over the recent decades? Ten, fifteen times?

Well, true, he *could* do it. His time was his own, wasn't it? All he needed was a little motivation.

At least when he was acting he was motivated to work out to stay in condition, so he'd look reasonably fit on camera.

But what motivation did he have now? That was another question he didn't have an answer for.

That gym he'd gone to recently (or *was* it recent?) just wasn't a real boxing gym. It wasn't what he wanted.

Time was like a river, as the novelist Thomas Wolfe had noted nearly a century ago, a river that flowed endlessly. Time held a mystery, though. It had a beginning, no? Must have. And perhaps an end – or not. God could keep time going as long as He wished. He could bring along whoever he wished, to experience it for all eternity. Hopefully, as the Bible says, Stanley was "saved by grace through faith." He would supply the faith, and the Lord would supply the grace. A winning combination.

He read, he napped, he went on the internet. Later, in his chair at his window, drinking a beer and reflecting on the valuable insights Primal Therapy had provided him, there was a pang of regret when Stanley recalled another sudden blow, the butt to his eye which, although he happened to win that fight, had caused him to slightly withdraw subconsciously, and not be as aggressive in his next fights. Who would, if they were feeling that incredible pain? His regret was that he hadn't known about Primal Therapy then, hadn't gone deep into the traumatic event's painful source and felt that blow's Pain fully, rather than suppress it. Oh, well. Such was not to be. Had he been free of that "reluctance," that slight withdrawal of his aggression – who knew how much farther he'd have gone, how many fights he might have won?

He drank, sadly, nodding his head. At least he had the realization now, and if he were to get into shape and spar, why, why, he'd definitely be as aggressive as he had been in his early career – (after the first round, naturally). (That first round was always hard for him for some reason.) "Slow-starting Stanley," a couple of people had called him. That probably was a result of something in his birth, some difficulty he'd had coming out, a difficulty that caused him to take things slow, at the start, always, during his life. But never having primaled about his birth experience, Stanley could only surmise about the Pain it encompassed. Wow, "encompassed." Now *that's* a scary word, he thought. Like a tight canal he had to struggle through in order to be born. Yeah, that's likely why he didn't care for that word…"encompass"…

Karen was leaving him alone, he hadn't seen any of the drug ring, he hadn't seen Marco – except *that* one Stanley never expected to run into ever again. Soon he would pull his car out, drive it as usual, and settle into the life he'd had before meeting Karen. But not yet. His instinct told him to continue to be careful, to watch his back, to play it cool. Cool Stanley, that was him.

It rained, which was a surprise because even though the weather people on local news had said it was coming, because of a hurricane further south, he had not believed them. He thought they were only making a remote possibility a strong one, to excite viewers and keep them watching. But it *did* rain. Not a lot, but more than for a long time.

Stanley stayed in, listening to the falling water, reading a detective story. He also sat at his table and scouted around YouTube in an aimless fashion, typing in names of fighters to watch any bouts that were posted. Of course, none of his were, because YouTube only had famous ones on there.

He also watched a few videos of Asian women getting massages, and decided it was time to get a massage himself.

Stanley's housekeeper returned after two months, and he was glad he had a housekeeper, but worried if the drug ring found him and came by to exact revenge, she would perhaps fall as a victim, by bad luck. So he kept out of the apartment whenever she was there working, so if they caught up with him it wouldn't put her in jeopardy.

He began to see how dumb he'd been to participate in Karen's scheme. Others were in possible jeopardy, not just the two of them (or, rather, the three of them, counting Marco). He could see Jerry and Tony carrying out orders and shooting whoever was with Stanley, just for good measure.

Why hadn't he thought of this beforehand? Dumb, that's why, like the *reason* he had his tax returns prepared by a pro – he was too *dumb* to do it himself properly.

But life went on, and it all looked pretty safe until Karen showed up, carrying a bag and asking to spend the night.

"Really?" he asked her, letting her into his apartment. "But why?"

"I can tell you but first I need a drink, okay?"

She drank wine – he had nothing stronger – and too much of that. She sat on his couch, he sat in his chair with a mug of beer.

She smoked.

"I don't recall you smoked."

"I took it up," she laughed.

"Oh. Well."

"Stanley."

"What?"

"How much do you care for me?"

"I – well, sure. Uh, enough to let you stay. To take the chance a shot will come through that door and hit me instead of you. Is that enough?"

She smiled that great smile and said softly, "I needed to hear that. You do care for me, don't you?"

"I suppose so. Why?"

"Well," she laughed, "that's not too convincing."

"Crap," he said, taking a drink of beer. "You can stay. Isn't that good enough?"

Karen looked ferocious all of a sudden. "No."

They were silent. Stanley had no clue where it was going, and yet, it pleased him she had asked that.

Finally she said, "Marco's doing fine, still hiding out. But Angel was so mad he smacked me around and threatened to kill me, but I knew he wouldn't, and then – she took a sip of wine – "luckily I was believed about not knowing where you live, or work, or anything. They didn't grasp how you could have been trying to get Marco away, so that was that. I –"

"Slow down, Karen. Relax."

"Sure. Thanks." She took a moment and then continued, "Well, so, Angel sent to look for your car around town, like we thought, and after weeks of that he gave up. Then Angel was on to other deals, sales...you know."

"Sure. Good."

Again she smiled. "Only – when Marco never showed up he got mad all over again and kicked me out, blaming me for it all."

"Wait a minute. How come your brother was so important to him?"

"I don't know, but good help is hard to find." She laughed and drank, and poured another shot of wine into her glass. Suddenly: "How many beds do you have?"

"One. I'll sleep out here if you want."

"Umm, no." She laughed again. Stanley could see he was going to have to come up with a little romance, a little sexual intercourse, and he hoped she'd be satisfied.

They did go to bed together and it was satisfying for Stanley, since he was able to perform. She was a little drunk so...she seemed to be happy. "Happy" isn't the word for Stanley though, because the feeling just didn't live up to the expectation. Why would he expect a different outcome after all these many years was a mystery – maybe some trick of the mind.

He noticed Karen was kind of passionless, which some women are – doesn't mean they don't like it. For Stanley the stress was minimal, and with the exception of the usual twinge of physical pain he always felt at orgasm, it proved a suitable encounter for both of them. Excepting of course his subtle melancholy afterwards – a plight which Stanley never felt like informing any of his sexual partners.

She felt no melancholy; she drifted off to sleep (after a trip to the bathroom) blissfully. Sure she'd had more vigorous sex in her life, notably with her first boyfriend in high school, but Karen had long since given up seeking for the passionate nearness of those days. Also, she'd drunk so much wine, so fast, she hardly noticed the details.

In the morning Stanley got out of bed as soon as he woke up, since past experience had shown him women will paw and kiss in an effort to prompt another encounter. That's not bad, but in Stanley's case it was another burden he preferred to avoid without hurting anyone's feelings.

He made coffee, instead, and waited for Karen to join him in the breakfast nook. It was a relief to him she hadn't called sweetly, urgently, to him from bed.

But she was sober now, and was slightly embarrassed about her behavior the evening before.

"Thank you for being so nice to me. I'm...at odds and ends. After I have some of this coffee I'll explain it to you."

She did, and Stanley fried eggs for them and made toast while she bathed.

So, Angel had told her to find her brother because he wanted to teach him a lesson. She'd said even if she knew where he was she wouldn't reveal it. Angel threatened her again. She'd left the house and refused to return, even when Angel called to request it. Angel thereupon told her in no uncertain terms he would kill Marco if he ever found him, just for running out.

Karen smiled. "Nice, huh?"

"So tell me where have you been staying since leaving that house?"

"Oh, with a friend in Silver Lake. But she couldn't put me up for long. Her boyfriend didn't like it."

"Umm. What now, baby?"

"Stay with you, get a job?"

"Umm." Stanley made a spot decision. "No, baby. No way. You should get out of town. Don't be stupid. It's only a matter of time before one of Angel's people or, you know, acquaintances, sees you somewhere."

She only stared at him, her mouth grim.

But Karen took his advice and got out of town. She realized he was right. She called him when she found a room in a Best Western a hundred miles away.

"Hi, baby," she said. She called him that now that he had started calling *her* that.

"How are you?"

"Not bad. Miss you," she said, a bit abruptly.

"I miss you, too."

"Anyway, I'll head out tomorrow and try to reach Phoenix and lay low. I know some people there."

"Not connected to Angel, I suppose?"

"Of course not. I'm not stupid, no matter what you might think."

"Take it easy, baby."

"All right. Anyway, I can get a friend to put me up, and I'll get a job – somehow – but don't you dare abandon me."

"What? Why did you say that?"

"Oh, well, I'm feeling sad and...rushed. Kinda wish I still did heroin."

"No way," he interjected.

"Yeah, not really. I'm just saying."

"Don't you even think about it."

Later, a week later, she called again. She indeed was moved in with a friend, a friend from school, one Angel and the others knew nothing about. She didn't have a job but could work as a housekeeper for now, she said. Stanley didn't like it but what else could he do to help her? He sent her a hundred dollars, though, which Karen sorely needed.

Meanwhile he had breakfast with Bill and Bill's workplace buddy Troy, an Asian. He was younger than Bill, and had a quick mind. Sometimes it felt like Troy was bored with the conversation, as if he wished he was doing something more mentally stimulating than hanging with the two old guys. But if that were true, why was he a mechanic and not a rocket scientist, or at the least a businessman of some sort?

Bill said his girlfriend had broken up with him, and he told about a woman who had brought in her car for a smog check, and how he'd conversed briefly with her as the test was being performed.

"Shortest skirt I ever saw," he exuded.

"I've seen shorter," Troy remarked, laughing.

To Bill's smile, Stanley asked, "Did you get her phone number?"

He shook his head. Stanley laughed. "Why not? Can't get anywhere without trying."

"I know," Bill replied, looking down at his plate of food, putting his fork into it and bringing some up to his mouth.

"That's okay. Next time," Stanley said. "If there is a next time. Does she come there regularly?"

Troy and Bill shook their heads.

"You should have asked her for her number. At the worst she says no and is secretly flattered," Stanley offered.

"That's right, that's right," Bill agreed, forking more eggs from his plate to his mouth.

"Do you do that yourself?" Troy asked. "Get numbers from strangers?"

"I used to. Sometimes. It's almost a waste of time when you are older, but..." He didn't finish. He thought of Karen.

Outside they said their goodbyes and once again Stanley said he would walk, patting his stomach and mumbling, "It's good for me." They nodded and climbed into Bill's car and drove off.

He again picked up a few items at the 7-11 and headed for his apartment. One of these days he'd remember to bring that cloth bag and not have to pay extra for plastic.

He walked along the alley behind his apartment building. He wondered what Angel and the others were up to. More of the same? He stared at his blue car in the parking spot. Soon he'd be driving it again.

He thought of Jerry yelling at Karen, that fateful day. What if he hadn't been in? He would have missed her, and certainly not recognized and interacted with her at the market, subsequently.

He was too shy around women. They wanted, respected, a little aggressiveness. They just were wary of rapists and murderers. Who could blame them?

Stanley trudged up the stairs and went inside, tired for no good reason. One day, he told himself, he'd drive his car again and hook up with some woman – Asian perhaps – who didn't require sex all the time! He wondered if Troy had a sister. A younger one?

Only, if she was younger than Troy, she wouldn't be interested in Stanley. Best hope he had a nice-looking *older* sister who wasn't too interested in sex. Good luck with that.

No more rain fell for awhile – the long drought continued. Predictions were dire. California could run out of water – agriculture devastated, wildlife and people with no water supply. But then he heard on the news that shipments could be brought in from other states paid for, of course. And desalination plants were being built. So Stanley relaxed. All he had to worry about was being spotted by drug dealers, and roughed up or possibly killed!

He read an old Zane Grey western, he exercised, he dreamed of dating Troy's sister, of writing another poem – he hadn't done that in many years – and making some more money somehow. The idea of training another fighter just didn't appeal to him. But quite possibly he could do another film or television part…

It was not easy to find Andrew. His number was changed. But Stanley called Andrew's old agent and found out who was representing him now. The new agency then told him they'd pass his number on to Andrew.

A week passed and Andrew called.

"What's up?" That rich, familiar voice.

"Not much. Hanging in there. How are you?"

"Fine."

"Say, are you working?"

"Now and then. Don't tell me you need a loan."

"No, man, no," Stanley replied fast. But the curtness hurt him. What if he had? Was that so awful between old friends?

"What I thought was, could you look around and possibly get me a job? Not a big part, but –"

"A job? Acting?"

"Yeah."

"Didn't we have this conversation before? I can't do that anymore, Stanley. Why don't you find *me* one?"

That was the last blow.

"Well...I mean you used to do it," Stanley feebly responded.

"Circumstances are not the same now," Andrew said.

"What do you mean?"

"Oh God!" Andrew sounded disgusted. "You've been out of action a long time and I don't have the same agent. This one doesn't want to help me find jobs for stray dogs." He laughed to cover up the unintended insult.

Stanley ought to have blurted, "That hurts me," but he didn't. He didn't for two reasons. One it would make him appear weak (a childish concern but one he held nevertheless), and two, there was truth in what Andrew was saying – who was he to expect favors after all the time that had passed? But he did manage, "You'll get ten percent, of course, like always."

"I can't, I just can't. What happened to your agent?"

"Oh, who knows? I'll call him and see." Stanley wanted to add, "since you are letting me down," but once again he knew Andrew was right. The old days were over.

George, his former agent, after initial resistance, agreed to look around for him. Nobody knows how hard it is for agents, the saying goes , until they become one themselves.

But nothing happened for two months, when George called with an audition for him.

Stanley tried; he read a scene for "tape"; he waited; he didn't get the job. And a very minor part it was, too.

He sat in his apartment. He'd used his car to go to the audition, at an office in Silver Lake. But he felt uncomfortable driving, even though it was very unlikely anyone would spot him, any of the drug ring who even remembered what his car looked like, after all this time.

He read an old Agatha Christie mystery, one Stanley had somehow missed all these years. *Murder on the Orient Express*. It was one of her most famous ones, and having seen the movie he was aware, unfortunately, of the ending, but he liked the Poirot stories and was enjoying the book, regardless.

And it distracted him from thinking about driving his Camaro, and about Karen, and Marco, and Angel, and all that.

He waited for his agent to find something, and he waited for a hand on his shoulder. But neither event carried much weight with Stanley.

He went to church a couple of times, prayed the Spirit would lead him, sang praises to the Savior, tossed money in the tray.

Then officers arrived at his door unannounced. Two Sheriff Department detectives. He let them in. What did he have to hide? Nothing much.

"Mr. Larson we have learned from Karen Bashor that you let her stay here one night. Last month?"

"Yes, that's true. Why?" They remained standing in spite of his arm waving them to the couch.

"Do you know where she is?"

He shook his head. "No, I don't."

To his unspoken question the policeman stated, "She vanished, at least for now."

"Well, I don't know, like I say."

"Are you sure? It's important." The taller one had done all the talking up until then, but the shorter one, the one not in a uniform, asked this question.

"I'm sure," Stanley said to him.

"Well," he pulled a card from his wallet. "Please call me if you can think of anything else, and especially if you hear from her."

He took his card, as the officer added, "Or have you heard from her since she stayed with you that night?"

He lied to the police. He didn't like any of this. They weren't telling him anything. He didn't like them. "No, haven't heard from her. We met in a bar as I recall, and she showed up here, after a few weeks, I'm not sure, and stayed. No, I haven't heard from her and I don't know where she might be."

The short one smiled. "Okay, pal. Thanks Call me." They left.

He got a beer from the fridge and sat down. Karen told them? Why? And obviously she hadn't told them everything. Had she run off again after speaking to the police? He couldn't figure it out, so he drank and pondered the future.

Next day he headed to the gym but found it had closed, for good, according to a sign posted.

There was a gym five miles away, a kind of fancy affair for women, mostly, with fitness equipment not in keeping with boxing, but it did have several punching bags in the rear by the back wall. He drove there and paid a high price of $10 to work out. He didn't care. He needed the workout and it was convenient. He brought his own bag gloves, old ones of course, and handwraps, also old. He liked the two girls at the front who, smiling, seemed glad to have a man, even of his age, in the place. They took his money, too, which may have helped their attitude.

His arms got tired sooner than he expected, and yet, and yet, it was a pleasure to recognize that his hands didn't hurt when he hit the bag, even into the second and third round. Of course there wasn't a three-minute-one-minute timer bell like at a real boxing gym, to guide him, but after all his years of experience Stanley could judge the length of time accurately enough for practical purposes.

He didn't shower there. Why bother? He had gotten what he wanted.

He drove through a Del Taco for two beef burritos and headed to his apartment, only bothering to check his rearview mirror for possible criminals three times or so.

He kept going to work out, every other day, and felt better for it. One of the women in the front came over to watch him punching the bag, and said he looked as if he knew what he was doing (when he stopped between rounds). He shyly nodded and smiled, but she persisted.

"Were you a fighter?"

"Uh-huh. You can tell?"

She laughed, "I'll say."

He smiled again, wondering will this lead somewhere, or is she only being nice to an old guy? Oh how he wanted to ask that right out, but he figured it would scare her, so he said, "Well, I had a few fights. Regular boxing, not Martial Arts. Can you do it?"

The woman, who had long black hair and might be half-Asian, flushed a bit. "I've tried. It's great exercise."

He started up again, and felt self-conscious. She walked away in a moment, apparently to attend to other duties. 'You're a fool, Stanley," he told himself.

At his apartment, preparing a dinner of green beans and Tri-tip, he realized two non-important things. He hadn't looked at the woman's hand to see if she wore a ring, and he hadn't thought to ask her her name. Not important because she was in her twenties, he judged, and wouldn't find Stanley of any interest other than that he knew how to box pretty well.

He showered, rested; thought again how his hands hadn't hurt (he knew they wouldn't, it was just the old Primaled-away concern that had tormented him since he originally hurt his hands so many years ago. Decades.) But it was still a pleasure to *know* they were not hurt, to feel the awareness in his entire psyche.

He knew he would return to hit the bag, and if that woman was there he would ask her her name.

He had to wait, though, because he found himself sore – his chest and back – from the exercise. So he took a few days off.

Karen called.

"Why, what do you say?" he responded cheerfully.

"Hi baby. It's hot here. I had to call to say hello, and...and...that's it."

"Sure, sure. Glad you have. Been thinking about you." He was trying to work up to telling her about the visit from the police.

"Nothing has happened. I guess we're all in the clear, you know –"

He suddenly felt angry. "Nothing has happened, really?"

"Why, well, nothing too important, no."

"Sure the cops didn't talk to you?" When she didn't respond he said, "They sure talked to me."

"Oh, yeah, don't worry about it."

"Just a minute. Pardon me. I don't care for that," he said firmly.

"Honey, don't worry about it. They tracked me down, is all, because they arrested Angel. He told them about me. The rat."

"Go on."

"Well, see, he must have been trying to make a deal with the police, turning in anyone he could. But they had nothing on me. I said I know Angel from a long time ago. That seemed to satisfy them – I let them search my room and my possessions."

"But how did I come into it?"

"Oh," she hesitated, "because I was making small talk to show I'd been in LA but not living with Angel. You covered for me, didn't you?"

"True. I didn't mention Angel, and neither did they."

"You're a sweetheart!"

"But how could they find you?"

Again she hesitated, and then said, "I don't know."

The conversation drifted around, and Karen hinted, by saying she missed him, that she meant she missed sex with him. And then she began to cry. When he asked her why, what was the matter, she said she didn't want to tell him, but did.

"I can't reach Marco. I haven't heard from him in over a week."

"That's not usual?"

"No! He calls me all the time. I'm worried about him."

"Do you think..." he didn't finish.

"They might have found him. In fact, I guess they have."

"You can't be sure. Take it easy."

She had stopped crying, and after a moment's silence, said, "You're my friend?"

"Certainly I'm your friend."

"And...well, I can't really ask this of you, you've done so much already –"

"Money? I don't have much, but –"

"No! Not that. Something else."

"Well, what?"

"I...if it's too much for you, say no. It's okay. But, could you possibly go to Big Bear, to check up on him? Please?"

"Drive to Big Bear?"

"Yes," she said quietly. "If you could. I'll give you the address, and you can see if he's okay."

That put Stanley in an awkward position, but he agreed.

He'd drive up on the weekend and look for Marco. Simple.

Hitting the bag at the gym and seeing the woman there, would have to wait. He didn't want to be sore or even tired when he made the trip. Who knew what he would encounter?

Then a bizarre discovery was made. He went to the drawer to fetch his pistol to take with him, and lo and behold, it was missing. It was not in its usual place, and no amount of searching revealed it. He guessed perhaps the housekeeper had removed it – why he couldn't imagine – but even putting a call to her availed nothing. She swore adamantly she never touched it. And he believed her. She'd never moved it before.

But a cold feeling hit him. Karen? She'd stayed in his bedroom, she'd had a small suitcase with her, and Stanley had not *seen* the pistol, after that. Well, he hardly ever looked for it, it being in a drawer he seldom opened.

The cold feeling turned to suspicion. He pondered the phone conversation. He decided to go to Big Bear on Friday. Why not? Why wait until the weekend just because Karen had suggested it?

He took a knife, in a sheath, one Stanley could carry on his belt if need be.

He began to dread the trip but held firm, along the way. He had the map, from the internet, he had a big bottle of water. He spent the midday getting to the lake, he drove around searching for the street. It wasn't much, only a side road. There weren't many cabins. He stopped at a safe distance. He walked toward the cabin. He heard hollering, and what sounded like a gunshot. He paused, and crouched, and listened. The front door of the cabin opened, and a furtive figure rushed into the pine trees to one side.

Taking a breath, nodding his head for no good reason, he proceeded toward the pine trees. He kept a distance from the cabin. No one else came out. He found a path and followed it around where the pine trees stopped. He saw the figure at the top of a canyon, a rocky canyon. He knew that it was Karen. She stood a moment, her back to him, and then threw an object into the little canyon. It clattered. She put her face in her hands, she was very still for a long moment, and turned again to the pine trees, making her way rapidly retracing her steps. Stanley was afraid to call out to her. He waited behind some bushes until he heard a car start up and then fade into the distance. He assumed it was her, in her car, but she must have taken the road in the other direction from his car, because the sound of her motor faded quickly away. He returned to his car. He stood in confusion, then made up his mind, approached the cabin door, and knocked.

There was no answer. Nothing.

Stanley made another fateful decision. After knocking a second time, he opened the door; he called out.

He entered. It was a plain mountain cabin with sparse furnishings, a table, a few utensils, a small TV and a broken-down chair, a stone fireplace.

He walked to the door of what he assumed to be the bedroom. It was open. He peeked in. On a bed lay the body of a man, his head half-covered in blood.

Stanley approached. It looked like Marco, but he wasn't totally sure. He held his fingers to the man's nose and mouth. The man was not breathing. Dutifully, Stanley picked up his arm and felt for a pulse. Nothing.

Stanley exited the cabin, wiping the doorknob with his shirttail.

He had little idea what to do but an instinct insisted he do something. The remoteness of the cabin and that wooded area might mean no one heard the shot, or perhaps didn't care, being used to a hunter's gun going off occasionally, this far from town.

But one thing was certain: he must attempt to find the shiny object Karen threw down into the rocks. Was it a gun? Was it a gun she used to kill Marco?

He looked around, saw no person coming, and hurried to the spot where she had stood. He wasn't panicking but he was quite nervous, and breathing heavily.

Had she and Marco quarreled? Had he shot himself? No, she would only hide the weapon if she had done it herself.

He found his way through the woods and gained the edge of the canyon, more or less where he remembered her sanding. He glanced down the slope. He drew a deep breath, looked around, and climbed, crouching, downward.

Nothing. So difficult to judge, so hard to find anything among the sparse weeds or whatever they were, pine needles, boulders, and small rocks. He grimly spotted, and turned over an old worn tire, not caring in the least how it had gotten there. He had to find the gun, if it was a gun.

Finally, nearing the bottom, and what appeared to be a dried up streambed, he sat on a rock and rested, shaking his head. If he even found it, what was he going to do? His duty was to go to the police, and to report what he had heard, and seen, of course.

After an interval Stanley stood, walked around the dry streambed, and hunted. Then, to his surprise, he found it. His .38, it looked like! Had to be. He picked it up, examined it, opened the barrel, saw several spent shells.

His gun! What was she thinking? That the police wouldn't conduct a thorough search? That they wouldn't suspect a gun might be...oh, it must be standard practice! Police investigators aren't stupid. She must have known that.

His word against hers. His revolver. His involvement in getting Marco away from the drug ring.

Again that cold feeling. Had he been set up? Would she do that? And why was she here if he was the one who was supposed to check on him?

Stanley glanced all around, and up the canyon, on both sides. Nobody.

The bullet will match his gun, of that he was certain. He made a decision, pocketed the weapon, and left.

Driving the winding highways down to the freeway, and west to Los Angeles, Stanley calculated two possibilities: she had killed her brother – if he *was* her brother – and planned to let Stanley arrive on Saturday, find the dead body, summon the police, tell his story, and then at some point be arrested after his pistol was found. Or, she had taken it but had not planned anything, had decided to see Marco herself, argued, and shot him. After all, she had been crying – or something, at the edge of the canyon.

Either way, what else could he do? The police would say *he* had argued with Marco and shot him. The weight of evidence was against him.

Should he go to a lawyer? Smart, proper thing to do. But still, he didn't want to risk it all on that hope. He'd have to get rid of his gun and then carry on like nothing had happened. She sure wouldn't reach him again. Would she? Either way?

Was not reporting a crime like that a crime in and of itself? Most likely, he surmised. But a minor one. Eventually someone would discover the body. He wasn't connected (if he hadn't been seen) and there was little chance Karen would confess when the police found her again and told her of the discovery. She *could* send the cops to him if she cared to, but that snub-nosed .38 wouldn't be found, as long as he got rid of it intelligently. Sure there's a record of him owning one, but...he'd say it was stolen years before.

He drank a serious amount of beer that evening. Too much. It was as though he'd won a fight and was celebrating, except Stanley felt no joy, no pleasure, not even a bit of contentment. He worried over the situation, and pushed away the worry with alcohol. Or rather, tried to. When he stumbled into bed the stress was lifted, sure, temporarily, but the sad state of things haunted him anyway.

In the morning he felt a hangover, but even more lessening of distress. Mornings will do that for a man. At breakfast he decided he needed to think his plan over – was he actually going to go through with it? What he disliked, he was becoming – a *liar*. A fake. Even a criminal of sorts. But what else could he do?

With a wry laugh, Stanley saw that many crooks had no doubt built a decision, an action, a scheme, on such an uncertain foundation. What else could he do, indeed!?

Well, first he could dream up a hiding place for the weapon, and then decide to use it or not. It had to be way outside of the city, far away.

Yet when it came down to actually stashing the gun somewhere (digging a hole in the desert, he'd figured), Stanley couldn't do it. He wasn't a criminal at heart. He dreaded to wait; if the cops showed up he'd tell what had happened and take whatever the ramifications were.

And Karen never called. He did sweat it out, though. Of course he'd have to hope the cops, the law, would be lenient about his circumstances. He had taken the gun because it made him look guilty. But of course they would suspect he *was* guilty.

Anyway, keeping the gun shows he isn't guilty, he figured. Unless they thought he was stupid enough to hang onto it after shooting someone. The twists and turns in his mind created major strain, but he put it in God's hands.

Manifestly, Stanley didn't want to lie. He detested lying. And it was one of the sins enumerated in the Bible. He had lied already to the cops about not having contact with Karen, and felt badly, and shy about going to church because of it.

He waited. No one called at his door demanding to examine his .38. No newspaper or TV report mentioned a death by gunshot in the Big Bear Lake area.

He went to breakfast with Bill, and Troy, and wondered again if Troy had a sister. He went to the gym and punched the bag, smiling and chatting briefly with what's-her-name.

He felt sort of sick about what he assumed Karen had done, and argued within himself concerning the responsibility he had as a citizen to report it. But then, would he be believed? Not likely.

If Karen wanted the killing to be blamed on him, she'd have to send the cops to his apartment. Would she do that?

And, another day, he implied to Bill that there was a tough problem he faced, and did Bill know any police? He did, he said. Two, as a matter of fact. Relatives of Troy's, both Asian. He stared into Stanley's eyes, waiting, but Stanley left it at that. He couldn't bring himself to tell Bill anything further.

"Talk about being caught between a rock and a hard place," Stanley muttered to himself later that day in his apartment. He could ask Troy to set up a breakfast with one or both of his relatives, and Stanley could explain it all to them. It would be easier than walking into a police station and talking to the desk clerk and...what? Telling it to a sergeant, and then...what? A detective. Of course he *could* do that, especially in case Troy's relatives recommended it.

He took a nap. He woke at five and ate pretzels and drank beer and watched the news for a long time. Nothing, still, of any body found in a cabin in any remote area outside of L.A.

But Stanley was angry at Karen. He wasn't positive she'd meant him to take the fall for Marco's murder, but he was almost certain. He didn't like to be mad at anyone, but there it was. His sleep was troubled, his body unnaturally weak when he rose up at dawn.

Over cereal he decided for sure to speak with Troy's police relatives, and called Bill, at work, about a meeting. A lunch, or something. Bill put Troy on the phone.

"Hey, man. Working hard?"

"Hardly working," Troy responded.

"So, uh, you could help me with a tiny problem – well, it's actually a serious problem. I –"

"Sure, man. What?"

"Oh, you have police in your family, Bill said."

"Yes."

"Uh, what about a breakfast or lunch with one or two of them, a get-together, so I can explain my problem?"

"Don't see why not," Troy replied, a bit warily, though.

"Well, I didn't do anything really bad. But I'm stuck between a rock and a hard place and need proper advice, you know?"

"That's cool. When do you want to meet up?"

"Soon. Anything. You guys can arrange it."

"Okay. I'll call you."

So the date was set, two weeks away.

He was very tense, especially after the time, day, and place for a late breakfast were confirmed, because Stanley hadn't felt the impending-ness of it until then. What would they say?

Would they look grave and recommend he go directly to the police station? Get a lawyer fast?

Would they laugh and dismiss his dilemma by approving of his quick action in light of such an obvious betrayal by Karen?

He didn't know. He just knew he had to tell them, and had to deal with the consequences. But what if Karen could not be found, could not be questioned – and, so what if she could? Who knew what story she may tell? – he would be the main suspect.

He prayed, he exercised, he drank beer and smoked some cigarettes, and waited.

The half-Asian at the gym turned out to have a boyfriend, Stanley learned when asking her to go for coffee "sometime." Oh, well. What was he going to do, anyway?

Once he was tempted to drive up to that house above Ventura Boulevard, for no good reason, for "the hell of it." He wanted to find out if they knew anything about Marco, or Karen.

He almost did it, too. What did he care, really, if they murdered him? What life did he have now?

But he didn't go. Probably that gang wasn't still there, having long since moved on to another spot to deal drugs. He'd sure tell the police the location, though. Maybe a tiny bit of good would come of all this ridiculousness.

But Stanley doubted the cops would be able to track them down, to arrest them, to convict them.

And while he waited, suspended in a realm of uncertainty and anticipatory gloom, the world appeared to carry on around him, quite unmindful, and always rambling, cars making noise, trucks making noise, children making noise, gardeners making noise, etc., etc. Ignorant of his impending collision with the law, the law-enforcers, the technicalities and formulae of the legal system.

One morning, the day prior to his meeting, Stanley awoke with a peace, a peace he hadn't felt for weeks. For some reason he didn't really care anymore; he cared less than he had, which was less than the average person would have, in his circumstances. Why, he did not know. Maybe God was blessing him with a last day of peace, and joy, before the harsh realities hit. He ate breakfast – cereal, toast, banana, coffee – in a pleasant mood.

He thought: if Jesus wants him to go to jail, then he goes. If He doesn't want him to go, he doesn't go. God always has a plan, Stanley figured.

That day he lay around, went out for a bag of groceries, in his car, and read the rest of his book.

Still, he drank a little too much – five beers – and watched a weird movie about a child kidnapping. Ha! The term "kidnapping" certainly applied to that plot. But...why did films seem, more and more, to be weird, to him? Was it just his aging or were they actually becoming weirder? More violence, less substance.

In the morning, he did his usual loosening-up exercises, his hand-clenching exercises, and showered. He ate toast and drank coffee until the time to leave.

He had become friends with a couple of cops when he worked as an actor. They were on the sets as advisors, and one was in a scene where his uniform and gun fit as part of the action. But finding them would be complicated, even if he could recall their names correctly – which he wasn't sure he could.

At least with relatives of a friend, Stanley had some chance at fair, or even more than fair, treatment.

The restaurant was one he and Bill and sometimes Troy had visited in the past. But mostly it had male servers, so they'd gone to other places, with female servers – just more pleasant that way. But the food was good at Emile's, and besides, Bill had suggested it would be less crowded than Denny's or Coco's, which was true. It was obvious to Bill and Troy that something was up.

Stanley had never been good at hiding things, as some people were. He could do it, but only with little artifice – only not saying things when saying them would reveal more than he wanted revealed. But to make up scheming lies to deceive others, he never cared to do and in fact, didn't do it very well.

When he saw the movie *JFK* he thought: Shucks, how have they kept all this complex stuff secret all these years? If bad people are so smart, what chance have the rest of us in this complex world?

Not that he wasn't a sinner – he knew he was. But certain lies outweigh others, don't they? If Karen had murdered Marco...well, he'd think about that later.

He pulled into the parking lot of Emile's, and situated his Camaro. He was five minutes early. He lit another cigarette. The strain was motivating him to smoke in a way he never did before, except while in the Navy so many, many years ago.

Sitting in his car, Stanley felt he was making a mistake approaching police with his story without having consulted an attorney. Yet, he wanted to put it all in God's hands and proceed. After all, isn't God a kind of attorney, representing the saved?

Troy parked, suddenly, next to him. He was alone. Maybe Bill couldn't make it. Usually they came in one car to these breakfasts.

He put out his cigarette and climbed out to greet Troy, who was smiling.

"Good to see you, Stan."

"Hello, man," he responded.

Troy looked around the lot.

"Guess we are the first."

"Yeah."

"My cousin Keith will be here but my brother-in-law had to work. Sorry."

"Oh. What about Bill?"

"He said he was going to be here," he said, scanning the lot again. "What's up, buddy?"

"Oh, I have a crazy problem. I need advice. I got mixed up in a mess, like I said."

"Really?"

Bill drove in before Stanley could reply, and after greetings, the three stood by the side of Emile's, waiting. Nobody said anything until Keith drove up, parked, got out, and was introduced to Stanley. Bill nodded hello to Keith, as they were already acquainted.

"Let's go in," Troy said, and led the way to the front door. Keith was a big man, 220 pounds or so, with short black hair. He only vaguely appeared Asian, at least to Stanley. They went inside, were shown to a table, sat around it, and waited for menus, which were brought quickly. They all ordered coffee, and Bill asked for water. In the drought it had to be requested, it wasn't served automatically, as before.

Stanley wasn't hungry. He looked at Keith's friendly face and wondered if he was carrying handcuffs. Certainly he was armed.

"So you are with the Sheriff's Department?"

"Yup," Keith answered.

"Cool," Stanley said weakly.

As they got coffee, and placed orders, Bill told Keith how Stanley had been a boxer, and told Stanley how in the Academy program the new recruits were required to box as part of their training. Keith nodded yes and Stanley asked, "How did that go?"

"They had an experienced boxer to work with us, and we all got beaten."

"Wow. That's not fair."

Keith laughed, "No."

Stanley recalled the many rounds he'd suffered indignity and hard punches as he'd learned the sport himself. Trainers seemed to delight in putting him to sparring with much more knowledgeable fighters, and those fighters (not all) seemed to regard him as a punching bag. He knew how Keith must have felt, and told him so.

By the time they were all eating a slight nervousness increased in Stanley's system, and he had to set himself for the task before him. His many walks down the aisle to the ring prepared him well. And that unique moment in a fighter's experience, after the referee's instructions, and the return to the corner, and the final (if any) words of encouragement from his corner-man, and the corner-man's climb out of the ring, leaving the fighter all by himself, and the bell, and the sense of aloneness, of emptiness, of moving awkwardly, or with grace (depending on the fighter's particular style and psychology), out into the ring toward his opponent, put there by chance or fate or sometimes connivance on the part of managers and/or promoters, to deal with, to confront, the unknown yet exciting, welcome even, activity, the initial encounter when whatever would happen would happen, and the spirit and the skill and the condition and the heart initiated the first punch, or block, or feint, or half or full jab, or swing, or even duck, however that boxer decided – all this too had prepared Stanley as he began his story, carrying on until the end, up to the present, as Keith and Bill and Troy only sat silently taking it in.

"What do you think?" he asked, finally.

"Not good," Keith said simply.

"What should I do?"

"You must go to the cops," he laughed, rather incongruously. Off Stanley's look, Keith said, "Not to me. Not the right jurisdiction."

"Oh, sure. But I don't care to report this..."

"I know. But you should have reported the body, you shouldn't have taken the gun, you shouldn't have left the scene. Of the crime," he emphasized.

Stanley said nothing, just nodded his head.

"Don't blame you, you know, considering...but at the least it is not good. At the most..."

"Illegal?"

"Uh-huh."

"Suppose," Troy intervened, "you call to Big Bear and find out what they know. If they found the –"

"I could," Keith interrupted. "*But* they will want to know why I'm asking, what I know about it."

"Sure,"Stanley said dispiritedly.

After a moment Troy said, "Look. It came from me, you can say honestly. I brought him to you. And just say it's a friend of mine who – who – heard his friend was there." He looked at Stanley. "That's okay, isn't it? To bring her – Karen – into it now? Sort of have to."

"Yeah, I suppose so. Why not? She certainly had my gun. I saw her. Will they tell you if a .38 killed him? I mean, if they have found him?"

"I need to give the location," Keith said.

"Okay, of course."

Keith smiled with his eyes.

"My friend, unnamed, thinks this woman was involved. A friend of *his*," Troy said to Keith.

"They will want me to get names from you. I'll have to commit to finding out for them, but they will probably agree to that, temporarily."

"Please just find out what you can," Stanley said.

It did rain again, though not for long. And Stanley tried to call the number, the last one he had on Karen, from when she left originally for New Mexico, her cell phone.

But it was disconnected – no surprise. He *did* contact and have a consultation with an attorney, but it wasn't satisfying. He paid $150 and found out very little. "Ride it out," Keith had advised, and more or less that's what the attorney said too, although using more and larger words.

Keith called with the news the body *was* discovered, and had been removed, and the boy's parents were notified and had taken the remains to San Diego for burial after an autopsy.

"What of his sister?"

"No record of him having one, Stanley. She must have lied to you about that."

"But why?"

"I have no idea."

"What about the local police? Are they still investigating?"

"I was told yes. But can't give you any information about it, sorry."

"Confidential?"

"Yes."

"Are you going to tell them about me?"

"Well," Keith said slowly, "since there is only your word you didn't shoot him, I have to. I am delaying because Troy can vouch for you, but really, it is a homicide, and he isn't an eyewitness, and...you know."

"I know. You have to."

"Correct."

But after that phone conversation, things moved fast. The next day, Troy called to say Karen had turned herself in to the authorities in New Mexico, and confessed that Marco and she had fought, that he was a drug dealer, that she had shot him in self-defense *with his own gun* (which was found in the cabin) and fled in a panic. Troy said Keith was going to wait and see, that at the moment the Big Bear police weren't pressuring him for anything.

"But man, the gun in the cabin matches?"

"It matched the fatal bullet, yes," Troy replied.

"My gun..."

"Didn't kill him."

"But man, it had other empty shells," Stanley murmured.

"You didn't hear a second shot that day? Or more?"

"No. I was just approaching, though. Could be she – oh, I don't know."

"I can ask Keith if they found other bullet holes somewhere in the cabin, but he may not know or won't tell me."

"Oh boy," Stanley groaned.

They were silent for a few moments. "How could she kill him with his own gun?"

"She grabbed it from a table, Keith told me, or just...anyplace."

"Karen's in big trouble."

"No kidding."

"But I can believe they argued and she felt threatened, and –" Stanley stopped himself.

"Let the courts work it out."

"Thank God it wasn't my gun."

"You can say that again."

The D.A.'s office accepted her plea of self-defense when a friend of Karen's came forward to claim she'd seen Marco slap her one night, six months ago, and that the two of them, Karen and Marco, had been dating for over a year.

The mystery of the spent shell-casings was solved at the court hearing when Karen testified she'd practiced in New Mexico with a pistol, which was now "missing" before going to visit Marco – to try to dissuade him from selling drugs (some of which were found hidden in the cabin).

Keith said he'd examined the court transcript and was more than satisfied. He would only tell what he himself was asked, and so far no one was asking.

Karen was free, and Stanley was glad, because he didn't think she was capable of actual murder.

She had lied about Marco being her brother, but if she'd told Stanley they were lovers instead, she might not have thought Stanley would help her get Marco away.

And frankly, he thought, that was true. He'd been a sucker and was lucky to have escaped unharmed.

The only problem, and Keith pounded it out at another breakfast gathering with Stanley, Bill, and Troy, was "that dang gun." She'd had it with her, which she hadn't mentioned in her confessional account of the events that fateful day Marco died in her father's remote cabin. Yet Keith wasn't too troubled. Had Marco died of a .38 slug, then he would be very troubled, he said. It was out of his hands, anyway. If Stanley ever wanted to go to the Big Bear police and tell what he'd done, he was free to.

"I believe her version of it," Keith told them all, at the table in Denny's. "Why not? She has no record of violent past acts. You," he pointed at Stanley, "can confirm Marco was associated with drug dealers, that he fled to the cabin, that she went there.

Why? Maybe as she said, maybe not. But if to kill him, she would have used the gun she brought with her, not his. Only his if he had provoked her. How did he? Violently? My feeling is, yes. And if the gun was in her purse, it was unavailable to her during the scuffle. *His* was laying around nearby, and she used it. Anyway," with Troy and Bill nodding in agreement, "she did the world a favor. One less creep, one less criminal, is fine with me."

Stanley didn't respond. Cops had their own stern attitudes in respect to the world they dealt with and if it seemed too cold-blooded to him, that was just how it was.

They all dropped the subject and the conversation turned to less serious subjects.

Outside, afterwards, once again Stanley thanked Keith and Troy, and Bill, for the incalculable assistance they'd provided.

He drove to the market, he bought a number of essential food items, and paper towels, and even vanilla Häagen-Dazs, which while not "essential," nudged at his mind and clamored for attention. Never seeing Karen again was a thought which irritated and depressed him. Frankly, she'd gotten under his skin.

At his apartment, putting food in the fridge and chips in the cabinet and a new dishrag in a drawer, he wondered about something. Why should she mention a gun, a now "missing" gun which she'd used for target practice? Since it was Marco's gun she killed him with, she could have just as easily left target practice out of her narrative. Unless she hoped it would be found!

He set a beer and a mug on the coffee table, lit a cigarette, and thought: she is a strange one. Had she really killed in self-defense? Then he belatedly grasped the purpose, possibly, for her target practice/missing gun story: to show the judge the danger she felt from Marco, and the reason she was able to shoot him so accurately that day. Those two factors helped support the self-defense claim. Sure they could well be true, but why throw the gun away at all? Why deceive the judge so?

He drank his beer and knew the answer: taking a gun with her that day looked bad, like she might have planned to kill him. Well, if she hadn't planned to, it was just for protection...but her lawyer may have encouraged her to lie about it to keep the question from coming up. A small lie, if she was no murderer, a big lie if she was.

He shook his head and drank more beer.

He could hit the bag harder. The primaling he'd done concerning his hand injuries provided the release from reluctance to hit hard, as the "deep" mind was freed from the notion that his hands were still in pain. So his training at the gym continued. He also smiled at the women who worked there, but never again asked any of them out. It was just the one he'd been interested in, the half-Asian one, anyway. But still, he liked the fact that they all were congenial, friendly, accommodating.

Stanley prayed, too, a few times, that all would be well, that he had done right, that Karen was as she claimed, innocent, that time would heal what wounds he had (and he did have some). He prayed in Jesus' name. He asked for forgiveness, should he need it, because a few minor laws were broken. At least, by him. God knows if Karen had lied, had killed in deliberate fashion, or however the law defined murder.

He also went to church and put money in the offering tray, hoping but not sure it might mitigate what was undoubtedly a series of illegal, or at best, questionable acts, for him.

He felt better, though, and took that to indicate God was forgiving him, and perhaps what he'd done wasn't so terrible. That was gratifying.

So he wasn't as apprehensive as before, he wasn't worried at all, he was as a matter of fact sort of joyous that it had worked out as well as it had.

He ordered more books from Amazon, more Agatha Christie and another Sherlock Holmes Magazine, and thought again about writing a poem, but put it off. Writing poems had lost their intrigue for him when the relationship with Rosy hadn't worked out. A poem had brought them together, one he'd written and left for her at the office of her business manager.

That seemed impossibly long ago, impossibly distant in the past.

So he pounded the bag, he hit with new-found energy, he put his heart into it, he turned those punches over as well as he had turned them over in his fighting days. Well...nearly....

The longing to be in a real gym – one only for boxing, or martial arts and boxing – kept a place in the back of his brain. It would be more comfortable for him, and more exciting, too. But where to find one? Online? He'd tried that once and come up with nothing, at least in the vicinity.

The idea struck him to ask the cute young half-Asian woman. What was her name? She may know of a place in the area.

She did. She was so bubbly he wondered if her boss would be mad she could be losing a customer. But what's-her-name was refreshingly straightforward.

"I can write the name down if you would like, Mr. Larson. Sorry I don't have the exact address."

"No, no. I can look it up. I may be old but I actually do know how to use that thing, that...'internet,'" he quipped and laughed.

"You don't seem old, Mr. Larson."

With that wonderful remark in his head he spent the rest of the day blissfully sensing how sweet the air smelled, how nice the people on the streets looked, how tender the lips of what's-her-name must be, to utter such ego-building nonsense. Or was it nonsense? Stanley actually felt pretty young, and aside from a few minor pains here and there, the old body functioned. Well, mostly.

He lay in bed that night wondering if she had meant anything more by it than a sweet compliment. That's the thing about women. You just could not truly be sure what they meant when they said something to you in a personal way. It was a part of their charm of course, and of their blasted mystery, but always one struggled to divine their meaning. Or meanings.

He found out she was half-Japanese, her parents were American, so so was she, and her name was Megumi. But yeah, she had a boyfriend and, whatever, even if he had sex with her he'd have to face the inevitable time when she wanted more and he wasn't forthcoming, as had been the situation with Rosy and many others, and they would drift apart when she concluded, "Yes, he's a nice guy, but...I need more from him."

It didn't matter – she had a boyfriend. And even if she was inclined to cheat, Stanley wasn't willing to be a part of deception like that.

There were times when Stanley regretted his position in life, in the world. More specifically, his lack of "real money," as Duke used to call it.

Many good fighters had made tens of thousands, some – a few great ones – millions. He thought he could have fit in between those someplace, with a little good luck rather than bad luck. The injuries, the head butts, had eliminated his chances of any "real money," or even "serious money." Not that he'd been *that* good of a fighter. But he'd been good enough to win a logical number of bouts – ten or so – until facing more talented fighters.

But no, the continued career hadn't materialized, and a few fighters who Stanley believed *not as skilled as he* went on to win more fights than he had – *their* hands not hurt, *their* faces not bothered by head butts, *their* subconscious not holding them back. But what Stanley had was something those fighters who he'd trained with and associated with around the gym did not: the "freeing" of Primal Therapy.

Not that he hadn't spread the word when he visited the gym, later, but only one person of the many he'd informed of the benefits of Primal Therapy actually took it up in any serious way. And that was not a fighter, but a woman he had befriended while an actor. She did it for six or so months (not enough, in his estimation) and quit. Too hard for her, too many painful childhood experiences coming to the surface and causing fear. But she'd gotten some results at least, unlike his other friends who'd listened interestedly to his advocacy, but refused to take it up.

Still, more money – riches even – held its allure for Stanley. A big house (well, it needn't be *so* big) a couple of expensive cars, a more complete wardrobe, travel to Europe and to the Caribbean, servants, etc., etc, had a place in his dreams. The acting jobs could have led to stardom if he'd been more talented, but he was not. And that was it (aside from poetry which brings in no money). He wanted to do nothing else. He wanted no business, no restaurant, no boxing equipment line of manufacturing and/or distribution. Nothing. The big house was not enough of an allure to make him work endlessly in some business to achieve that goal.

So his life was what it was, boring and inconsequential, like many others.

He felt a satisfaction, in some way, because he was relieved of the need to be aloof and refined – two necessary requirements of being rich (or at least, he naively saw them as requirements). And another fearful flaw he foresaw in being rich, an inevitable change: the twisting around of the view (proper) that money was a *means* and not just an *end*.

Part II

"What can I get you, friend?"

Stanley wasted no time joking with the waitress when she pointed out, to his naming the 'Big Scramble" as his to-go order, that a choice of four forms of it were listed under the title on the menu.

"Oh, I have to pick one! Well..." he said, "I'm too old to make such decisions anymore."

When she failed to laugh he quickly added, "Not really, hah, hah."

He chose one – the one with ground beef, and told her.

"Hash browns or home fries?" she asked.

"Uh, home fries. They're good, aren't they?"

"Yes," the little trooper responded, and wrote on her pad.

Undaunted, he asked, "How are you today?"

She smiled, "Oh, it's one of those days, you know."

Not really knowing, he said, "We all have 'em. Tired?"

"Yes! And I had an early class," she closed her eyes, "and could hardly stay awake."

He nodded sympathetically, feeling abashed she was in school and he was trying to engage her in banter, in a type of flirting without her suspecting it. Or, maybe, she did suspect it and wasn't bothered. She was certainly friendly enough.

He sipped his decaf after she left to put the order in at the kitchen window. He tried to keep his eyes off her because a trio of men at the end of the counter – two standing behind the counter and one sitting – were looking at him. Or at any rate, Stanley *felt* they were. And he surmised they were employees from their attitude and dress. Why they weren't in fact working he couldn't imagine, except the place was not too busy.

Finally she brought him his packed bag of food, and said "Follow me, sir," as she walked behind the counter, toward the cash register.

He dutifully abandoned his cup of decaf, picked up the bag before him, and proceeded to the cash register.

This had a unique feeling. Normally one finished one's coffee even after the bag of to-go food was presented.

As he paid, using a credit card, and began to write a tip on the merchant copy receipt prior to signing it, he asked, "Well, now, how much did I tip you the last time??" and suddenly mid-sentence recalling he had *never* dealt with her before – it was *another* young waitress the last time.

"I don't remember," she said anyway. Naturally, she couldn't be expected to recall every old guy she served in there.

He wrote a generous tip, added it up, signed, and when she said, "I hope your food doesn't get too cold," Stanley tried again with a joke of sorts.

"Oh, that's okay. I'll heat it up. That's the way I cook, heating up take-out orders." She smiled but didn't laugh.

"I'm half-joking," he added very quickly, since he felt she must have thought it a serious remark.

"I know. I chuckled inwardly."

As he left, Stanley thought, "now that girl is definitely interesting."

It meant little. A charming waitress (in his eyes) who was less than half his age – a third his age – may find his humor appealing, or not. She may dispense her charm along lines of "interest" to herself, and her tips. After all, she wasn't foolish. She was working for a reason. Stanley recalled working while attending college himself, even though living with his sister he didn't need to pay rent, and insufficiently paid into the grocery bills. But...he'd been invited into that arrangement. She may have felt compelled to pressure their mother for the extra money for Stanley, because she herself was receiving expenses from their mother (who was remarried to a wealthy physicist).

Stanley's sister (half-sister?) attended college full-time, and Stanley had taken a slightly reduced class load. He delivered pizza part-time and spent all his Navy discharge pay and savings until giving up school to try other things.

Like boxing. Like taking acting classes as Andrew advised later. Like writing short stories. Like working full-time at a gas station or two, to make ends meet. He hardly wanted to ask his mother for anything – she made it seem like such a big sacrifice for her even though her husband made a seriously high salary as head of a scientific research facility. And she made him feel like a beggar by her use of words – as she had, always.

Money was too important to her. She admitted so, even blaming it on her childhood suffering through the Great Depression. And so it may have been, but Stanley figured that was only an excuse she used to justify her plain love of money, her greed.

"You can't find a nice job, a better one than a gas station?"

"No, not really."

"Really?" The doubt in her remarks hurt him, as if he wasn't trying, wasn't truly interested in finding one of those many "easy-to-obtain" jobs out "there," implying there was some serious flaw in his nature, some wretched laziness which may cause him "deplorably" to depend on her "own funds."

The acting classes didn't cost much and as a matter of fact, when Stanley had turned to boxing at age 23, Andrew gave him a hundred here and a hundred there to help him eat properly and buy equipment, and pay for training. Later he discovered paying for training was unusual – more normally a trainer would "adopt" a prospect and teach him (or her) in the hopes of earning money later, should the prospect turn professional.

But as with most things in life when money is available and offered, the willingness to do, and energy accompanying it, is enhanced in the recipient. Andrew knew that fact, being older and possessing more experience than Stanley. So the trainer was offered the money, and accepted.

But time passed and he turned pro and he acted in a few films and a series, and yet now the bank account was way low but not empty, and the memories were mainly pleasant.

Stanley watched videos online, YouTube and other places, even sexual ones. But he didn't like porn. It violated a certain sensibility of his. He could enjoy soft porn, however, and was fond of one titled *Japanese Soft Core '99* with a lovely girl, Nana, cavorting half-dressed showing her terrific body for more than an hour. She had a great smile, too.

He supposed soft porn was less painful for him to watch, less evocative of the fact – the problem – of his weakness: lack of physical feeling during sex acts. *Seeing* them only brought that back to his consciousness. It was all too obvious the pleasure (fake or not) exhibited in sexual videos in no way matched his own.

It was difficult to enjoy something at half measure. Like coffee diluted to the point of being half as tasty, half as full-bodied, half as rich as one hoped it to be. But in Stanley's case there was an even greater detriment: the twinge of pain he felt during ejaculation. That made it all the more disagreeable to him.

So, he avoided the viewing of it, and tried to dismiss the awareness, the recognition of it, from his mind, as much as he could.

There was a hope, though, that because the pain from other traumas had been felt, the Primal Pain, and his sense of well-being and freedom had increased, gradually, he decided to do more primaling as it applied to his genitals, his groin, in the wishful thought there may still be a little progress to be had in that area. Perhaps.

Avidly, he dreamed of that, and set his heart on it, knowing at the same time he may be badly disappointed. Because regarding sexual feeling, primaling hadn't done much over the years. It *seemed* there was more feeling down there, it *seemed* he felt freer and not as reluctant to try, but at the same time he knew he was not feeling that much, and wasn't that free, and still was reluctant to try to have sex, to enjoy it. The sad fact was (perhaps) the damage was permanent to nerve endings there, right in that area, and the problem was just physical instead of psychological.

But for sure there was more pain to be dredged up – he could tell. And the more Primal Pain he felt from any injuries, there would be a positive value.

He only had to make himself "bring" it up, feel it, and release it, as much as there was.

It rained again, and the thirsty ground soaked it up, the hills put forth new growth in a day or two, and yet the long drought remained. News channels foretold a coming El Niño condition from the Pacific with potential of *too much* rainfall, and flooding.

But Stanley did not fear. He stocked up on canned foods; he already had a grill powered by propane. He brought another set of propane bottles to complement the six-pack he had. While the little grill had been purchased in an effort to prepare for an earthquake, and no electricity, it would serve well the possibility of a storm ravaging Southern California and interrupting the area's electricity. He felt prepared.

What he wasn't prepared for was the announcement at breakfast one day that Bill was deciding to move in with his parents and join their real estate company, giving up his job as a mechanic. And Troy? He wasn't quitting his job, he said, no way.

"It's good work. I can put something aside." When Stanley nodded agreeably, Troy added, "I want to get married someday again, you know."

"Sure," Bill said. "Why not?"

Not for Stanley, though. He left the coffee shop, and drove away after saying goodbye to his friends, feeling sad. Marriage was not for him. Unless the woman didn't care for sex much – and good luck with that!

Tomorrow is another day, a spunky female character said in a movie once. "Scarlett O'Hara, yeah," he thought. Stanley headed for a reasonably remote stretch of road in North Hills, parked his car, and recalled, again, an injury he'd had once, trying to high-jump a rope placed across a rear entrance to the barracks when he was stationed in San Diego. It was late at night, the rope was up to signal that returning liberty-takers needed to use the front entrance at that hour. But, having been drinking down in Tijuana, he felt rather rebellious, and loose, and stupid. He ran and jumped, throwing his right leg over the rope. But he hesitated because he saw that the pavement and then the steps, on the other side of the rope, were not conducive to landing and rolling on – something a more sober Stanley would have noticed before jumping. His face and groin struck the rope, which did not give – it was well-secured at either end – and he bounced over onto his back, the pain in his face and his groin excruciating. Not to mention his back.

This was the event he primaled about that day, on the side of the road, in his car. He screamed and yelled, reliving the moment.

It didn't take long. He had a small cushion he pressed against his face to muffle the sounds, and he'd rolled up his windows. It hadn't looked like anyone would drive by, but at short intervals he stopped to take a breath and scope out the street in both directions. If a car was coming by, he'd merely wait for it to pass and then recall the feelings, the action of leaping over the rope (but not making it), of landing hard on it, and then he'd release the pent-up pain again.

The process, the method, he was quite familiar with. It was the specific trauma that changed. Of course he'd had to repeat the primaling a lot, over the years, when a trauma was deep and extremely painful. Funny thing was, one never really knew for sure how deep or painful a given event/trauma/circumstance was until it found its way to the surface. Sometimes certain events would be surprisingly painful.

Instead of being a victim of abuse or torment or negligence by someone else, this time the painful experience had been caused by himself alone, many many years past. Not that it made much difference – whoever caused the trauma, whether it was intentional or unintentional, mattered not in the least...the only issue regarding who and why pain had been inflicted was the further pain which needed to be felt, if it was inflicted by someone who was expected to be on Stanley's (or anyone's) side. A victim of betrayal, of trickiness, of fraud in unexpected fashion, had the deep emotional hurt (of such betrayal) to deal with, also.

But not in this case. No one had told him to high-jump the rope, no one had tricked him into doing it.

Willfully he waited for days, hoping for a change. He knew from past results that it took time: weeks and months.

He returned to the same road and parked and primaled a second time, because the healing factor, the change from old psychological condition to new was not to be rushed or forced or pushed by mental effort. He vainly held his figurative breath, yet willfully demanded of himself the change.

Yet, still, he gave up waiting, and sat in his car on the remote street again, and watching out for passersby, in vehicles or on foot, he dredged up the memory of the jump over the rope again. When it rose in his mind, so did the pain, and he once more experienced excruciating pain, a hurt he had not fully re-experienced the last time. He yelled into the little cushion, and then breathed heavily.

Another memory sprang up, and he went with it, feeling it, too. A sharp pain in his foot, a scraping sensation on his forehead? Why, he noted, it was during a fight he'd had as an amateur, and the opponent had stepped on his foot and tossed a punch which Stanley just partly ducked. And he'd fallen down backwards, and the referee had counted it a knock-down even though Stanley had sprung to his feet shaking his head "no" at him, and at the judges sitting watching him, ringside.

He'd lost that fight by a close margin (he suspected), one of the tough ones to lose, in his mind. Now he knew how he could have gone down like that, a mystery to him until this moment. He'd not, at all, recalled that foot on top of his foot, and the loss of balance it caused as he attempted to move – but now he saw: it was a trick some trainers taught their fighters, a dirty trick, illegal as can be if done deliberately. Whether it was deliberate that time, Stanley couldn't know, but certainly he suspected such. That had been a skilled fighter he was in there with; not likely he'd be sloppy enough to step on his foot by mistake….

Nevertheless, as time went on, the "reaction" to his previous primal continued – a bizarre feeling of irritation combined with listlessness. Always like that, he noted, in varying degrees, after all primals. The feeling between his legs hadn't noticeably improved, but that didn't mean it wouldn't, after more weeks or months. The mental healing process took hardly any time at all, or a longer time – by what rules it transpired Stanley could not know. Perhaps a therapist at the Institute could explain it, or even Dr. Janov himself. It didn't matter, really, how many days or weeks or months the healing took, just as long as it did. But he couldn't be sure how much it would, in this instance, because he didn't know if the tear on his penis that happened when he was twelve had damaged nerves or not, and should *that* be the case, how then could primals about *other* pain improve such physical damage? He could only hope progress would be made.

Meanwhile the Social Security and Pension Plan checks continued to come in, and he paid his bills and saved a little. He did get a massage, and she did rub him there, and he felt something but not enough, and wasn't even able to come – so he stopped her from touching it, finally.

He decided to wait a considerable amount of time before trying that again.

He punched the bag, he ate with Troy and Bill, he read another book (Edith Wharton), spoke on the phone with an actor friend from the Western series – who wasn't finding any work – and drove out to the beach, one day, to see the lovely sea.

Winter had arrived, cooler temperatures prevailed, and Stanley didn't know it, but adventures – two actually – came surprisingly into his life, one with deadly consequences. Then another appeared on his horizon, this time with less deadly consequences – although a broken nose for him (once again), at the gym.

It wasn't that girl who was working there, the young one who had a boyfriend, Megumi. She always gave him a sweet smile when seeing him, and he responded in kind. As a matter of fact, Stanley didn't usually smile much – he had to make himself do it. A lot of times he'd forget, even when joking with someone. Why, he didn't know, except he suspected it had something to do with his boxing career disappointments, or perhaps it went further back than that, a disappointment now unconscious.

Primaling didn't seem to help that. But maybe someday, if he kept at it.

Megumi must have liked his smile though, because she would pause at whatever she was doing and sort of stare at him until he walked over.

No, it was a man, a much younger man who was punching the bags too, now, who broke Stanley's nose.

Stanley introduced himself, and found out he called himself Pedro.

He was stocky and appeared to be Latino but had no accent that Stanley could catch. He hit the bag rather poorly, so after a few visits to the gym he asked Stanley what was he doing wrong?

Stanley showed him how his feet weren't placed correctly and how his punches were way too wide to be effective. Straighter punches were stronger, they used the weight of the body more – not just "arm punching" as it was called. Pedro didn't quite get rid of the habit, though, even after instruction. Well, some people just didn't have the talent for boxing. But Pedro thanked him repeatedly for his assistance.

Meanwhile, Megumi had observed this, yet said nothing. She approved of people helping people. In fact, that was why she had her job at all – she felt motivated to help others, help them help themselves, health-wise, by exercise. It was a simple formula she had, one she'd learned from her parents: exercise, nutrition, fresh air. She saw Stanley instructing Pedro and hoped she could see improvement in Pedro's workout.

She didn't really know the man, a co-worker had spoken with him when he first entered the gym and signed up, just recently.

Bill wanted to have breakfast earlier than had normally been the case, because he had to meet his parents for their daily (almost) confabs concerning their property interests. Bill would never say how rich they were, but apparently buying, fixing up, and later, selling houses could be lucrative if handled correctly. Bill had not cared to pursue those interests and was more drawn to cars and guns (of which he owned a few) but at last his (very old) parents had succeeded in drawing him into their business.

Troy objected to the two-hour earlier meeting time, and was often not at the restaurant with Stanley and Bill, now. He needed his sleep he said, and even on a day off rising early was beyond his "natural" compliance, but he did manage that occasionally.

Stanley asked Bill if he might invite Pedro, and Bill readily agreed. There was something in the quiet manner of Pedro which lent itself to an easiness, a friendliness while in his presence, so Stanley concluded he would be a fine breakfast companion in Troy's absence. Or perhaps, even should Troy show up earlier, a fourth voice in the conversation couldn't hurt, could it?

Before that happened, Stanley gave Megumi a present of Trader Joe's all-natural fruit bars, six to a pack, for no good reason he could think of except he'd learned years (many years) ago that women had a soft spot for gifts, no matter what they were, and Stanley still wished to be on her good side even if she *did* have a boyfriend. Being nice to her didn't have to lead to anything – in fact he wasn't quite sure he cared for it to, although he held off going to that other gym.

But if it led to something, he'd have to stop coming to this gym, right? To avoid the feelings of inarticulate awkwardness which would follow him having to tell her he couldn't sustain a sexual relationship in the way Megumi might wish?

She gratefully accepted the gift (a bit less enthusiastically than he'd hoped) and said "Thanks, that's sweet. But why?" The question surprised him and he could only shrug and say, "Why not? You're always so pleasant, and...I don't know." This lit up her face for no reason he could grasp, but in her mind the fact he couldn't express it meant he had feelings for her beyond the usual, and it flattered her. Not many people gave her anything, and this small gift touched her, even if she didn't want him to see how much.

The last thing she needed was a guy pressuring her to go out – hadn't he asked her once already?

The car was running well, and Stanley took a long drive up the coast, to north of Santa Barbara. He didn't care for how crowded L.A. was these days, very different than in the 1970s. He stopped at a café and ate lunch, thanking God for this pleasant experience.

He'd always enjoyed sitting in cafés, or coffee shops, rather than big restaurants or bars. More comfortable, physically, and even emotionally. Except the day he found out Elvis had died – he was in a small restaurant then. The waitress had asked him, "Aren't you the one who told us Elvis just died?" or something like that. It might not have been very hard to answer, this case of mistaken identity, but for the fact that he knew nothing of it, and he felt it was a pretty bizarre way to find out such news.

Or when he'd read in the paper the owner of the gym – who Stanley considered a friend – had just been murdered. That was while sitting in a café also. The news hit him hard, and the crime was never solved. Both of those events occurred in 1977.

He returned, in a relaxed state of mind, down the coast highway to the San Fernando Valley, picking up beer and cereal and a turkey sandwich at a local 7-11 market. A homeless-looking fellow was loitering outside and, stopping him before he could ask for money, Stanley asked, "What do you need?"

The man, in his twenties, dressed shabbily, smiled. Before he could answer, Stanley asked, "Are you hungry?

The man replied, "Yes, I am, but – " and before he could ask, as Stanley assumed, for money, Stanley removed the packaged turkey and cheese sandwich from his bag and handed it to him. "Here, buddy."

The man smiled more fully and gratefully took the offered gift, whereupon Stanley turned to re-enter the 7-11. "Thank you, thank you. God bless you," the man shouted after him.

Stanley nodded and went in to buy another sandwich. He didn't care to give beggars money because for all he knew they would purchase alcohol or worse with it, and so he tried always to give food or on a hot day, a bottle of water instead. Sometimes they said they weren't hungry (but not often) and he'd see if they wanted coffee. It was worth the extra effort. After all, "there but for the grace of God" – or the will of God, or the luck of the draw, or something – it could be him loitering, broke, weak, destitute, unhappy, dirty, thirsty, or some such type condition.

In his apartment Stanley placed his newly acquired items in places appropriate to their role – beer on the floor, cereal in a cabinet, sandwich on the kitchen counter. He exercised a bit, drank water, showered, sat at his coffee table drinking his first beer and watching the local news. To his dismay, a murder had been committed nearby – a scant half-mile – while he was away on his short road trip.

A woman was found slain in a parking garage, a bullet through her neck, which had somehow proved fatal. The newscaster didn't explain why, but Stanley assumed due to loss of blood. Her age and identity were being withheld, but police said she was known in the office building there, an insurance company, but gave no more information.

A crazed boyfriend, Stanley assumed, or rather, guessed, was the culprit, and would be tracked down and arrested before too long.

Other news bored him, so he switched on Turner Classic Movies to see what it had for prime-time fare. A musical, a sweet one with Bing Crosby and Mitzi Gaynor. He watched it. He drank more beer, he ate chips and half a banana, and his sandwich too.

The morning brought a feeling of peace and he remembered to say a couple of Bible verses as recommended in Norman Vincent Peale's book on positive thinking. He strove to think positive.

Breakfast with Bill was early again. Bill said he was having a bit of trouble with his parents, who were stuck in their way of doing business, and he chafed against the pattern they had established for choosing property to buy and fix up.

117

"Just tell them you'd like to do it differently – what's wrong with that?" Stanley asked him.

Bill just shook his head. "They won't budge. They're old."

The two of them ate in silence for a while until Bill said, "I might have made a mistake giving up my job."

Stanley didn't want to push it, didn't want Bill to feel any worse than he already did, so he didn't say anything to that.

They paid and walked outside. Bill shrugged and stared out at the street. Stanley wished he had brought cigarettes but he seldom smoked anymore, and hardly ever carried them. But the oddness of the moment made him wish for one.

"Look, man – it's not working out?"

"What?" Bill asked.

"The deal with your folks."

"Oh...no, it's fine," Bill replied.

That was as far as the two of them were going to take the subject, but Stanley knew there was a real problem, only his friend was not willing to discuss it in detail.

Life was like that sometimes. Even often. Things which needed to be discussed were left unattended, even between friends. How more productive the world would be if important, though personal, issues were addressed more openly.

They nodded goodbye and went to their respective cars silently.

Stanley considered Bill a good friend, and good friends are supposed to help each other, but he was at a loss how to help. He needed more information. He needed to know the exact nature of the conflict. Only then would Stanley be able to think constructively about a valid solution – if there was one. But until he got Bill to open up about it there was no prospect of helping him, aside from quiet emotional support.

But it was awkward to put pressure on Bill, who was sometimes a private person. Still, it had to be done – especially the one question which must precede the pressure Stanley needed to apply: did Bill even want any help from him in this situation? One always must ask that question, Stanley had learned. Just assuming the task of assisting a person without his consent was wrong.

One day, as Stanley was punching the bag while women quickly walked, and one ran, on the treadmills, and one woman lifted weights on a machine, Pedro strolled in looking disheveled and distressed. He nodded to a supervisor at the front counter and made his way to the rear where the heavy bags were.

Stanley noticed him and smiled, then returned to his work, jabbing efficiently at the swinging black bag. Pedro appeared out of sorts while waiting until the new time clock-bell (on the floor near the wall) rang out the signal for the end of a round. Megumi had arranged for the business to buy the timer, at Stanley's suggestion.

119

"Man," Pedro said then, shaking his gloved hands downwardly, while Stanley paced along the wall. "Good stuff. You got a great jab."

"Yeah, lucky that way."

"Someday let's spar and I wanna try to avoid it, ha ha ha!"

Stanley couldn't decide if Pedro was serious or not, but nodded, in silent agreement.

Pedro stepped closer and held up his hand, palm outward. "Please, amigo. May I borrow twenty dollars? I'm in a – a – " he couldn't finish. The bell rang to begin the round.

"Trouble?" Stanley asked, seeing it was rather more than a minor problem.

Pedro smiled embarrassedly, put his hand down, and Stanley nodded.

Turned out his father hadn't sent the check he usually received the first of the month, and he was short of funds. Sure, Stanley lent it to him, even asking if he needed more, since twenty dollars didn't go so far in the modern world. In the '70s, perhaps.... Anyway, as Pedro hesitated, Stanley pulled another twenty from his crumpled wad of bills and Pedro grandly bowed and thanked him. They accomplished this transaction outside in the parking lot behind the gym.

"As soon as I get the check I'll be sure to repay you, amigo," Pedro said somewhat formally.

"No sweat, amigo." It sounded odd as he pronounced the word "amigo," because Stanley was not exactly sure if Pedro was his friend. More an acquaintance, really. It was one of those idiosyncrasies of Stanley's, trying to understand a complicated, nearly impossible to understand world. A sinful world, a deceptive world, a world heading for great tribulation in the unknowably distant future. Or, not so distant.

Anyway, Stanley often made the evaluation: was a person just a stranger, an acquaintance, a friend, or a good friend? He had his own definition of each level. Most people didn't bother to think about it to that degree.

But a stranger owed you nothing, except common courtesy, an acquaintance owed a general kindly acknowledgment, a friend, a deeper fondness and communication, and a good friend an even fuller give-and-take, a willingness to support the other no matter whether a return in effort (or funds) would result. A good friend, of all relationships, should be expected to give of him or herself regardless of any expectation of personal gain, when the other needed help. The first three levels were not to be held to such an exacting standard.

That's how Stanley viewed it, anyway.

Pedro wasn't at the gym the next week, any of the three times Stanley went in. He didn't ask Megumi because it would have been uncomfortable – why should he care that much if Pedro had been in or not?

Forty dollars wasn't *nothing*, but still it wasn't that significant to Stanley. If someone was going to scam him out of forty dollars...well, tough shit, he figured. He remembered when he'd swiped carburetor cleaner from the shelf when he worked at a gas station, thinking little of it. People stole, people repented, things changed. He was sorry, now, but if Pedro was at a mental point in his life where he didn't grasp the wrongness of taking from others – who was Stanley to judge?

He'd ordered another volume of the Sherlock Holmes Mystery Magazine. He'd read two or three of them. And in his bizarre characteristic way had forgotten which numbers of the series they were, and if he ordered more he *should* dig them out from wherever they had gotten to among his many old books stacked up around his apartment, to make sure he ordered one he'd not gotten yet. Only a fool would just keep getting them and not pay attention, to take care, not to get duplicates – but then again Stanley didn't worry about the cost of that foolishness, like other people would. He didn't care – though he ought to.

And little did he know before long he'd need some of the skills, and the deductive reasoning methods, of Sherlock Holmes himself, to figure out the mystery that was to engage him shortly.

He got a call from an old friend (in both senses) from his acting years, a nice outgoing actor who had not made it very big but had worked more often than Stanley. He'd gotten Stanley's number from Andrew. He'd be in town next month. He was mostly retired, but took an occasional audition, and had one coming up, and there was time in his schedule to visit with Stanley, so could they get together?

Could they "hang out," could they "catch up," could they "touch base"? He used all the clichés, and after the conversation Stanley felt a bit manipulated, and wondered what Robbie had up his sleeve, if anything.

A lunch at a Hollywood restaurant was proposed, when next Robbie called, but Stanley felt an aversion to well-known Hollywood restaurants. A compromise? "Whatever," Robbie said.

They settled on less-trendy but respectable Highland Hills, a coffee shop just north of Sunset Boulevard. "So be it," Stanley observed, and a date and time was agreed upon.

Meanwhile a conflict arose in his mind. Did he want to ask Robbie to see if there was a role for him in the project Robbie was auditioning for? Tricky, since the role Robbie was going in for may be the only one Stanley would be fit for, age-and-physical-wise. But perhaps there was another part…? Or he could just get the name of the project and ask her agent (if he would take his phone call) to look into it, if his agent cared to….

But would Robbie feel put upon? Used?

By the day of the lunch he still wasn't sure if Robbie would mind, so he decided to follow his intuition during the conversation.

They both had cheeseburgers. They would have both had coffee, too, but Robbie ordered a beer. The talk was jovial enough and still, Stanley hesitated. Then he found an opening.

"So, you haven't done shit since – what – the nineties?"

"Oh," Stanley replied, "I worked a couple of times in the – you know – in the zeroes."

"Oh. A couple of times?"

"Small parts."

Robbie laughed, "That sucks, man."

"No kidding." As he watched Robbie drink his beer, he sprang to action. "Any parts for me in this thing you're doing?"

"Umm...I haven't got it yet, but..." Robbie looked away, thinking. "No,, not really. Well, an ex-con who gets shot up by the cops. Not much of a part."

"Yeah, well, that's all right. Thanks anyway," Stanley said.

"My part's pretty good, though. Even a romance. Old guy, old woman. Having a fling."

"Cool," Stanley offered, wishing he hadn't asked anything about it. A pang of envy passed through him, but it vanished quickly.

What the hell did he care, he asked himself? He hadn't been pursuing an acting career for – for – years.

"Hope you get it," he told him.

Afterwards, Robbie called to say he *hadn't* gotten the role, anyway, and that they should have lunch again in the near future. Stanley agreed, but thought he'd have to call about it himself and not wait for Robbie, who like most actors would fail to follow up on plans. It was the boxer in him that saw things through, unlike most actors (and actresses) he'd met. They were slightly odd and inconsistent types – more full of imagination than practicality.

But he didn't have to make the call! A week later, he was at lunch with Robbie, this time at Denny's in the valley, listening to a crazy story: Robbie had been invited to attend a party (an indoor barbecue of all things) in the hills above Hollywood. Could

Stanley go with him? He didn't feel right going alone, and anyway, some producers and other film types would be there – it could "lead to jobs," he said.

Plus it was a two-day invitation (with two nights in the "mansion," as Robbie referred to it), a "wonderful place."

So, he went. A big house, automatic gate, a circular drive inside (around a fountain in the center), two stories, wide in appearance and with balconies. Steps leading to the entrance. When Robbie parked behind a Honda near the fountain he said, rather condescendingly, "That's the maid's car. Frederick's luxury rides are in the garage."

They pulled their two small bags from the rear seat and heard a loud "Hello" from the now open front door.

Stanley saw a smiling, short, dark man (Spanish?) on the top step.

"Hello, Frederick. We made it!" Robbie slammed his car door and advanced to Frederick, while Stanley followed.

The two men hugged and Robbie introduced Stanley.

"Welcome! Come in!" They made their way inside, and the rest of the afternoon was a blur for Stanley – a well-furnished, European-style layout, a big bedroom with two beds, for Robbie and him, a wife who didn't descend to the living room for twenty minutes, beer and jokes, and a sense of unreality for Stanley, who felt the wealth around him and the strangeness and the odd congeniality of Robbie who behaved as though he was a family member instead of a "friend" with this pair of – what were they? – rich people.

Dinner was out, though, at an Italian restaurant. Pleasant enough but boring conversation for Stanley. Or...not truly boring, it was...too formal. Stanley was informal by nature, and formality irked him, pained him. Yet Robbie fell into the groove and spoke in the measured tones of his friends.

The subject of boxing came up. It was unavoidable, actually, because his hosts asked him questions – polite questions – about his life, his history, etc. But a tight look in Mrs. Pace's eyes told him she didn't approve, and a blank look in Mr. Pace's eyes told him *he* didn't care.

Strangely, Stanley thought, if he smashed a left at him, right there at the table, he *would* care. The idea shocked him, to have such an idea at all, but there it was. Perhaps he was feeling negative toward these people, and toward Robbie too, for some reason.

Robbie drank too much scotch and laughed loudly at comments that weren't funny. And he leaned toward Stanley in an overly friendly manner, even touching his arm, and the horrifying thought came to Stanley, "What if he was bisexual, or just homosexual, and had designs on Stanley in the bedroom they shared? Had he invited him here for that?"

The men and the classy woman returned then to the fancy house in the Hollywood Hills, Stanley aggrieved over how to deal with a potential situation. He knew he must say *something* to Robbie – but what?

He could be wrong and would upset Robbie. But he could be right, and still upset him. At the house they all were saying goodnight when Frederick asked the guys if they wanted cigars on the patio. They declined, but Stanley caught himself and switched his position.

"Sure, why not? It's still early." A lie, but then again, was it? It wasn't "late," because he didn't want to have his planned conversation upstairs with Robbie. It *was* early, looking at it that way.

"Excellent!" Frederick responded, obviously wanting a cigar himself. His wife smiled and made her way to the staircase.

"See you fellows in the morning," she said to the guests, and vanished upward, quietly.

The gentlemen sat on the patio, which provided a view of homes, hills, trees, shrubs, and sky. A half moon was out. The air was neither chill nor much heated – good weather to relax in.

Frederick provided a container of cigars, large or small, foreign or domestic. He attempted to identify which was which but the two guests really couldn't have cared less. They lit up, they sat in comfortable chairs, they puffed contentedly.

Except for Stanley who dreaded what he must say later. He knew why, too. Once, in the service, at a private house off-base when a friend had taken him to meet a hot girl called "Blondie," he'd learned a lesson. There was no "Blondie." The owner of the house had lured them in with the promise, however. The friend knew him, had met him some way or other in town, and Stanley assumed all was well. They drank, and the owner, a very nice type, rather prosperous and kindly, put the young men up for the night, and apologized when the girl he'd invited hadn't "shown up."

In the night, in a bedroom by himself, Stanley slept soundly, having, however, drunk too much. They were both under drinking age, these two sailors, and booze never was easily procured. A certain wildness attended any drinking, as if each isolated time was somehow to be the last. And with the chance of being sent into the war in Vietnam, an undercurrent of uneasiness flowered in the minds of the servicemen, so when given the opportunity….

But out of a deep sleep, Stanley was roused – the man who owned the house was climbing into his bed, saying, as Stanley opened his eyes and began to sit up, "Don't worry, fella. You're going to enjoy this, and –"

But Stanley leaped clumsily out of the bed, to the other side, yelling almost incoherently, "I'm not fucking Jimmy!" There was a shocked look on the man's face, and he ceased positioning himself into the bed.

"What?"

"I'm not fucking Jimmy!"

Stanley had quickly calculated that Jimmy was a betrayer, had been in this man's bed and perhaps sent him to Stanley's bed. Who knew? Alcohol distorts impressions and conclusions, but that was what he thought.

And the man backed off, a step backward, saying, "All right, all right, easy." He held his hands up, vanishing from the room.

So Stanley slept, and in the morning the man drove both boys to the bus station – as if nothing had happened.

And it was like nothing had, on the bus ride returning to base, until Jimmy announced, "That creep. He said that blonde girl would be there, and he lied." He turned to Stanley, sitting beside him. "He fucking lied, I'm telling you. He just wanted to get us out there."

To this Stanley could but nod in agreement. He had little if any interest in telling the story of the previous night to Jimmy.

But Jimmy already knew. As the bus bumped its methodical way through the streets, Jimmy let out a laugh. "When that bastard came back to bed he told me you scared the shit out of him!"

"Oh, yeah," Stanley muttered, thinking: "Bed? They were…?"

But Jimmy answered that unspoken question, "Yep, he got me into bed earlier. I was drunk." He shrugged.

Stanley, aghast, had kept his mouth shut. In a moment Jimmy continued, "He went down on me. I let him. What the hell?" He stared out the window and added, "It's disgusting, really."

The rest of the way they spoke of other subjects. Except once more Blondie came into Jimmy's mind.

"I really believed him. I'd heard of her before, from – well, never mind. Someone who said he'd been out there and she was there." He was quiet for a moment or two. "Hell. *He* must have lied too. Just to cover up what he'd done!"

"Lied because…?" Stanley asked, stupidly.

"Yeah, man. He lied to me to cover up his own doings with the guy! A homosexual. I don't want to say who he is, I don't want –"

"Sure," Stanley interrupted.

"But fuck. I'm not like that. It was only…." He said no more.

"Sure, man. I won't tell either."

Jimmy made a face and let the discussion drop.

It didn't matter to Stanley, though. He wasn't sure if Jimmy was one or not, but he didn't care. People did what they felt like doing, one way or the other. As long as they didn't impose it on him – that's all.

So he had to tell Robbie the way it was to be: Robbie had to keep his hands off him if Robbie had any plans along those lines, now. But should he use those words, or some others?

In the room after separate trips to the bathroom, the men undressing, Stanley made himself say, "Look, you know, uh, I feel I must mention that, uh, I don't know about you but I'm straight. Just don't be offended."

The words stopped Robbie as he sat on his bed untying his shoes. He chuckled. "Are you crazy?"

"I'm just saying."

Robbie made no remark, other than a muttering, "Uh-huh."

The night wasn't quite sleepless but it wasn't a wonderfully sound sleep, either. But there were no problems.

The morning was sunny, the coffee good, the talk friendly at a large wooden table, with the four of them. A servant served. It was curious to Stanley. He thought maybe breakfast would be handled by the wife, and/or the husband. But no, they were just too wealthy for *that* relaxation of standards.

Frederick's business came up in conversation as a topic and yet, oddly, the information about it was very scarce.

As Stanley learned later, Frederick didn't care for strangers knowing about his work, or his "company," either. Some kind of clothing manufacturing, from what he could gather. Hip clothes and jackets, especially, for men and women. With outlets here and...somewhere else, South America?

The main happening soon after breakfast was the arrival of another house guest. Miss Crowley, a producer of TV and film. Her boyfriend (who was to join them all later at the barbecue, but not spend the night), was described as a "black gentleman" by Mrs. Pace, "So don't be shocked, please."

"Oh, no," Robbie laughed in embarrassment, "That wouldn't shock me."

When she looked at Stanley he shrugged, as if to say "whatever" – a word he wished he could say but felt constrained. Many people, older people, took it as a kind of insult, or a slight, because it had years before become a cute saying among youngsters, a saying which tended to confuse the older generation. Was it confirmation? A rebuff? Stanley thought of it as a word of compliance, yet didn't know if Mrs. Pace did. So he remained silent. It slightly surprised him she even considered a black man a possible subject of significance, but these were rich folks, and such did have ways and mores generally foreign to him.

Miss Crowley arrived in a flurry of activity, her hair askew and her bags being dumped inside the door by a surly limousine driver who left with instructions to return the next day.

"Sure, lady. I know all about it," he said as he backed out the door.

"Darling," Mrs. Pace breathed gently, embracing the new guest, and adding, "Wonderful to see you."

Miss Crowley smiled warmly but professionally, issuing an air kiss and a perfunctory, "Great to see you. I packed in a rush."

"We have anything you may need. Come, I'll show you – oh, here's Calvin! Will you bring this lady's bags upstairs?" She led the way.

Miss Crowley was young, healthy looking, not overly pretty, but then again she was a producer, not an actress. She wore white slacks and a white jacket, no hat, an expensive watch, but no wedding band. They climbed the staircase as Calvin, the part-time bodyguard, all-around assistant who'd been called to service due to the barbecue, grabbed the three suitcases and followed the women.

In the kitchen, noise and cooking smells abounded. A trio of cooks expertly fashioned a meal for eight – pork, beef, fish, rice, beans, salad, and even vegetarian hot dogs. The hamburgers and steaks were to be grilled early, at Mr. Pace's insistence. He wanted the party to be a party, not a staid dinner with courses provided in formal fashion. Today he would wear a cowboy hat indoors, and boots, like he did as a young man at his parents' ranch, years ago.

But there was racquetball first, at the outdoor court, which Mrs. Pace prevailed upon Robbie and Stanley to participate in, with her daughter, who mysteriously appeared seemingly out of nowhere. As it turned out, she lived not far away in a small but lovely house. A beautician who was "going her own way" after dropping out of UCLA, Robbie told him.

She had blonde hair, a too-prominent nose for a rich kid (not kid, really, at 25, but full of energy and laughter). Obviously a nose job was against her bohemian principles. But she wasn't entirely bohemian. Belle (her real name) was also a product of fine schools and summers at a beach house in Balboa, where smoking weed, and sex, were not unknown activities – hidden, of course, from parents and relatives.

Belle also read books – literature, history, romance novels – and saw to it that boyfriends behaved well even when she didn't, always. She had a tendency to quarrel and even holler, when she felt like it. Spoiled to some degree, always getting money from her father, always showing affection for both her parents, and respect.

She just wanted to do nails, hair, and make-up for other women. It fascinated her. She loved to chat with women, to joke as females joke, about the disgusting traits of men.

She had little ambition, a fact that irritated her parents, and she didn't seek marriage, no matter what bachelors came her way.

Yet she enjoyed being at the big house and joined in the life there when she could. Racquetball was great exercise, everyone said. And she excelled at it.

She had no trouble beating the two old guys her mother matched them with. Her mother was a fair player, so the two together, a formidable pair.

Stanley enjoyed it; he felt strong from his workouts at the gym, and had enough wind (not nearly as much as in the old fighting days, since he didn't run much) and his old competitive spirit (which had not been up to par for his trainers and managers, but was sufficient for him to excel to an extent).

Stanley never had cared so very much about winning – it was the joy and invigoration of participating that appealed to him, the sense of being alive.

"Damn it!"

"Sorry, Belle."

"Never mind."

The women exchanged remarks as they panted around the court. Robbie laughed rather than spoke, and Stanley confined himself to occasional grunting. While racquetball may look easy, it certainly wasn't.

"Belle, get back."

"Be careful."

"I am, I am!"

But as the festivities were soon to take place, the four of them had to give it up, and none too soon for the old guests, who were starting to tire. Mrs. Pace, slightly younger than them, and used to the sport, appeared happy and refreshed. And Belle, who played the best, seemed tireless.

Matter of fact, her red cheeks and smooth legs drew Stanley's attention more than once or twice. Robbie was less interested in her, but charming nonetheless, calling her Billie Jean King and evoking laughter from Mrs. Pace, who asked, "What about me?" Belle pretended not to know who Billie Jean King was, no doubt only to tease Robbie.

They went upstairs to bathe and dress, and Stanley pictured Belle in the shower, but quickly drove that image from his mind.

He was glad he needn't appear naked in front of Robbie, who did go naked for a moment in their room, and hit the shower first. But Stanley had brought a robe and donned it while Robbie was showering. He didn't care if his fears of Robbie had any basis in fact, or reality – they were there, they haunted him, and while he held a democratic view that Robbie or anyone else, for that matter, could be whatever they felt they were (short of hurting anyone, children especially), still a worry afflicted his psyche, and he behaved accordingly.

He showered while Robbie dressed, in sport jacket and tie. Robbie was on the patio smoking while Stanley dressed in his own version of a sports jacket – a khaki military-looking affair and black jeans.

He combed his hair and wished he had shaved, but changed his mind. Why should he be so formal? It was a barbecue, wasn't it?

Indeed it was. More guests had arrived, men without ties, one of the women in shorts. It was not as formal an affair as Robbie'd suggested.

They were a pleasant group, young and old.

"Darling!"

"How are you?"

"Love your hair!"

"Making any money, ha ha?"

"Give me a hug."

"Sit here."

"Need a drink? Ask the maid there."

"Did you see the movie about – what's the name? About the pig?"

"Let me get you some more ribs, Darling."

"This is Stanley. He was a boxer. Friend of Robbie's."

"How do you do?"

"I'm fine, thanks. You?"

The food was good. Steaks, hamburgers, fish, ribs, corn, fried potatoes, milk, wine, beer, iced tea, coffee, bourbon, scotch, whiskey, etc.

The people listened to, oddly enough, a dose of rap music, but also Sinatra, Lionel Ritchie and (surprising Stanley) a masterpiece of the not-too-distant past, "Walking in Memphis" by Marc Cohn. Some of the guests danced in a small but adequate ballroom adjacent the dining room. Miss Crowley and her boyfriend had the most fun of all.

Another producer, Sam Lister, danced with Belle more than once. But Belle found Stanley, laughed at him for sitting by himself, and led him protestingly to the floor to make him dance whether he wanted to or not, twice.

The loud scream from outside ruined everything, of course, but it was fun for awhile.

Several guests hurried toward the pool area, several held back. Stanley froze, then followed Belle, who dashed through the open double patio doors, and when she had proceeded no more than a few seconds, yelled:

"Mother! Why – "

A new but less vociferous scream came from Mrs. Pace, who then said, "Look!"

"Oh my God," a man said, and his wife repeated the exclamation.

As Stanley exited the doors and approached the now gathering group at poolside, he saw Belle kneel down beside an inert body, a man, soaking wet, at the water's edge.

Sam Lister had just pulled him out.

Mrs. Pace stepped back behind Belle. "Is he alive?" she asked.

Belle put her ear to the man's mouth. "I don't think so," she replied, tremulously.

"It's Bruce," said Mrs. Pace. Mr. Pace now advanced from the ballroom, a strange look on his face: obviously a problem was causing this disturbance, and he feared to imagine what it was. Robbie was behind him, his face blank.

"Let me in there. What is it?" Mr. Pace demanded, pushing forward.

Belle stood; Mr. Pace took her place. "Shit, what happened? Did he fall in?"

Later, after the paramedics had failed to bring life to the wet body, and the policemen were questioning everyone, Belle clung to Stanley's arm with one hand and drank whiskey with the other from a glass. Photographs of the area were taken, the body was removed, the guests stood around helplessly. The music had been turned off.

Belle was shocked, a tearful look on her face. Stanley had seen a bit of death before, though not much, and it sustained his reaction of cold evaluation, of reserve, of calmness. And Belle clung to *that* as she clung to his arm. The group of barbecue-goers dispersed. Mrs. Pace pleaded with Robbie (and by extension Stanley) to follow the plan of spending the night.

Mr. Pace sat in a soft chair drinking whiskey, speaking with his friend Raymond, a business friend, a comfort to him. Raymond sat near him, in a chair pulled from the dining table. The maid, the kitchen help, were allowed to depart.

"Let the clean-up wait," Mrs. Pace had said (when the police were there). The maid still put items in the dishwasher, and the cook put away much of the leftovers, but neither of them wanted to stay after speaking with the police (very briefly). They were notably stunned.

Not a single one of the guests said they had seen Bruce in the pool, or heard a sound indicating he (or anyone) had been in the pool, by accident, choice, or otherwise. The policeman in charge was rather of a mind Bruce must have had too much to drink, and the marks indicating a blow (from him slipping and striking his head) were noticeable; the cause of his drowning (if he had) would await further investigation.

Stanley had not bothered to ask what might have occurred – he overheard police tell others they just couldn't say at this time, repeatedly.

"Was he a friend of yours?" Stanley asked Belle. He saw no reason to avoid the subject, as she was relaxing rapidly, due to the alcohol.

"Not so much. I knew him a little."

"You parents' friend?"

"Thank God he's single," she said, not answering his question.

"Well, he fell in, I'm sure."

"You are?" she asked.

Stanley saw the sweet look in her eyes, half-pleading with him to make it so "simple."

He wanted to ask, "What else?" but instead murmured assent.

Robbie approached. "The cops are finished." He had a glass in his hand, also.

At the door, Mrs. Pace said goodbye to Sam Lister and his wife Rachel, a small woman in a pale blue dress. She looked somber while Sam was repeating, "You will be okay? You promise?" to Mrs. Pace, as they went outside and down the steps.

"Oh, yes. Thank you."

Miss Crowley and Roger sat quietly on the couch. Mr. Pace brooded. Robbie rose partly to the occasion, telling him to stop worrying. But he didn't put much enthusiasm into his words.

Belle sat at the now-empty table, a cloth of purple and white still draped over it, a bottle of wine (red) and one of champagne looking lonely there, with two empty wine glasses nearby.

"Nasty," Stanley said to no one in particular, as he too sat, finally, in a comfortable chair, against the wall. He wanted a beer but felt slightly disrespectful about it, so closed his eyes instead, wondering if Bruce had been held under the water by someone – odd thing to think, he told himself. But there was a nagging idea, a memory, teasing around his brain.

Then it came to him. One of the guests, while eating – who was it? – had elbowed Bruce Montana when Bruce had told him, "What wouldn't I give to spend the night with that Miss Crowley."

Oh yeah, he said it to Raymond, Mr. Pace's business friend, who'd poked his elbow into Bruce's ribs and remarked, "Knock it off."

"Why?" Bruce had responded. "Jealous?"

"Of you? No, stupid. But Crowley has a boyfriend."

"So what?"

Stanley had not heard any more, but now he glanced over at Raymond, still sitting near Mr Pace. Something caught his eye, and he rose to advance on the dining room table, poured a glass of red, stepped back, and sat on the floor near Mr. Pace.

"Are you okay?" he asked him.

"Oh, yes, thanks. It's only the shock of it, really. But I knew Bruce quite well."

"Did you?" Stanley asked, but looked down at the floor. He was glad there was no answer to his question. He wanted to get a good look at Raymond's pants cuffs. Sure enough, they were wet. Not too obviously, however, because the pants were brown. But no doubt about it.

He drank from his glass.

Mrs. Pace moved to her husband, placing her hands on his shoulders. "Why don't you go to bed, Frederick? Get some sleep, if you can."

He looked around at her face. Smiling, he said "No, you, dear. You go get some sleep."

She shook her head, patting him. "Not yet."

Suddenly Stanley realized that Raymond's shirt had been rolled up at the sleeves, up to the elbows. He tried to look casually, to examine the rolled part. They *appeared* to be dry, but were they?

Mrs. Pace kissed her husband on the cheek, turned and stepped over to the sofa. She sighed very audibly. "Oh God," she said, slipping onto the sofa, asking, more to herself, "What has happened?"

And Stanley, wondering exactly the same, stood as he placed his glass down. He thought there were two ways to find out if Raymond's shirt sleeves were wet. Ask – ask to examine them – or grab at them impolitely.

What would Sherlock do? "I think he drowned," he said to Mrs. Pace. She jerked her head, and her eyes, to Stanley.

"Certainly," Frederick said. "He fell in, but...why? Couldn't he swim?"

Stanley lunged at the sleeve nearest him, with his left hand, grabbing suddenly and firmly. Raymond tried to pull away but being unable to, slapped at Stanley's hand. "Hey, lay off!"

"Your shirt is damp," Stanley yelled. Frederick began to rise, but Stanley smiled and released his grip on Raymond's arms. "Damp with pool water, I believe."

"What?" Mrs. Pace exclaimed. "So what?"

"He wasn't near the pool with us, that's the problem. He stayed away the whole time." Before Raymond was able to speak, he continued, "Pool water on your pants, too," he said, pointing down.

Robbie had come forward to stand beside Stanley, as Raymond spoke. "You're crazy. I was in the kitchen, I rinsed some glasses, I –"

"You argued with, uh, Bruce. I overheard it, you hit him with your elbow. About Miss Crowley."

Belle now stood beside Stanley. "What?"

Raymond jumped up, but Robbie put his hand to his chest. "Take it easy, man," he said.

"That's absurd," Raymond said to Stanley. "Miss Crowley?"

"Yes. You poked him with your elbow. Sit down – I'm sure the cops can find out if you have pool water, or tap water, or your clothes. Quite easily."

Raymond turned to run, away from Robbie, but Robbie lunged after him, putting his arms around his waist. Mrs. Pace gasped, Mr. Pace stood and took one of Raymond's arms. "Stop!" he hollered. Raymond did stop struggling, but yet Robbie held him with both arms.

"You pushed him in there?" Stanley asked. "And held him under?"

"No!"

"I don't doubt it," Belle said. "He liked Miss Crowley. Didn't you?" she asked him.

Raymond refused to answer.

"You dated her, didn't you?" Belle asked. "Of course you did. Of course he had, right, Mother?"

Mrs. Pace said, in a rush, "Why, that's true. And she told me you were upset when she broke it off."

Raymond wrenched his arm out of Frederick's grip. "Lay off me," he shouted, and struggled to escape Robbie's hold.

"Why don't you just sit down?" Stanley asked, stepping over to him.

"All right," Raymond replied, and got to his chair, with Robbie alongside. He sat. Robbie had released his grip but stood where he was.

"You did it?" Mrs. Pace was dumbfounded. "Drowned him?"

Mr. Pace went to the phone on the table by the sofa. "I'm calling the police."

"Yes," Mrs. Pace told him.

It had certainly been a long night, the police arresting Raymond, taking statements, clothing as evidence, etc. etc. Mr. Pace did most of the talking but had to let Stanley give his version, his story, about overhearing the argument, discerning the wet pants and sleeves. That frankly impressed the two officers, one of which shook his hand respectfully and firmly, when they were leaving.

Raymond had been cuffed and put in the back of a cruiser, and driven to the station.

So all was well in the world, it seemed. Mrs. Pace left the group early, claiming tiredness and a bad headache. Belle had made coffee and sandwiches. Robbie sipped whiskey, looking bleary-eyed and pale.

It was so late, if they hadn't been so fatigued, the group might just as well have stayed up until dawn.

The dogs had barked from their pen at the commotion outside, the police radios, the engines firing up, and the two vehicles driving off. But they soon quieted down when the house became silent.

In the late morning events and people were stirring; Belle was up with Miss Crowley and Roger. They had breakfast prepared by the maid Leticia, and by eleven Mrs. Pace joined them, followed by Stanley and Robbie and Mr. Pace, looking haggard.

Belle had filled the early risers in as to what had transpired after they'd gone to bed. Naturally, Miss Crowley and Roger had heard the commotion of the returning police officers, but wisely had opted to remain in bed, listening.

It was shocking to Miss Crowley, of course. "What a maniac," she aptly described Raymond. She looked on the verge of tears, but managed stern control. "What a wonder you are, Stanley, figuring it out."

"Nothing, really," he said in Sherlockian false modesty.

They all exchanged phone numbers. Miss Crowley feared she'd be called in to make some sort of statement about dating Raymond, and Roger patted her hand.

"Don't worry. I'll go with you."

Stanley liked the man, but didn't want to impose himself by asking what he did for a living. He decided to call him sometime and have lunch and ask a few questions. He told Belle he'd call her, and thanked the Paces for having him over, and said fairly sheepishly, "It was a good visit, regardless."

He went into headquarters later to sign his statement. Two reporters got his number and called for him to comment, but Stanley begged off.

A month went by, he worked out at the gym, he drank water, he read books, he got a massage or two, and Robbie called to say a trial would *not* be taking place, that Raymond had pled guilty to manslaughter and was sentenced to ten years.

Seemed like light punishment, to Stanley, but what the hell, the D.A. must have felt the evidence was weak, and Stanley was glad not to have to go in and testify. The defendant's attorneys would surely have tried to trip him up on the stand about the argument he'd overheard.

Since it *did* turn out there was chlorine in Raymond's shirt and pants, Raymond may have felt it wasn't worth the risk to plead not guilty and be sentenced to life – or worse – if convicted.

Meanwhile Pedro still didn't pay back the money, and finally Stanley asked him about it.

"Could you say when you might pay me the $40?"

Pedro was working on one of the bags and turned his head, looked at Stanley, and replied, "What put a bug up your ass?"

"Huh? It's been quite awhile, man."

"I don't have it," Pedro growled. "Leave me alone."

"I'm asking *when*."

Pedro walked over to him. "I don't want to talk about it."

"Why not?"

At that point, Pedro shot a right cross and it hit Stanley on the nose. All he could do was pull back a bit, but not far enough.

As Pedro stared, Stanley stepped in with a jab and a sharp uppercut, whereupon Pedro covered his head with his gloves. "Uhh," he groaned. It had been a hard punch. Even the jab had stung him.

"Okay, okay!" Pedro spat out, moving away.

That was the end of it, except for a week Stanley's nose was sore and even putting ice on it didn't bring down the swelling. He knew from experience it had been broken. He didn't really care too much, but was annoyed he'd not even blocked. That's what happens when a fighter doesn't spar. He loses his speed for reacting to attempted hits.

He'd have to find a gym with a boxing ring and do some sparring no question about it. But he never saw Pedro again – who'd quit coming to the gym. And of course he didn't repay the loan.

"Whatever," Stanley thought. Just another adventure with him being slightly the worse for wear.

The ironic part of it all was that Stanley had helped the guy learn how to punch like that.

He looked around for a gym with boxers and rings, but didn't succeed. He looked on the internet with little luck – such gyms were far away. If he was still a fighter, an active one, then the distance would have not been a deciding factor. But at his age, and temperament, he wasn't about to sacrifice *that* much.

God, he trusted. Christ, he trusted. Even the Holy Ghost, a more weird element, to a man's understanding, he trusted. The Spirit led him. The Bible says that Jesus sent the Spirit when he, Jesus, ascended to Heaven to be with the Father. Okay, we have a "counselor," the Bible says. So Stanley relied on that.

Praying was fairly simple; the prayers were directed at God, in the "person" of the Father, of the Lord Jesus, of the Holy Ghost. Which one answered the prayer was difficult to say. And yes, many prayers went unanswered, because they weren't God's will.

Stanley prayed for greater health, for more peace, for more love both in his heart and in others', and yes, more money.

The big contacts, at the house in the hills, the producers, etc. who were supposed to help Robbie and Stanley get jobs...well, that just didn't happen. How could it with a murder taking place?

He didn't feel like speaking with Robbie, anyway. He still felt uncomfortable the way he'd touched him and leaned into him that first evening. *Probably* just his imagination supplying reasons for Robbie's behavior, when it was only alcohol and friendliness.

He should call him. But he didn't. They had talked over the phone during the weeks right after the events at the house, and had agreed to meet again for lunch, but neither followed up. Stanley believed it was because he'd told Robbie he wasn't interested in a – what to call it? – a match, a coupling, a fling? A homosexual one. So of course, Robbie would not follow up on any plans to be with Stanley again (if that had been Robbie's hope). But had it been?

It didn't matter, Stanley's life went on slowly, as normal. He'd had a momentary vision of a new acting job – but that vanished when Bruce was drowned. Raymond in his plea bargain told of overpowering the short man (holding his hand over his mouth), banging his head on the concrete around the pool, putting him unconscious into the water, and holding him under until he stopped sucking in water. Whether Bruce had choked back into *consciousness*, Raymond hadn't said. But Stanley believed it to be the case, and all the murderer had to do was bang his victim's head against the side of the pool and force him underwater once again.

But no, Raymond wouldn't admit to that if he hoped the court would be at all lenient – yet Stanley felt somehow, in his mind, that a second part of the assault had taken place, although he couldn't explain why he thought it. An intuitional conclusion, likely.

He went through his routine – shopping, exercising, eating, reading, etc., having breakfast with Bill, and occasionally Troy. Longing in his heart for a woman friend, and waiting for the primaling he'd done to take effect.

He got his hair colored and cut. Stanley didn't like the grey to show. What man did, as he aged? Well, some of course, some who didn't care and others whose wives wanted their men to have a distinguished grey-haired look.

But while lacking in vanity in most areas, this Stanley felt strongly about: age. He looked younger than his years, and wanted to keep it that way. He didn't mind *saying* he was old – he often did that at the grocery store when he asked for a bag to carry his beer in, telling the clerk it was easier to carry "for an old guy." They usually asked him if he wanted to carry the six-pack by the handles. He usually had a cloth bag, but the purchases didn't always all fit in it. Hence the need for a paper bag – which cost a few extra cents, maybe ten cents. He didn't really pay attention.

He drank his beer after a shower, noting his hair looked dark. Darker than it had actually been when he was younger. He'd asked for "dark brown" at the hair salon, as usual. After a few washings and exposure to the sun it turned more medium brown, anyway.

He watched the news. Lots of political talk as the campaigns were heating up during this election year. And of course the war against ISIS, or ISIL. Bad dudes, very bad dudes. What motivated them Stanley couldn't really imagine – unless it was the devil himself controlling them.

Whoever won the White House, Hillary Clinton or someone else, they'd have their hands full. That's how he judged it, drinking beer and staring at the TV screen.

He wanted to go to the theater and see some of the films in contention for the Oscars, but didn't have the energy. He wanted to drive to the beach, to walk on the sand, one of his favorite things to do in the past, but couldn't bring himself to do it for some reason. He wanted to write a poem, and *that* he did do.

It takes time; one had to return to it many times over to get it the way which seemed correct. And yet it became only another poem he put in a flat large envelope filled with many others, and put in a desk drawer.

He wanted to go on a date, but who could he ask? A waitress? A masseuse? A cashier at the market? He didn't have the gumption, although a few of them did appeal to him. Not that he would satisfy them sexually if it came to that. But a date was only a date, not a major commitment. So he took the idea into consideration.

He'd had a number of dates when working on location in films. Dinner dates, usually at the hotel where the cast and crew were staying. Easy. You met in the dining room at a certain time, ordered drinks, ordered food. Talked, joked, told a story or two. He didn't invite many of them to his room after, and so, seldom knew whether they would have gone, or not. One or two did.

And one, a hairdresser, had invited him to *her* room. Bold. But he said no thanks, he was tired, he appreciated it, but...she must have thought he was insane.

He preferred to get a massage, and when he felt aroused, would ask for more gentle, intimate, treatment.

Meanwhile, he got another book from Amazon, one he'd been putting off reading for so long he couldn't recall when, and who, it was recommended it. A difficult book, a complicated book, a book on the long, convoluted U.S. entrance and participation into the Vietnam war, from our people's, the American people's, the Washington people's, the military people's, perspective. Naturally he'd put off reading it. Who wouldn't want to? But he wanted to know what it said. It was from *after* the secret Pentagon Papers were published, so much truth would be contained inside its many pages. A man named David had written it, a journalist, Halberstam. Stanley didn't know who he was, but he was *somebody*; he had researched and had interviewed and had considered and had written, and so long as he was honest, it didn't matter that his wasn't a name most Americans knew, like Lyndon Johnson or *some* Americans knew, like Robert McNamara.

So, he began reading it when it arrived in the mail, and it opened his eyes to many things.

One thing was how the men around the presidents (Kennedy and Johnson) followed along with the program toward Vietnam, and yet the ones around Johnson failed to object to the bombing and the troop escalation as might be expected. Johnson was too forceful, his advisors, and bureaucracy, just gave in after voicing (some number) their fears and doubts about it all.

Kennedy was more opposed to entering into combat in Vietnam than Johnson, but Kennedy was killed, and after the landslide election of 1964 Johnson had the power to send in troops to fight and airplanes to bomb: the shady deal of using the Tonkin Gulf incident to get Congress to authorize combat by American forces was the key to Lyndon Johnson's strength. He could claim legitimacy before the American people and the world for his military escalation. The war was on, it wasn't just advising the South Vietnam army, the South Vietnam government. It was not what Kennedy had wanted, as Stanley knew from other reading, and it may not ever have been what Johnson actually wanted, according to *The Best and the Brightest*, but it was what Johnson ended up approving. Don't look weak in the eyes of the world, don't let the communists take over, don't let the right-wing senators howl at you for being soft, etc., etc. And, it appeared to Stanley (although the author didn't suggest it), don't let those big oil men in Texas turn against you and make your life miserable.

Had Kennedy lived, and served two terms, would this misguided losing strategy of escalation of forces have occurred? Some say yes and some say no, Stanley had found over the years, when such speculation took place in conversation or on the news. It was more rare than he might imagine, because, no doubt, few people cared to delve into the question. Too painful, too frustrating.

Stanley knew his position, his conclusion to such a speculative question: he believed Kennedy was smarter than Johnson, and in fact braver and stronger, and would have resisted the political pressure to attempt to win in Vietnam, would have taken it on the chin if need be, initially, and gotten us out of the war there, and let the South fall if it had to fall.

But speculation is just a calculation, and only when he got to Heaven would Stanley know for sure – he would ask around, to get the answer.

The hardest part of reading the book was seeing how the actual numbers of the North Vietnamese troops were hidden from the civilians in Washington. General Westmorland, in Vietnam, didn't like the huge size of the potential reinforcements from the North, and told the intelligence officer, a colonel who had put together the estimate of the North's capacity, to revise the report by *lowering* the number. Otherwise, he might not get his war, his increased troop level, his wanted escalation. Whether Johnson knew about this trick was not known.

Stanley considered the book's content reliable, because it had the secret Pentagon Papers, as one source. And interviews of participants (after the fact), the fact of more than 50,000 American dead and many more wounded. If the escalation had been refused by the civilian leadership...there would have been far fewer casualties. But that's a matter of speculation. And Stanley had another speculation: what small part he'd had in the war might not have resulted, and the pang of guilt he felt, which made him want to drink more beer, now – well, that wouldn't even exist.

One day followed another. Stanley's birthday in March came and went as it always did. He knew of course, one day I would pass by and he wouldn't be alive, he would be passed on to Heaven – if he kept his faith.

Death wasn't an issue; it had ceased being an issue one "gone past day" he couldn't recall. He had stopped fearing death, perhaps as his faith in Christ grew, or perhaps when he'd been knocked out, or perhaps when he primaled about his difficult birth with its visions, of near-death experience images, and sensations. He knew he *had* feared death, had feared it in Vietnam on seaplane patrols, especially at night. But one day, in the 1970s or 1980s, when he was boxing, and he was beginning primaling, and solidifying his belief in salvation, it left him, mysteriously.

Not that he wanted to die. He clung to life as all men and women do (mostly). But he didn't care when it would happen. He'd accomplished some things in life, he'd helped some people, he'd made a little difference.

The natural *alert* system was functioning – he'd look twice around him in dark areas of the city, or over his shoulder if he heard a strange sound, a voice raised in intensity which could mean danger. But that was reflex.

One Monday morning, he discovered on the internet that it was close to St. Patrick's Day. He only knew a little about St. Patrick, but what he knew was impressive. And didn't it mean good luck? He wasn't going to celebrate by drinking more than his usual three or four beers but he wanted to do something. He was part Irish, too...so he was supposed to do something.

It would be on Thursday. A trip to a bar was not to his liking, but, something...special.

He asked Troy and Bill what they were up to. "Nothing."

So they talked it over, each to the other, phoning and texting, and decided on a movie at Bill's. He had a large TV screen, and couches. Troy brought his girlfriend. Neither Bill nor Stanley had any prospects, but Stanley asked Bill to invite his sister. All that idea produced was an "I'll find out."

If he was lucky, she'd be free and willing to join them. So he waited. The choice of which movie to watch would necessarily be Bill's, with a bit of input from the others.

Having only met Bill's sister once, Stanley felt nervous – and why not? He'd have to make an effort, he'd have to try to be charming, he'd have to be smiling and manly and funny and strong and...all that which he knew women liked. And lingering back of his mind the dread: if it went really well she might want to go with him to his apartment for sex, and he'd have to do that too, as best he could (like always).

But would it actually lead to that? No, no, she'd be careful because her brother, her older brother, would be right there in the house watching the movie, and watching her – and watching him, no doubt.

Fictitious fumbling foolishness, crazy idea in the first place! But what could he do now – he'd made the request, and must face up to the consequences, whatever they were.

Perhaps it would be all right, he told himself (over and over).

And he waited for the primaling results to kick in. But that was a chance he deemed unlikely. If feeling hadn't returned to his groin area it would take *more* primaling, and there wasn't time. He'd have to be nice to Joy at the movie party, and fend off any signs of aggressive interest on her part, if such there was. What mattered another minor embarrassment on his part? He'd been subject to that, as he recalled, since high school, anyway.

Then a reprieve: Bill called to say Joy wouldn't be able to attend.

The dread persisted, though. The problem wasn't solved, only a delay was in effect. It was to his advantage however. He'd be motivated to plunge into that Primal Pain again. And soon. No good putting it off!

Maybe, he hoped, this time he'd feel the Pain, whichever traumatic experience it came from, and be free of it.

Nevertheless he prayed, and had a little fear. He drove to the street where he usually parked and brought up in his mind the memories of past traumas as he usually did, and struggled to release the emotion. He saw himself being kicked in the crotch, and yelled out into the small cushion, and then saw himself being kicked in the crotch years later, in high school (a memory which was vague) when he'd pushed another student who had insulted his girlfriend. The guy didn't take kindly to that and swung up his foot before Stanley had enough time to react, and in the car Stanley yelled, hollered, and moaned with the pain, into the cushion.

It was his fault, of course. He had started it. But dirty fighting is still not acceptable, in his mind. After the primal, driving away, Stanley realized he needed to forgive that guy for what he did. Even 50-plus years ago. So he forgave him.

He drove to a 7-11, got a bottle of water and a six-pack of Pacifico and drove on to his apartment. The tiredness which usually followed a primal struck him, and he felt glad about it, as he usually did.

But the next day the strange irritation that followed a primal struck him, dogged him, as usual, made him slightly misinterpret the sounds outside his apartment as the source of his irritation, of the thoughts he had about life (which were closer to the truth being the "cause" of his irritation but were not actually it). He knew the unearthing of old long ago Pain was crossing into his conscious mind, and producing a conflict within – with a meeting of reality *now* and the "reality" of *then*.

It was an empty feeling, too. Like his world was empty, he only crisscrossing the boundaries of mental and physical dimensions, as if a dose of LSD had been slipped into his coffee. A small dose to be sure, but nonetheless a "tablet" producing mysterious illusions and confusing interpretations. But that reaction faded, and in two days his life appeared very normal again.

Bill said he had to go out of town to help his parents restore a house they'd purchased, to watch over the restoration, really. It was the very first time Bill had been entrusted with such responsibility, and he felt elated. They said goodbye outside the coffee shop as if he was going off to war. Or at the least, boot camp. Stanley felt sad, for some reason, like he was losing his friend permanently. It made no sense, but there it was.

He had to take aspirin because his arms hurt after workouts. A mean turn of events, because all his boxing career when his arms were sore he just toughed it out. Not now, though. He was old and didn't care to go through the day or two of suffering consistent with that painfulness caused by overexertion. Boxers knew they could "work out" the soreness by more exercise, and mostly left it at that. He was ashamed of himself but there was no one to blame. He asked God to heal him. He waited. It all turned out all right, so he went to the gym again, making sure he didn't do too much. Was that to be his life now, not doing "too much"?

Part III

There was no time to be whimsical. He watched the news and pondered the possible presidential election results. He only cared for his country – what was best for it – and by extension, the rest of the world (to a lesser extent). He loathed terrorism, he loathed poverty and hunger, he loathed greedy corporations if they were in essence huge sharks taking bites out of the "little people." He wasn't sure who the "little people" were except they were victims with low wages and even lower expectations.

Hence he approved of Clinton when he heard her speak. He also approved of Sanders, though his ideas seemed impossible to carry in a congress which may be more center, and right, than he.

He didn't like the Republican front-runners who wanted to step up the military attacks. He feared that would lead to greater troop levels, greater combat, and more loss of American lives. He'd had enough of that in the 1960s and early '70s. What good was fighting for the middle-east if we would only partly contain the enemy, the Islamic terrorists? It was like Vietnam all over again.

Stanley struggled through these ideas and prayed the leaders would have wisdom to deal with these important issues. He also called Roger about having lunch. The man was friendly, and agreed.

They decided to meet at a place in the Valley – Roger said he needed to be in the area anyway, he'd arranged a talk with a TV producer about an idea for a show Roger had been developing. A comedy. So seeing Stanley was convenient for him.

But the lunch didn't turn out as expected. Roger brought up the current political campaign, and surprisingly, to Stanley, announced he was not a Democrat, but instead a staunch Ted Cruz supporter – a Republican. And a conservative one at that.

At a table at Lulu's on Roscoe Boulevard, the two of them thrashed it out.

"Why so conservative?" Stanley asked him point blank.

"The leadership now, of our country, aren't doing enough. They are mighty weak, I think."

"How so?"

"Look, we have an enemy. The Muslims. They want to destroy us."

"Now, wait, man. Not all of them do. Only a small percentage."

"Oh, come on. Everybody knows they all hate us. They just pretend they don't. But anyway – listen. You wouldn't go into the ring and only fight halfway, would you?"

"No, no. But...are you talking about ground troops in Syria?"

"Yes," he said. "Anywhere. I was in the army. We were ready to go and fight, if we were ordered to. We should – "

"But Obama is conducting a whole lot of air strikes."

"That's not going to do the job," Roger insisted.

They left it at that. Stanley was shocked that a black guy would be so hawkish, but he was no doubt stereotyping Roger in a reverse fashion. Roger was adamant. He wanted to use greater force to combat terrorists and terrorism.

They paid their bill, splitting it, and shook hands outside.

"Good luck with your meeting, with your project," Stanley said.

Roger smiled. "Thanks a lot. I'm hopeful!"

They drove away, each in his own car, and each with his own beliefs.

He wanted to call him again, since there was a pleasure being in his company. Black men had comprised his main friends and associates at the gym, in the '70s, and he missed the particular mood and banter and support and yes, individuality they afforded. Most people would say Stanley was being somehow racist by this willingness, this partiality, but be that as it may, most people never had the – most *white* people – never had the opportunity to be friends with black men on such a constant, active level.

Stanley was able to see, to know, beyond the surface, these men (and their women, occasionally), in a way many white men never could, short of employment in a predominantly black work circumstance. And so he felt a kinship, a bond, with the black experience in America, at least in that limited way.

It was the struggle against the silent (and not always silent) biases on the part of whites, discrimination by the more powerful, with the honorable way *most* of the black fighters and trainers at the gym dealt with it that Stanley learned of and respected. Had *he* been in a minority, held back in promotion, or even denied a job in the first place, because of bias against him, he hoped he would be as brave and honorable in the face of that as these other men were.

They confided in him, after a period of time, after they got to know him, after they trained with him, after they saw his genuine interest in their success, their friendship.

What he learned was the reality of their being glanced at suspiciously on the street, in the stores, on the buses. And occasionally summoned taxis failing to stop. And police being harder on them than on whites. But the police, Stanley thought, *had* to be suspicious, considering the crime and poverty in some areas where blacks lived. The police were more suspicious of the Latinos, too, he noticed. But wasn't that because of a higher crime rate in the close, poor Latino neighborhoods?

Nevertheless, he found those friends at the gym fun to be around even more so than the few white fighters. Perhaps it was due to the *need* blacks were conscious of, to overcome prejudice and the resulting oppression, wherever the whites, including himself, didn't need to make themselves acceptable to the surrounding cultural environment in Los Angeles. They were already accepted, *nearly* everywhere they went, automatically.

So he phoned Roger once more, he chatted, he said they ought to get together for lunch again and "argue politics." Roger found that humorous, and agreed to meet soon.

So, one or the other had to call to arrange the future lunch. Who would do it? From Stanley's past experience he felt Roger would not be the one to do it. Those friends from the gym had been agreeable to "get-togethers" also, but Stanley was the one who followed up. And due to his shyness most often the sociable get-togethers didn't happen, unless it was to go to a match at one of the local arenas, or to run together in the morning somewhere.

So he stressed about it. He waited. He felt the old reluctance to do *anything* social with *anyone*. Shyness, mostly gone (compared to in his youth) reared its ugly and isolating head.

It was like in high school when he avoided friendships, and girlfriends – *anything* except a few people who reached out to him.

He called Troy. Since Bill was out of town, and had always been the one to invite Troy to breakfast, it was now up to Stanley to reach out, because Troy was not someone who had ever called, even though he had Stanley's number.

They met for a late breakfast.

"Coffee?" the waitress asked them. She knew them, and they said "yes," and she walked away, leaving them to read the menus.

By the time she'd returned with the coffee they each had decided what to order, and did, and she walked away again.

"What you been up to?"

Troy smiled, "Work."

"Yeah."

"What about you?"

Stanley shrugged. "Same old struggle."

"Ha!"

Life went on. Peace was there, an uneasy peace once in awhile, but mostly of a "tenor" to Stanley's satisfaction. He primaled again, having felt there was little progress on the sexual side. Maybe, he surmised, God didn't want him to enjoy sex, that such would lead him into troubles. It certainly had for many people, and yet...yet, there was no pressing guidance from the Spirit telling him to leave it alone, to not try to primal away the mental restrictions. He believed if God wanted him to leave it alone, to let it go on as it was, God would make a stronger impression about it on his heart.

God was mysterious, that's for sure, but on our side. These two factors provided Stanley with enough energy and strength, internally, to get him through each day in spite of feeling lost sometimes, and bereft, and yes, inconsequential.

"The peace that passeth understanding." A notable item from the Bible which while abstruse, meant he could have peace anyway, whatever the circumstances, whatever the problems, whatever the failures, whatever the lack, whatever the disappointments, not having to understand it.

"The same old struggle." Would that it wasn't the case! But one way Stanley knew he could carry on: by the knowledge of all the others who had gone before, who struggled much more than he, and *also* had to carry on. He'd read enough history to know of the grieving men and women who had spent toil and time and endless effort to raise themselves and others up, to make the world a place of value to all.

And he was acutely aware of the blood and treasure spent in war. Most acutely to him, the Vietnam war, but also each of the others.

Of course, he was not a political leader, not a journalist, not a speech writer, not an anything. Only a lowly citizen with little money. How could he change anything? Affect anything? Voting, of course, and sending in small contributions. He didn't care to join any organization. So, that was it.

Major events, laws, challenges domestically and abroad, were all beyond his reach to influence.

So it was he watched the news and ate alone, or sometimes with friends, and hit the bag at the gym irregularly, and came to remember the time he visited Andrew in San Diego when Andrew was portraying Richard III at the Old Globe Theatre, and they had both been recently doing some Primal Therapy when it was fresh and new and exciting to them. And why, once, in Andrew's dressing room after a performance, Stanley dared to speak grandly of the prospects of Primal Therapy, if it took wind and caught the interest of the public in a large way.

"You know, it's wonderful," he told him. "I...could probably cure drug addiction with this."

But Andrew took the idea badly. "What? You are bold, man. That's arrogant."

"No, no. *We*. I mean, not just me. People could rid themselves of their pain and not need drugs."

Andrew stopped what he was doing, removing his make-up, and turned to Stanley. "It's this arrogance! *You* will do it?"

"Not by myself. I mean, start –"

"Surely not!"

"What's the matter?"

"Look," Andrew said. "You say 'we,' but you mean you, with or without help. What's so special about you?"

"Nothing," Stanley replied.

That had been a strange and disconcerting experience, one which he thought about later, several times.

Really, he hadn't felt very arrogant, or full of himself, or like a big shot, or however Andrew had taken it. He had just felt a lot of people were suffering, and based on his (and Andrew's) experience with the healthful results (slow as they may occur) of the crying and yelling and screaming away former pain – Pain – then why not? Why not spread the news, bring it to drug addicts, get them to do it? Wasn't past Pain making them need soothing pain-relieving drugs?

But, well, was he too bold, too quick to think he (and Andrew) could somehow form a company, or a foundation or such, and get addicts to do Primal Therapy? Go to the Institute and see about proceeding?

The rebuff bothered him; he decided Andrew was wrong about it.

Yet – he didn't do anything. Didn't pursue the idea. Didn't create a groundswell, didn't even approach the people at the Institute about it.

He did hold a bit of bitterness in his heart as to Andrew "Don't call me Andy," a friend who had rejected his idea. Stanley had a particular dislike of being rebuffed. It went back to his childhood when his parents made much use of nasty and pitiless views (of his imagination, of his desires and plans). He learned not to express them, so often were they rebuffed. By his teenage years he wasn't telling anyone his goals and plans, should he have any, because of that.

It occurred to him now, in his room, at the table near the window over the alley, that this was a good subject, a fertile area, to primal about in the future: the pain his parents inflicted rejecting his voiced hopes and dreams.

Noteworthy in all this period, he had as of yet not found a girlfriend (or woman friend, more accurately) to spend time with, to converse with, to date, to dine, to imbibe booze with, to bed perchance; and for sure he knew the reason: dread. Yet, why not? Why not befriend someone and let all the chips fall where they may?

What did he truly care if she left him, dissatisfied? He could say what he had said before when a relationship loomed before him: that he wasn't very good at it, "so don't expect much." And *this* time, Stan, he told himself, don't laugh after telling her that, to make light of it. Let the import of it strike her consciousness fully, for a change.

But as with most plans, he found the struggle of accomplishment eluded him. He spoke with clerks, waitresses, fellow shoppers in the grocery store, but nothing came of it.

He shied away from the internet, from dating sites. It felt scary and impossible. That sort of woman would be interested in a more complete type of "hook up" than he was willing to brave.

Even at church, the women he saw appeared "out-of-reach," beyond him. He could start a conversation, for sure, but to what avail? Soon as they found out he drank (and smoked once in awhile), they'd run as fast as they could, even providing they were not married, or didn't have a boyfriend. Oh, well, Stanley reminded himself, it's all up to God, and he could just have to wait patiently for a blessing, if one was meant for him.

Still, he exercised and drank water and fought the good fight against growing old.

What was he going to do for the next ten years? It felt like that's how long he could reasonably say he would live. Perhaps longer, sure, that's what all people wished in their hearts. Well, most people. Some were so unhappy or guilt-ridden they *wanted* to die.

Ten years – he hoped to be well enough so that he could do something of value, of importance in such time. But what? He had no idea. No inspiration. He'd keep reading and perhaps find a plan in that. An idea. Maybe one of his friends would come forward with a good suggestion. He'd kind of hoped it might be Roger, due to his being a new person in his life, a new mind to hear from. But...it didn't look promising now.

He could go to church and pray for guidance – maybe that would be more productive than praying at home, in his apartment.

Yeah, that's it, he told himself. Go to God's house to ask for it.

He waited until Sunday, and went to a new small church – "Christ's Abode," it said on the unassuming front – and entered at 10 a.m. It was half-full. Or half-empty, whichever was preferred. Young people, mostly couples, conservatively dressed. Quiet. They hardly chanced a glance at him. He sat on the side, not all the way back. A white woman sat beside him. A black man and his black female companion were to his left. He didn't feel hemmed in, they were all so kindly-looking.

A woman in a white gown led a hymn, from the stage. A group, a few children, an older man, sang from the side of the stage, apparently the choir. It wasn't a hymn Stanley knew. The words, nevertheless, were on the front of the little program he'd picked off a table near the entrance.

He sang along; another hymn followed. Spiritual stuff.

Finally a young man appeared from behind the stage, through a curtain.

His hair was short, his arms were short, his eyes were warm and brown.

175

He gave a sermon about the love believers should have for each other.

"In this abode we love our fellows, our brothers and sisters, and as Jesus died for us, providing for forgiveness of our sins, so each one of us are to forgive those who sin, who abuse, who steal, who commit any transgression against us."

"Amen," several of the congregation replied – including Stanley.

As the preacher continued, Stanley prayed earnestly for a path, a sign, a leading, in his life, according to God's will.

He contributed ten dollars, acted friendly, and walked out the door.

One week passed and no great revelation came, and no individual event sprang forth to reveal a path, a mission, an "assignment" for his searching. He checked out the gym Megumi mentioned but unfortunately it wasn't to his liking. So be it. Time will tell, as the wise saying holds.

He had breakfast again with Troy. But it was uneventful. He got a massage, finally, but discouraged the masseuse from playing around on his penis, since his energy was lacking; the need was suppressed (involuntarily). So be it. Time will tell.

There was a notable process in his search: he had to demand of himself faith, and look about expectantly. As he did so the following weeks, Stanley grasped the concept that *all* of us ought to live this way. But most people did not. They trudged forward, if forward it was, on a path to the grave. Sad commentary, that.

One morning, he rose, the light pouring in through his curtains, a bird or two outside making early chirps, a few cars running by on the street at the top of the alley, and hunger in his stomach – but yet, what was that indefinable notion nudging at his half-awakened brain? It was a cross between dread and excitement, a sort of early warning system of some new thing looming ahead. What, he didn't know. Even after a few exercises and a cup of coffee he didn't know. He *hoped* it was an announcement, by the Spirit, of an answer on its way. Yet there was a tinge of alarm to it.

Would his phone ring? Would he meet someone important to his quest? Would a powerful idea strike?

"To God's glory," he reminded himself. Let it be to God's glory, not his own, whatever it be. "Make it that God is first," he told himself.

But what was the objective past that? The big goal? Not fame and millions, not vast recognition and acclaim. It would be more along the lines of love for others, for helping others, for putting others in the path of the light of God's love. But how can one do that?

The phone did ring, but it wasn't anything important. It was Bill saying hello, he was still up north supervising remodeling of his father's property. It would be done soon. They'd sell it and Bill's life would return to normal, until there was another place to remodel and sell. But his father was tired of all that, so not inclined to ever do it again. There was lots of money in the bank, anyway.

So Stanley said, "Great! See you soon, I hope," and the conversation ended, no special doorway opening for him to walk through and reach a position of "directed discipleship."

It was such "directed discipleship" he fervently desired. The problem was, it needed to be given by the Spirit, so Stanley was not able to take a hand in its method, or its ends, or its content. Except to obey the best he was able.

He watched an old movie one night – a film from 1945, "Escape in the Fog." Kind of crazy plot, a woman having a premonition and then later meeting the man in her dream / premonition. Stanley wondered if his instruction was to come in the form of a dream, also.

He had lunch with Bill and Troy. They tried a new place, which had a couple of young Latina girls as waitresses. It irked Troy the way Stanley half-flirted with them.

"How come you don't go for a woman more your age, man?"

"Well," Stanley told him, "I'm not doing much, just joking around."

"Sure, sure," Troy responded.

Bill smiled. "Have at it. I'll watch," he said.

Troy laughed, "Oh, he always has an excuse for his behavior."

"I do?" Stanley asked.

"You do, like now, you weren't trying to hit on the waitress." Troy held his tone firm, staring at Stanley, and then chuckled.

"Wasn't!" But with further thought, Stanley conceded, "Sort of."

"Uh-huh," Troy murmured, satisfied. "I think so."

The restaurant was new, with new counters and tables and booths, a trim and serious male cashier, and of course, the two young waitresses. The food turned out to be good, yet still the place was mostly empty, a fact noted by Bill.

"Yeah, word hasn't spread, I'd say. They only opened a month ago. I know because I checked online," Troy said, a bit smugly.

The neighbor below knocked on his door one day. It was a warm L.A. day and Stanley had opened his windows to feel it. He hadn't put on the air-conditioner. Why should he unless it was too hot for him?

The neighbor, a tall dark man who probably was European (but Stanley couldn't place the accent), looked sheepish. Someday he'd ask him where he was from, but not this day.

"Do you have a minute?"

"Sure, what's up?"

"My dog – my dog is ill. I can't, I don't have the cost of the vet, you understand? I – "

"Need a few dollars?"

"Need about sixty dollars, yes."

Stanley wanted to say no, but, after all, the guy was always nice whenever they spoke, and the dog was quiet – so quiet Stanley hardly was aware that he was downstairs. So, he said, "Okay, man. I'll get it."

He went to his bedroom and pulled cash from a plastic receptacle used for the purpose of hiding money. From whom, he wasn't sure, probably an intruder. He returned, thinking suddenly he could face a drawn weapon and have to give up *all* the cash he had, but, well, should he have closed the door on his neighbor's face? No. Anyway, there was his neighbor, just outside, as he'd left him, now with a look of gratitude on his face.

Stanley handed him the bills. "Sixty, buddy. Hope your – "

"Oh, thanks *so* much. You're a blessing," the man said, taking the cash.

"No problem."

"It was bothering me, I want my dog to be well."

"Of course you do."

So he shook Stanley's hand and went down the steps to his apartment. Stanley felt good.

Yet he ought to know the guy's name. And tell him his own.

Meanwhile, the political season went on, and Donald Trump surprisingly made more progress toward the Republican presidential nomination. And Hilary Clinton progressed, although not surprisingly. Passions were heating up on either side, among those paying attention, as Stanley noticed on TV news and on the internet.

Did it matter? Could any person solve the international woes that faced us? Hunger, war, greed, social disputes? Maybe, if God so willed.

Stanley kept his faith. He trusted. He hoped. He prayed.

A light rain fell, he drank coffee, regular and decaf, all day, he read an old Henry James book, he thought about boxing, he thought of those times when his back wasn't sore, when he ran in the hills, and had avoided his crazy landlady, and slept all night without waking up, and woke up fresh yet pensive, as was his nature. Those times seemed like just a year ago.

He went out the next day after that day of remembrance, that night of not sleeping so well, of lying awake from 2 a.m. to 3:30 a.m., of dozing until sunrise. He went out to face the new day and felt determined to accomplish *something*, to gain the edge on the large world around him, to pass the time in an agreeable enterprise.

But Stanley found nothing but the same old, same old. Cars on the road, buildings, parks, people going about normal Southern California living, content or otherwise, legal or otherwise, headstrong or otherwise, stressed or otherwise. He then stopped at a 7-11 and purchased some supplies, chatted with the friendly clerk, overheard a cell phone call by an obviously angry young man outside in the parking lot, looked longingly at a nearby burrito / taco shop, put his bag into his car, went to purchase two burritos and two tacos, drove to his apartment conscious he had done *something* but not found what he was looking for, thought of the song by Bono reflecting sentiments to that effect, did a series of sit-ups and a few minutes of shadow-boxing and stared into the alley, reflecting, stared out the widow, wondering, wondering, and wondering: what next?

The night of fitful sleep, the twisting and turning, the small nightmares not amounting to much, had led him into dawn. A bird on the sill had sung a brief moment and fled. It reminded Stanley of Rosy, for some reason – a painful memory.

She too had fled, and not due to any fault of hers, like the bird was not at fault in any way. The bird, a winged creature, a sweet thing, had to carry on as best it could – and so had Rosy.

He'd lifted himself out of bed, joints protesting, headed to the bathroom thinking: what losses had he had due to that groin injury, the nerve injury? Was it unfixable? Permanent? That's the big question. Probably, he thought sadly, when he returned to the bedroom, donned a dirty robe (why didn't he let the housekeeper wash it?) and tramped slowly to the kitchen for coffee. He turned on the stove, put a little water in the kettle, placed it on the burner, returned to the bathroom to splash water on his face and brush his teeth. Another day, another dollar, as they say. Another chance to find out his mission in life.

But yet, did he really have a mission? Did any of us have one? Was searching for it futile, like staring out into the alley?

When the kettle sounded, he went to make his instant coffee, and sat in the kitchen, still wondering.

He could go to a movie. Maybe *something*, some word or line or action or landscape or piece of music would provide a clue – if a clue were in fact possible – to his mission.

He could ask a waitress what was the good of life. He'd wanted to do that very thing, in the distant past, but always hesitated. She'd think him mad, certainly, and fail to offer a profound answer.

But maybe not. Maybe the Lord would reveal it to him in a waitress's answer. Maybe the risk of asking was the very step God wanted him to take, in faith.

His resolve to ask was fallen away when he actually had the opportunity. A waitress at Coco's brought him his coffee, and took his order, and during that time he almost asked her, but it felt wrong, it felt embarrassing. She walked away, and he saw how the question would fail if he made a joke of it. He must ask in seriousness, and that was nearly impossible. "Nearly," he said to himself, but not "completely." When she returned, later, with his order, placing it in front of him, he made himself ask. But first, she said the usual "Enjoy. Anything else you need?"

"Well," he began "can you tell me something?" She nodded. "What do you think is the good of life?" But she laughed, assuming it had to be a joke.

"That's what I'd like to know!"

And she moved away.

He ate nervously. It wasn't at all how he'd expected. Next time he'd have to say, "Really, seriously, not kidding, etc. etc."

Funny about women. Half the time when you are joking, they think you are serious, and half the time when you are serious, they think you are joking. But he'd keep at it. He had to find an answer to it all.

Finally a big moment, opportunity, came his way. A little coffee shop on Topanga Canyon Boulevard, a bright waitress – or so she seemed to be, anyway. She spoke hurriedly yet to the point. She had little if any trouble with his order, which included take-out in addition to breakfast there. She even suggested he was a "picky eater," in a not unfriendly way!

They joked of prices, how what he wanted would cost more the way he ordered it (modifying the menu).

"It always costs more to get something good," he told her. She agreed, nodding kindly.

"Cheaper is usually lesser quality," she whispered.

He waited, he drank his coffee. Could he ask her the little question?

He ate. She dealt with other customers. He was at the counter, yet she handled a few tables, too. And took payment at the cash register. Efficient, fast-working. He commented, "I don't really care if something costs more. Within reason."

"That's fine, but I have a daughter. I have to count pennies."

That statement made him feel the question about the "good of life," the value of living, was inappropriate. She wouldn't be philosophical, she'd be practical. So Stanley left without asking her.

He thought, too, was she looking for a husband? A father to her daughter? Was that why she had been so friendly with him?

Surely not. Surely she didn't want an old guy. Yet...maybe anything would be acceptable to get her away from waiting tables. He couldn't tell. His personal radar was so messed up – like usual – he hadn't any answer.

Some days passed. He began to hate the quest which offered so little result. His hair grew faster than any results of his quest appeared.

He watched the news, of course. He read in a Sherlock Holmes Mystery Magazine. He scouted around the internet for anything interesting. He even searched out the words "life" and "meaning" and "good of life." But the quotes he found were unsatisfying. Sure, he could read the long articles that popped up on the web – but he didn't have the energy. He was led to believe that his answer was simple – a phrase or two – and it would show him the path he must take to work a work of positiveness, as God wanted him to.

But what it was he just was not able to determine, until he spoke with Bill again one breezy Saturday morning outside Coco's.

They were near their cars, just saying goodbye, and Stanley felt moved to ask, "Hey, man, what's the good of life?"

Bill laughed. "Not much."

"No, really."

"Uh, I guess, to lead a beneficial life, to –"

"No, man. I mean what's the *good* of it, not what we should do."

Bill twisted up his mouth in an effort of reflection.

"I don't know. It can be enjoyable."

"Yeah," Stanley agreed. He moved to his car. "There must be more than that," he tossed over his shoulder.

"Preparation," Bill yelled.

Stanley stopped walking. "For what?"

"You know, the next life."

"Oh, uh-huh. That's true. Thanks." He went to his car, oddly at peace, more peaceful than recently.

It made sense. The next life, whatever it was (and the Bible indicated it was terrific, sweet, unimaginably pleasant), we now were preparing for it. Developing, growing in faith, overcoming obstacles, learning, being trained, guided, reproved, hurt even, to reach an understanding, a grip on our hope for the future, beyond the grave.

That's what the struggle was for, the pain of daily life. To edify, to promote the individual's certainty, knowledge, skills even, for being over there, wherever it was, with God, face to face.

The little heart palpitations were an annoyance at first, then a concern when he felt them, in bed, before going to sleep. A kind of thumping, not strong, but *there* when it didn't seem it ought to have been. So finally he gave in and went to the doctor, who recommended a test – ultrasound, was it? And after that he had to take a white pill every day, with a name he couldn't even pronounce right and had trouble remembering.

That settled down the trembling in his heart area. It was almost like his diaphragm was doing the vibrating, but no, the doctor called it a "heart flutter," so Stanley had to accept that; he didn't want a heart attack, especially he didn't want a stroke, which could be caused by the increased blood flow (or was it decreased?) which could make for plaque build-up in his heart, which could break free and head to the brain.

"Screw that," he told himself. "Boxers may get brain injuries but we sure don't have strokes. That's for inactive folks, isn't it?" He'd have to ask his doctor about that.

Meanwhile, the downstairs neighbor walked up to pay back the $60 loan.

"Fantastic!" Stanley almost shouted. "Come in for a beer or something."

The neighbor replied he just couldn't, he had to go out for awhile. "But another time, friend."

"Okay," Stanley said, a bit sadly. Not often did he have the chance to bring anyone inside his little place. "Another time."

He put the money in his hiding place, sat again in his chair in the living room, and smiled to himself. *See there,* he thought, not everyone is a greedy asshole.

The next day, two momentous events occurred. Well, more like one and a half. His stomach was bothering him for some reason, so he went to Rite-Aid to get a pack of Tums, and inside the store saw a waitress he'd liked years ago, with a child in a stroller. He avoided her. So she'd gotten married and had a baby? Naturally. He bought his Tums and went outside to eat one in his car.

Sure, married with a child. Why not? That's what many normal people did in their lives.

He drove to Carl's Jr to get a couple of "all-natural" burgers, and picked up more Pacifico Clara at the nearby 7-11. Then outside, driving away, one of his old Primal Pain memories kicked free. It did it like that, sometimes, years after the Primal, for reasons he didn't understand. But this release, this opening up, was indeed momentous. Stanley had basically forgotten about the trauma and the primaling of it. Now he smiled. The memories rushed back, but without any accompanying "sting," as it was called. He didn't "care" anymore. He was free of it.

It had been a fall, a sudden shock and hurt to his arms as he'd caught himself falling to the ground, with his hands. His hands had hurt; he'd primaled about them, and his arms (hurt also when his open hands had struck the pavement). It was outside a bar after a night of drinking in Tijuana. He had tripped on the curb. Boom, he'd fallen forward.

Now, driving in Los Angeles decades later, he felt his arms loosen up, the old unconscious restricting of movement, lack of free moment, that he'd suffered from since that fall, left him. It was palpable, the freedom was noticeable. And it was quite joyous. He had a freedom of arm use he'd been denied since 19-years-old. Getting it back showed just how much – 20%? – he'd lost at the time.

Part IV

It was funny to him how the time he'd spent acting in films, as little as it had been, nevertheless, had left Stanley with so few acquaintances to call on now in his retirement. But it was his fault. He'd not gotten numbers, addresses, emails. He just drifted along unattached to his immediate surroundings like mainly he'd done all his life. Pathetic.

What the source of this unusual, almost inhuman, style of living was, he knew not. None of the traumas uncovered and dealt with by Primal Therapy shed light on it. In fact, he couldn't recall a time in his life when he *was* normally attached to friends, reaching out and holding onto them as most people in society did.

He had some friends, yes, but when you really came down to it, the question was: why so few?

He hadn't spoken with George for many long years. He knew he wasn't working at the auto shop as he had been, in the '70s and '80s, and the address the owner gave Stanley in 1990 led to one thing: an apartment rented by someone who didn't know George. He should have asked the manager but hadn't pursued that idea at the time, planning on returning another day.

But like the unconventional loner type of person he was, Stanley never went back. Should he now? 25 years later? That manager won't even be there, most likely.

He paid his bills, he drank his beer, he smoked on and off, he went to the chiropractor, he kept a look out for a companion of the female sort, he prayed to the Lord and continued to read books.

Nothing important came in the mail, no one important called, just texting from his two friends to meet for breakfast, usually not Troy texting, but Bill, who was more aggressive.

Terrorism, politics, local crime dominated his news viewing. He needed to get some more movies on DVD. He needed to go to the gym.

He did notice a difference in the freedom while he took items down from shelves, and put them away in his apartment – he felt that freedom in the use of his arms. "Thank God," he said to himself when he recognized it.

Then one day there was a knock on his door. The tall neighbor, to ask for more money? No, he saw as he opened the door, it was a small woman of perhaps forty or fifty years, smiling up at him. Thus began another adventure.

"Hi! You don't know me but I'm Troy's friend. You know Troy, don't you?" She kept smiling through the short discourse.

"Troy?"

"Yes. May I come in?"

"Well, uh –" Stanley looked past her to see if there were any others. There weren't. He continued to hesitate. "What's this about?"

"Nothing so very much. He said I should ask your help if I ever needed it. I do. We do."

"Well, come in, except I ought to call him first."

"You can, thank you," she replied, not moving.

"How come he hasn't called *me*?"

"You can ask him. He gave me your address and – please, let me in."

"Sure, come on. I don't want to be rude, but how do I know, well, that this isn't some scam?" He stepped back and the little woman stepped in.

"I'm Annette," she told him. As she walked in Stanley closed, and locked, the door.

"Please, sit down."

She did. She wasn't pretty but she had a certain look which drew his attention – like a woman who had charm and style. She wasn't dressed like that – but she expressed it in the way she moved and sat.

"Nice place," she said in a small voice. "You have known Troy for many years?"

"Many," he said, nodding.

"So, he – " she stopped. "He is aware I am here. He has become mixed up in a mess. He's being accused of stealing tools at work."

"Tools?"

"Yes, well, expensive ones, I'm afraid."

"Who accused him?" The –"

"The boss, yes," Annette interrupted.

When she paused he felt sorry for her. Whatever her mission here was, it was unpleasant, he gathered. "Of course he hasn't stolen them," he said. "Troy is an honest and honorable man."

She dipped her head, agreeing.

"So," Stanley urged her, "there can't be any real evidence against him."

"No, suspicion mostly, since he often worked late, alone, and could have taken things out of the shop."

"What about other mechanics?"

"There are only three others, and they never work late, alone."

"So...how much are these things worth?"

"Ten thousand," she said.

"No!"

"Yes."

"What were they? Oh, never mind, it couldn't mean anything to me anyway. Shouldn't I call Troy?"

"First I need to ask you a favor."

"Okay."

"He can't make bail," she said.

"Oh my God."

"We need you to put up the whatever it's called, to the Bondsman."

"Yeah. How much?"

"A thousand?" She made it a question. He sank into his chair.

"I assume you came to me because no one in his family has it?"

"That's correct, Mr. Larson. They are all broke, or –" she stopped suddenly.

"Or what?"

"They refuse."

That was pretty much all of it. He withdrew the cash after speaking with Troy, in jail. There was a piece of evidence Annette hadn't mentioned. Troy informed him one of the other mechanics told police he'd asked him to participate in the robbery, but the other mechanic had refused. It was all a lie, Troy told Stanley.

Of course, Troy wouldn't be so stupid as to think he could get away with such ridiculousness.

195

And Stanley only thought later, why hadn't Bill been called upon to pay for Troy's bail deposit? It was an annoying thought, first because it could show a sign of aging that it hadn't occurred to him until later, and second, wasn't Bill a closer friend, with a more readily available money supply? He decided to ask them both about that the next time they three had breakfast.

And of course, he was rather fond of Annette, and having her phone number, he spoke with her several times during the transaction.

He wanted to ask her to lunch sometime but figured he'd best wait to question Troy regarding his friend's status, relationship-wise. She could be closer to Troy than she let on, which would be awkward.

Meanwhile, he continued to do a little exercise in his apartment, and plan to, God willing, return to the gym.

He stressed about Troy's condition – who was guilty? The other mechanics? An intruder who left no trace? How can an intruder break and enter and leave no trace? They could have a key, but what about the alarm? *Was* there an alarm?

Could the boss have done it, for some reason, perhaps to score money and get rid of Troy? Why, though? He'd have to ask Troy if he got along with the boss, and if he thought the other mechanics had stolen the property, using a duplicate key after Troy had left.

Yet Stanley had a slight intuition there was more to it all. He sat in his room pondering, but soon recognized he'd have to get a lot more information.

The police no doubt weren't searching for alternatives. Why would they if they have a suspect charged?

He met with Troy and Bill at a deli, Brent's, for breakfast. Troy looked sad. They ordered and sat quietly until Stanley asked, "You are working now, I suppose?"

Troy didn't smile. "Hell, no."

"Your boss believes you did it?"

"He won't say, only that he can't have me in the shop for the time being."

Stanley sipped his coffee. Bill said, "Hang in there, man. It's all bullshit –"

"I know," Troy said, and at last offered a brave smile.

"No jury will convict you," Stanley added, an immediately regretted saying it, evoking a trial and a jury and the question of guilt, at breakfast. Just then the waiter brought their food dishes, so they ate silently.

"How did you get along with your boss – what's his name?"

"Marshall. Got along okay," Troy replied, rather disconsolately.

Stanley said, "This guy could have framed you."

"Why? He can't get much out of that," Troy responded.

Stanley ate, then said, "He can sell the stuff *and* collect the insurance."

Both Bill and Troy looked at him afresh. They hadn't thought of that.

"We have to follow him, see if he leads us to the goods," was Stanley's answer to their unspoken question. And he decided not to ask Bill why he hadn't chipped in with bail money, when suddenly Bill offered to follow Marshall's SUV when he left at night. He said he'd actually tailed people before, and his experiences would help. It was a girlfriend he'd followed several times, a couple of decades ago,but still, he remembered how to do it. Just close enough to not fall behind and lose the target, and just far enough away to protect against being spotted and suspected. Especially since Marshall knew Bill from when he worked there.

Stanley readily agreed – he didn't think he could even accomplish a tail job if he tried it himself.

Bill got the exact description of Marshall's new SUV, and Troy even had a vague idea of the license plate. So Bill would wait down the street from the front entrance of the shop, which was how Marshall generally exited for the day – at 6:00 pm or so.

Stanley napped in his apartment, and read, and listened to music, and of course exercised, and showered and drank water, and cooked a frozen turkey dinner in his microwave, and put the surveillance activity out of his mind the best he could.

He watched some news but turned it off, smoked a couple of cigarettes and drank four Pacificos slowly, thinking of being overseas in the '60s, and the girls in the small town of Cavite City who worked in the little bars, and his motorcycle, and various other aspects of that memorable tour of duty in the Philippines.

In the morning a thought came to him – if the possible cache of valuable tools was espied, if Marshall led them to a garage or shack or old rented warehouse, should they notify the police, who would need a search warrant, if they chose to take Bill's word for it? Or...should they check the place out on their own to see if the goods were even there?

That meant...uh...*breaking in*, that's what. No, no, Stanley did not want to do that. They'd have to go to the police, no question about it.

Anyway, breaking in was a risk not only due to its illegality, but suppose a guard was in there? An armed guard?

Three days later it seemed like a moot point anyway, because Bill reported to them that Marshall had not gone anywhere suspicious but merely to his house, except on one evening he stopped at a bar on the way, presumably for a casual drink. He wasn't inside more than fifteen minutes.

Stanley felt another night of surveillance was a waste, but Bill offered to do it once more, for good measure. Maybe Marshall had little reason to check up on the stolen property, but might do it periodically out of anxiety. Troy agreed with that, although he was mainly convinced his boss wasn't guilty, "Wouldn't stoop so low," as he put it.

Unlike Sherlock Holmes, Stanley was unable to figure out any alternative potential thief – unless it be one (or more) of the mechanics. He still believed it was an inside job of some form. But that was an intuition, not deductive reasoning.

The one idea he did have out of the ordinary, and somewhat Sherlockian was to meet again with Annette. She may know more than she had shown.

He talked to Troy on the phone.

"You guys dating, or…?"

"No, man. She's my friend. I don't think she wants to date Asians!" He laughed, but it sounded a bit weak.

"Well, see, I just liked her, and wanted to ask her out, to lunch, or coffee, you know."

"Okay with me. Thanks for the thought, though."

"She doesn't have a boyfriend?"

"Not any more. Did."

"Oh, so I'll just call her."

"You do that," Troy said.

He called, she accepted, they met at Denny's. They had coffee, talked a bit, and ordered lunch. Burgers. Not so exciting, but good enough for a beginning. Annette had driven her car – "Why should you bother?" she asked, when he told her he'd pick her up. She seemed like an independent sort.

"Put me at ease, Stanley," she got right to the point. "You have no doubt of Troy's innocence?"

"No, none. I thought you knew that. Did he say otherwise, did he –"

"No," she interrupted. "I mean, not actually. Only he was wondering how you could just trust his word so fully."

"Me? I know him well enough to be shocked beyond belief he would steal so much. Maybe a can of oil once or twice," Stanley laughed. "Kidding."

They continued the lunch in a friendly manner, but the question he wanted to ask put an end to that.

"Annette, listen. I have to tell you what's bothering me. The police don't have enough to convict him – not that I know much about criminal trials, but I know *some*. A jury has to convict beyond doubt, well, reasonable doubt it's called, and that's the problem I have. There is reasonable doubt."

"But that's good, isn't it?"

"Yes, for us," he told her. "But not for the prosecutor – a jury won't convict, in my opinion." He sipped his coffee as the waitress suddenly appeared to take away their empty dishes. He told her yes he'd like more coffee, when she offered.

While she was gone he said, "So, I think there's more to this than you or Troy have said. More evidence, I mean. Is there?"

"Like what?"

"Good evasive response! You know I don't know what it could be."

She glared at him, but didn't deny it. "I can't…."

"What?"

"I'm not at liberty to say."

"Really?" He watched the waitress pour him more coffee. "That is, Troy wants you to keep quiet?"

"That's none of your business," Annette said firmly, and stood. "I think I will leave now. Thank you for lunch. Goodbye."

She quickly stepped away, headed for the entrance, and never looked back.

Stanley returned to his apartment.

Naturally, he had no idea what was the further fact, or facts, that remained hidden. He thought it over, however. One thing struck him: if there was more evidence, it may be enough to prove Troy *had actually committed the crime*.

And she was covering up for him. But why? If the police knew, what did it matter if Stanley knew?

This sort of personal trouble Stanley hated; he guessed they were just keeping the facts from him due to Troy's pride. Stanley couldn't care less about that. And wasn't it all going to come out later in the trial anyway? Suddenly he was mad at Troy.

He called him but there was no answer.

He went for a walk – it had the effect of settling his nerves. He decided to ask Bill about this all.

The dark thought that Troy was guilty and didn't want his friends to know lurked in the back of his mind.

He did his usual reading and back stretches and shadow-boxing, and turned on the news. There was coverage of the Republican Convention,so he watched it.

He was tired, more tired than usual in the morning. He couldn't figure out why but the necessity of calling Troy loomed in his mind, so that was a good guess, the deed disturbed him, confronting his friend, and just could cause Stanley to feel weary.

But he bucked up. He had coffee. He ate breakfast at the café around the corner, he smiled at the waitress, he walked to the liquor store to get beer and packaged cheese and microwave popcorn.

In his apartment he put off calling Troy until eleven, hanging out on the internet. He watched a couple of old fights on YouTube, but oddly they bored him. Maybe he was getting bored with boxing. It could happen, all the years he'd spent around it.

At last he called Troy, who had not returned his call from the day before, in spite of Stanley leaving his name. Which he didn't have to do – he knew for a fact that Troy had his name and his number in his phone.

"Yeah, hi, pal," Troy answered.

"Hi. How are you?"

"Good. Can't talk long, though."

"Fine, I only have a question."

"Okay," Troy responded.

Taking a breath, Stanley jumped in. "Annette got upset after I asked her if there was more evidence against you than I know." He waited, but Troy was silent. "And, uh, what might there be? Have you told me everything?"

"Why wouldn't I?"

"No reason I can think of," Stanley answered firmly. "But well, it seems as if the case against you is thin."

"Hell," was all he said.

"What?"

"Leave it alone, would you?"

That stopped Stanley for a moment. "Really? Why?"

Surprisingly, the phone went dead.

"Hello?" he asked in vain.

What was he to do now? It might be he should do nothing, for the entire circumstance was none of his business. If Troy was guilty what was Stanley to it all?

He wanted to call Bill to discuss it. But should he? If Annette and Troy wanted him out of it, he should stay out of it.

No wonder tailing Marshall had led to a dead end, a waste. Marshall wasn't involved in it.

And even if he was, it was some deep stuff. If Troy and he had planned and done it – what was Stanley to do? Jump in and get hurt, possibly? So he left it all alone, he wanted only to see if perchance Bill had found anything.

Meanwhile he looked again on the internet for a new gym to go to. He was tired of the one he'd been at, it had no other fighters, really, it had no boxing ring, it was just not a good place to train, in his opinion.

But all he found was a new one on Ventura Boulevard. It was the only one that looked promising. He'd seen mention of it before, but had not gone by to check it out.

Nevertheless, the first thing to do was have breakfast with Bill, and find out the latest, whether it be conclusive or not.

They arranged to meet two days later. It was at the usual hang-out, and while Stanley feared the possible appearance of Annette and/or Troy, that chance was slim.

They ate, they spoke of various topics, including the presidential race, and then the talk turned to the case at hand.

"Obviously, you didn't find out much by following the boss?"

"No, nothing. I stopped after that time I told you about – the last one I would do. It sucks, really, tailing somebody. I don't know how private detectives can do it."

"Maybe they don't have to now, with electronic devices," Stanley offered weakly.

"Yeah? Radar, you mean?"

He laughed, "I don't know what I mean."

They finished their eggs and Stanley dove in, "You know, there's more to this than I figured at first."

"How so?"

"Did Marshall go anywhere except home,or to that bar?"

"He did, he went to a grocery store that final evening."

"Did you go inside?"

"No," Bill replied.

"He could have met somebody. He could have met Troy."

"Huh?"

"Look, there has to be more evidence than we've been told, Bill. When I asked Annette about that she got mad and left the table."

"Strange."

"There had to be something."

Bill sat silently for a moment. "What do you mean, more evidence?"

"Well, they don't have much on him. Would a jury convict so easily?"

"No...that's true. They may be just reaching, though."

"Yeah," Stanley admitted. "That could be it. Hoping the jury will see it their way."

"Maybe," Bill agreed, but rather half-heartedly.

It was a "wash," he felt. He couldn't find out anything. All he knew was Marshall had gone to the grocery store on his way home!

But something was nagging at him. The behavior, the abrupt negative behavior, of Annette and Troy was only part of it.

So Stanley strolled into the auto shop and asked a mechanic for Marshall. The mechanic, a tough-looking Latino, pointed with a wrench to the office on the side of the building. "In there," he said, holding the wrench tightly in front of him, almost as a weapon.

The door was closed, but of course it would be, considering the noise coming from the work in the shop.

Stanley opened the door and walked in. The man he assumed was the boss looked up from his chair behind a littered desk. He put on a smile, he waved Stanley over.

"Hi, I'm Stanley Larson. I figure you're Troy's boss? I'm a friend of his."

"Sure. How are you? What can I do for you?"

Now came the hard part. The man looked stocky, appeared to be around forty, with thick arms, resting – poised – on his desk.

"Well, this trouble, this charge against Troy, you know," Stanley began, haltingly.

Marshall nodded. The smile was gone.

"I don't know much about it, but seems to me the case is weak. He's not the type, and he doesn't have the tools, apparently."

"No, but what 'type' are you talking about? Thieves come in all types."

"Uh, sure," Stanley said. "I mean he always seemed an honest fellow."

"But what do you want here?"

"Uh, well, is there some evidence to link him to the crime? That's what I don't understand."

"Sure," Marshall said. The smile was back on his face. "He told one of my employees all about it."

"You mean that, that lie how he was planning on doing it?

"Lie? You want to say that to Pete? He's outside."

Stanley laughed. "No, I just don't believe it, that's all."

"Do you believe he told him *after* he'd done it, that he had?"

Stanley was speechless for a moment. "No, well, no. Is that what happened?"

"That's what happened. You want to ask Pete about that?"

"Well...yes, if it's okay."

Marshall laughed. "You do? After calling him a liar?"

"I won't say that, no sir."

Marshall shrugged his thick shoulders. He rose, ushering Stanley out the door into the work area.

"Pete!" he hollered. "Come 'ere!" The noises ceased with the sound of the boss's voice. The three mechanics at work all stopped, and a tall Latino man came forward, a dirty rag in his hand.

"This is a friend of Troy's who wants to hear it from you how he said he'd robbed me. Took the stuff."

The tall man, with very short hair which contained a bit of grey, eyed Stanley suspiciously.

"Hello. I'm trying to find out what I can, I..." Stanley was at a loss what else to say.

"Work for the cops? I told 'em everything."

"No," Stanley offered quickly. "Just me and Bill, a friend also, can't understand what happened. So –"

"All right. He came in here the next day bragging how he'd done it. Like he was a big shot. The police were on the way, so he spoke fast. Said he'd put the tools and the machine into a van by himself and left the big doors here open, and took off. That's all."

"You don't know where he took it all?"

"Wouldn't tell you if I did. Just the police." He played with the rag, appearing nervous.

"Well," Stanley commented, "he must not have told you since the stuff wasn't found."

"So that makes you a smart guy, doesn't it?" Pete remarked sarcastically.

No one spoke for a moment and Marshall reached for Stanley's arm. As soon as he touched him, Stanley flung Marshall's hand away sharply.

"Hey!" Pete moved to hit Stanley in the stomach, but he blocked it, and counter-punched, out of habit, with a jab to Pete's face, which connected. It didn't do much good, because Pete immediately drew back his right to throw a big roundhouse. Stanley ducked it easily and realizing he had to come on strong, hit Pete with three punches, a left, a right, and a left, and then Marshall punched Stanley from the side, and the mechanic who held the wrench grabbed Stanley and pulled him away from Pete.

"Stop it!" he yelled, holding Stanley by both arms. He was much younger and stronger than Stanley, and that was the end of it, since Pete, bleeding from his nose, did nothing more, and Marshall grumbled but said nothing.

"All right," Stanley muttered. He stared at Pete. "You know more about this, don't you? Did you steal the stuff? I bet you did. And you're trying to pin it on Troy."

Pete opened his mouth, but no sound came out.

"Did you?" Marshall snapped at him. "Did you?"

"I want a lawyer," was all Pete said, at last.

"Yeah, and get the police to check his property, wherever he lives," Stanley said to Marshall.

Pete smiled. "That won't help you any."

"Tell me, man," Marshall said to him. "We can make a deal. Just return it. You've been a good worker."

Pete looked ashamed. It was obvious he wasn't experienced as a thief. "You bastard," he said, glaring at Stanley, and wiping the blood from his face with the rag he retrieved from the floor.

"You have got to be kidding me," said the mechanic who had the wrench. He let go of Stanley quickly.

So once again, Stanley provoked a confession. He had to make a statement to the police the next day. Marshall retained a lawyer for Pete – he did like the guy, after all. As for finding the tool stash, that happened without incident. The lawyer was urged to make it as easy on Pete as possible, and Pete was to say it was his "conscience" that got to him, not Stanley's punches. Again a reporter called, but again, Stanley begged off commenting.

It took a few weeks but Troy admitted it was his ego, sprinkled with embarrassment and humiliation that kept him from saying Pete had told the cops the lie about Troy claiming to have been the thief – because, what if his friends had believed it? And he'd asked Annette to hide the information, too.

Both Bill, and then Stanley, tried to assure him they wouldn't have believed it, no matter what.

One day another book of Louis L'Amour short stories arrived in the mail, and Stanley holed up in his apartment reading it, tired of going out, tired of even the quite limited socializing he did do.

One thing he was happy for, the freedom he'd noticed in his arms when he'd thrown punches at Pete. That was a result of his recent primaling, and he wondered what else there was left to do in regard to past trauma; it never appeared to end!

The internet, the news of the election, the books, the breakfasts with Bill and Troy, the prayers, the beer, the looking for a new girlfriend, halfheartedly, the food purchased, the memories, the music on the radio – these aspects of his life led him along, currently. He looked in the door of the gym on Ventura Boulevard. It seemed all right. Someday he'd "venture" in and work out.

There was church, too – he knew he needed to return at least occasionally.

He ordered a DVD from Amazon, he ate popcorn, he wondered how Andrew was doing. Not finding much work now, considering his age? Oh, well. He'd worked a lot, compared to many struggling actors. And certainly compared to Stanley.

Funny, it struck Stanley he would like to be in another movie. Or an episode of a TV show. He didn't usually think about it. There were good memories, there were bad ones, as to his acting in shows. All water under the bridge, Stanley reflected. But yet – he did want to try it one more time. "I mean," he thought, "how do I know how long I will live? One more acting job sure would be like...icing on the cake."

Still, he didn't have an agent now. He needed an agent to find him the job. He had to think about it, to arrive at a plan.

He thought about one of his jobs, a very small part in a movie. He liked doing it, but didn't like the director, who'd treated Stanley like a nobody. Which he was, sort of, but that director didn't have to ignore him so much, did he?

On the set he'd barely said a word, and pointed where he wanted Stanley to stand. It was frustrating, but what could he do? Complain to him? Lot of good that would have done.

Hopefully should he get any more acting jobs, the new director will treat him like a human being, and not a moving piece of property. Or "meat," as the saying goes, as actors are sometimes referred to.

Beyond that, he received notice to go in for jury duty. It wasn't a thing he hated, it was kind of okay in his mind, and it would give him something meaningful to do. He had to call to register, which he did, and wait for certain dates, to call again, to see if he had to show up at the Van Nuys Courthouse for orientation (which they provided a way to accomplish on the internet, but since Stanley's printer was broken, and he didn't feel up to running out to get another one, he wouldn't be able to provide the printed evidence he'd completed the orientation online.

So what? It meant he had to show up an hour earlier at the courthouse. It gave him a chance to observe others, which he most always liked to do in the past. People were mainly interesting to him, even if they were only sitting, and listening, and looking bored.

He called the old number for his old agent, and left a halting, broken message on voicemail. He guessed the agent wasn't doing too well if he hadn't an assistant or a secretary – was that good? Or bad? Would the guy be willing to try to find him a job or would he be dismissive, since Stanley wouldn't make much money even if he did find one, and the commission would be a pittance?

He prayed God may be willing to make it happen….

He saw Clinton was ahead of Trump in the polls. Trump was making ridiculous comments. He just couldn't help himself, Stanley thought. Politicians are supposed to take care what they say, like John Kennedy did. It's one thing to speak spontaneously in regular life, but if the voters and all are watching, carefulness with words is mandatory.

Not that Stanley would want to be a politician. First of all, you have to wear a suit most of the time, and ask for contributions half the time, and be nice when you might not feel so nice.

Anyway, if he could just find something more to do, new to do, during this "preparation" time, he'd be happy. But what? He guessed it would come to him eventually, and wow what a moment of triumph that would be. So he kept on the lookout.

He did call Annette once, and had a good conversation. She thanked him profusely for what he had done.

"Really, I mean this. Troy thought he was going up the river."

"Uh-huh, I gathered that. But his ego was the thing. He ought to have told us what was going on." Stanley replied. "He told you. Why couldn't he tell me and Bill?"

"You're *men*, that's why!"

"Oh. That makes a difference?"

"Naturally," she answered.

"But...oh, screw it. I understand. A proud heart."

"Sort of like that, yes."

"Pride is not good, as the Bible tells us."

"You rely on the Bible?" she asked.

"Sure. I believe. Don't you?"

"Uh...not so literally," she answered.

"Have you read it?"

"No...just heard things, quotes, and stuff."

"Try reading it. I'll get you a copy if you wish."

"Okay, Stanley. That's nice of you. I don't know where to start."

"Fine. I'll get the New King James Version. It's easier to understand than the old translation."

"Okay, Stanley," she repeated.

But after he bought the book online, she declined to accept it. People are funny. She said it wasn't a thing she was comfortable with; she was grateful he'd tried, but all that Jesus stuff turned her off.

So he hit her with it, "You'd rather stay unforgiven, then?"

"Huh?"

"Sin is falling short of God's glory. It's in the Bible. We all sin."

"Fine. I'm no big sinner, though," she said. They were on the phone. He feared she'd hang up on him.

"Most of us aren't, but are still sinners."

"You are? How come Jesus doesn't stop you from it?"

"Because he lets us go our own way. He wants us to make decisions for ourselves. He died for us as sinners, but we can't help doing it. Pride, envy, lying, you know. I try but it's difficult."

"You keep that Bible, but...tell me more sometime, okay?"

Later, Stanley wished he'd named more sins to her. There were plenty mentioned in the Bible, including the "puffed up" attitude he'd tried to avoid most of his life (when he first saw it mentioned). Anyway, he'd speak with her again; he wanted her to be saved.

Lunch with Bill and Troy the next time was uneventful. Troy was critical of Clinton, and Bill seemed okay with that. Stanley said she was going to help working people, he had heard from her speeches, and Troy shrugged, not willing to reply.

Stanley saw they both thought the system was broken, but he was old enough to remember how good the 1990s were, with Bill Clinton as president. Congress didn't seem so obstructionist then, but maybe he wasn't recalling correctly. Obama's dark skin may be why Congress was so opposed to him, but nobody was willing to 'fess up to it, so Stanley had no basis of facts to go on. Maybe it was just political persuasion, as the congressmen and senators who voted against Obama's proposals said. But he thought otherwise. He'd heard enough racial remarks in his life, even from his parents, to know it was usually a secret attitude people tried to keep from strangers. And that would include keeping it from voters, he figured.

Days went by. He took his Camaro in for an oil change, and a transmission flush. Not exciting events, but very necessary. He held off calling Annette. He'd let her think about their conversation for awhile. Not that he even knew if she *was* thinking about it.

The political campaigns carried on. He wasn't smart enough to see what the differences were with immigration policy. Why weren't the laws enough? Like traffic laws, they only needed to be enforced. Maybe more agents were the answer.

He felt sorry for those coming over the border – why did they have to? Why couldn't their own countries provide jobs? Somebody must know, but it wasn't Stanley.

Was someone stealing money in vast amounts in those countries? Why couldn't they have thriving businesses?

It was too much for him, so he hoped Clinton would work out a good program with Congress when she got into the White House. It didn't look like Trump was going to make it. He seemed mean, anyway, like some fighters who threw elbow punches, and butted with their heads. Of course, that was just Stanley's feeling. Maybe Trump, as weird as he acted sometimes, actually wanted the best for all Americans.

Nevertheless the constant political news led Stanley to want to watch a good film, but he couldn't think of one offhand. It was easy to order used ones from Amazon DVD, but which? A western? A comedy? The recent movies didn't appeal to him. A consequence of growing old, no doubt.

He could watch the many copies of the series "Naked City" that he had purchased years ago. But now he had a distaste for crime, having seen a bit of it in his life these recent times.

It just had to be a comedy. But...he needed a suggestion. He had to *ask* someone who was a fan of comedies. Must be *some* old friend who fits that category....

He thought of an old black man who lived in the apartment house next door. They had spoken only a few times but the man was jovial, with a sense of humor, and could possibly be a fan of comedy movies.

As it turned out, the old guy was not that much older than Stanley – maybe five years or so – but surprisingly responded with the recommendation of Fred Astaire movies.

"They are funny, but with lots of dancing and singing," he said. Stanley had knocked on his door and just asked his question.

"Sure, and like I say, I live right up there. My name is Stanley Larson." They shook hands.

"I see you around," he answered, "sometimes. I'm Walker. I might suggest fun screwball comedies from the '30s, too."

"Oh, I've seen several of those. Cary Grant, Jimmy Stewart?"

"You've got it," Walker smiled.

"Let me give you my phone number. If you need anything, call." Stanley, not having a pen or paper, just stood there.

"Nice of you. Hold on." Walker went inside, returning shortly with a pad and pen.

Stanley told him his number. The old guy was so friendly and kind-looking he didn't feel any compunction about giving his number out. "I'll get a musical, like you say. This may seem crazy but I just don't have any ideas and thought, hey, that guy over there might know."

"Fine. Makes sense to me."

Later, the thought that he had expected a recommendation like "Rush Hour," or something with a black comedian in it made Stanley feel vaguely racist, and vaguely ashamed of himself.

He ordered a Fred Astaire film, an old musical, and waited for it to show up in the mailbox.

And Walker didn't call him, which was okay, because if he wanted anything from Stanley, it could be money, and Stanley was tired of giving people his money. Not that he really cared, but he only had so much, and didn't want to run out, even with Troy slowly repaying him. Didn't everyone fear running out of money?

He did his partial sit-ups, and his other exercises. He called the number and found out he had to report for jury selection on Monday. He sort of dreaded it. He was feeling tired, like a recurrence of that old Epstein Barr virus (or *was* it a virus?) he'd had years ago, and he did recall the weakness, the odd form of sleepiness, the unusual tiredness, that accompanied it. Poor timing.

He was unhappy about it. The doctor had told Stanley it may come back once or twice, but he didn't expect it now.

On top of that, his battery wouldn't start his car the morning he was leaving for the courthouse. He had to call the Auto Club, and while the driver got it started he told him the battery needed to be replaced, and may not start that afternoon. Which it didn't. He'd sat around in the jury assembly room and was finally told to return in two days, and when he went to the parking structure his car wouldn't start, and he called the Auto Club, and the technician who showed up put in a new battery for him.

All this while feeling tired.

He got to his apartment and managed not to feel sorry for himself, because he knew things could be a lot worse, and he was lucky, in a way.

He was lucky he even had a car – some people didn't. He was lucky he had a few dollars to pay for a battery, and food, and drink – some people didn't. He was lucky he had his wits about him – some people didn't. He was lucky he could walk, and talk, and see, and hear, and...and...well, whatever else – some people couldn't.

He was lucky he had a nice place to stay. It wasn't so great, actually, but it could have been a lot worse. He knew fighters, ex-fighters, who lived in rundown boarding houses or old apartment buildings with the john down the hall – the way Stanley had lived when he was starting out fighting amateur.

He had Medicare. He had Social Security and the small pension. What else did he need?

He cringed, starting his car the morning of returning to the courthouse, but it did start. He stressed about being late, but he wasn't late. He parked in the big structure, he pulled himself from his car, walked to the Superior Court building, went through security, up the elevator, all the while feeling weak and insufficient for the task ahead.

If he was chosen for a jury it would be hell, feeling this way. But, whatever, he told himself. Fighters had to be tough, even in the tenth round of a ten round fight. He had seen his friend from the gym, Lonnie, win a fight in the tenth round. Stanley sure didn't feel as weary as Lonnie must have then!

There was a crowd of prospective jurors outside the door of the courtroom in the hall. He joined them. He then realized he was sent here with them because they'd been given a specific trial to attend, if chosen. He'd forgotten that from Monday. The Epstein Barr made thinking more mixed up than it usually was. He put on his juror badge. He'd remembered that at least.

They were called by name – he responded "yes" when the woman at the door said "Stanley Larson." Nobody was late, so they all went in. He was led to the jury box, since he had moved up to the front when his name was called. The other people had held back, mostly, not wanting to be on a jury at all. Stanley didn't either, feeling this way, but had moved forward anyhow. Holding back wasn't going to make any difference, he was still smart enough to realize. It was the judge's and the attorney's questions, and then the answers, that determined how a selection was made – who was dismissed, and who wasn't.

He sat down in the comfortable jury box chair, and when the box was filled, the rest of the people sat in the spectator section of the courtroom. The attorneys were standing up by their tables, the judge was sitting behind his bench. He welcomed everyone and explained the trial may be a long one, weeks, and that those who felt it would be an economic hardship had to fill out forms (questionnaires) explaining their issues.

Stanley had no hardship, but for feeling weak. That was one issue on the form, too, medical reasons for not being able to serve. You needed a note from your doctor to pull that excuse off. Too much trouble, Stanley decided. He'd just tough it out.

A large number of people took the forms (when they were handed out) and pens, and began to fill them in. He just sat there.

He thought of his doctor, of the treatment – a series of shots in the butt, he recalled, by a cute nurse. Vitamins? Yeah.

He'd have to go in for that again. He had a different doctor now. It had been decades since that last sick episode.

Finally, the questionnaires were filled out and collected at the door as they all walked out to leave for the day. Another short day.

He got to his car; it started. He got to a Mexican restaurant for food to go, got to a 7-11 for beer, got to his apartment. A half day and he was tired. How could he sit on a jury for an extended trial?

In the morning, he woke up to the alarm clock, dressed, and headed for the courtroom. He stopped for donuts, very uncharacteristic of him. There was a cafeteria in the court building which served breakfast, but Stanley was just not that hungry early in

225

the morning. It wasn't really *that* early, they had to be there at nine o'clock, but to him it was early.

He was just as weak as the day before. But he wondered what the case was about, he wondered if he would be selected, wondered how the attorneys would make their cases, how the deliberations would be if he was on the jury, at the end of the trial. But mostly he wondered how he ever thought he could get to the end of it, feeling this way.

The "voir dire," jury questioning and selection, lasted a couple of days. He was picked. Or more precisely, he was not sent away. The trial started on Monday.

It was a civil lawsuit trial, the plaintiff claiming he'd gotten asbestosis from the asbestos in the stuff he'd been working with, the stucco he'd applied to interior walls in a housing project. The defense had to show they didn't know the stuff was dangerous. It had to show it wasn't liable, that in the 1950s when the worker was exposed, it didn't know asbestos hurt people.

The plaintiff's attorneys put on witnesses to explain how it was asbestos caused the illness; the attorneys showed how sick the plaintiff was, by calling his doctor to the stand.

Stanley got bored by the second day. He took the breaks out in the sun, eating quesadilla from a food truck. He spoke with other jurors, but not about the case – the judge had told them in no uncertain terms, and often, not to discuss the case with anyone, and for sure not to form an opinion as to the guilt or innocence of the stucco company.

They sat and listened, in the jury box, taking notes occasionally, with the alternate jurors sitting patiently nearby. If one or more of the original jurors couldn't continue, then an "alternate," or more, had to step into his or her seat – so they had to pay attention as if they would make a decision, later. Which they might.

There were mostly younger people on the jury with Stanley. He knew some about them because he'd sat listening to their answers to the attorneys' questions – do you know the plaintiff, do you know the company, have you any negative ideas towards corporations, do you think monetary awards are too high, generally, can you be fair and impartial as you hear the evidence on both sides, etc. etc?

He wanted to leave, yet he also wanted to stay to see how a trial actually turned out, up close.

He sat at a table in the cafeteria during a break, he listened to the juror who sat next to him in the box tell about his past employment, and he smiled at the jurors outside the courtroom in the hall as they waited for the roll call to go back inside.

He stopped caring about asbestos when he had to see slides on a screen to accompany the witness's testimony. He looked at the plaintiff who was sitting in the spectator section. He admired the judge's control of the proceedings, and he watched one juror for fun – she was sexy-looking. But too young for him.

He wondered how the defense would explain why they didn't know the stuff was dangerous, because the plaintiff experts said there were published findings about it, even before the 1950s. But he didn't get the chance to hear the defense testimony. After a lengthy meeting (in the area beyond the doors at each side of the bench) with the judge and the attorneys, they returned and the judge announced that a settlement had been reached between the two parties and the trial was over. Just like that.

They were excused, after the judge thanked them for doing such "an important civic duty," and that if any juror wished to speak with the attorneys they'd be out in the hall in a moment.

Stanley didn't feel like speaking with them – what would they say? What the settlement was, and why? No, he doubted that. He headed to his car, went to a 7-11, went to his apartment, and then remembered he'd been told to go to the jury assembly room and check out. Oh, well. He'd do that tomorrow.

He did his back stretches, his short sit-ups, his warm-ups, and even took a shower. Then he napped. Then he had coffee. He did wonder about the settlement, who gave in – did the plaintiff agree to less money "damages" than he'd started out asking for, or did the defense agree to pay a higher amount than they'd wanted to start with?

But it was all water under the bridge, now.

He watched some news and some of *Jeopardy*, and clicked around to various channels and drank beer and ate what Mexican food he had left from the day before. And was grateful he didn't have a problem with asbestos.

The next day, he got down to the court building, parked, went through security once more, got to the assembly room, stood in line at a window, felt relieved he didn't need to attend the trial still, turned in his jury badge holder, was told he'd receive a check in the mail. Jurors got a paltry $15 a day for their service. He wished again he had pull in Sacramento and could get them to raise the pay to 20 or 30 dollars a day.

But he was just another retired has-been, and couldn't influence any elected official that he might know of, or about. Sure, he could call one of their offices up there, or send an email, but the futility of that crushed him like a bug under a passing truck's tires. Well, maybe that was an exaggeration, but still, as he thought again, what could any citizen do to bring about change in the system, other than vote, and send in a small donation once in awhile?

The DVD arrived; he watched it all in one evening.

Sometime he would thank the neighbor for the suggestion.

He wanted to see if the weakness would vanish (as he hoped it would) because he didn't want to call the doctor and go in. Even though he had Medicare, and all the benefit it gave, he was egotistical enough to expect his own body to toss off the problem. Like Sugar Ray had said to him so many years ago, while he'd sat in the gym, weak and tired from no doubt the same malady: "Kick it! Kick it!"

Good advice from a great boxer who had trained and fought for more than two decades, always in top shape. Training was rigorous and it kept the fighter strong and healthy.

But still, being weak, Stanley had a difficult time kicking it, and yet, in a few months, he was well.

Sugar Ray Robinson must have meant for Stanley to "kick it" by working out and running often, but such was very tough. He was working then, too, and so had diminished energy. But he did get over it, and returned to the ring.

Now what was he to do? He couldn't run like he used to, he couldn't train like he used to, he couldn't spar like he used to. In that experience of the 1970s after Sugar Ray had said, "Kick it!" he could still run at the track, off and on, and hit the bags, off and on. Now he didn't feel like doing anything like that. He could shadow-box a bit, and he did, hoping for the best.

It was fun to shadow-box, particularly now that his hands and arms felt free of old Primal Pain. But the weakness slowed him up, made him quit sooner than he wanted to.

But time would tell, as the saying went. Time would tell.

After a week, a thought came to him – a feeling, actually – that in his right hand was a dormant pain. From the fight when he had lifeless gloves, and knocked down his opponent, and later realized his knuckles had hurt with that punch, and many years later he primaled about it, and yet, and yet...now in another "spot," in his hand, behind the knuckles, in the bones, he felt a reminder of pain, of hurt, and he went to the street where he usually primaled, parked, rolled up the windows, thought about the fight so long ago, and the punch, and put the little cushion to his face, and voila, there it was, rushing up, the pain inside his hand from that punch long suppressed. He yelled, he howled, he let the pain come out, he released it, and that was that.

He not only felt that past pain, but that of other punches during the fight; it was the one punch that decided it, though. The others merely contributed.

He drove away happy. He drank water to soothe his vocal cords. He napped in his apartment.

Now he had to wait – weeks, months, whatever, for the results. And yet he knew he'd be able to hit the bag harder, because he wouldn't be holding back as he had subconsciously done, after that fight, for years.

He felt sad because he knew he'd have been a better fighter if that hadn't happened that night, if those gloves had been tossed out earlier by a discerning official down in the storeroom at the auditorium.

But such things happen in this life, and we must make do with what cards we are dealt, so to speak, and trust God to see us through our difficulties.

It wasn't right, no, the many mistakes made by others that lead us to further difficulties. But who can say our own mistakes at times haven't led others, even strangers, into difficulties?

Stanley knew he'd been rude to his own sister (half-sister) as a young boy, calling her ugly, and made her cry. What unconscious meanderings in her later life were a result of the emotional pain he caused her? What words or actions had she avoided, words or actions which could have helped her in her life, if she was *not* carrying that repressed pain?

So with all of us. It's the reason God sent His Son to be born in Bethlehem, to save the world, the world that sinned, that so often ruined its chances for peace and love and harmony.

The shepherds heard the message from the angel, that a Savior was born, the One who would finally take away sin, in the last days. Stanley sent an apology to his sister, on her Facebook page, but didn't expect a reply.

Keeping at his plan of watching to see if the sickness, the weakness, would go away as he exercised, he waited. It seemed he had been waiting all his life for a good thing to happen, a good time to arrive. But what else was there to do? If he had secret enemies, or evil energy tossed at him by the big enemy Satan, he'd just have to fight on, with the help of Jesus.

He slept well. Too well, in fact. But he forced himself to drink extra water and shadow-box a bit more each time, every two days, and in a month he was almost sure he was well.

He celebrated by buying a couple of large bottles of Pacifico and re-watching *Some Like It Hot*.

In the morning, he didn't feel bad at all, he felt like the virus was kicked.

His body was tired but it was a tiredness different than the virus tiredness. It was like the tired feeling the day after a fight, not the tired feeling of sparring in the gym, of walking to the shower wearily, and afterward dressing and leaving the gym to go to work the swing shift, which he'd had to do more often than he cared to remember, as an amateur. That was the training weariness, not the satisfying tiredness of having accomplished a goal, a bout.

Now retired, his fights behind him, his jobs behind him, the gas station, the factory, the taxi he'd driven for a number of months, his acting parts, all behind him, he figured.

What was in front? His almost marriage was behind him, his partial schooling was behind him, his brief service to his country was behind him. What now?

A spark of life still burned, still glowed inside. A longing, a need, a hope.

But as memories and teaching, the past was gone. The future loomed, but he saw no hill to climb, no valley to cross, no road to follow, no nothing. He could write a book, a novel, of course, but the motivation was not there.

Did he need to struggle for it, the preparation for the next journey? He decided to expect a solution, a blessing, as many of the songs he heard (and falteringly sang along to) at church, implied.

A blessing, a blessing. That's the thing to wait for.

But none seemed to arise. Just the same old day-by-day life.

Food, exercise, reading, news.

He got x-rays taken at the dentist and found out he had another cavity. And more bone loss. No blessing there.

He bought more vitamin D-3 at Whole Foods. That was supposed to help bones.

One day he felt a strange kind of awareness in his left forehead, or rather, on the surface of it. A punch he'd sustained in the past, he guessed, now surfacing from his subconscious memory. Something to deal with, he assumed, to primal about. But he put it off. Didn't he just get through feeling the old pain in his right hand?

But the sensation on his forehead, above his left eye, continued to make itself known, occasionally, so he knew he couldn't put it off indefinitely. A memory of sparring with a fighter surfaced. A pro, when Stanley was an amateur. Did he pop him with his elbow? Could his knuckles have been that powerful, to hit through the glove and the headgear so much it became suppressed Pain? Possibly. They were only sparring, and Stanley wasn't sure now about it all, but he could find out by primaling. The details would be revealed then.

After he did that, he would take a long drive. Where, he didn't know. Maybe out into the desert. Or to Arizona. Why not? He had an old friend who lived in Phoenix.

Right now, he texted Bill a couple of times, and hung out on the internet. It was boring him, though. He knew he could find some action if he'd walk into that gym on Ventura, but….

Something held him back, so he reminded himself to get out and primal about that punch. Tomorrow, he thought. Or the next day. He realized it must have been a "good" one, if he was avoiding it. Or a "bad" one, depending on how you saw it. Funny, though, the conscious memory of it was minuscule. Just a vague feeling/sensation.

He wondered what effect it had had…

Was that why they called him "Slow-starting Stanley"? Why he never charged forward and fought hard in the early part of a bout?

Had he always been that way? It was not easy to remember. His mind seemed to be playing tricks on him. A few fights, a few fights...his early ones. Was he "slow-starting" *then*? When had this sparring incident taken place? Who was the sparring partner? He was a stranger! It had, in fact, been in San Francisco, a gym he only went to twice. He'd been up there to visit an old Navy buddy. Well, not old, not then. They were both young men, and had talked a lot about the experiences in Cavite City, the girls there. He'd had Stanley over for a week, at his house. He was married, with two children. And Stanley'd gone to the gym in town, in the city, to keep in shape. He recalled it now.

At least that much of it: the second time he'd gone to that gym he asked a tall, trim black fighter there did he want to spar, to "move around a little?"

Now he had to get to the road he usually primaled at, and do it. To focus on the pain of the hit, to let it come out of his subconscious, to fully feel the Pain.

Still, he put it off. He sat in his place reading a Zane Grey book, one he didn't really care for. He went to breakfast with Bill. Troy was working. He drove to the beach, saw the sweet Pacific, drove back, ate at Cable's, did a few stretches and sit-ups, showered, drank beer, hoped for the best, went to bed.

The next day, he went to the same street, as usual, and primaled. The Pain came up surprisingly fast, it was just there below the surface, waiting to be released. He yelled into the cushion as usual, he watched out for cars. Should one pass by he'd have to stop the cries in case someone saw him or heard him and became alarmed, and stop to check – a long shot, but you never knew. He finished when he felt finished, put down the cushion, started the car, drove off. He felt satisfied he'd done, at least, probably more than, half of it. More than half the Pain. And he was convinced the opponent had struck him harder than need be in a "moving around" sparring session. Why? Perhaps because Stanley was white, and he was black, and racial grievances ran deep with some black youths. So he'd banged his headgear with the heel of his glove!

The results were slow, as it was the case sometimes, especially with long-repressed Pain. But the slow healing process was occurring, he was sure. The reversing of behavior he'd adopted since that "improper" punch would begin, would change him back to the person he was before that punch, in many ways. He already felt, in just a few days, the old spirit return, something he hadn't even been aware he'd lost. But he noticed it now.

A bitterness had engulfed him after that punch, and now he saw it had made him withdraw, be less willing to engage the world, so to speak, yet went unnoticed by him. And by his friends, he wondered? They no doubt didn't feel compelled to remark, since the change, the withdrawal, was subtle.

Now perhaps, his friends will not notice a change in him, a greater willingness to engage the world, for that too would be subtle. But he would notice it, and be grateful for it. It came as a blessing from God, to be more the person he had been prior to that crazy life-changing punch.

And of course, his friends at the gym then wouldn't have noticed any subtle change in his behavior. They were boxers and former boxers and were used to things, and people, changing. They wouldn't have cared anyway, just gone on with their own lives and...yet, he had not gone on to fame and glory as a professional, as he'd expected. No, and others had expected it, too. Or *said* they did, at any rate. But that failing wasn't alarming to them. It was just the way it went. It was just how things turned out – some succeeded, others didn't.

But now he knew why. He'd been on the edge of greatness and been turned back, by a stranger who hadn't liked his looks, and had the ability to inflict a wicked blow for the hell of it. What to do now, forty years later? Or was it more than forty years? He knew he'd been in San Francisco, what year was that?

Not important. Not material. Not necessary to remember. What was he to do now, with this new freedom, this revelation, this wonderful piece of information, and change?

Yeah, he'd been an amateur, still. But it wasn't important. He felt a growing resolve as the days went by, to turn his past weakness into strength. And it *had* been weakness, of a type. He'd avoided some fights, *of all things*, yet forced himself to have them, because in his heart he wanted to have fights. It was only a reluctance in his dumb subconscious that told him his forehead still hurt, a lot, when it actually didn't, and who with a real pain in such a way would want to climb in the ring to, in likelihood, suffer more of it?

No one, probably. But not knowing consciously what was the cause of the reluctance, Stanley had simply forced himself to keep boxing.

And who knows how much he held back in the ring? To avoid another hit like that one, to protect his forehead because part of him thought it was still hurt?

Why, hadn't Sammy, who had known Stanley from his first coming to the gym, and trained him, complained Stanley hadn't been aggressive enough in that first pro fight (in Bishop)? A fight he lost? And Stanley hadn't really known what he'd been talking about. But now, sure, Sammy had been right about it, after all. He had seen something even Stanley was not aware of at the time, something Larry seemed not to have noticed, either. But Larry had been handling him for a couple of years, and Sammy had moved on to take care of a pro fighter or two, without paying as much attention to Stanley after initially teaching him and getting him started fighting amateur. He happened to be in Bishop with his fighter James, and helped Larry in the corner, and got a good look at Stanley up close that night, and saw he was different, aggression-wise, than he had been in his earlier career, before Sammy had asked Larry to handle him, *and before that landmark "cuff" in that sparring session in Frisco had done its subtle damage.* Sammy had a sharp eye – but of course good trainers do. Larry was not to blame – he hadn't seen Stanley's first few fights, before the change occurred. But now what? What good will this do now?

He had won fights after it occurred, he'd done quite well, actually. But the "loss" was there, he knew now. He would have done even better. But now, how can this freer feeling assist him in a life where he's old, and has little to do?

The questions remained, but he carried on, looking for something to do, a life to live, a way to go as he prepared for the next life, the one promised to believers who made it in faith to the last, on Earth, and were taken to be with the Lord forever. He watched the news, he read books, as always, but nothing special came to him.

Life sucks, he thought. Life is a tough experience. He'd have to wait for God to show him what he was to do. He'd already known that much, but this time he felt it more deeply, and quit trying so much to figure out what it was he was to do with his life. Let it be that God shows him, let it be that God takes him along. Let it be that he seeks and finds.

The next day it rained. Good, sweet rain that was desperately needed by the area. He put on a light white rain jacket and ventured out. His ball cap protected him somewhat, but he liked having raindrops get on his face.

He wandered along the street, he stopped at the café, he ate a small breakfast, he dreamt of being with Rosy in the early years, he tried not to feel sad, but good. That partially worked.

He went to the mini-market, he returned to his apartment. He put a couple of items in a cabinet, he sat in his chair and watched the rain beyond his window. He told himself to take off his shirt and pants even though they weren't that wet. He'd put his jacket in the bathroom. He thought of Rosy, he thought of Linda Ronstadt, he thought of the 1970s. And he fell asleep, damp and cold, in the chair.

Part V

Time was not an "enemy." He was relaxed about it. He was surprised how weird the presidential campaign had gotten, but even that didn't dispel his positive feelings about the future. He just knew something good was coming for him.

Not that having another errant tooth pulled didn't bother him. It did. He sure didn't want to lose any more. He was taking Vitamin D-3 for his bones, and prayed it would keep other teeth from getting loose, and needing extraction.

Maybe that head butt to the mouth had weakened the hold his bones had on his teeth – he didn't know. Maybe it took decades to be manifested. He didn't know. He tried to forgive the head-butter, though. That was the Christian thing to do.

Moreover, Stanley wanted to shelter no grievances. He wanted to be free of them. If his teeth all were pulled, or fell out, due to that obviously intentional head butt so many decades ago, so it would be and he would deal with it. A terrific shame, of course, but not to be used to hate the world, or even hate that dumb fighter who didn't risk having to win by fighting according to the rules.

He still had enough teeth to chew food with, but implants were advised. How he would be able to pay for those expensive replacements, he wasn't sure. The dentist's receptionist said she'd call Stanley's insurance provider and attempt to ascertain whether or not they would cover implants.

It was nearing the election, the day he would vote. No question he didn't trust Trump, so it made his decision easy. Anyway, Stanley was mostly a Democrat, wasn't he?

Regardless of the controversies, lies, wrongdoing that Clinton was accused of, he felt in his heart she was okay, and would try to help the country, and was capable of helping it.   Bill didn't agree, and neither did Troy. They were opposed to Clinton. They denied it was because she was a woman, but rather, they didn't trust her based on the many stories going around, the many accusations against her.

Stanley declined to have breakfast with them the last two weeks of the election campaign since the conversations infuriated him.

"Happy days are here again," he thought, as Clinton held onto her lead in the polls (generally). He hadn't let go of his idealism, from the JFK and RFK years of the 1960s, and he may be fairly old but he believed in good things for everyone, not only the wealthy minority.

Monday, the day before the election, he drove to Whole Foods Market once again. Why not? He picked up some things, he kidded with the cashier, he drove to his parking spot, he went up the stairs to his place.

The next day he'd vote. A cherished act that not everyone felt like doing, unfortunately.

His neighbor from downstairs knocked on his door, just as Stanley was finishing his partial sit-ups.

"Hello," he said to Spencer. "What's up?"

The man looked tired. "Nothing. Only...I must speak with someone."

"Come in, by all means."

They sat, the man was silent for a bit. Then he said, "Well, I had an argument with my sister, she lives in Tarzana. She wanted me to come over to dinner but I told her no. I said I was having dinner with you."

"With me?"

"Yes, it's all I could think of."

"Ha! Fine. I'm having meatloaf. Care for any?" Stanley rose without waiting for an answer. As he approached the kitchen, he heard, "No, don't trouble yourself."

"No trouble," he yelled back. "Like a beer? I'm having one."

Spencer didn't reply, so Stanley brought him a beer anyway, after he put the Whole Foods' prepared meatloaf in the toaster oven to warm. It didn't require much.

He poured beer into his mug after sitting down, indicating Spencer do the same with the bottle and mug he had placed beside him on the coffee table. But the guy didn't do it. He stared with remorse-filled eyes at Stanley.

"She has problems. I don't want any part of it," he said.

Stanley sighed. He probably didn't want any part of it, either, but what could he say? Christians are supposed to help others.

He tasted the beer. Was it going to be a long talk?

"You see, she has to pay her car payment or they will take her car," Spencer said slowly. He didn't look at Stanley.

"Oh, now, hold on," Stanley said. "I can't give you any money, I'm about broke myself." He took another sip of beer, feeling bad.

Spencer smiled. "I understand." He shook his head. "Not only that, her daughter, who still lives with her, is pregnant." He looked at the beer bottle on the table.

"Um-hmm," Stanley murmured.

Spencer looked at him with appeal in his eyes. "I gave her a few hundred. She has a job as a housekeeper, like the one you use."

"Um-hmm."

"She can't make it without her car. They are going to take it if she doesn't pay."

"What's she owe?" he asked, but wished he hadn't.

"Only five hundred."

"Uh-huh."

Spencer poured some beer in his mug, at last. He doubt he now felt he had done what he had wanted to. He drank. "Very good. I've not had this brand before." He even smiled, he was feeling so relieved.

"I like it," Stanley replied, wondering what was coming next.

At first nothing really did. They spoke of other things – the landlord, the election, the price of gasoline.

Until Spencer finished his beer. Then he asked, "Can you help with only some of it? I know you said you are about broke. Well, so am I. But she can pay you back when she gets a couple of paychecks."

"I doubt that, really. She must have other expenses. Insurance, phone, food, you know."

"Well," Spencer said. 'Yes. Maybe it will take longer. But she's a good person." He gave Stanley those pleading eyes again.

Suddenly Stanley asked, "How do I know I can trust you? That this is the truth?"

Spencer grew red in the face. "Oh, really. Truly. I'm not making this up. I'll take you to speak with her yourself."

"No, no, I can't afford it."

"How about two hundred?"

Stanley sighed and drank his beer and silently asked the Holy Spirit what to do, and felt the Spirit tell him: "Go ahead." So, he shook his head but acquiesced.

"All right. I can afford two hundred. But hell yes, I want to meet her first. *And* her daughter."

"Yes, yes," Spencer said, smiling.

He went down to Spencer's place – a sparsely furnished abode – and after a phone call to the sister, Julie, they just waited for her and the daughter to drive over. Tarzana was not far.

A lot of a to-do for a couple of hundred bucks, Stanley thought. He went upstairs for two more beers and brought them down. Why not?

"How far along is the girl?" Stanley asked.

"Along? Oh, you mean...so, that would be...I don't know precisely. Five months."

"Uh-huh." Stanley felt odd. If it wasn't a scam, he ought to come up with more than two hundred. It wouldn't hurt him. He asked the Holy Spirit again, as he sat in a big comfortable chair, looking at the ceiling. He held the beer bottle in his hand and waited. The Spirit told him an extra hundred would be okay.

He'd have to go to an ATM, but that could wait. He really wanted to check out the faces of the women to see if they appeared honest and sincere.

Spencer mumbled on about the election. He said he preferred Trump. He didn't like Hillary.

"Baggage. Crooked and corrupt," he said.

"You watch Fox News?" Stanley asked him.

"Yes, I do."

"Uh-huh."

Julie showed up without her daughter. She appeared unhappy and concerned, but smiled for the introductions. She was tall, nearly as tall as Stanley.

"Sit down, sit down," his neighbor ordered. "We must get along. We must be friends."

She sat on the couch, and he sat beside her. Stanley resumed his seat.

"Well," he said.

"She has a problem," Spencer said; then, to Julie, 'I have explained it all."

"Oh," she replied simply.

"You know," Stanley launched in, "it's not my usual action to loan money to strangers, but, well, I do know Spencer, and so – "

"Thank you," Julie interrupted. 'We wouldn't ask but for the pressure."

"Okay," Stanley responded. "You can't make the payment? For your car?"

She shook her head. "No."

"Uh-huh. I can come up with some of it. But, excuse me, Spencer said you are taking care of a pregnant girl?"

"I am."

"Wasn't she supposed to be here? Don't be offended but, you know, I wanted to see for myself."

She nodded. "Brook wasn't feeling so good. She is at the apartment, though. If you want to see her, let's go there. No problem. Thank you for even considering it." She looked down at her feet. Her concern had transformed into embarrassment.

He followed her in his car to the apartment in Tarzana. A typical one bedroom place in the Valley. Brook had moved into the bedroom and her mother was sleeping on a cot in the living room. Brook was a nice, sweet girl of twenty, and it didn't take long for Stanley to go to a market nearby and withdraw $200 from the ATM, and combined with $100 he'd brought with him, he handed it over to Julie in the parking lot.

"Thank you so much," she said to him, and hugged him. They parted friends, with Stanley hoping he'd done the right thing.

Well, it *seemed* right. But one never knew. It could all be fake. Nevertheless he felt the Spirit was telling him to do it.

The next day he voted, confident in Clinton's victory, as the polls were showing her ahead of Trump. It was a narrow margin though, and as he'd told Troy, "Anything can happen."

He napped, he read in the latest Sherlock Holmes Mystery Magazine he'd received in the mail, he exercised. He put off turning on the news coverage as long as he could. Being in California, he wanted to have as many states' voting finished, and the counting started, before he sat in front of the TV. So he spoke on the phone with a friend, one who lived in Palm Springs. It was a pleasant call, as the friend, Ryan didn't have his TV on either. Little did they know what was happening, that many states were reporting Trump was doing better than expected.

He also did his back stretches and shadow-boxing, and showered, and sat down finally to watch the returns.

It was shocking. Trump was leading and after awhile Clinton had no chance of catching up, even with the electors from California. Stanley shut off the TV, wondering what in the world had happened. He almost called Ryan but decided against it. He went to bed shaking his head. The polls had been wrong? The country was going in a new direction.

Spencer let him know Julie had paid for her car, and was enormously grateful to Stanley. Well, he had known, or expected, that. Still, it was hard to drop the doubt he'd felt as to the transaction. He had to accept the Spirit had led him rightly, and forget about it.

He bought a six-pack at the 7-11, filled his tank with gasoline, and tried not to feel bad about the election. That took some days, however, because it was questionable what Trump knew of being a president, and if his advisors could urge him to do the proper things. What if he made foreign leaders mad at him? What if he made divisive comments about various factions of the US population?

Weeks passed. He continued to be uneasy. He received no money from Julie. He did, however, keep exercising and reading and looking for a path in life to satisfy his craving for reward, activity, some type of fulfillment.

He drove by the gym on Ventura again. It beckoned to him, it called to him, but he feared it. What pain would he feel, entering it? Such pain as his less-than-stellar boxing career would signify. That is, his *professional* one. His other career was certainly stellar.

But...that didn't satisfy him. It *should*, he knew, and he had God to guide him in life, so why fear entering a gym? He must wait until God led him to enter it.

A strange thing happened, though. The neighbor called him, said there was a problem. He'd tell Stanley later in the day, if he was available. Stanley said he would be. But that evening Spencer didn't show up.

No sweat, right? He'd visit some other time. Stanley's philosophy was "go with the flow." He'd learned that as he became older. So he'd only wait for him to contact him.

Yet, two more days went, and no contact. Should he call? No, it was whatever it was – Spencer had a problem and would let Stanley in on it, or ask his help, when he was ready to.

Only just let it not be a need for more of his money, or a scam to get more of it.

Meanwhile, he took his heart pills, he drank water, he read, he watched TV, he ate burgers; he longed for a few more bucks. But didn't most people?

The day he was going to go to look at the gym came – he felt it was a guidance in his belly somewhere – *but* Spencer knocked on his door first.

"Sorry," he said when Stanley let him in. "I been in the hospital."

"What?"

"Yes. May I sit down?"

"Sure."

Spencer sat in a chair, smiling. Stanley went to the small couch.

"What happened, can I ask?"

"Oh," he began. "Stomach ailments. I'm okay now."

"Uh-huh." Stanley felt a scam coming on.

"My sister Julie begs your pardon but cannot pay any money now. The baby needed more tests."

"The baby."

"Six months now," he nodded.

"What? Oh, the pregnancy. That is a baby, I suppose. Okay."

"Thank you. But now I have a problem. It isn't money, so don't worry. It's the former wife...problem."

"She's bothering you?"

"Why, yes," Spencer replied. "A guess?"

"Yeah, but it isn't tough to arrive at."

"Well, my life is not good."

"Why?" Stanley asked, the suspicion growing.

"No big deal. She calls and she..." he paused.

"Needs something?"

"Why, yes," he replied.

Here it comes, he thought, in spite of the denials. He refrained from saying, "Uh-huh."

But Spencer looked at the floor, at the carpet.

"Go ahead," Stanley urged.

"She calls."

"Uh-huh." He couldn't help saying it.

"She wants the apartment."

"Really? Don't you rent?"

"Yes."

"Well, what...she wants you to move out, and let her move in?"

Spencer nodded. Stanley laughed.

Spencer looked oddly at him.

"Just tell her no."

He shook his head. "I am not getting anywhere with that."

"Listen, my friend, you tell her no, that's all it takes."

"Sadly, she threatens my life. She does."

"Oh, come on, man."

"Stanley, she means it, she will kill me."

"Bullshit."

Now Spencer laughed. "Of course it seems like it, but I think she –"

"Oh, come on! And why does she want to move in down there?"

"So I will pay the rent as I normally do."

"Ah," Stanley said. "That is it. You are in a tough spot."

"Yes, but you can help. *You* can tell her no, she may accept that."

"Just a minute. Why me? She doesn't even know me."

"That's not essential. You can tell her we are friends, you are watching out for me."

"Oh boy," Stanley said.

"Please."

"And what's the reason? You can't move because…?"

"Oh, well," Spencer began. He pursed his lips. "I don't know."

"We need a reason for why you can't move out, obviously."

"Should we say I'm sick and it will cause too much...much…?"

"Difficulty?" But Stanley held up his hand before Spencer even nodded. "No, I don't care to lie. You don't want to move because it's too great an inconvenience, but you're ashamed to tell her that."

Spencer clapped his hands together. "That's excellent! Done!"

"Uh-huh. What's her phone number?"

He spoke with her, a dry voice on the line, but not an unpleasant one. She waited while he explained his identity, and how Spencer had asked him to call.

"Well?"

"Uh, you see, for him to move now is just too difficult, he says. The inconvenience of it, the...he isn't feeling that well, and...hopes you will understand."

"Oh, but, he could have told me all this, couldn't he?"

"Not really. He isn't up to it," Stanley offered, creatively, he thought. It was true, for sure.

"You ought to be ashamed," she said. Stanley looked at Spencer who was staring at the carpet again.

"Now, uh, no. I'm doing a friend a favor. You will need to find a different place to live. I'm sorry."

She gasped, said "Screw you," and hung up on him. So much for that.

A day or so passed, without word from Spencer, but then he called and said his ex-wife had agreed to keep looking for a place to live in for herself, and not pressure Spencer any more. He told Stanley he had thought it would work.

"Well," Stanley thought, "he knows the woman, that's for sure, and could know what method would work on her." Spencer thanked him again, and said he'd make some soup for Stanley the next day. But Stanley didn't care for any soup, and told him so, thanking him in return for the offer.

Why did he make women hang up on him, he wondered? She wasn't the first one. He guessed it was the directness he used, a hold-over from his boxer's attitude, no doubt.

He would probably need to soften that manner in the future. If he was able.

He spoke with Ryan in Palm Springs, who was reconciling himself to Trump winning. He figured the Congress and the Supreme Court, the balance of power idea, would control Trump if he actually tried any reckless behavior on a grand scale, in office. Stanley wasn't so sure. But it all remained to be seen. Stanley in fact held out his unspoken hope that there was time for voting calculation fraud to be revealed, thus denying Trump the office, but that time was short.

Still, the polls had shown Clinton ahead,and yet...the vote tallies, the state-by-state counts, refuted them. If voting machines had been tampered with, such evidence may surface. Or it may not, maybe it would be such a scandal, if machines in some states had been hacked and their votes flipped, that the leaders would rather hide it.

Stanley felt his life was all right but still as yet he hadn't found the goal he aimed at, the activity, the work, to "own" him, so to speak. Thoughts of acting roles, women, perhaps training a young fighter, writing something more, and others, floated past his brain like leaves, flowing in the wind towards a sweet rest upon a hill or in a meadow, or dramatically in a slow stream, to sink or wash ashore God knows where.

He read the Bible some. He saw how Christ healed and preached up until his death on the Cross. He saw how the religious leaders tried in vain to trick and trap him. Not an enviable position to be in, but one He took willingly.

Stanley drove around the city, still seeking an activity to "complete" him, as he perceived it. But he found none. Not one part, even, of one.

Was it a waste of his time? A dumb pursuit he'd made for his life, now? Should he just give up and watch TV, and meander along until his own death?

No, he kept searching. He was sure God had a place for him still, a part to play in the scheme of, the plan of, his life. But what was it?

He walked to the gym from the parking lot near the Verizon store. He peered into the front window. A ring was there, empty, and some exercise machines, one occupied. He dared not enter. It seemed, in fact, hardly the right moment. An old guy in a boxing gym? The manager would walk from the back (where he saw punching bags), and inquire as to his being inside. He'd have to tell him, "Why, only looking around, but interested in working out, sometime."

Stanley wasn't up to that conversation yet.

So he went away, morose and feeling weak. One day, by God, he would go in there. But not this day.

He ate, nearby, and returned home.

Trouble was, he *wanted* to work out. Seemed a bizarre paradox – not willing to go inside the gym and yet at the same time, wanting to train.

Not the first time in his life Stanley had faced conflicting and disparate facts affecting choices.

He slept well that night, nonetheless, because he had, at the very least, gone to the gym and looked in the window. He'd even looked in the glass of the door, though not opening it.

It was sure getting colder in the Valley. He welcomed it as a positive change from the hot days, weeks, and months preceding. It rained more too, a blessing for the dry ground. Stanley felt compelled to continue his search, but knew nowhere to conduct it.

He could call Ryan in Palm Springs, but to what avail?

The part-time housekeeper showed up, apologizing for missing so many days. It wasn't important to him. She didn't have to come by to clean but every two weeks, or three, as far as he was concerned. She had another job – full-time – and if she didn't need the money, he knew she would not show up when she had promised. He was too old to care, he suspected. He didn't have to have clean underwear, or socks. At least, not much. If she didn't show up for a month, well then he had to wash them in the shower, because he didn't feel like taking laundry in to a shop. But he could, if need be; it wasn't difficult, just sort of inconvenient, to do that.

He could run the dishwasher, and water the plants on his small patio outside his door. That was not a big deal, but he'd rather she did it.

He watched *A Christmas Carol* on a cable station. The good one, the very first one, from 1951. Great stuff. He didn't buy any gifts, though. Who could he give them to? He hoped that didn't make him like Scrooge.

He spent the holiday alone. What did he care? A couple of old friends left him texts about having a Merry Christmas. He didn't have enough energy to text them back, for some reason. He did it the next day.

Also, on the 26th, it occurred to Stanley that his downstairs neighbor may be alone and unlike him, Stanley, not caring for it. So he rang his bell to say hello. But there was no answer.

He walked to the liquor store to get beer and beans, and a banana, and a bag of chips. He could make a roast beef sandwich from his last "to go" order, and read his book and maybe go on the internet to see what YouTube had to offer. And of course, exercise and watch news, and a movie he'd gotten in the mail, another DVD he'd ordered recently.

Something he heard or read that day sparked a memory of Vietnam. He thought about it after going to bed.

It was just a brief moment in time, the memory. His Navy friend Bill had been getting Stanley on his flights, since Stanley wasn't an actual crew member, but the pilot permitted it. Just a few flights, patrols up and down the coast of Vietnam.

Stanley was woken up early one morning by Bill, on the ship they slept on, the Seaplane Tender. Bill said, "Come on, we have a patrol. Now." Bill had forgotten to tell him the day before as he always had.

Stanley, deep in sleep, wasn't about to force himself to get up and dress and rush to the launch and go out to the plane on the water in the middle of the night like that. And he didn't have to, not being a regular crew member. So he begged off. He said, "Oh, no! Man, forget it. Go on."

Bill stared at him and then turned away from Stanley's bunk, and Stanley went right back to sleep.

Later that day when the plane returned, and he saw Bill in the ship's mess hall, Bill told him they had been fired on during that patrol. But not hit, apparently. Stanley felt a twinge, more than a twinge, of envy. He'd wanted to see some action and was sorry he'd refused the early morning request to participate in the patrol. He saw some action later, though, on another flight, his last one before returning to the Philippines to serve out the rest of his tour of duty. And yet….

Except he couldn't feel but so much jealousy because he decided if he *had* joined in that flight, the circumstances might have been all different, the shots may not have been fired, and he wouldn't have been a part of any action. Stanley thought, just his extra weight on the seaplane might have changed, a bit, their speed, or direction, and therefore the timing, of the patrol, so they could have been somewhere other than where the enemy had been in order to take shots at them. So he didn't feel too bad – might have gained nothing.

Or, looking at it from a different angle, they might have been in a worse position had he joined the flight, and gotten shot down. So maybe God kept him from going. It was possible, he decided, lying there in his bed in the Valley that night, before dropping off to sleep.

In the morning, he thought, regarding the incident, that the next time he has a request, and feels less than inclined to accept it, he will make a greater effort, will proceed, as long as it seems God's urging.

He knew he *could* have dragged himself out of his bunk that early, dark morning, and dressed hurriedly, and gone with Bill. Perhaps he should have, or perhaps not. But the next time he'd be more determined to go with the flow – asking the Spirit for guidance first, of course. At that time, in Vietnam, he'd been far less religious than he became, in the 1970s, anyway.

His phone rang. He answered – he was up and having breakfast.

"Dude," the voice of Ryan in Palm Springs said.

"Hey," Stanley replied as laconically.

"How are you?" Stanley hated that question, but answered anyway, "I'm okay. You?" He would prefer to say, "not great, but who gives a shit?" But he didn't say it.

"Good, man, good," Ryan said.

They spoke a few minutes. Ryan was coming into town that weekend and would meet up with him if possible.

"Sure."

They picked a restaurant, they chose a time, they said goodbye, and hung up.

Stanley wondered as to this sudden trip, but hadn't asked Ryan why he was coming into L.A., because he had not volunteered the info himself.

Stanley sat in his chair and thought, "It has to be important, though." He could ask him about it in person.

As it turned out it was, indeed, important, and Ryan had been hesitant to mention it over the phone.

They met at the Daily Grill, in the hotel Ryan decided to stay at, and had lunch. Ryan was taller than Stanley, of the same age, and grey-haired. They'd met on a movie both had done, both having roles as the friends of the leading characters.

The café was quiet and Ryan ordered fish, Stanley ordered plain hamburger and fries.

"Good to see you!" Ryan said a couple of times.

"Same back at you," Stanley replied a couple of times.

They talked of past events, of hanging out at the beach house Ryan had rented in the '80s. Ryan asked him if he still did any boxing, and Stanley had to say, "no."

While they ate, Ryan happened to mention a problem he had. A woman problem.

"She's terrific, really, but she left me. We'd been living with each other for...months. A few months."

"Uh-huh," Stanley responded.

"She left without any warning."

"You must have been having a problem, come on."

"Hell, no. But she acted bothered in regard to *something*."

"No idea what?"

"No," Ryan said firmly. "Everything was fine. But, well, she may have had another boyfriend, here in L.A., because she came out here once in awhile.'

"Oh. That."

"Yeah," Ryan looked down at his food, nearly finished. "I'm guessing."

"But did she pack up and leave without you knowing?"

"Yes, that's right." He looked at Stanley. "Man, here's the thing. My car – she had been driving it – has a locator, you know? I could see where she'd been. And –"

"You mean, during her trips?"

"Yep. And she didn't even know I could do that, because I caught her in a lie. I told her I knew she hadn't been where she said she'd been."

"Hello, Ryan! That's what was bothering her."

"Oh, okay, sure. Right. Must have been," Ryan acknowledged. "She didn't tell me that, though."

"Why would she? If she knew you knew she'd been someplace and lied about it..." Stanley threw up his hands.

"Right."

"Pissed at you, or at herself. And either way, she felt compromised."

"And took off," Ryan added.

"Uh-huh," Stanley confirmed.

"But no call? No text? No notice of any kind?

"So you are saying you are wondering..." Stanley didn't care to put it into words.

"She would have notified me, I am positive. To explain, at least."

"And because she didn't?"

"A crime, dude. Flat out. A bad dead."

"Hurt?" Stanley asked.

"Yeah. And don't want to call in the cops because she's gone, and maybe only extremely angry at me. And that's what I'm doing here. To ask you to find her."

"Huh? Me?"

Ryan pushed his plate away, at the moment their waitress arrived to take their plates.

"Would you care for anything else?" she asked.

"No, no," Ryan said. "Thanks."

She left, and he stared into Stanley's quizzical face. "Why not?"

"Well, uh, what for? Can't you hunt for her better?"

"No, she doesn't want to see me. You know May, and she won't be hiding from you."

"Wait, man. She knows we are friends, and –"

"Fine. You can speak with her if you find her."

Stanley frowned. "Okay, just where do you think I should look?"

Ryan pulled a note from his shirt pocket. "This is a couple of addresses you can start with." He handed the note to Stanley, smiling. "Good luck." His smile disappeared. "I only hope she's not dead."

"What? Cut it out. She's okay."

"Probably," Ryan allowed. "Let's get out of here." He searched the room with his eyes, for the waitress, to get the check.

Outside he pressed two hundreds on him. "Here. Expenses."

Stanley hesitated, but took the bills. If he was going to act as a detective, why not be paid as one?

He had to look over the places indicated by Ryan's note. That was the very first order of business. Not to venture into the places, only view them. From that, he would make a plan, an approach, depending on the circumstances. Ryan had not said much, if anything, about them. Well, at least he hadn't said "Be careful." But perhaps there may be danger, Stanley cautioned himself. So he'd have to put his gun in his car.

He went to his apartment, that day, with a few misgivings. Why had he agreed? Friendship? Stupidity? But then again, as always in his life, it seemed, he didn't much care what befell him. And perhaps this was the right path, the goal, he had been searching for.

He drank a few beers, stared at that paper with the addresses, and determined to do the best he could on this new task.

In the morning, he was even less sure about it all than the night before, but stuck to his plans. He ate, dressed, took his pistol and some bullets to the trunk of his car, and drove to the first address. It was West Los Angeles, off Santa Monica Boulevard, close to the 405 freeway. A business, looked like, as he pulled around the corner and saw a boring-looking building. He parked in a lot, climbed out, went to the front of the building. He saw a sign over the entrance.

"Chase Photography," it read.

He wished to enter, but should he? Photography? He could pretend he wanted some pictures of...anything. His car. Himself. That's it, of his car *and* himself. He entered.

A large room, a cluttered counter, a workplace in the back, papers and equipment at various places. A corner alcove set up with lights and a chair: a spot for portraits. Possibly May worked here. Or her boyfriend.

"Excuse me?"

"A moment!" a voice from the rear announced. Stanley felt nervous. This was not his normal line of work, to be sure, but he had to carry on, once decided, "come what may." That phrase in his head struck him as curious, since Ryan's girlfriend's name was May.

He felt like leaving, but didn't. An Asian man entered, smiling, to nod at Stanley, leaving the back room door open.

"May I help you?" That word again! It caused Stanley to flinch involuntarily.

"Well, uh...I guess you take photos? Like of people and cars?"

The man returned his smile. "Anything!"

"Oh, so, I would like a few pictures of my car and me," Stanley said.

"Can do."

"How much?"

269

"With the car or separate?"

"Oh, with the car, I guess."

"50 dollars," he replied. "For three different ones."

So it was he posed with his car and had photos taken. He also asked a couple of questions, and found out the man, Rey, had one female assistant but her name wasn't May.

He paid after picking up the pictures the following morning. They looked good, in fact.

So he needed to go on to the next address. Later, he might need to return and attempt to get a gander at the female assistant, no matter her name.

But what was he doing? He is supposed to have a photo of the subject, isn't he? Stanley had read enough detective novels to know that much. Why hadn't Ryan thought of that? Did he really want to find her, or…?

"Now, don't get paranoid," he told himself. "Take each step one at a time."

He drove past the other address. A big house in Calabasas, an imposing house of brick and wooden beams and a huge front yard, all gated, of course. He'd have to come up with a story when he rang the bell in front.

He returned to his apartment before he called Ryan. Had to leave a message. Said he wanted a photo of May, maybe more than one.

He read in a Sherlock Holmes Mystery Magazine, appropriately enough, exercised, showered, sat down to have a beer, and turned on the TV, all the while thinking Ryan would return his call at any moment.

But that didn't happen. He watched the news. Trump was president now, causing turmoil already.

Stanley microwaved a turkey pot pie, had another beer, taking his time. He needed that story, to get into that house. The photos of May would be important – he could say he was looking for her, but couldn't divulge the source of his information. Yes, that would do nicely.

The next day, he wasn't all that confident, and Ryan hadn't returned his call. He didn't care to proceed minus a photo of May, no way.

He did drive around, his cell by his side. He ate some eggs at a Denny's on Topanga Boulevard. He thought of trying Ryan again, but why bother? The man must have heard his message. It was a bit mysterious, to Stanley. Wasn't Ryan in a hurry?

Out in the streets, he happened to stop at an intersection, a red light, while schoolchildren passed before him, in the crosswalk. They looked somber, they looked happy – all types. He heard joking from some, as schoolkids are wont to do. One boy waved at him, and leaned backwards, hands out, indicating the car. Stanley interpreted it as a sign of compliment. He smiled at the young teenager and had a glow from the "compliment" as he drove off with the green light.

Later, he pulled into the parking lot of Marie Callender's and went inside for a to-go order. Like a fool, he hadn't called ahead to order it, so he had to wait after he told the hostess what he wanted – but that he didn't mind. He felt like he had to wait for his prayers to God to be answered too, and that wait was much more frustrating – yet had to be endured.

A young woman came in the front door, limping, with a cast on the left leg. Stanley stood aside to let her by, and said, "Oh, wow. A sporting injury?"

She chuckled and replied, "No, just being a dumb ass."

He said, as she walked to the hostess, "Well, I've done that, too!" It was a silly remark, but she was courteous enough to laugh at it.

He didn't want to oppress her, so he looked away as she arranged to be seated by herself. He saw, after a responsible interval, that she had taken a booth near the front. So he could look at her while she sat, now with her phone out, as young people are generally wont to do. She didn't look up at him. He wandered around in the area near the front desk-cash register, thinking she too must in fact be waiting for a to-go order. But his came out, he paid for it, and left. She hadn't looked up at him, but kept her eyes, and fingertips, on her phone.

Probably looking at photos of her boyfriend, Stanley sardonically surmised. Of course he had no way of knowing, but it was the thought that came to his mind.

Well, he'd had his own young years, too, so what did he have to be ashamed of? He went to his car.

He wished he was able to speak more with her, yet it was not in the cards. He wasn't quick-witted enough to play that game of clever conversation that some men are able to do, even when there was a profound age gap, or perhaps, especially when there was a profound age gap. Some men can make a way with women where it looks as if there is no way.

Stanley waited in vain for a call from Ryan, so gave up and tried again, and left another message, "Please, man, I must have a picture of her. If you don't have one at any rate, let me know."

He didn't update him on his search. There wasn't much anyway. If Ryan provided no photo, he'd simply go to that house and take his chances. What could happen? Well, he might be shot, of course – that was something. So of course he'd have to take his gun with him. Why not?

He slept well that night, after repeating the Lord's Prayer – which wasn't the Lord's prayer at all, He gave it to his *disciples* who were to pray it. Stanley didn't think Jesus prayed it at all, He didn't have to. He'd no sins to be forgiven, for starters; Jesus was sinless, as far as he could determine from reading the Word, and hearing it preached in churches. Stanley had to forgive, and had to receive it, too. Christ died for our sins but we obviously still do some, and need an all-encompassing act of forgiveness.

Also, Jesus didn't need to pray to be delivered from temptation, did he? Not really, since as God He could avoid, stand up to, temptation, while the rest of us must struggle with it, and hope to get assistance fighting it.

So he slept well, and awoke refreshed, ready for what should come.

Ryan finally called. It was a brief conversation. He'd been "busy." He had a photo or two of May – recent ones, as a matter of fact. He'd scan them and email them to him.

"No, my printer is broken. Just put them in the regular mail."

"Snail mail? Ha-ha. Okay. Any luck so far?"

"No. I don't care to approach the house without a photo of her."

"Yeah, right. Fair enough."

That was about it. Ryan said he had Stanley's address.

But did he sound tense? Yes. But that could be explained: his girl was missing.

Stanley knew her, of course, but had not seen her for – what? – ten years? He just needed a photo. She could answer the door and he might not be able to recognize her. In theory, at least.

So he waited. Yes, there were bullets in the gun. He hoped he wouldn't need to use them.

Finally, the picture arrived in the mail. He remembered her from it. She was older but still pretty, with the hint of Asian in her looks. He would approach the house, say he had known this woman, wanted to speak with her, and that someone he'd rather not identify had provided Stanley with the address.

Might work. If anyone at the house knew her, fine. If not, or if they did but denied it, he'd have to say they could give her his name and number if she "showed up."

That was the plan, and he carried it out. A voice from a metal box at the front fence, the metal gate, was what greeted him that afternoon.

It was raining. He had no umbrella, just a ball cap and a rain jacket. The voice, a male voice, after asking, "Yes," was silent as he explained his purpose, until he said,

"Her name is May White. I have a –"

"No one lives here by that name."

"Oh, okay, but will you please look at the photo I have of her? She might be using another name."

More silence. Then the gate door buzzed, clicked, and the voice from the box told him, "Come on in." He took a breath, a sudden one, and walked through as he pushed the gate open. He walked a wet path to the front door of the house. He was hoping he could get out of the rain. The big door opened and a football-player-sized fellow stood looking at him. Frowning.

"Hello," Stanley preemptively said. "Larson's the name." He felt foolish saying it that way, but it came out like that and he had to live with it.

The man, in his thirties with blond hair, nodded. "So you have stated. Do you wish to come in?"

"Yes, thank you." Stanley did go in, when the football player took a large step backward. The room was not well lit, adding to Stanley's apprehension. He remembered to smile at the last second, and he held out his hand to shake. After a slight hesitation, the man complied, with a firm grip, and gruffly said, 'I'm Peterson." What his position in the household, servant or friend or family member, was, he didn't say. He did shut the door after Stanley entered, however.

The place was large, with chairs and sofas and tables. Uncomfortable looking. Like a meeting room, not a living room. Two staircases led up, on either side of the room.

Stanley felt nervous, but pulled the photo from his pocket, showing it to Peterson. "This is the woman, recently."

After a slight look of curiosity at Stanley, the big man stared at the photo in his hand, and smiled for the first time. "I know her," he stated. "But who is she to you?" He returned the photo.

"As I said, I used to know her." Stanley didn't want to say more until he had an indication Peterson was willing to open up.

"Yes, well…."

"It's important," Stanley said, hoping it was sufficient.

"Why?"

"Can't say until I speak with her."

"Go to hell. You show me an ID first. And tell me what's so important, and then you *might* be able to talk to her."

"Hmm," he replied. "Okay." He pulled out his wallet, and then his driver's license. Peterson took the ID and scrutinized it. "What's your story, pal?"

"Oh all right, tough guy. I know a close friend of hers who is worried about her. He hasn't seen her for a few weeks."

"My, my, what is all this?" a strong female voice asked, from the stairs on the left. The men turned and saw the beautiful May standing a few steps from the top, dressed in white. White sweatpants, white pullover, white sneakers.

"Hello, Missy. This man says he knows you."

She smiled. "Certainly. Good old Stanley, the boxer, isn't it?"

Peterson took a more than casual look at Stanley, because of this comment. He looked him up and down, but didn't appear impressed.

"Right. It's me. From long ago."

"Oh come on, it hasn't been all that long." She descended the staircase now, still smiling.

Stanley nodded graciously, following her with his eyes as she walked to Peterson, placing her hand on his arm. "Relax," she fairly whispered.

"Whatever you want, Missy."

She turned to stare at Stanley. "What brings you here, as if I didn't know?"

"Well, you can guess, Ryan's worried, but, uh, unable to come on his own."

"Ha!" she laughed. "He didn't *ever* like to come on his own." She giggled and glanced at Peterson.

"Excuse me." She put her hand to her mouth, then took it away, asking, "Would you care for some wine? I most certainly would."

Without waiting for Stanley's answer, she walked to a small bar under the staircase. She grabbed up a wine bottle which had been standing by itself on the counter.

"Please allow me to do that." Another voice, this time from a doorway, on the left. Stanley saw a rotund man of probably fifty, wearing a dark jacket and grey trousers.

The man advanced on May/Missy and took the wine bottle from her hands. She meekly withdrew, turning to Peterson with a shrug, and for Stanley, a blank expression. The man proceeded to open the bottle, groaning a bit while doing so. "Humph!" he exclaimed, pulling out the cork with the corkscrew. He turned triumphantly to the three others, gave them a slight bow, and said, "Who wants some?"

May/Missy held up her arm, Peterson shook his head, and when the man looked at Stanley, asking, "Who are you, anyway?" with a short laugh, Stanley answered, "I would rather have a beer, if that's okay, and my name –"

"David, allow me to introduce an old acquaintance, Stanley...oh please, I have forgotten your –"

"Larson," he supplied, feeling uncomfortable.

"Glad to meet you, sir," David said politely. "We will look forward to hearing all about you. And a beer we can provide, of course." He took a wine glass from a shelf and poured. "I myself, as Missy will confirm, prefer Jack Daniels."

He opened the refrigerator under the bar and withdrew a Beck's bottle, opened it with a small opener, and took a tall glass from the shelf.

"Thanks," Stanley said. He advanced to the bar and waited as David filled the glass. Missy also advanced, taking her glass from David while Stanley took his.

A straight Jack Daniels, no ice, was quickly arranged by David's deft hands, and a toast was proffered, "To long life," with a smile at Missy and Stanley, and just a quick glance at Peterson.

They drank. David consumed his entire glassful, Stanley a fourth of his, and Missy a long gulp but less than half of her wine. She took a breath, made a face, uttered a moan, shook her head, and said to David, "Wow, this tastes like shit."

He laughed a bit and told her, "Well, you picked it, darling."

She went to place her glass on the bar, nodding to him. She took up the bottle to read the label, as if to confirm she had selected it. She put it down, frowning.

"I'd rather have a beer like Stanley's. By the way," she said, turning to him, "Is Ryan all upset? He knew I was restless. He hasn't tolerance for –" with a gasp she stopped, put her hands to her head, felt a spasm in her arms, clutched at her chest, moaned, and fell to the floor. Peterson ran to her. David shouted, "What the hell?"

Peterson turned her over. She looked purple. Stanley also advanced, but Peterson held out his arm. "She's not breathing," he said. They then all tried to help her, to no avail.

Days later, the autopsy results were reported in the newspaper, strychnine had killed her. The police questioned everyone and the house had been searched.

But only weeks later was an arrest made – Peterson. A small, plastic bag was found in his closet upstairs. It contained a syringe with traces of strychnine. Police confirmed they believed he'd injected it into the wine bottle through the cork, knowing May (her true name) would choose it to drink, as she normally had (or so David Corso told police).

Stanley was never, at first, considered a suspect, having only just arrived at the house, with no opportunity to place poison in the wine bottle. It was found in the bottle, police said, in lethal quantities.

Stanley had explained about Ryan, who was questioned also, at length. It turned out May and David had been married for five years. Ryan cursed vehemently on the phone to Stanley when that information was revealed, (in spite of his pain regarding her death). It was, in fact, a strong "motive" for Ryan, but the lack of opportunity saved him.

Yet that didn't keep the police investigators from questioning Stanley to be sure he hadn't been sent by Ryan to "do her in," as one detective phrased it. It was a bad grilling, Stanley thought, but they gave up on that idea. The tainted syringe was the main evidence, although Peterson claimed innocence.

Why would he have done it? Stanley had too little information to know the reason, and the investigators certainly were not sharing theirs, except Ryan had an idea.

"She could get under your skin," he told Stanley on the phone one day. "She had a way. That guy – bodyguard or whatever he was, being in the house and always nearby, fell prey to her wiles, I bet."

"Could have," Stanley agreed.

"If she cheated with me for months, she might have cheated with that guy right there."

"And...he couldn't have her all to himself, so he did her in?"

"She could make men crazy, trust me."

"I suppose you might know."

"Ha! No kidding, Sherlock."

"But man, that stuff in his closet? Stupid, wasn't it?"

"Yes," Ryan said. "It's quite dumb. But he was acting crazy, anyway."

"I suppose so," Stanley agreed.

Days later, another idea occurred to Stanley. What if the bag was planted, what if...someone else poisoned the bottle?

But if David had, it was impossible to prove. And him stashing the bag would have been very risky, with Peterson around.

But...if he'd had lots of time to do it, days or even weeks, and poisoned the wine some *other* way...even that afternoon....

Yeah. His back had been turned half the time he was at the bar. He sounded like he was opening the bottle, and perhaps he was, but he had time to pour strychnine in there. From a vial from his jacket, maybe. He sure had a deft way of fixing drinks, as Stanley had witnessed.

He might have been jealous. He might have – probably had – known about Ryan, too.

The next day, Stanley phoned the detective who'd questioned him, Bernstein. He got back to Stanley within an hour, listened to this idea, and promised to check it further.

And of course, it took a long time to hear any results. But Bernstein called to say thanks, they'd made an arrest. Corso confessed after they found another suspicious death in his past, a woman in a band he used to be the drummer for – the singer. Unsolved strychnine poisoning. The lead guitarist even told police he'd always thought David Corso had killed her, but there was so little evidence....

"Wow," Stanley said. That's all he could think of. And another confession, like before when he'd been close to, solved even, a crime.

Lucky, he thought. But maybe not luck. When the facts are against someone, they ought to give up if they are guilty,and make some sort of plea bargain.

Bernstein was extremely grateful, offered to take Stanley to dinner for a reward.

"Glad to accept," he told the Sergeant. "Whenever you'd like."

It bothered him though, the murder, the whole episode. He sure wished such experiences would not happen to him any more, after this.

Life went on for him. Slow and uneventful, which he didn't mind. He had to make peace with many failings, falling short in some areas. Everyone must have to deal with these disappointments, he figured. What was so special about his falling short of his goals, such goals as he'd had in his lifetime? Nothing.

He smoked some cigarettes, more than usual. He ate nachos from Denny's – not the best take-out food but since he considered himself to be an ex-athlete, not a current one, it didn't matter. He drank beer. He drank his usual three bottles a night, however, not more, except one Saturday night when he had four, for no apparent reason.

Life meant suffering, he knew, and joy, he knew, and he was very blessed not to live in a poor country or one with a dictator. In spite of how some TV commentators viewed it, Stanley didn't believe Trump was a real dictator.

Getting policies enacted was always the goal of presidents, he figured. Doing it with class, like JFK, or without class, like Trump, was just a part of the overall picture.

What the results were, in terms of aiding or hindering the American people in general – in safely and honestly pursuing happiness, and living in liberty – seemed to him the main matter when evaluating a presidency.

Such ideas flowed into, and out of, his mind. A memory here, a concept there, a pain, a pleasure, a process, a passing, an appeal to the Lord, a sense of discouragement. Each in its own way, facets of his journey.

And so again, his birthday passed – came and went like all the others – now with even smaller fanfare. He determined to make new friends and have a more rich social life. After all, he wasn't that old. Time to liven his journey up.

But such was easier said than done. He only knew to watch TV, and shop. "Ha ha ha," he told himself. If he couldn't face that boxing gym, and didn't want to walk into a Senior Center, he had to strike up a conversation *somewhere,* somehow, with someone.

And make a friendship, or at least a functional approximation. But where? A coffee shop? A store of some kind?

He decided on an old place he hadn't been in for years. In the Lake Balboa area. Cherry's was the name. Plain old coffee shop, a step down from Denny's.

He went in. The hostess/waitress behind the counter did look familiar. She was of average size, and had brown hair. The counter was empty, but a table had four people in it. Stanley sat at the counter, not wanting to take up any of the empty tables.

She was fixing something, with her body partly turned to him. She looked over as he sat, and asked, "Menu?" He nodded. If she wasn't bothering with "Hello," why should he?

She brought him a menu and returned to her work preparing a food plate, and proceeded to take it to the table of customers. He opened the menu.

A man came in the side door, which faced the small parking lot. He too, sat at the counter.

Stanley steeled himself to start up a conversation. The man said something he couldn't catch, as the waitress/hostess passed him and went behind the counter. She said, "Nice to see you again," and got him a menu without asking. But the man didn't need it.

"Meatloaf," he said. She asked, "Gravy?"

"Yes, gravy, please. Don't I always have gravy?"

"Sure. Coffee?"

"Just a Coke." She went to fetch his drink, and had time to glance at Stanley and ask, from a distance, "What would you care to drink?"

"Coffee. Black."

Stanley tried to think of a method to make contact, conversation, with the man those few seats away, but failed. He knew he could say anything, more or less, but for it to lead to an important exchange, to a significant talk which could lead to anything major, anything life-changing or even close, became too much of a requirement, a burden, to achieve. So he said nothing.

Even the woman didn't provide an opportunity, being busy with her other work. He ordered a pastrami sandwich and ate in silence, tossing various ideas around in his head.

Finally, he volunteered, 'This place is like the old spots in the 1970s, isn't it/'" The man turned to Stanley, shrugged, and went back to his meatloaf.

That finished it. Stanley paid and left, deciding that tack was forsaken. He should try it with a woman, anyway. In another place, at another time.

He arms felt good, like he would be able to use them when (or if) an occasion arose to – to fend off an attack, or save a damsel in distress. That thought unfortunately caused a pang of emotion, as it made him think of May (Missy) and her untimely, cruel demise. Stanley forced his mind away from that memory, although he was happy he had a role in the apprehension of her killer.

He sat alone, and sulked, however. He didn't want to think about May, or Ryan, or any of it.

He watched TV. *The Incredible Hulk* was on. Another re-run.

And he drank beer, remembering his boxing days. His wins, mostly. And a few head butts. Would he ever get free of them? He'd primaled enough. Why did those memories still haunt him? One in particular, the butt to the mouth. Why, it was as if that guy had *rushed* him,solely to do it – he'd had that in his mind as he advanced on Stanley and thrust his head forward. Too bad the ref had been behind Stanley, at that instant,and had missed it. It was out of town and only the ref was the judge. There were no other judges at ringside, who would certainly have seen the violent infraction.

Whether the fighter had done it on purpose, Stanley would have to wait until he got to Heaven to find out, most probably. Unless the guy somehow came up to him and admitted it. Oh yeah, *that* was likely to happen!

There was bitterness in his heart over it, but Stanley tried to forgive the guy, whether he'd done it deliberately or not.

He went to sleep thinking of it, and forcing forgiveness into his heart.

Not very much happened the next day except he went to Whole Foods again, for various items, including organic instant coffee. And food.

The cashier irritated him – kind of gay – and while Stanley tried to be tolerant he knew inside him lurked a modicum of homophobia. A couple of jokes, which Stanley didn't exactly understand, and the comment "Sexy!" came from the cashier. And when he asked to have the beer put in his cloth bag (to make it easier to carry), the cashier said tartly, "As you wish," and Stanley said, "You can call me crazy but it's easier that way," and the man said, "Oh, I wouldn't call you that even if I thought so," and laughed.

"Paper bags, too?"

"Yes," Stanley told him, since he needed extra bags for all the groceries, and he only had one cloth bag. He took out a dollar bill, even though he paid by credit card, and asked, "Will you do me a favor?"

The cashier, bagging Stanley's items, said, "That all depends on what it is!" and laughed again. It sounded like innuendo, and Stanley just didn't know how to deal with it, so he only answered, "I need four quarters."

He went out to his car with the quarters and groceries, not feeling all that comfortable. But, he told himself, it was no big deal – "don't obsess about it."

But he did, for awhile. The gay guy (if he was) had been too pushy, and that not only bothered Stanley, it threatened him, some way.

A fear of further pushiness pervaded his mind, ridiculously. Really, the guy wouldn't attempt anything more than banter, would he?

It's a throwback to innuendos and more he'd felt abused by in his younger years, at school and in Hollywood. It discomfited him then, and was a lingering unpleasantness he felt. Of course, since he wasn't bad-looking it was inevitable. He didn't actually blame men for being attracted to him – it was only something in their nature. Women had to put up with far worse in society.

At his apartment, putting the groceries away, he blanched, almost literally, at the realization how fortunate he was never to have gone to prison.

Next day his California tag (sticker) arrived in the mail, so he put it on his license plate. That was comforting because he didn't wish to be pulled over by the police for an expired registration. What if he somehow was to get into an argument with the police and end up in jail? And then in a cell with a big bad con? Oh no.

He didn't think it was his imagination that was running amok. He thought such craziness could in fact happen within the framework of the "proper" circumstances. Hadn't innocent people been sent to jail? And some suffered unfair treatment? It was occasionally on the news. Rare, yes, but not impossible.

He went to Bob's Big Boy for some take-out, and to a 7-11 for some beer. That would hold him for a couple of days. And nights.

But what of his extended future? That was always the thing he would keep coming back to – without an answer. There was no way he could get another acting job, was there? And he as yet wasn't ready to go into that gym on Ventura Boulevard.

So what could Larson do? Sleep and eat – but what else?

Part VI

Larson could struggle on, as he always had, and pray for help. Why, didn't Jesus suffer? Assuredly, and for others. So Larson suffering was actually no big deal. Even a community of sufferers was no big deal. Wasn't sacrifice and struggle the hallmark, the history of Jesus' followers?

He wasn't facing hungry lions, was he? Or chains, or hard treatment at all. That was the wonderful result of a country following freedom of religion; the "free exercise" clause of the 1st Amendment guaranteed that, and America steadfastly defended it.

Even with a newcomer like Trump in office, religion was safe. It was in the hands of our democracy (or republic). It was embedded in the fabric of our way of life.

He worked on a poem, one he had abandoned. But his heart just wasn't in it. Poetry had been significant in his younger days, but now not so. The reverse of many people, he suspected. Most people who liked poetry were older, and had disliked it when young – too many other exciting activities, and too much work to focus on. No matter – he had always been on an unusual path, he knew, all his life. Stanley Larson didn't mind being different – he was very used to it. "You're a strange boy," one of his elementary teachers had said to him, when he'd mussed up his hair before posing for the yearly school photo. She had put a dab of Brylcreem in his hair just prior to that. He couldn't stand it, for an unexplainable reason. So then she attempted to smooth it back in place at the last moment – with very limited success. His hair looked odd in the school photo – uncombed and greasy. But Stanley didn't care.

He sent an email to Ryan asking how he was doing. He didn't want to speak with him on the phone, but was concerned about him, after what had occurred. Ryan had been a good friend in years past. It took a couple of days, but Ryan sent a terse reply: "Fine, I guess. You?"

Stanley replied he was okay, too, and that was that. He hadn't felt like saying more.

Funny how friendships wax and wane as years proceed. Especially for a relatively shy person, which Stanley was. That doesn't help sexual relationships, either, even for people of normal physical functions. Which thought cast Stanley into a funk. His primaling hadn't been of great advantage when it came to that. Again, he was left with the discomfiting potentiality that his low sexual feeling was due to the real injury, more than the psychological effect of a series of emotional hurts. Once again he thought, if there had been actual nerve damage, back when he was twelve, and being kicked by that older boy...primaling wouldn't cause a recovery of physical feeling.

But he put that out of his mind and slept. After all, he could primal again about that pivotal attack, and hope for the best.

He made a decision to pray for Trump, even though he didn't like him. The Bible encourages praycr for leaders – like in 1 Tim.2, as Stanley well knew from hearing it preached about, some years before. He didn't care for the directive, but complied with it anyway. He found himself praying for the president to have insight – into human beings, into humanity at large – a quality, a trait, Stanley thought Mr. Trump lacked. It may allow him more compassion for regular people, and for making more compassionate decisions.

Also the spring, after good rainfall in California, apparently ending the long drought, was very warm, in Los Angeles at least. A comfort for Stanley Larson. So he tried not to reminisce, back to his boxing days, or the few movie sets he'd acted on, or Rosy, or Amy, a fun girlfriend he'd had before her. Instead he tried to think of, once more, what he should do now. Yet the warm spring in some weird way paralleled his days, now, with days past, likely because he felt good in warm weather. He guessed that was due to his fondness for being out of school, in the summer, during his early life, but he was not sure. No matter. Not all mysteries needed to be solved, did they?

But, he felt good. The warm (sometimes hot) spring weather wasn't conducive to clear thinking about his future, and in a way he had to create his future out of "whole cloth," as they used to say.

But fortuitously a letter arrived in the mail which led him to activity, and a revelation from Spencer, in spite of initial stress. It was without indication of the sender, aside from it being from Long Beach.

No return address. Might be only some solicitation, but upon opening and reading it he found this:

"Dear Sir. We at Trans-Nation News Service want to show our gratitude for your recent note of interest. Anytime we find a fellow reader of our newsletter who wants to complain, we deal with it philosophically. But in your case, and in the case of all compliments, we extend thanks and well-wishes. Yours sincerely, David Dublin, Editor-in-Chief."

Ha! Stanley knew nothing about the organization and for sure had not sent any type of congratulations or compliment to it. He couldn't write back, either.

A day later, there was yet another letter from the Trans-Nation News Service. It was even more brief.

"Dear Sir. Sorry for the mistake. I regret our last note was mistakenly sent to you. Yours Sincerely, David Dublin, Editor-in-Chief."

Creepy, he thought, creepy.

But he didn't have to wait long. Looking for the company on the internet turned up nothing, but then one day his downstairs neighbor Spencer paid a visit.

"Stanley, my sister wants to give you this." He handed a large number of fives and tens to him, at his door.

"The money? That's fantastic!"

"Yes," he replied. "She got a job, she saved it up for you. Thanks again for helping."

"Sure, sure. I wasn't expecting I'd see it," Stanley laughed.

"I suppose not."

"Do you want to come in?"

"Okay, just for a minute."

They sat and chatted. But surprisingly when Stanley asked about Julie's new job, was it housekeeping, Spencer told him, "No, no. She's working as a proofreader for a newsletter."

"Uh, yes? Is it the Trans-Nation News Service, by any chance?"

Spencer appeared shocked. "It is! How could you guess that, I wonder?"

Stanley laughed. "Just lucky. Here." He handed him the two notes he'd received in the mail. Spencer read them, shaking his head. "I'm confused."

"Me, too."

"Do you want me to ask my sister about them?"

"Do. I'd love to know if she can explain it."

"You could call her yourself," Spencer said.

"No, no. You'd better. You know her."

"Okay."

"And please thank her for the repayments," Stanley said.

"Oh, I will."

Several days went by and Stanley didn't hear anything. He didn't hear a sound from Spencer's apartment, either. Was the man even in there anymore?

Then he received a phone call. "What's your day like tomorrow?"

"Same as today. Nothing very much doing. Why?"

"Julie told me about that newsletter. It's a scam."

"Really?"

"She may quit them. They were sending notes to people, and then following up with stealing their personal info."

"How?"

"You didn't get a third letter because she put a stop to it when I spoke with her. A third letter gets you to receive the weekly newsfeed, by mail, and internet. They hack into your system after you provide them with certain information. Lucky they never got your email address, and credit card number."

"Yeah, no shit," Stanley replied bluntly. Then he asked him, "But she provided my address here?"

"Didn't think that was a bad thing, at the time. Maybe you'd actually want a subscription. Part of her job, you see."

"Oh, I see. Not her fault they had a scam going," he laughed.

Later in the day, Stanley called him to ask what he was up to, if he'd like to go out for coffee? He wanted to ask another question about Julie's work. It was stressing him out. But Spencer said he couldn't, he was busy online with something. So Stanley asked his question then.

"Can't she get into trouble participating in that theft of personal information?"

"I guess. I'll call her and tell her to get away from there."

"Okay, good."

But after they hung up he had another question. Could be getting old, how could he forget it? Stanley wanted to know where the business was, what was the real location, because he couldn't find it searching on the internet.

That stressed him out. Where had his two letters come from? Where was Julie working? She had to be working, she'd paid back the money he loaned her. Or...was something else going on? Had *she* sent the letter, made up the whole thing for some bizarre and dark reason?

People were worldly and not always honest, he'd learned, even as a child. There'd been lying and deception often in his youth, his household. It still left a bitter taste in his mouth, so to speak. Yet here he saw no cause for deception. Even if someone were to gain access to his private affairs, to his money, they wouldn't gain much. His bank account was low, merely $1500. His life was devoid of secrets others might wish to uncover. Whatever had Stanley to hide? He loathed hiding things anyway.

Hiding things never helped, unless you were trying to put something over on someone.

Which turned out to be the case. Spencer climbed the stairs and yelled for Stanley to open his door. It was dawn. He entered when Stanley opened up, grouchy from the earliness. Spencer sat in the chair.

"She cleaned out my savings. Seventeen thousand," he said. "Crazy woman."

Stanley made coffee. Spencer didn't say more until he had a cup of it in his hands.

"She used the sneaky methods – don't ask me how – of that news business. I guess they had computer hacking skills."

"No doubt," Stanley said.

"She played innocent. Now she's gone." He sipped his coffee. "With my savings."

"Gone?"

"Can't find her, believe me. And her daughter."

"Uh...are you sure it was her?"

He laughed at that. "Too much of a coincidence, buddy."

"Yeah. The bank said...what?"

"Account closed by me, they said. Money transferred to another bank. *Hers*."

"Oh, boy."

"Yeah, and I can't do anything."

"What do you mean? The cops can catch her," Stanley said firmly.

"Naw. I don't want to get the cops into this."

"Why not?"

"Oh, hell. I love her."

So that was that, except he dared to ask him why he'd been pleading lack of funds to him all this time when he had seventeen thousand put away.

"Oh, Stanley, I was wanting to hold onto it no matter what, for retirement. So, I lied. No one even knew – except Julie."

Later the man admitted it was actually more money than that. It further pushed Stanley away from him. Deception was a no-no in Stanley Larson land. He'd seen and been hurt by too much of it as he grew up, to tolerate it in his later years. "Twenty-seven thousand dollars," she was now accused of stealing. The man was so secretive about it he hadn't even told Stanley the full amount!

So be it. One more person in Stanley's life to avoid. Would there ever be an end to it?

Day by day, he looked for his true purpose. Yet still, it eluded him.

He read about Paul's sufferings spreading the gospel through the world around him, and how Paul ended up in Rome in prison. Fine turn of events!

Stanley shrugged off the bad prospect of never finding what his "assignment" was. Many people – most? – never discovered theirs. In fact, most people on Earth didn't hear the Good News, or didn't hear it clearly, anyway.

He couldn't travel and spread it. He couldn't go on the radio or TV to spread it. In fact, Stanley doubted he was even supposed to do such evangelizing – he only felt compelled to talk to individuals about God and the Bible. No, it was something else, he was sure. But what, he didn't know. God had to show it to him, was all he really knew.

The housekeeper came and cleaned his apartment and did his laundry and ran the dishwasher and put water in the plants on the window ledge and the landing and asked for a week's pay in advance because she was having difficulty making her rent payment this month, and he complied – after all, she was so sweet about it. What did he care? She would come the next time and work and they'd be all even. It had happened before.

Trump seemed to be causing confusion and dismay each day, but Stanley didn't mind so much. He shook up Washington and made ridiculous statements but...was it very important? Couldn't the real workings of government proceed in spite of him? Unless he got us into a war, or caused riots in the streets?

He took his Camaro for gasoline, and drove it through the automated car wash, with sadness in his heart, thinking how wasted his life was now. But he had health, a valuable condition at his age. He had the chiropractor to help him when the need arose – a sore back or neck – and the TV to show him what was going on in the city and the world. But that was it, aside from God, music, and books. And a few precious memories. Oh yeah, and YouTube.

His health was the big issue, society told him, and the pills for his heart condition kept him safe. And paying his bills every month.

But yet, his goal was unmet. Perhaps always would be.

He did receive a call from an old friend – maybe this was his opportunity. That would remain to be seen. Don was his name, he had been in a couple of the Western episodes with Stanley. They'd struck up a friendship but grown apart as many actors and actresses do. But Don said he had wondered what Stanley was up to, and tried his number. He said his wife had asked him to call him, but never got around to it.

"So sorry, pal."

"That's okay, Don."

"You never called me, either!"

"True enough. What's up with you?"

"Not too much. Still trying to get acting jobs."

Stanley laughed. "I quit."

"Well, I've had a few. A good part in a Hallmark movie a year ago."

"Great," Stanley acknowledged.

"Let's meet up. What do you say?"

"Good. Lunch?"

"Lunch," Don replied.

They got together at a place of Don's choosing – a Mexican place Stanley had never heard of, much less been to. La Mañana Café on Ventura.

Stanley was early and waited inside near the entrance, standing, and saying to the hostess his friend was to be there at one. She smiled. He watched her behind the front counter, seating people when they came in the door, and he sat on a bench across from her.

"You know, you look like Linda Ronstadt," he told her. She stared at him.

"I'm sorry. I don't know who that is, but hope it's good." She laughed.

He laughed, too. "It most certainly is. You don't know who she is? A famous singer from the '70s and '80s." He could have as easily said, "and '90s," but didn't want to embarrass her any further. But she sure looked like her, with dark hair and flashing eyes, and pretty lips.

So Don and he enjoyed the meal, and afterward, when Stanley tried to take the hostess's photo with his cell phone, she said no, it made her uncomfortable to have her picture taken when she was in need of make-up. Not that he thought she needed any more, but rather than be a jerk and snap it anyway, he resisted the temptation, even though he had his phone in his hand, and had set it to photograph, before reaching the front counter. Don thought the whole thing amusing, but he didn't.

"Okay, it's up to you. Some other time." She smiled again. She didn't seem to be bothered in any way. "You won't mind if I come in, say, Friday to take one?"

"No," she said. "I don't mind."

Outside, later, Stanley was confused. Would she purposely put on extra make-up for work Friday, or had she meant it wouldn't matter then?

He couldn't figure women out, so he let his confusion fade away like smoke from a fire being doused. It wasn't a crucial point, anyway.

Seeing her again was the plan, although a resistance developed. He found out speaking with Don a few days later that there was the potential for being seen as a "stalker."

"Oh, bullshit," Stanley said, over the phone.

"Have it your way. I'm only warning you in a friendly way."

"Thanks. She sure is lovely, won't you say?"

"Yep. All the more reason to take care."

"It's only a photo!"

"It's a danger if she has a boyfriend…."

"I know, I know."

"Gotta go. Good luck."

Later, Stanley had one even more scary idea: what if she was married?

Nevertheless, all he wanted, in fact, was a picture. So he steeled his nerve, asked God if this was all okay, and went in on Friday. She was there behind her counter. The place was getting crowded even though it was only four in the afternoon. Good food will do that. And good margaritas, he assumed.

He approached her, he held up his phone, he grinned when he believed she recognized him.

She was just vaguely, and sweetly, resistant.

"Can I?" he asked.

"Umm – all right." He quickly took it, as she curved up her lips, posing.

"Won't you smile more?"

"I smiled!" she told him.

"Okay – thanks." Boy was she shy about it, he thought.

Out in his car he realized how nervous he was. It made him want to laugh, but he didn't. He was so happy he was surprised at himself. Driving away, he hoped her husband wouldn't be mad, if she had one, and told him about it all. But she *did* look like Linda Ronstadt.

He drank beer and gloated over his success and ate a Carl's Jr. California Classic burger. He watched TV news, turned it off, and thought about a few fights he'd had, again wishing he had access to any which had been videotaped for television. They *must* exist, he told himself.

One memory persisted in his mind that night. One of his bouts as a pro, where he'd luckily received the raised glove due to landing a surprisingly solid left hook that wobbled the opponent, causing him to clinch for the rest of the round. Silly, Stanley didn't push him away, partly because he was tired himself and welcomed the slower pace of the action, and partly he expected the referee to break the clinch, which he didn't do. Anyway, he won the round and the next one, because the other fighter just didn't have any real gumption in him anymore. It was a close fight – a four round bout – because the first two rounds had been fairly even.

Glad for the victory, he had hugged the other fighter when the last bell sounded, even before the decision.

But now, sipping beer, he thought over that sharp punch. It showed how actually old Primal Pain is a false idea in the subconscious, "telling" him of his left hand "hurting" him. The subconscious had convinced his mind that it still hurt from the *previous* trauma (with the soft gloves) and he hadn't, in fact, been hitting as hard for several bouts. Yet this guy had been starting to move in, and Stanley's punch struck much harder than he'd expected, certainly harder than his subconscious had expected. He should have known that afterward, but he didn't think about it. His trainer did, though, at least to the extent that he said, "Way to go! Great left hook in the third round," later in the dressing room. Such was the way it went. *Now* Stanley knew, regrettably, his punches could have *all* been sharper if he'd primaled away all the pain in those days of his active career. But he hadn't. He only did that within the last year, or so.

What remained to be done was to go to the gym and find out just how hard he could hit *now*.

That pleasant thought lingered as he opened a new beer and took a sweet gulp.

Days vanish, age progresses, time takes us along on its perpetual path. Hope helps, hours come and go, life has twists and turns, choices are good and not good. People can think they know it all, learn otherwise, and grow in grace if they make their hearts available to God's will. If they don't, they fall deeper and deeper into the world's pernicious and hidden (and deceptive) ways.

Stanley tried valiantly to keep free of worldly lusts, or desires, if you call them that. He didn't love money, which was the root of them, so he had a few steps on the enemy, the sinkhole of trickery and hate and greed and yes, deceit, for how else could sinful natures explore crimes and other negative practices without lying and cheating?

He read mysteries, which gave him a view of the good and the bad, and thought it over as best he could.

He read Shakespeare plays occasionally, but they were hard to comprehend, even with footnotes explaining certain words and phrases. Stanley indulged, though, because the lines and the expressions were so enriching, when understood.

At Whole Foods Market he got a Western-style hat off the rack. He tried it, it fit; he liked the shape of it. At the checkout counter, before putting his other items onto the conveyor belt, he put on the hat again, asking the woman behind him, "How does this look, all right?"

She examined it briefly, and replied, "Yes, it looks good. Quite good, actually." He thanked her, saying, "That's sweet."

Later, outside putting bags into his car, Stanley wondered, should he have kept talking to her, and then asked her out? Oops, he thought, he forgot to look for a ring on her finger.

The next day, he wore the hat around wherever he went. It was black, it made him feel like a cowboy. But of course he had no horse, he had no cowboy boots. When he'd been in the Western series, he'd had boots. And a gun, sometimes.

Those days were long gone. He'd never do any more acting – on film, at least.

He ate at the café beside the bowling alley. He didn't care to bowl, it might aggravate his back. But he wasn't depressed. He only needed a path to be on, to seek his "mission" in life before he died.

He had a clue, at any rate. The way he'd felt overseas. Whatever the reason for it, Stanley had felt strong, and a special kinship with life. While others on board that seaplane tender in Vietnam had longed to return to wherever "home" was, he'd felt otherwise.

He hadn't wanted to go "home" – he had none as far as he was concerned. Yet he wanted to hit Los Angeles or San Diego and go to Junior College, as they called it then. Maybe study journalism. Working on a newspaper seemed romantic and exciting. Or at the least, satisfying. But then later, he didn't like the unromantic stories he knew he'd have to write, after only a couple of months in that college class, so he'd looked to other jobs.

But, overseas, he'd felt happy, and though not sure exactly why, it set him apart from most of the others around him there.

But what did it mean? That he was cut out for an unusual road in life. Boxing showed that. And getting into Primal Therapy did, too.

The clue was, he was different. Beyond that, who knew? Luckily, he was no criminal, no ne'er-do-well. So this led him to think of a plan.

A novel. He would write a novel.

He never had (although he'd started one or two many years past). It takes so long, he'd given up. But now he had nothing but time, as they say.

He could write about anything. He could take as long as he wanted to finish it. Like those long Thomas Wolfe novels he'd read. *The Web and the Rock*, for instance.

But he felt uncomfortable just jumping in with no idea. He had to come up with a story of some sort. So he pondered for a couple of days. He figured a mystery with a boxer being involved, that should do it.

But would a murder need to be part of it? So gruesome. It was one thing to read about them, like in Agatha Christie stories, but quite another to *write* about one.

He decided to hold off on that. He'd write about a strange event in an ex-boxer's life, and take it from there. Yes, a strange event....

He didn't come up with a story first, so he sat down at his table with paper and pencil and wrote a sort of introduction, about the character, and his surroundings. It would be in and around L.A. Why not?

A man on Social Security, and savings from a successful career fighting, more successful than his own. And who occasionally trained fighters at a made-up gym, and had an ex-wife, and suffered...what? Some physical ailment from boxing. Stanley couldn't figure that out but he wanted the guy to be at some disadvantage when the "strange event" happened, so he'd need to call on reserves of "inner" strength to "overcome," to beat the bad guys. Or just one bad guy? A mean criminal. But not a genius one because Stanley couldn't think up a big, complicated crime. He knew he'd have to make it a less-than-genius type mystery. What did he care?

The ex-boxer could come up against a smart crook. That's all he needed. And a cute dame, of course, who is "bad." That would work.

He left the table and his introductory notes and exercised. He showered. He made a dinner of pastrami and cheese and Pacifico and sourdough bread, and mustard, all the while thinking about his book.

In the morning he took a walk. He ate at the café, he bought beer and canned beans at a liquor store, and shuffled back to his apartment and his book, spending an hour on it, then taking a short nap. Writing was actually tiring. He'd only written poems, short stories, or assignments at school. Nothing like this. Later, he pondered. Having created a few more introductory essentials – age, size, living conditions, for the character, he thought of a good name – Rio. Why not? It was distinctive.

Then he hung out on the internet. He couldn't spend all his time thinking about Rio. But the book called him back.

He had a hard time coming up with a crime idea, a mystery. He just felt it was too vast, the scope of a full story with bad guys, cops, etc. He sat and took things one step at a time, unsure where it was going. He prayed God would guide him.

Finally, he settled on a bizarre account of an aged man alone in a house on a hill above the ocean, a rich but reclusive man, with two loyal servants, who has a heart attack and stays cooped up in his bedroom, being given medicine, being visited by his doctor, watching movies on a wide-screened TV, eating as much as he can force down, waiting patiently to die.

Then his great-niece arrives to help look out for him. And her fiancé. They move into separate rooms but sneak together at night.

The old guy gets worse, and calls in a private detective because he wonders if the fiancé, who he doesn't care for, is poisoning him. The private detective knows the ex-boxer and confides in him about the situation at the house.

Somehow, Stanley needed to bring Rio into the scene, to the house. But then what? Have the old guy die and the police arrest the great-niece and her fiancé, because she stands to inherit a large fortune, but it turns out it wasn't them? Stanley needed a few more suspects, he figured. That's how Agatha Christie would have done it, and Erle Stanley Gardner.

He wrote in the "gardener," so that now three servants worked there. He wrote in the old dying man's brother, who stood to get money, too (he turned out to be the murderer). All this became pages of notes that Stanley referred to as he wrote the story out, over the next weeks.

He made the butler an evil-acting type, who *could* be the poisoner. He made the housekeeper/cook a sweet lady who smart readers may think would be the killer, as a surprise.

He wrote about an hour (or so) a day. It was all he could manage. The difficulty of the effort precluded him from spending more time than that on it.

Stanley well knew there may be no significance to this effort; he didn't care, though. Life was wide open for him now and he meant to step into it with as little, as minute, reservation as he could.

Summer and fall developed, but it was hard to distinguish which was which, due to the heat that pressed on Southern California. And bad fires raged to the north, and a couple of fires right there in the Southland, which made Stanley uneasy. Most people were uneasy, as far as he could determine. The winds made fires hard to put out, and who could say what devastation they would inflict before the brave firefighters could subdue them?

After his housekeeper vacuumed the carpet he'd lay upon it, to ease his back, for sitting and writing took a toll on him, not only mentally but physically.

No matter. He enjoyed it. He dreamed his book would be a bestseller, and make millions of dollars (for him and the publisher). Why not?

Ryan called and talked about his life. Stanley mostly listened and feigned more interest than he in fact felt. Ryan again said he'd drive to L.A. someday for them to have lunch. He didn't mention May.

He wrote as fast as he could but it wasn't fast by any stretch of the imagination. In fact, it was slow.

His mind worked slowly. Not like in the ring in the midst of the action. Oddly, though, a bout seemed like slow motion, in one way, but terrifically exciting in another. Writing was the opposite for him. It felt rapidly charging forward as he did it, but as if it had been hours, after, when it was only less than an hour, most times. A bout felt fast, in other words, *after*, but slow-motion during. Writing "fast," during, but long and bewilderingly painstaking as he looked back on it, each time.

At least he felt accomplishment, and who knew? This could be his life mission. This book, or another one later.

Meanwhile, he still wanted to primal about his birth more, and he knew he was putting it off. It was so painful he dreaded going into it again. He felt there was more, and he knew already that as he'd struggled to come out, then, he'd felt so crushed he'd feared death – feared it hugely, ominously. The more he'd attempted to get out, the more pressure was applied to his head. Or, at any rate, that's how it felt to him. But he *had* gotten out, he had not died. Nevertheless, if he'd felt he was dying, Stanley needed to re-experience that Pain, that awful moment, or moments, to be free of them.

He wondered about Bill and Troy, but didn't call them. He didn't want to argue, to hear them defend Trump. It was bad enough watching the news and the latest unpresidential comments the president was making.

Of course it wasn't as bad as Nixon, who dragged the war in Vietnam (our part) out until 1973. Stanley didn't think Trump would actually provoke North Korea into conflict with America – not armed conflict. Too dangerous.

But one never knew.

Part VII

Hot weather dragged L.A. into October and November with patterns of cooler weather, sometimes, back and forth like a tap turned on and off.

He spent time on a movie chat site but gave it up – he didn't have anything to say about current films since he didn't watch them.

He went to the dentist, got an implant, charged his credit card, and hoped he could cover the cost.

He drove by the gym again, longing to hit the bags, to move around on the floor or in the empty ring. "Someday," he told himself once more. "I daresay there is still time for that."

He thought about his birth, and still put off primaling. He was unsure why his mother had tried to crush his head when he was coming out. She didn't want him to live, but why not? Was he illegitimate? He'd thought of that possibility before. A probability, really, considering how little he looked like the man who raised him, who was supposed to be his father, and the coldness with which he dealt with him often.

Stanley had asked her if that was true, but his mother denied it.

One more thing, like who killed JFK, that must wait to be answered when Stanley got to Heaven (he figured).

One day, after writing, and while taking his walk, a horn honked. He saw a large woman inside as the car passed. She hadn't honked at him, but he could see no car blocking her way. She pulled over to the curb, though, and rummaged inside her purse, it appeared to him. She then honked her car horn again. He walked past her and she looked over at him. He returned the gaze. She was indeed large, fat, really, in a loose white dress. Her hair was white also. Her expression made him hesitate – her face was screwed up as if in appeal, somehow. He continued walking but stopped, deciding to be a good, sort of, Samaritan. He went to the passenger window, which was halfway down, and leaned toward it.

"Are you all right?"

The woman nodded yes. So Stanley was in a fix. Take her nod for it? Ask another question?

But then a fat *man* rushed up, pushed Stanley aside, and opened the door. Stanley grabbed the man's jacket collar. "Wait a second," he told the man, who threw back his arm, striking Stanley's, and proceeded to climb into the car. The woman made no movement.

Stanley yelled to her, "Is this okay with you?" She was frozen. He put his hand on the fat man's right shoulder, again saying, "Wait a second."

The man, flushed, looked up at him. "None of your damn business," he said.

"True, but maybe she doesn't want you in there."

The man pushed Stanley in the stomach, turning to the woman. "Well? Drive away!" He reached out, to pull the door closed, and then Stanley punched him in the face. Nevertheless, the woman *did* drive off, the passenger door slamming shut, a car behind her slamming on its brakes, and Stanley watching, his mouth agape.

Nobody in the vicinity made a comment or approached Stanley. Leave well enough alone, was the average reaction in America, he figured. Don't get involved, is what people generally advised. Oh well, he thought, they have a valid point. It can be dangerous to involve yourself in other people's business.

Two weeks later when he saw the fat man again, outside a liquor store, begging for change. Stanley pulled his car in and parked. An odd spirit of curiosity propelled him. He put his hand in his pocket, for change, after he exited his Camaro. The fat man waited. Stanley approached him, taking coins in his hand, holding his hand out to the man, who then had a weird look on his face.

Stanley gave him the coins, asking, "Do you recognize me?"

"No, sir."

"I hit you in the face awhile back."

"Oh...yeah." The man turned away.

"Hold on there. I want to know what it was all about, you and that woman."

The fat man stopped, turned back, and looked grim. Mad, in fact.

"My ex-wife, if you have to know. Thanks for the money. God bless." He walked further along the building, and leaned against the wall a short distance from the liquor store entrance.

Stanley mentally shrugged. He knew domestic beefs were best left alone. Yet, this may not have even been one. He returned to his car and drove away – still curious.

The evidence indicated a domestic problem, but Stanley felt it could easily have been something else. A drug deal, for instance. She'd honked to bring the man to the car, and she'd been nervous when Stanley showed interest. He also felt guilty punching the guy, even if it wasn't such a forceful punch. All the man had done was push Stanley's arm away and then push him in the stomach. Big deal.

Lucky the guy hadn't had a weapon on him and used it. Surely, Stanley hadn't thought of that, in the moment. Don't be crazy, he told himself, now. Watch out for that in the future.

The day dawned the morning following, and he was glad he had no bullet hole in him. He had a cup of coffee and wondered: was he stupid? Too many rounds in the ring?

What was that woman to him? Oh, well. He didn't care, he was sort of chivalrous, in his own working-class way.

Lunch at Lulu's. To-go food in the bag, a drive around town, thoughts of the story he was building. A pang inside about something...what? The primal he knew he had to get to before long? Sure, a painful one. And hey, he might die doing it. He might be so crushed (in the memory of it, the blatant intensity of it) that the force she exerted on his tiny head would cause a shock, now, and send him into oblivion. Or rather, the land of the free, on the "other side," as some people refer to it. But certainly he wouldn't die – he'd merely *feel* like he was dying.

Stanley thought of the time he'd been knocked out (after a low blow, unseen by the referee) and been out until the smelling salts. He saw deep in his unconscious, when he'd primaled about that event, the murky, then clearer, vision of a grassy hill and an opening in a wall and the great light beyond it – but the vision disappeared with the nasty smell of the salts in his nostrils. Someone administered them while he was out cold on his back in the ring. So...perhaps he'd died momentarily. He didn't know. It sure *seemed* like a "near-death" experience, as he'd heard described on TV once or twice.

Could be it was what happened to him during his birth, too.

He walked into the gym, he looked around, he walked out. It reminded him of the first time he'd gone into the Main Street Gym downtown. He'd been a little nervous then, in the 1970s, and was a little bit nervous this time. Could be the mind conjured being hit with punches, but not overtly. More on a hidden, secret level. It wasn't the same as thinking about it when someone – Sammy or Larry or Duke – would put gloves on him and help him up to the ring. *That* awareness of being about to be hit with punches was real, as the sparring partner was either already in the ring moving around, or just about to climb in himself, probably feeling the same anxiousness Stanley felt. Of course that went away as soon as the action commenced.

Anyway, Stanley drove off that day satisfied he'd walked in. Better than nothing.

He held on to hope but without much reason. Only faith, faith in miracles. The housekeeper came by and cleaned, put things in order, did his laundry, made the bathroom fresh again, took money, and left. He was happy about that. Clean dishes! Clean clothes, clean towels! All may not be well in the world, but it was pretty good in his.

Yet Stanley felt the awareness he had few friends! Or *any*, really. When she smiled and left that day, it struck him that he was alone. Normally he didn't care, but this day it bothered him. Getting old could have something to do with it.

He hoped he could return to the gym, and there make a few friends. That seemed like the most natural place.

But he was reluctant. He'd have to work out, not only hang out, and that wasn't his instinct at this time.

So when could he make friends? Did all old people face this? Most have families to rely on, children and nieces and nephews and siblings and...oh well, he ought to reach out to his sister, at least. They used to be close, as children and as teenagers. But she took his mother's side when Stanley pulled away from *that* conniving and selfish woman, many years ago.

How to patch it up now that his folks are dead and it's only his sister and him? He put that off for another day. He got food at Wendy's (a triple burger and a taco salad) and got into his apartment, and wrote awhile, and did some sit-ups and warm-ups, but skipped the shower, and turned on the news.

Trump was still up to his weird comments, and there was a fire north of the San Fernando Valley – way up in Ventura, so he wasn't too worried about that, except the winds were powerful, very powerful....

He used to like the feel of the Santa Ana winds. Still did, as a matter of fact – but they spread brush fires, so people complained about that particular weather condition, and rightly so.

Stanley thought about his time with Rosy, for some reason. The romance, the laughter, the joy, even. She didn't like his boxing but wanted him to do well, at least. She didn't like the bruises on his face when he returned from sparring with them (on occasion). She cared more about his looks than he did.

She had done what she could to help him enjoy sex – but it was too deeply entrenched a problem for physical caring, for physical attention, to solve. It of course put a damper on their relationship. Saying "I love you" to her only could go but so far.

They split up over it, in his opinion, more so than due to boxing.

Stanley bought four cheap books at the used bookstore he liked to go to. They would hold him awhile, in lieu of friends, until he found one or two of those.

He continued to write. The book was coming along. He felt okay about it. He wasn't quite sure how he'd finish it, but that didn't bother him; he had an idea about the end – that's all he needed right then.

The fires grew worse – there was one encroaching on the Valley, not too many miles from him. The sun was a bizarre shade, due to smoke in the air. The loss of homes he saw on the news was disheartening. And he waited apprehensively should a policeman come to his door and tell him to evacuate, as many thousands of residents (where the fires were) had been, and continued to be forced to do. But the knock on the door never came.

He curtailed his exercising, such as it was, due to the unhealthy air. He stayed inside as much as possible, as news broadcasters advised. Staying indoors was easier now, due to internet access, which gave him, and most people, something to do if they needed it. Many people had to go to work, of course, but Stanley could stay in and read and write and watch YouTube and comment on discussion sites. Of course, he didn't do very much of that – he hardly knew where to find such sites. But there were a couple, news places and entertainment ones, like IMDForum.

They said the dry weather, the strong winds, the growth on the hillsides, made things worse for firefighters. Burning embers made it to rooftops, and houses burned. Bad luck, Stanley believed. Just bad luck – unless the fires were caused by arsonists. That would be bad luck too, in the larger perspective. Rotten bad luck.

But the several fires around began to be contained, except the massive one up in Ventura hung on – very stubborn.

Christmas was coming, too. He had no one to buy gifts for. He'd give the housekeeper an extra $20. He *could* send his sister a card. Funny, he didn't even know if she was married or not, now. She had been. When his mother was alive she had been, and had gotten a divorce. But enough time had passed for his sister to find a new husband.

The temperature began to drop, finally. Not that he cared – but for getting sick. He didn't want a cold. He made sure he was warm enough at night. And took vitamin C each day, as usual.

But a weird thing happened. He saw the fat man again, this time in front of a 7-11 asking people for money. Stanley gave him a dollar and said, "Hey man, how you doing?"

It appeared he remembered Stanley. He gave a smirk, took the dollar, and said, "Good. Thanks."

Stanley had pulled in, parked his car; and walked up to the guy. Now he went inside the store, thinking it was odd for him to be overweight (most homeless types were not). He wanted to ask him why – and another question: had he seen that woman lately? But both questions were vaguely rude. Personal.

Inside he got Pacifico, a bottle of water, a small container cup of Cheerios, and then at the counter, cigarettes. Two packs. He paid with cash and put the stuff in his cloth bag. Outside the fat man was nowhere to be seen. At his car, however, a short younger man walked up. He was dressed in a shirt and tie.

"Excuse me," he said.

"What is it?

"Just a word."

"Uh-huh."

"Many people sin, and die without knowing Jesus –" he began, but Stanley cut him off.

"Don't bother. I'm a Christian, I'm saved."

"But do you know for certain your sins are forgiven?"

"Yes, I do. The Bible tells me so," Stanley laughed, because it reminded him of the children's song.

"Oh, beautiful," the short man said, and was going to ask for a donation to his church organization, but Stanley cut him off once more.

"Look, tell me, did you see that fat homeless guy out here? Did you speak with him?"

"Well...I saw him, uh, but didn't speak to him, no."

"No? You ought to have, pal. Or should I call you brother? You should have. Me, I'm already saved. But he looks like he needs it, too."

The man had little to say. He nodded, and then, "Yes, sir."

"I gave him a dollar. Where did he go?"

"Where?"

"Where."

"Well, beyond the bus stop, in that direction." He pointed.

"Thanks," Stanley said, closed his car door after putting the bag in, and walked off, locking it automatically from his key remote.

He went along the sidewalk, past the bus stop, looking for the fat man. Not that he could have said why he did, exactly. He was a bit curious and then he laughed again. He had to find a friend, didn't he? Then he realized the man in the suit was a potential friend also.

When he saw no sign of the fat man, Stanley returned to the 7-11 parking lot, but the other man was gone, too. So much for making any significant acquaintances that day.

The following day, he spoke with the counterman at the café he went to off and on. He dared to ask his name.

"Jim."

Stanley nodded and told him his. But that was it, he couldn't think of anything to say, to further the acquaintance. He decided the next time he went in he'd make more conversation.

It was three days later. The man was tall and dressed in the white shirt, showing his employ – the name of the café was on the front. Stanley decided the guy was

Armenian or some such, due to his accent. As it turned out he *was* Armenian – at least in background. He had been born here; he was American because of that.

"Hello, Jim," Stanley said when he sat at the counter, taking the menu someone had left nearby.

"Hello!"

He gave Stanley information when asked – quite friendly.

Stanley ate and left, once again not knowing what more to say to procure a type of friendship. That is, other than asking him what his accent was, and finding out.

Nevertheless, it was all to no avail, as the next time he went in, and was told by Jim that he was born here and by God didn't want "illegals" crowding in and taking his "position," "no way."

"How so?"

"How so?" Jim laughed. "They work for cheap, Stanley. You don't know that?"

"Oh, sure. But your boss can't hire them, can he?"

"Are you dumb? My boss can do what he wants. But –" he stopped. "Excuse me." He went to get a plate of food from the small window counter behind him, when the cook placed two plates there. He took the food to a customer further down, to Stanley's left. When Jim returned he took the other plate and placed it in his food preparation area, and with his back turned, placed on added items to the plate – tiny butter containers and jelly containers. Then he put the plate even further down the counter for another waiting customer. Finally he came back.

"Well, it's going to be okay," he started right in again. "Trump – he will send the illegals back to their own country."

"Uh-huh," Stanley replied. "Really?" He wanted to ask: "All of them?" but didn't.

"Sure. It takes time though. Trump has the damn Democrats to deal with."

Stanley took a breath and said, "I'm a Democrat. Moderate, of course, but still –"

"You are? Sorry to hear that." Jim walked away. That was the end of their budding friendship.

Outside driving away in his Camaro he pondered: what was this about? He used to have friends of all political persuasions – or no political persuasion at all. But now the divide was more extreme. Trump had seen to that. Even unpopular, according to opinion polls, he wielded power. He drove people on the left crazy. He had staunch supporters who felt the Democrats were weak and stupid. There was far less middle ground, space for getting along, for talking and for give and take. Or...did the news media exaggerate it all? Once again, Stanley had to admit he didn't know enough to figure it out. But he was smart enough to know the mood of most Americans was more negative than it had been. And we were not as cooperative with each other as we had been.

And terrorism made us less wiling to abide the smallest affront.

But, however, the economy was not bad; the stock market was swinging up; despite grumbling, the people were well enough off to allow each other room to be irritated, yet not be violent, in general. The holiday time saw gift-giving, and robust sales to put smiles on the faces of business leaders, even if the poor were not any better off. But time would tell. A rising tide lifts all boats, a smart person said once. Stanley couldn't recall who that person was, but he did recall John Kennedy had quoted it.

Maybe the irritation and non-cooperation he saw on news reports of the country's social and political state would dissolve as the economy continued to improve, and the idea reviled by Democrats, the "trickle-down" theory, would work. He doubted it, though; it hadn't worked in the past, when tried by our leaders.

Stanley didn't like being so stressed out – who did? – so he made the effort to focus his attention on his novel, and finding a few new friends. He continued to watch the news on TV but restricted the amount. That helped as far as his stress level was concerned.

One day, the downstairs neighbor left – moved out; didn't say goodbye. The place was "foreclosed." Stanley didn't know that but the new neighbor informed him so, when they met and spoke, accidentally, out front on the street. The new neighbor's name was

Bell – Jud Bell. He was not very friendly but Stanley didn't care. He'd open up after a few more meetings, Stanley was certain.

Jud Bell was an odd person though, and kept so much to himself that Stanley seldom saw him. Once at the carport he did, and once at the mailboxes in front. Both times Stanley said a greeting, "Hello. How's it going?" but got only a nod in response. The guy was brown-white, and well-dressed, and drove a fine car, a BMW, black and fairly new, but he sure didn't care to engage in a conversation. The first time, Stanley had initiated it, asked if he was all moved in, and had he seen Spencer, etc., but after a few replies and the answer, "yes," to Stanley's question, "Have you got the place in foreclosure?" the man walked away, waving.

Well, he was youngish, in the old mind of Stanley, a fit-looking forty or forty-five. Perhaps Jud wanted nothing to do with a guy who had grey beard stubble, and grey hair.

It wasn't that, though. Jud didn't care to converse with his neighbor because he had serious and unfixable problems (he thought) with a couple of crooks who had lent him money for a failed business venture, and now Jud was not able to repay them. Not immediately, that was.

He didn't care to tell anyone, including his upstairs neighbor, and he felt sad he had this issue to deal with.

Christmas came and went. Same uneventfulness for Stanley. His New Year's resolutions, of course, were those to be expected: go to the gym and work out, primal about his birth, make a few new friends.

It would take time. He didn't know, either, when he'd complete his book. He knew he would be spending more time on it, even when he finished the first draft. It needed to be in shape to be typed up and – what? Read by someone who could offer whatever advice or criticism was called for. Stanley didn't care for criticism – who did – but realized it was to be sought, and adjustments made (if he agreed with it).

The New Year began. He faced it with courage and resolve. What would it bring?

He tried again to make a Facebook page work. It hadn't been easy, and he'd given up on it. Not enough action, and too much stuff to work out – it wasn't worth it. Except now he wanted friends, and it was a way of gaining some. But, he tired of it, even when he found some ex-fighters, and actors, that he knew, and connected with them. The conversations dwindled after the first telling of doings and life, back and forth on the pages. As days wore on, Stanley saw Facebook was not working for him. The new year led nowhere as far as that was concerned, but in another way it *did* lead to somewhere. He met a sweet girl at the nearby 7-11. She laughed at his jokes, and always reminded him to take his credit card out of the scanner when he used it. He asked her name the third time he saw her. Mel. Short for Melanie, he guessed. She had brown hair and was about thirty years old, he figured.

That meant, at his age, he didn't have to deal with the romantic relationship stuff, just the friendship stuff.

And the third time he was in there, also, he asked her if he should grow a beard.

"Sure!" she said, in a delightful way.

So he let his beard grow. It was already a three-day growth when he asked her. And that was New Year's Eve day, so by the middle of the month of January it was starting to look like an *actual* beard.

But then she asked him if he knew any rich people – she needed money to pay for her car or she would lose it (a large payment).

"Oh, no. I don't. And I sure don't have any money myself. If I did, I'd help you out. You seem trustworthy."

"I am!" she said, in her enthusiastic manner. But he felt bad. Was it a scam? And hadn't his housekeeper said she needed money for *her* car payment? Stanley's memory was not perfect, by any means. "It was Spencer's sister who'd needed money for a car payment," he told himself. "Or was it for rent?" He couldn't recall. Spencer was gone, and Mel was here. That is what mattered, he told himself. But nevertheless, no matter how she would implore him, he couldn't afford loaning anyone any money.

"A rich person?" he asked himself. No, no, he knew none. Well, Bill had come into some inheritance when his father passed away the year before – but they'd had a "tiff," so to speak, about Trump and Hillary, and Bill would not take kindly to loaning Stanley any money – even if Stanley asked him, which he wouldn't. He liked Stanley, but not *that* much.

So he'd told her no, he knew no rich person. He was just a lowly member of the lower class – sad to say. And prospects for a change in that were dim. He had to live with his choices. It recalled the frown, or more correctly, the *scowl* on his mother's face when she talked about his boxing, and even his entering into the life of an actor. She'd rather he be something much more "substantial" than that.

Well, it mattered nothing now.

The book grew, the beard grew, the back and forth between North Korea's leader and Trump grew. Stanley plodded along. And he set a day to go to the secluded street where he could primal about his birth. He'd felt some of the Pain of it before, but now he was determined to get through it to a degree not attained in those previous sessions, even should it take him several attempts (which he expected) now.

Meanwhile, he went to the 7-11 and saw Mel again. She was behind the counter and said hello when he entered, passing her. So she recognizes me, he thought pleasantly. He fingered his beard and she said, "Fine!" and then helped a customer in front of her.

When he arrived at the counter she was busy, unfortunately, and the other clerk, a man, tabulated the prices of his beer, Cheerios, ice cream, and chips, and took his money.

Stanley left morosely, feeling the crazy melancholy that was more often his lot, now, of a wasted (mostly) life and feeble fate. His spirits were low, but he forged on.

Why worry? He'd speak with her another day. She'd known him when he came in – "certainly that's enough for now, man," he told himself. It was only for a friendship, wasn't it?

Jud Bell was not to be seen in front of the apartments, but Stanley heard him talking on his phone – Bluetooth? – when he went upstairs. Couldn't make out the words, really. Was Jud angry or only being forceful? Stanley couldn't say which. But the voice was loud and insistent.

Oh, how he hoped there wasn't going to be a problem. Screw that, he told himself. He was mighty tired of problems.

He exercised, and watched the news, and drank beer. He'd written for a while earlier. He grinned when he thought of Mel saying "Fine!" in respect to his beard. She cared, then? Or was that too much to hope for?

In the morning, he heard Jud on the phone again, yelling, denouncing who knew what, for around ten minutes and then it ceased. In fact, Jud was arguing with his friend Jason who refused to loan him money to pay off the crooks he owed, even when Jud told him they'd threatened violence.

Stanley had an urge to speak with Jud, a mysterious but strong notion to find out more about him, but didn't have any idea how. If God was making him feel this, Stanley relaxed and decided God would show him a way.

So he did nothing for the present, in respect to it.

A curious event transpired that week, one which defied reason. Stanley, driving to the dentist for work on a tooth which had decay, saw the fat man sitting on a bus bench. He pulled over. He parked. He approached the man.

"Hey, you! I want to ask you something," Stanley announced.

"Huh? Oh, you!"

He sat beside him. "Look, I am wondering, do you need a friend? I'm looking for a friend." The man said nothing. "I just, I mean, it's not easy to explain. I'm older than you – I need a friend, I –"

"Leave me alone. You are weird," the fat man replied, looking away, up the street, for any sign of an approaching bus.

Stanley stood. "I can take a hint." He walked back to his car, feeling ashamed and embarrassed.

Was he losing his mind? He sure hoped not. When he glanced back, prior to climbing into his Camaro, he saw the man was not on the bench. He was not to be seen anywhere, even though a bus was now approaching.

Stanley cursed under his breath. Twice the fat man has vanished like that? "Not reasonable," he added, after he got into his car, shaking his head. He drove to the dentist's, perplexed, mostly by his own silly behavior.

It surely was trivial, in the scheme of things – not portentous. Yet for some reason, it felt so. The elusive man, the man who called *him* "weird."

Stanley hoped he was rid of him.

After the drilling, and being told he was in need of a root canal, and making another appointment, and trying to eat something, on impulse he drove to the street he did his primaling on, parked, looked around to make sure he was unobserved, put the cushion up to his face and began making noise – groans, hollers, even, after a period of time, screams, while periodically halting and checking around him, waiting for any car to pass by, and dredging up the suppressed memory of his mother crushing his head as an infant as he pushed his way out of the womb, to get "to life," as it felt to him then, and feeling the awful squeezing she applied, contrary to his infant wishes, and felt defeat, yet kept at it, finally to emerge.

That was all he would do that day – it was difficult enough. It didn't take long. It was raining, too, which in fact prompted Stanley to drive off as soon as he could, and return to his apartment.

He felt relief. The numbness from the dentist visit had quickly vanished, and he had food to-go he'd gotten earlier. In fact, it all felt like that old phrase, "All was well in the world." But who said that, he wondered? He couldn't recall. And was that even the right phrase?

The next day the Primal "relief" sustained itself. He wanted to congratulate himself about it all, but refrained. He wasn't positive it would continue – sometimes the good feeling after a primal didn't last, although the benefits definitely did. And, additionally, Stanley gave the true credit to God, and to the originators of the Primal Therapy theory and practice.

He worked on his novel. He deliberately tried to sprinkle it with expressive words, and "big" words, too, but gave up doing that, thinking it was pretentious. A few big words were good, they fit the flow of the narrative when they were called for, like "perfunctory," and "complacent," but basically he wanted to use everyday language.

He put personal reflections in the story, as ideas of the characters, but in a limited way. It was a line he didn't care to cross, to go from fiction into non-fiction.

His beard grew. He went to see Mel in the 7-11 but she wasn't there that day, disappointingly. He saw no more of the fat man. He received no phone calls from friends or ex-friends or acquaintances, other than the dentist's office.

He had to find more to do. He struggled to come up with an idea.

His neighbor Jud still had loud phone conversations which came through the floor of Stanley's apartment. One day, Stanley knocked on his door, to invite him to lunch somewhere. Jud declined the invitation, however.

As the rewards of the birth primal settled in, he felt better. Subtly, of course, as usual, but noticeable nevertheless. A relaxation of sorts, in respect to life. It was a feeling of freedom from an anger he had subconsciously felt at having been crushed, mistreated, in that way. A feeling that had stayed with him all his life, affecting him unconsciously.

And later, as a man, he had concluded who they said was his father was *not* his real father, that Stanley had been born illegitimately, he now felt that *that* was the reason she'd tried to make him a stillborn child, to not have to have him, due to her guilty conscience. But he didn't know for a fact, only suspected.

It was that he didn't look much like his so-called father, and that, in fact, his sister (half-sister?) did. And that his so-called father was less than loving, as most fathers.

Though he'd asked his mother once, she dismissed the idea. That did not convince him. In fact, it furthered his suspicions because she hadn't reacted with shock at such a suggestion. He thought she'd failed to realize a bit of "shock" was called for, if his idea had been ridiculous. She could have been more earnest in denying it because an honest person would have felt very much the need to correct such a false idea (if it was one) in their child.

He took a drive, he bought another burger at Carl's Jr., he thought things over. Who should he call? Oddly, he felt no motivation to call anyone. He did think of the gym, but again felt a weird resistance to go there, to work out. Maybe God was stopping him. That is, temporarily. Hard to say. But pretty much, he felt, such was the case. God held him back. God was in control, for sure, and who was Stanley to force anything like that?

Thus, he humbly accepted life as it was – as long as he thought God, the Spirit, was guiding him.

After shopping at Whole Foods and putting the groceries away, he worked awhile on his book, did a little exercise, and sat down to see Trump's State of the Union speech.

Stanley had watched some of Obama's, so why not this one? He expected he could learn a few things, although he knew, at his age, that such speeches were as much propaganda as they were anything else.

First, before turning on the TV, he partook of the Lord's supper, by getting a piece of cracker (as bread) and sipping a little brandy (fruit of the vine). He focused his mind on the body of Jesus, who had said, "Do this in remembrance of me."

So Stanley struggled on, not making sense of the world, but yet writing his book. Could be something good may come out of it – something helpful to this world. This world controlled by the rich, exploited by the rich. If this book shed any light on that, and helped people to see the error of always thinking only of themselves, of their material needs, and instead turn to spiritual visions, pursuits, endeavors, efforts – well, that would be wonderful. If people would love their neighbors as themselves – that would be especially wonderful.

Yet Stanley knew he often failed in that effort; he didn't always love his fellow man. But he attempted to when he remembered to. What else could any of us do?

He looked for Mel again, and again she wasn't there.

"What happened to Mel?" he boldly asked the clerk behind the counter. "Does she still work here?"

He got a questioning look. "She? Mel?"

"Yes."

"Oh, yes. She works here still. Not today."

Stanley let it go at that. He felt strangely, asking about her, anyway. Not that he should feel that way. But perhaps the dude standing there was her boyfriend? Or only being protective.

"So what?" he thought to himself. If she still works there, he will see her again. Not that it meant anything. He only liked her demeanor, her lilting attitude.

And Stanley did see her again, a few days later. She said Hello to him as he passed from the entrance to the refrigerated section to pick up a few big bottles of Pacifico, to walk further to get a container of Cheerios, to grab a turkey and cheese sandwich, and return to the front.

"How are you?" he asked, placing his now full cloth bag on the counter.

"Okay," she replied, with not much enthusiasm. Not her normal way.

As she looked into his cloth bag, and he helped her by taking out some items, he decided then and there to be forceful. "Are you all right? Do you have a problem?"

She glanced sharply at him. She didn't answer. She rang up the items and then gave him a look he couldn't interpret. She told him the amount, he handed her cash from his pocket. She shook her head, as she got his change from the register.

"You needn't trouble about me. I'll make it." Strange words, to his ears!

"Well..." was all he could say, and "thanks." He left, confused. She obviously didn't wish to confide in him, yet equally obvious, she had a serious problem. Her past earnestness was missing. He wanted to know why. He wanted to help.

That could wait until next time, he hoped. Meanwhile to his amazement, as he began to drive away, he saw Mel run to a car, a black Honda, put a small item inside, and turn to re-enter the 7-11. He was on the street by then and wasn't able to see her after that. He drove to his apartment and parked, wondering about it all. To say the very least, his curiosity was piqued.

Was that her car? No doubt. What was the tiny package? Drugs? Money? She locked the car when she left – he saw the lights flicker from her using the remote.

Praying about it comforted him. She had a trouble, she darted out to her car with something – almost furtively. Here again, Stanley found himself starting to get involved in an area that wasn't his business. He asked God to show him what to do, if anything.

In fact, he expected that the next time he saw Mel, and asked her if she wanted help, as he felt he ought to, she'd likely tell him to forget it, and he'd have to. Until then he felt compelled to act.

Mel drove home after calling her husband at work. He told her he'd pick up pizza on his way; he knew she was tired and didn't feel like cooking for them.

She was tired, she only wanted to drop off the payment before going home. Her brother had forced her under threat of exposure, to write a check for three hundred dollars, leave it in the register overnight, but take out the cash for him. He would, otherwise, tell her husband about her past as a prostitute.

Of course, she knew there would be more demands, later, if she complied. But she had no choice. Her brother was a creep, had always been a creep, and would surely tell on her if she refused to pay.

Big deal! She was a hooker for awhile when she first came to L.A. from Oklahoma. She'd needed the money. Her brother followed, moved in with her, and lived off her. But now he was working in a car wash, living alone, needing rent money, he said.

She didn't want her husband to know her brief past history of providing sexual services. No telling how he'd react. He was a good man and Mel didn't want to lose him. So she took the money to Red, and didn't say a word to him, only just handed the envelope over and drove home.

Her problem was asking Patrick for three hundred dollars, to replace what she'd been forced to remove from the 7-11. The day's receipts, the cash, *and* her check, were by now in the safe. Before the manager was to deposit it at the bank, the next day, she'd have to get the check from the bag. Luckily, the manager didn't deposit the day's profits in the morning, as most 7-11 managers did. He was too tired, usually, and lazy, and his father owned the franchise lease, or whatever it was called (Mel didn't care, she only wanted that check, to tear it up, and to replace the money).

She'd done this once before; and had not been caught – but still, she was nervous about being fired, or worse, facing criminal charges. She only needed to tell her husband she'd lost her Visa, and needed some money, some extra money to tide her over until payday, until getting a replacement card.

It worked out fine. Mel was clever. The next day before the manager Steve came in (he was always late), she opened the safe, took out her check, replaced the three hundred, locked it up, breathed a sigh of relief.

But she knew it was only a temporary reprieve. Red would want more. And this was too great a risk to continue taking. If Steve decided to come in early, as he did infrequently, she'd be caught when he went to the bank, or later, when the teller found her check and called the 7-11 about it.

She wanted to kill Red, but certainly that was out of the question, wasn't it? She'd had a hard life, true, but never killed anyone, especially a family member.

Meanwhile, Stanley walked in, took items to the front, even asked Mel if she wanted his help with anything. "You appear to be bothered," he said.

She tried to act calm. She was oddly touched by his concern, but there was no way she would bring him into her mess.

"Thank you; but no. I can handle it myself," she told him.

"Okay," he replied, taking his change from her, putting things into his bag with her assistance. "I'm only offering."

She smiled warmly. "I – I do appreciate it – Stanley, is it?"

He smiled in return. "Yes."

But that was that, until he saw what appeared to be her car, at the bowling alley, when he went there to eat at the adjoining café a day later. It resembled what he thought was her Honda, at least, and he went by it to peer inside for any sign it was hers.

What he saw in the driver's seat was a human form bent over, into the passenger seat. On instinct he pulled open the door.

"Hello?" he asked. The form didn't move. He decided it was *not* Mel, it was a man in a dark shirt, with longish hair, but not Mel. Asleep? Passed out? Or…? He touched the man's shoulder, having to reach in to do so. Nothing. He shook it. Still nothing.

"Hey!" he yelled. But a cold feeling swept over Stanley. The shoulder was so limp, it was lifeless. He pulled himself out of the car, slammed the door for no good reason, looked around. He saw no one nearby, so went into the café and approached the waitress behind the counter.

"Say, excuse me. I think there's a dead body in that Honda out there. Or someone just passed out, but he's all slumped over." The woman was momentarily speechless. "Check it out if you don't believe me. I gotta go." He turned and left, half-expecting her to yell for him to return, but she didn't.

He wanted out of there. His car was around the front of the café where he usually parked it, close to the side street nearby. He went to it, unlocked it with the remote, got in, rather excited, and started it. He asked himself did he truly want to rush off like this? Yes, he told himself. That guy was probably dead and that could be Mel's car and he wanted absolutely nothing to do with any of it. As he drove to the side street, he saw the café manager in his rearview mirror, walking straight to the black Honda.

Of course it was on the news later. Man found dead in car. Stanley sat with a beer and thought, "God, oh God."

The man's name was not given. The cause of death was not revealed. But crime scene tape surrounded the car in the lot, he saw, and police vehicles abounded. "Mysterious death." The news reporter even said an unknown "individual" had first informed "workers" inside the café and left quickly. He was wanted by the police for "questioning."

The next day, Stanley read the paper. The waitress said she'd recognized Stanley but didn't know his name. He'd been a return customer, "always sitting by himself."

Stanley dreaded being found out. Why? Could he be considered a suspect? *Likely*, he thought.

The man in the car had chest injuries which turned out to be puncture wounds, as from an instrument of some sort. It wasn't found in the vehicle. But whose vehicle was it? The newspaper didn't say, the police wouldn't say, and they no doubt were locating the owner now, to question him or her.

Fine spot Stanley was in. If he went in now, to say he'd only been – what? Nervous? Afraid? Ha! That could work, but it wasn't the real truth. Of course, if it wasn't Mel's car, then the police wouldn't care as long as he had no connection with the murdered man. But what if it was her car, was someone Mel knew? He'd have to say he didn't know him – but why then was he afraid to stick around for the police to arrive, they'd want to know.

And if he didn't come forward now, but was identified in one way or the other? Too suspicious. The police would believe he had "something to hide," as they say.

And what if Mel killed the guy? With an ice pick for instance, and it was hers, and the police then would (could) think Stanley was her accomplice?

He spent the day stressing out, but didn't turn himself in. He just couldn't.

Mel didn't care to go to work, so called in to say she was sick with a bad cold. It was true she didn't feel well.

She lay about her place, wishing she'd accepted that old guy's offer of assistance. He could be here now feeding her, picking up food for her, but no, her husband might walk in.

But anyhow, she didn't know how to reach him. *And*, he could have more in mind for her than "help."

She drank brandy, she'd told Patrick she had a cold, smoked cigarettes, watched TV, and slept.

She'd have to return to work on Monday. For now, the stress made her feel sluggish.

Stanley crept through the next day, refusing to buy a newspaper. He ate at the old Denny's he used to frequent. He got fried eggs to go, also. He felt weak.

Mel'd drunk too much, had a mild hangover, took two aspirin, hated her brother, and called a friend who told her to come over for a visit. Ericka. Another person who'd left their small town and ventured into the wild territory of Southern California. Married now, two kids.

Mel declined the invitation. She dearly wanted to tell Ericka she'd been blackmailed by Red, but how could she without revealing she'd worked as a hooker? Ericka would simply freak out, no doubt.

She took out the trash and walked to a liquor store for more brandy. She felt confident she'd be okay by Monday.

The Honda, however, turned out not to be Mel's. The local news told Stanley that important fact. The owner's name and photograph were revealed. A manhunt was on, the owner missing. The apparent murder victim *was* known to the (now) suspect, and missing car owner, and his family and friends claimed total ignorance of his whereabouts. Stanley sighed in relief. Even if the café waitress identified him somehow

– he was safe. No connection to the two men – he'd never heard their names before. And he was glad Mel wasn't involved.

If the car's owner had killed the man found inside, that would be that. No one would care much about the "witness" who alerted the café worker of the body. Hopefully.

So he wandered into the 7-11 one day, looking for Mel. He attempted to not be obvious about it. He put beer and Cheerios and milk and bottled water into his bag, and went to the front. She was there. He said Hello to her.

She didn't look so good – drawn and watchful, as if stressed by a secret passion. She perked up a little when she saw him, acknowledged him. He tilted his head, as an unspoken question. She began to ring up his items.

"You okay?" he asked.

"Sure," was the terse reply.

Boldly, Stanley remarked, "If you say so." It brought a short laugh and then a frown from her.

She said, "Could be better." He gave her money and begun placing the items into his cloth bag. A couple of customers were standing behind him so he wasn't able to speak longer.

"My offer still stands," he said as he walked away. She nodded. That was of some comfort to Stanley.

But what could he do? Give her his phone number? Ask for hers?

A day or so transpired. He felt an emerging sense of threat. Was Mel in some kind of danger? Or was this feeling merely his imagination? That was the rather perfunctory question. Yet the sensation of threat around her – and him – was pervasive.

Imagination or not, he must deal with it.

Stanley continued writing his book. The story grew, the mystery made sense to him. Soon he would "resolve" it. But what of the mystery around Mel? How could he resolve it? Only by approaching her another time. If she rejected his sincere advances, he'd let it go. He had the will power for that. He'd had an overflow of will power all his life – it was a result of his making it out of his mother's "crushing" womb's killing attempt, and forging ahead into life, a damaged and mistreated entity, to be sure, but a strong one – inside, anyway.

Mel was there in the store the next time he went. She glanced at him as he headed to the cold box to get Pacifico to put in his bag. He trembled inwardly. Would she laugh at him when he suggested again how he wished to help her?

No, she didn't laugh. After she asked him how he was, and he replied, "Good," she took his items and rang them up. When he asked her, "How are you?" she nodded as if to say "Good," but he interjected, "Not so good?" She shrugged. She told him the amount he owed. He said "Okay," handing her a few bills, and then made the inquiry, "How may I help?" She didn't look at him. She made his change and said, "Oh, probably you can't. Thanks, anyway."

"I'd sure like to."

That stopped her. "My hero?"

"Call it what you want. But confide in me, can't you? I'm not a bad guy."

She smiled at last. "Sure not, I reckon." Then he laughed.

Luckily, there was no customer behind him. Stanley said, "Will you call me at least? I won't ask for your own number. I simply want to hear your problem.""

She hesitated, looking at him, wondering, was this dude for real?

Then she nodded, handing him a pen, and a scrap of paper. He wrote his name and phone number on it, then handed it to her. She said, "I'll call."

She'd wanted to ask, "Are you married?" because it was an issue she feared at that moment, but did not ask, realizing he may get the wrong idea about it. Mel didn't care in the usual male female way, she cared because if he was, his wife might not like her calling. But she let it drop. When he left, she watched him go to his Camaro, but by then she had a new customer to tend to, and didn't see him look back at her before driving off.

She felt a relief. He maybe could help if he would speak with Red, and insist he lay off, stop the blackmail. She'd have to tell him – what was his name? Stanley. Have to tell him her secret. But that wouldn't matter. She sensed he was a kind soul and the news would not mean much to him. The task of dealing with Red, however, *that* Stanley may not wish to do. But it was worth a try. Something had to be done.

Red was tall, but not so powerfully built. He wouldn't want to oppose Stanley. He was a bully with her, but with another man? It was worth a try! The guy had offered his services, hadn't he?

Meanwhile, Stanley managed to go to the gym and enter, and ask the man behind the front desk how much the monthly dues were. Fifty dollars. There were big bags to work out on, there was a ring in case Stanley ever got in good enough condition to spar a few rounds.

He was glad he asked a couple of questions. Even with a grey beard, Stanley had felt no animosity or mocking on the owner's part – if he was the owner. That was a question he hadn't asked. It wasn't important who the guy was.

Stanley had told him he used to work out at the Main Street Gym. Had the guy ever heard of it? No. Fine. That meant Stanley wouldn't have to answer many questions, either.

He drove away, remembering the good old days – training, visiting George (Jorge) and Alicia, running at the high school track, boxing at the Olympic Auditorium, pursuing Rosy.

He picked up a fried egg sandwich and a San Francisco burger at Marie Callender's on Tampa. He waited while they cooked it; he sat inside watching the front door. It was raining again.

People left, people came in, the way things worked in America, and other western countries: commerce, trade, capitalism. The terrorists hated it. They wanted to bring us down. To end our grip on the resources of the world.

What did God want? Stanley wasn't sure. Peace? Stability? Love? Hunger? Poverty? Violence? Were we all learning a lesson? Were we all supposed to suffer until Christ returned? Was that God's will?

He took his food and made his way to his apartment, driving in the rain, and thinking.

Mel waited for her brother to call. She'd left a nasty message. She wanted a showdown. Until that happened, she didn't need to call Stanley. She cursed under her breath as she prepared dinner.

But Red hadn't called by the time she fell into bed beside Patrick. He was awake, but not for long.

Mel was glad for that. Sex wasn't on her agenda this evening. Once more, laying restlessly, Mel thought of killing Red. She could shoot him with Patrick's gun, couldn't she?

No, the cops would certainly investigate, would ask her and her husband if they had a weapon, and Patrick would turn it over cheerfully, incriminating her (and him) so she'd be forced to tell the truth. Okay, Mel thought. That idea was out. She'd have to see what Red said when she informed him she wasn't paying anything more. She had decided not to wait for him to ask. That was her nature – aggressive, not waiting for life to overtake her.

Stanley awoke, exercised, had coffee. He felt good. Not old at all. He thought about his book, he thought about Mel. What could her problem be? He had no idea.

Rain dripped on something outside his window, repeatedly. It began to be an irritation but he felt no desire to look for the cause and maybe remedy it. The "pink-pink" thing was an irritation he could handle.

He ate an egg, frying it in a pan and tossing a small amount of lettuce with it on the plate, toasting a slice of bread, sitting at his table, wishing Mel would call.

She wouldn't, he figured, and decided not to return to that 7-11. There were many of them around town; he had no reason now to go to that one. If she didn't call, that was.

Mel took her ringing phone away from the main room, where Patrick was watching TV. She sat on the bed with the door closed. "Hello," she said.

"What is it?" Red asked.

"Nothing, but I can't pay you anymore. If you were going to ask."

"Me?" He chuckled. "Now that you mention it, I –"

"Stop there. No more money. You're a pig."

"Ha ha, that's good, coming from you."

"Stop, Red."

"I only need a couple of –"

"No! Tell him if you dare. He may knock your head off."

"You think so?"

"He loves me," Mel said, and hung up. She felt satisfied. He'd gotten the message. He was too much of a coward to tell her husband. She hoped.

Red had been a problem to her growing up in Oklahoma, and he was a problem now. But need she phone that old guy with the beard?

Well, we'll see what Red's next move is. He'll probably try again. She'll refuse. Then what? Mel dreaded him going to Patrick...so she'll have to try that guy Stanley before then.

What was tricky was not scaring the guy off, not letting him think Red could be dangerous. She'd just say Red was a weakling, that a few choice words of warning would suffice to stop the blackmail. Yes, that was the way to do it.

She called Stanley, she tried to sound weepy, she appealed to his manly instincts. She explained.

"I'm sorry, man. My brother needs to be told to lay off. If you want me to tell you what he has over me, I will. But...I'd rather not."

"Uh, well, I should know," he replied. "I can't go in without some idea, you know. He may doubt me if I am not knowledgeable, you know."

"Yes, yes," Mel said, putting a tremble in her voice. "I will call you again. I need to get up the guts to tell you. I'm embarrassed about it."

"Fine, fine. Call me again."

"Okay. Thanks. Goodbye."

"Goodbye." He hung up.

Crazy. Another woman, another problem with her brother, like Karen and Marco. So what the…?

And yet, she did call, the next day. She told him the sordid tale.

He regretted hearing it. Not that he hated prostitution so much, but he hated such a perfect target it was for blackmail.

"Can't you deny it to your husband?"

Mel chuckled. "He always knows when I lie to him. I've kept this from him, but once I have to talk about it, he will know."

"Oh," Stanley responded. "So I will insist your brother lay off and if he won't, then what?"

"He will. He's a scaredy-cat."

"Oh." Stanley hadn't heard that term in decades.

They planned the meeting. Red would expect her, at his apartment, but the two of them will show up. Full of forcefulness. Yeah, and see what the result was after telling Red to back off – to desist. Would he implode, or would he explode?

Mel arranged it with Red the next day. And she phoned Stanley, giving him the news. Stanley wanted to pull out, but he didn't say so. He was stuck. Just like you, he told himself, getting in dumb predicaments, and afraid to retreat. You have to make the best of it, be as careful as you can.

It wasn't until the weekend and he had plenty of time to think what to say. But what? Lay off, that's all he could say, lay off of Mel....

The weekend was there hardly before he knew it. Too soon. Since he didn't know if it would turn out well, or badly, he should pull out of it. He didn't know this guy Red – could be he'll become violent. Oh, screw it, he told himself. He was committed now.

Stanley wrote a little in his book and steeled himself for the meeting, the confrontation. Mel showed up in her Honda to drive over to Red's. Her idea.

She spent a few minutes in his apartment, looking it over.

"Nice," she allowed.

"Thanks," he replied. "A drink?"

"No, not yet." She laughed, putting on an act. Best to keep Stanley calm, not worried. He'd function better that way.

He had a cigarette, hiding his nervousness. Best to keep her relaxed, not tense. If Red puts up resistance, let it come all at once, he thought. Let the guy blow off steam.

Redheads are volatile, aren't they? Mel's hair was *sort* of red, he noted. He pressed his lips together between drags, for some strange reason. Well, not so strange, he admitted. It was how he felt. He avoided her eyes, but asked, "I wonder, Mel. Do you suppose he'll go for it?"

She nodded yes.

"I can't threaten him with much of anything. Don't want to. It's illegal," Stanley remarked.

She gave him a concerned look, but didn't speak, just watched him.

And finally, as he stubbed out the cigarette, Mel said, "Ready? We ought to –"

"I'm ready," he interrupted.

They left the apartment and headed for her car. It made him think of the body he'd found, with knife wounds. A bad omen.

They reached the place where Red lived. They parked and entered the front of the cheap-looking building. She led up a flight of stairs.

"Screw the elevator. It's broke." She took him to a door down the hall. She inhaled sharply and rang the bell. Nobody came to the door.

They waited. She sighed, "He is supposed to –" The door opened. A tall, redheaded, crazy-eyed man glared at them.

"Hi," Mel said.

"Hi," he responded, "who is he?"

"My friend."

Red shook his head but opened the door more, to allow them access, and backed away. "Whatever," he muttered.

So the game was on now, Stanley thought. He walked behind Mel, who then reached around to close the door. "How you been these days?" she asked her brother.

Red sat in a black vinyl chair. "Good enough, so far."

"I'm...this is Stanley. Sorry. That's Red, we call him." She waved her hand to him. No smile.

"Sure," Stanley said, nodding, when Red signaled a greeting with his right hand, pushing his hair from his eyes with his left. "What's the deal?" he asked Mel.

"Uh, maybe I will let this man answer that."

Stanley stepped toward Red, who tensed visibly. "A conversation. A notice," Stanley said. "Lay off her. I know about you squeezing money out of her. It must stop."

Red pursed his lips. "So say you?"

"Me and her. So say we."

"You got any idea what you are saying?"

Stanley smiled for the first time. "Kinda. Blackmail, her past, your squeezing. That much I know."

Red was quiet. He looked from his sister to the guy with the beard, calculating. "I guess you can force me to do as you want?"

"I have a friend, a bad person, who will make life rough for you."

"Oh. I see," Red responded. "A bad person, as in a criminal type?"

Stanley just nodded, thinking it was more effective than a spoken word. It worked.

"No worries," Red announced with a sound of acceptance, a sound of emphasis, a sound of, it seemed, full compliance. "I don't need any more money from her."

"Good," Stanley said, feeling relieved but wary.

"We're done here, then," Mel announced, and yet continued to watch her brother, who turned his face to the front door.

The victors left the man sitting in his chair, went to the Honda, and returned, whilst checking behind them for any sign of a car following persistently, to the relative safety of Stanley's apartment.

They hugged outside her car. There was little to say; they parted, bonded and guardedly happy.

He'd come up with the "criminal type" to further the threat against Red. It just suddenly had come to Stanley, who thought of the Fat Man for no apparent reason. But the actuality of an unusual type, in his mind, added to the sinister sense of danger he conveyed to Red.

Mel would probably ask him about it sometime – who was the "bad person" he'd scared Red with? It would be fun to tell her all about it.

He sat in his own chair in his own apartment, drinking a beer, and feeling quite pleased about the whole episode.

Provided it was successful, naturally, as successful as it had looked.

But before going to bed another thought occurred, suddenly. He'd left fingerprints on the other Honda's door handle. Yikes. Didn't police dust for prints at a crime scene? In books they do. Can they trace him?

Oh, boy.

Part VIII

Regardless of any worries, any problems, Stanley felt a freedom as the result of the primaling he'd done recently on his painful birth. He was born in pain and anguish, and his life had followed a track, a road, in such a way as that – from one episode of anguish to another. Always intermingled with days of happiness, though. And now if he could stop being subconsciously influenced by the torment of his birth (expecting more of the same), he might just make a newer path, one of relaxation of mind, of peace and harmony. At any rate, it felt like a strong possibility.

Don't expect torment, he told himself. "Expect something good."

His instincts told him to stay away from the 7-11 with Mel inside. She would call if there were difficulties, wouldn't she?

Certainly that was no difficulty, for she felt fine, now. Red never bothered her after their visit to him. She did wish Stanley would come in sometime – she wanted to thank him, again. But she understood, in her heart, that he may want to stay away, being as the entire situation was at best, unpleasant and unappealing, and at worst, risky for him.

Red was unpredictable – mostly meandering through life in a fairly docile way, but *sometimes* provoked by circumstances into a rage. He attacked the mailman once, in Oklahoma, and hurt him rather seriously, for failing to deliver the mail-order magic kit Red had ordered – the money coming from his after-school job sweeping floors at the town's lumberyard.

The mailman pressed charges, too, and Red spent a week in the county jail, learning a lesson (he said). But Mel had doubted it. The box of magic – toys, really, for youngsters – showed up later. Red smashed it when he found it on the doorstep. He cried to Mel, "I only wanted it to impress people. I don't care now." She'd attempted to piece the tricks and secret items together for him, but Red refused to touch them. She stored it in the garage. Her mother only shrugged it all off.

"He has a bad temper, don't he?" she remarked privately to Mel.

"You think?" Mel laughed.

But now, after the occasion of pressuring him out of blackmailing her, she wondered about that temper. Could it cause an outburst in the future? Darkly, she again thought of killing him, but once more cast the thought away. Not capable of it, she decided. And furthermore, the risk of a lengthy prison sentence loomed unbearably, crushingly lurid, in her mind.

Another book arrived from Amazon – a Rex Stout mystery. Stanley hadn't enjoyed Nero Wolfe stories as much as Poirot ones, or Sherlock Holmes, but still, he wished to give the big guy another chance. He was glad to get the book. He could only write his own but for so much, every day, and anyhow, he might get an idea or two from Rex Stout, an accomplished and very successful writer, to help in his own writing.

Life therefore dragged on uneventfully after the Mel episode. He wanted to relax, anyway. As low on funds as he was, he yet had enough to live – that was what counted in his mind. Enough money to get by. As he "got by" he still dreamed of going to the gym. It wasn't the Main Street Gym from the '70s and '80s, but it was a boxing gym, and he wanted to train.

Still Stanley put it off. Too tired, he told himself. Maybe a recurrence of Epstein-Barr, like when he had jury duty....

He drank plenty of water and carried on with the daily routine; he read and wrote.

He thought of Rosy sometimes, and even of his red '57 Chevy. Both long vanished from his life – but fine memories, examples of how even a drifting erratic life has fond moments, lovely characteristics a person can cherish alongside the weaker moments, the troubling times (as when he felt cheated in his first pro bout) (that was a bittersweet memory; he'd lost unfairly, but Rosy had come into his life again, unexpectedly).

He thought now more sadly of her than of that bout, yet both of those memories had a touch (or more) of pleasantness. It was a good fight in spite of the weight difference, and being with Rosy was generally sweet.

Like after the shots he'd fired from the plane off the coast of Vietnam. When the Marines had boarded the junk, and found supplies intended for the Viet Cong in the south, Stanley was told by the seaplane's flight captain that no, there were no dead found on board. His aim had been "unsatisfactory." Well, fine, because Stanley was not familiar with using, aiming, the .50 caliber gun. Fortunate, too, because, years after, he definitely had negative thoughts of the U.S. involvement over there. Not that any soldier (or sailor) who killed enemy Vietnamese ought to be blamed. They (he or she, as the case may be) were only doing their duty. It was the higher-ups (whoever they may have been) who pushed the war, *knowing* how unnecessary (and thereby wrong) it was, who were the responsible ones.

Meanwhile, he still felt tired for no reason he could determine, and sat in his chair at his computer, on Facebook, and looking at pictures from the Olympic Auditorium, and some famous fighters, and even a good past bout now and then on YouTube. He himself wasn't shown on YouTube; he hadn't had a career that justified it. But it didn't make him feel bad. His time in the ring, while not fantastic or stellar, was satisfactory, in spite of having been shortened because of hand injuries and head butts. He wanted to have done more, *of course*, but took it in stride. A lot of hopeful fighters hadn't got as far along as she had. Stanley didn't pity his career, or himself. At any rate, not overmuch.

He considered seeing the doctor as he kept feeling tired, but said no to that idea, for the time being.

Stocking up on supplies, food to prepare himself (although he didn't care for cooking), and a store of to-go meals, he kept inside for well over a week. Why not?

The respite helped. He rested, wrote, read, watched the news, and slept a considerable amount. When Stanley finally emerged from this reclusive period, he was refreshed and almost himself. A couple of weeks of exercise and he should be quite ready, he judged, for another adventure.

The call of the wild! He went to the beach, cruising sweetly in his '70 Camaro, walking on the sand, eating a burger from a small spot in Santa Monica, then cruised a "path" along Sunset (as he often had) and slipped over the canyon to the Valley. At one point, he felt the urge to visit the Griffith Observatory (of James Dean *Rebel Without a Cause* fame), but it was too far. He wasn't 30 years old anymore; distances were an issue now.

Stanley felt happy, though. He'd had a good journey for that day.

But what to do next? Check on Mel? Shop for more groceries? He needed something "important," but he only could think of mundane activities. No one called him, so he should call out, reach out, to someone. But who? Stanley's mind was a blank, so he watched the news. Crazy stuff about the special counsel, the congressional hearings, witnesses all around, specious words about Russian non-interference with the election of 2016. Of course they had tried to interfere; if that had turned the result in favor of Trump remained to be seen. Stanley felt a conspiracy, a flipping of the election, was completely possible. There were lies and more lies, it seemed.

He smiled grimly at the TV. Who was lying? That had to be determined. Which side was being dishonest? The Republicans? The Democrats? Or, God help us, a little of both?

After a few weeks, he took an envelope to the post office – it was a job he didn't feel safe leaving to the collection which supposedly occurred from a slot at the side of the apartment mailboxes. No delay was desired – he'd taken too long to write the check for the DMV and get his car smog-certified. The deadline was approaching and he didn't care to get charged if he was late.

So at the post office, which was closed, naturally, on Sunday, he was about to put the letter in the outside box when a voice behind him said, "Don't mail it there! Go inside." He turned to see a stocky man, around thirty-five or forty, pulling open the door to enter. And sure, it opened; it was only the P.O. windows inside that were closed.

"They put a sticky in there, on a string," he told Stanley, "And pull out the mail at night. Better to put it in here." He pointed inside. Stanley followed. He was confused – the P.O. takes the mail out with a sticky? What?

The man kept talking – he explained what he meant – "thieves."

"It happened to me. They took and cashed a check I mailed!"

Ah, that was it. Stanley then waited until the man had placed his own envelopes into the inside receptacle, and deposited his.

"Thanks," he told the guy, who, walking away, grumbled, "It's getting worse, it's all getting worse. What can you do?"

Stanley began to follow him outside, but the man hurried off, with one last remark, "Can't do anything about it, have to just keep smiling."

That brought a smile to Stanley's face. "Keep the faith," he replied, but didn't think the hurrying man heard him.

Stanley walked to the market near the office, and thought, "Bizarre, but probably true, nevertheless. Good advice."

Later, he regretted not stopping the guy for more chat, and then trying to befriend him. Wasn't it Stanley who wanted to make a new friend? But he'd not thought of it – he was taken aback by the whole event, and not able to befriend the guy. "Next time," he ordered himself. "Make a friend."

But as always, he was the slow-starter. Perhaps it had kept him out of trouble all his life, yet he wasn't so sure about that. It wasn't so good in the ring, if he got "caught" early; he hadn't much chance to retaliate until later rounds. But so what? He asked himself. He'd come on strong, later, if he hadn't been knocked out early. In life, slow starting was a flaw, too, by causing things to slip by, losing the opportunity a chance encounter or an idle but significant remark presented to him. That caused Stanley to wonder, sadly, "What moments last? God knew. What paths missed? What joys forever unrealized?" The people in the gym, even one sports writer, had used the nickname on him. Well, perhaps he'd do another Primal of his birth, and presto – no more "slow starting" in life. There could sure be a cause, there, he assessed to himself, that very night, drinking beer and flipping the TV channels around.

The next day, he finally finished the book, with the brother being as he'd planned, the poisoner. Now he had to go over it all from beginning to end, rewriting, as he'd learned in school. Creative writing class. Oh well, it was a good way to spend time.

He waited a day to start the rewriting, no need to hurry.

He took a long walk. His back kind of hurt, he couldn't understand why. He hadn't been doing any strenuous exercising. Or lifting. Or having sex, for sure.

The day was sweet, warm; soft sun from behind a very slight but extended overcast. He went in an aimless manner. He found himself at a clothing store, going inside to buy a new pair of Levi's. And a pair of socks.

He walked back to his place. He shook his head as an image of Rosy came to his mind. Forget her, he told himself. He checked the box for mail, finding a package (a book) from Amazon, and walked upstairs. The door, however, was half opened. He stood and listened. No sound. He peered in. Not wanting to surprise a thief who could be armed, he yelled, "Hello?" Nothing. "Hello?" He then walked inside, nervously.

A bit of a mess, yep. Furniture moved, desk drawer open, a box from one closet in the bedroom lying on its side with the contents scattered around it. He searched, to no avail, for a hiding marauder. The little kitchen was fortunately not a mess. Whatever they'd wanted wasn't likely a kitchen thing.

Stanley closed the front door. What would Sherlock do? Look for clues.

He tried to find a clue – a piece of paper, a clothing item, a hair, even. But nothing. Should he call the cops? No, what was missing? Not anything.

He wondered how the door had been unlocked. No sign of entry by force, so another key? The landlord? A pro lock picker? But Stanley just dismissed the break-in from his mind. Even his pistol was not taken. He decided to have the lock changed. And ask his downstairs neighbor had he heard anything?

So the lock was changed. His landlord approved it, on Stanley's word alone. The neighbor was not easy to catch up with – it took two weeks – but he said he'd noticed nothing suspicious.

Fine. The guy was not paying attention to Stanley's apartment; he hardly knew what Stanley looked like, probably.

Maybe Jud had gone into his place looking for money? In fact, that is what happened. Jud was ashamed and brooded for awhile, and one day resolved to admit it had been him. He figured Stanley would not care to tell the police, and he was correct. When he told Stanley, pleading stress and stupidity, Jud saw to his relief that Stanley was willing to accept it, to forgive.

"But don't you still need money?"

"I do," Jud replied. "A lot."

They were in Stanley's doorway.

"Good luck. And as you learned, I don't have any money to spare, either."

He was happy Jud had not discovered his hiding place, where he kept a little cash.

"Don't try it in the future, I won't let you get by the next time."

"Certainly. I surmised that."

"Tell me, how'd you get in?"

Jud smirked. "A lock pick. From my younger days. Sorry."

"Breaking and entering was your habit?"

"Had to. My heroin habit. No more!" He held up both hands.

"Yet you owe somebody?"

"Old debt. They have made it the issue. A threat."

Stanley said nothing to that. He didn't care to know any more. When Jud went downstairs, Stanley thought, "Well, well, I've got a new friend. Sort of."

"Hopefully he won't be killed by dealers," he said to himself the day after. "If it is dealers he owes."

But he felt all right about this, other than a fear his part-time housekeeper could be caught in the middle, possibly in the crossfire. "But that's dumb," he told himself. "Very very unlikely."

Still, he decided to stay away from Jud, new friend or not.

He didn't want murdering dealers to think he was close to Jud, and therefore a candidate to cause them trouble. He would call 911 emergency if he heard gunfire, but that was the extent of it.

He heard no gunfire for the next weeks. He heard conversations Jud had on the phone through the floor or the windows or wherever the neighbor's voice was getting up to Stanley's apartment, but that was all. He couldn't distinguish exact words – except one or two, sometimes. Good. The less he knew, the less he chanced being involved. He wasn't a real private detective, after all. Only an amateur. And he wished to keep it that way.

He kept rewriting his mystery novel, copying and changing what he had onto fresh pages. A laborious process but fun. The rest of the time, he dug into a new Sherlock Holmes Mystery Magazine and a religious book about the gospel of Matthew. And watched the distressing news: shootings, bombings, severe weather, congressional investigations that seemed to go nowhere. Was the end of the world near, or only looking so?

His back was okay, his teeth not bad, his spirits fine. One day he'd walk into the gym, he told himself for the hundredth time, it seemed. Only his old friends wouldn't be there. Fine. He'd have to make new ones. So be it.

A day came he decided to check on Mel. She was in the 7-11, behind the counter. He'd gone to other 7-11s for the past three months, avoiding her.

She looked pretty. He smiled, and she returned his with one of her own. After collecting his usual items, Stanley approached her, put his bag on the counter, and smiled once more.

"Your beard has grown," she remarked as they took things out of his bag. She rang them up. He didn't know what to say. He was shy, or something. Finally he blurted out, "No more trouble?"

Mel laughed, so he took it to mean, "No." He stuck his credit card into the little machine. "Cool," he said a bit too quietly. That was it – he *did* feel shy, he realized, going outside. But she'd looked good, and he knew for whatever reason, it was okay to keep going in there, now. He felt happy. No trouble. Other than his fingerprints on that car – but he guessed that issue was passed. "Praise God from whom all blessings flow…." It was a hymn, wasn't it? The words occurred to Stanley as he drove up to his carport and parked the Camaro.

"No trouble, no trouble. Praise the Lord," he said when he climbed the stairs.

But there was trouble. Not from the police, not from Red, not from Mel, not from Jud, but a new and mysterious person – a bad hombre, as some would call him. The evil offspring of a long ago boxing buddy of Stanley's. The guy called Stanley up.

"Got a message from Preston. Do you remember him?"

"Sure do."

"He's in a nursing home. But I'm supposed to say hello for him. My dad."

"Your dad?" Stanley hadn't known Preston very well, and sure didn't know he had a son. "Well, we were at the gym in the '80s. Didn't realize he had a son."

"No problem. He said he worked out with you. Says Hi."

"Cool. But...won't he call me himself, or...?"

"Not doing too well, that's why. I'm just a messenger."

"I see," Stanley responded. "He's not doing well?"

"That's how it goes. Too many punches."

"Uh-huh. I remember he fought for the, uh, the WBA...?"

"Light-heavy title. Lost by knock-out. 1986, I think. I was just a kid."

"So..." Stanley started. "If he needs me to visit I'd be glad to."

"Not that," the son said. "He needs nothing. Just to say Hello, like I told you."

"Okay. Hello from me. What's your name, by the way?"

"Arnold."

"Okay. How'd you get my number, by the way?"

"From your old trainer and manager, Larry."

"Fantastic. I need to give him a call."

"Listen," Arnold said. "There is a favor you might be able to –" he stopped.

"Yes?"

"Dad's in a spot. A tough spot."

"Oh," Stanley said. "If it's money, believe me, I don't really have any."

"You don't? He could use some."

"I can spare a hundred, but –"

"Fine. Can I come get it? We wouldn't ask but the bills pile up."

"Uh-huh. They sure do."

It was a rip-off, of course. When Stanley went to visit Preston, the old guy knew nothing of any money Arnold has asked for. In fact, he hadn't seen Arnold in months.

He'd given a hundred to him when he stopped by Stanley's place.

"Here we go again," he thought when he left the boxer at the nursing home. "Yes, you dupe."

A sharper person would have spoken with Preston before handing over the cash. Oh well, live and learn. Lucky it wasn't more than it was. So, he'd been taken advantage of. Stanley tried not to think it was due to Arnold being black, but part of him couldn't help it. Was he being racist, or just sensitive to the plight of blacks and how they'd been taught by the negative circumstances surrounding them, *to be*? Stanley hoped it wasn't racism but felt – accepted finally – that part of it was. He'd reacted with the old "that figures" because Arnold was black, and disliked himself for it. "That figures" what?

How? Due to Arnold's race he was bound to lie, to trick, to take money from another person by subterfuge?

Ha! Whites did that also. So, that resolved, Stanley began to feel better about himself. He got Arnold's phone number from his phone, and tried to think of a plan. To reprimand Arnold but not demand restitution. He'd tell him to keep the cash if he needed it so desperately.

Stanley sat in the armchair as the night infused the daylight with dark. He sipped a beer, he made his plan. He'd be harsh but not mean.

He called. No answer. He left a message. "Well, man, your dad said he knew nothing about sending you to get money from me. I hope you are sorry. Keep it. You must need it bad, to trick an old gym friend of Preston's. I guess your loyalty stops at the water's edge."

He hung up, wondering what the last part meant. Ha! He took a sip of beer. "That's what this stuff does to you, pal," he said half-kiddingly, and looked at the mug.

A call came in the following day. Preston himself.

"My boy, you have stirred up a hornet's next. My son –"

"What?" Stanley couldn't help from interrupting.

"My son, he's pissed at you and wants to settle things. He's saying I *did* ask for money from you, a lot, but I can't remember because of too many punches."

"Well," Stanley replied, "it might be true."

"Fuck! My brain's as fine as anyone's. Been examined, I'll have you know. He's just prevaricatin'. You like that word?"

"Sure. I don't know what it means, though. Lying?"

"Sort of. More like hiding the truth, which is, I asked *him* for some money. He went to you on his own, to keep from handing over any of his own money. Cheap. Always has been."

"Oh, I see."

"We're stuck, boy, and he's going to pay you a visit."

"For?"

"To pound you into 'a pulp,' he says."

"He ought not to try it."

"Aren't you old now?"

"Yes, but my gun isn't."

Preston was silent. Then, "Can't talk him out of it. I tried, but…."

"That's bad," Stanley said grimly.

"Yep."

Of course, he could call the police. They could speak with Preston and pick up Arnold for questioning. To what avail? None other than maybe scaring him off. Like Red? Stanley doubted Arnold was going to be scared, even by a visit by police. Well, when and if the dude showed up, Stanley would have his pistol near.

But he didn't show up. Days passed, no creep at the door. And when he went out, gun tucked in his waistband under a loose-fitting shirt, there was no Arnold behind him in a car or on the street watching. If he was, he was pretty sneaky about it.

But finally they met, in a parking lot outside Rite-Aid. The dude looked angry.

"Put up your dukes," he yelled. "I'll get you for ratting on me to Preston!"

"Bull. I just asked him about it." Arnold had his fists up.

A woman shouted, "Stop it!" as she walked to her car. She kept going, of course. Smart.

Stanley decided to fight. The guy wasn't *that* much bigger. Only marginally.

They swung on each other, both connecting. Stanley, to his great surprise, fell, severely stunned. But Arnold only shook his head.

"Want some more of that?"

Stanley rose to his feet, and advanced. Might as well try it one more time. He ducked Arnold's next punch and went to the body as he'd been trained to do against a hard hitter. Three sharp blows and Arnold was stumbling backwards.

The woman screamed "Stop it!" again as she drove away. Stanley jabbed but Arnold shook it off and straightened, fury in his eyes.

Stanley danced a few steps and thought, "Don't be slow. Could be a mistake." But Arnold came at him and swung wildly, so Stanley covered up and took a step back. He threw another punch, a right hand, to the body. It connected. He still got caught with a right on the side of his face – the dude could hit, even when in pain.

Stanley jabbed again, quicker than the dude could make any other move. It hit him in the nose, hard.

"Break it up," another citizen said, nearby. They paid no attention to him.

Arnold moved forward, blood coming from his nose. He missed with his left, which Stanley ducked, and with his right, which Stanley blocked. Arnold panted, pausing.

"Break it up, I'm telling you."

Stanley glanced over, saw a young man to his left, pointing a finger at them.

Arnold charged, knocking Stanley off his feet. He kicked at his head, missing. Stanley rolled quickly and tried to jump up, but another kick caught him in his back. He fell flat. Arnold stomped at him – and it felt bad – in the ribs. The young man grabbed Arnold from behind.

"Lay off!" he hollered. Arnold pulled himself away.

"All right, all right. I got what I wanted," he said, and with a scornful look at Stanley on the pavement, marched to his car, holding his stomach.

Later that afternoon, the rescuer, Dan, left Stanley in his apartment, fitted with an ice pack and a tray of coffee, cheese, and cold roast beef he'd found in the refrigerator. He'd given Stanley his phone number, accepted his thanks, and told him to call if he should feel worse.

"You're a good Samaritan," Stanley informed him, as he went out the door. He was 25 or so, with short, military-style hair, and dark pants with a white long-sleeved shirt. Said he lived near that area.

"No doubt a veteran. Or on leave," Stanley surmised. "Brave."

Next day his bumps and bruises were subsiding nicely. Getting beat on was not new to him, though getting stomped and kicked was. He felt no wish for revenge – probably the grace of God, the spirit of forgiveness, in him. What did he care, really? Not very much harm done. And he knew for sure he'd delivered several hard blows himself. Lucky (sort of) he'd given up taking his gun around.

He did want to report to Preston. Shouldn't be a secret, what his son did. So Stanley decided to call the nursing home to tell him.

They said, however, he couldn't come to the phone.

"Can't you just hand it to him? It's mobile, is it not?"

"Sir, he won't speak with anyone. Those are his instructions," the receptionist answered.

"But – oh well, all right. May I leave a message?"

"Yes," she replied. Little did she realize it would contain a vivid description of the parking lot assault.

"My, my," the woman said, as she finished writing it down.

"Please deliver it intact, ma'am. It's important to me."

"I would not doubt it," the woman replied in a serious tone.

"*Thank* you," Stanley said, empathically, to urge her on to her task.

"May I say I'm sorry, sir? For what happened? Between you and me, I don't care for Arnold very much."

Two days passed and Stanley felt certain that was the end of it. "God knows how the message was interpreted," he thought. "For well or ill…."

But no, that was not the end of it. Arnold showed up at his door, face twisted into a mean grimace.

"I'd love to kick your ass again, but my dad ordered me to..." he mumbled, handing Stanley a small envelope. "Don't spend it all in one place," he added, after Stanley had taken it. He turned away.

Stanley opened it and saw it contained a hundred dollar bill.

"Thanks," he yelled, after Arnold descended the staircase. No response.

Inside his apartment, it occurred, strangely, to Stanley, that if he'd heard any sort of agreeable reply – even "you're welcome" – the whole event would be more acceptable.

As it was, it was not acceptable, since he still felt soreness in his back and in his jaw.

The hundred he threw on his dresser. He didn't feel ripped off, now. Only, circumspectly, irritated. Beat up by a guy who obeys his dad, at his age? There could be more to this than meets the eye. "If I was a private detective, I'd figure it out," he told himself. But for now, all he felt was confusion.

He worked on his book. He watched the news. He wondered how Arnold had hit so hard. Maybe his dad taught him something. Lucky he hadn't showed him how to avoid a jab. Or perhaps he had, but Arnold couldn't manage it. Stanley smiled at that – Arnold wasn't the only one who had a tough time blocking, or slipping, that jab. Nice to know Stanley still had it. And probably the primaling factored in, enabling him to jab like he had early on in his career.

But the drama wasn't over yet. He got a note in the mail from Preston. He, wrote, in bad handwriting, that his son was acting weirdly, making threats. Would he come to meet with Preston and Arnold at the home?

It didn't require much thought. *No.* Stanley wanted nothing more of it. "Let the police know," he wrote back to the father. "That's the better way to handle it."

No reply came in the mail, so Stanley had no way of knowing if Preston had followed his advice. But he couldn't get drawn into it. That old fighter's son was dangerous.

Rewrites on his book were a struggle. But having enjoyed any English class he'd had in school, for him this work was not unavailing. He had a talent, a turn of phrase (or so he felt). Others could be the judges of how interesting it was.

Keeping track of the flow of the mystery was difficult. Couldn't let the reader in on too much. His notes were sparse. A real mystery novelist probably kept lengthy notes while working. Anyway, he made Rio a hero.

The donut shop girl was sweet and friendly (her job), but Stanley knew his white beard told her all she needed to know: old dude. He had her make him a couple of roast beef sandwiches, without cheese (the stuff wasn't tasty to him anymore – maybe his age changing his palate).

She put a couple of donuts in a small bag, and he paid, going outside with the sandwiches, also, in a large paper bag, happily anticipating his immediate future. He got beer and cigarettes, and returned to the apartment. Such it was for provisions, for the free and easy American life – as long as one had enough money.

And so much for the bruises on his back and ribs, where he'd been stomped – they were fading, he noticed after taking a shower and turning to see the reflection in the mirror.

What was that young guy's name who stopped the kicking he had been getting? Stanley asked himself, as he sat down to a beer and the local news. His number was laying around somewhere. He jumped up and saw it on his table-desk. "Oh yeah...Dan. Have to buy him lunch or something."

Then he watched the news. What was going on? Actually, the mess was beyond him. Beyond his ability to grasp. He switched from station to station. Claims and counter-claims. Clever statements, clever responses. The Congress, the FBI, the foreign leaders, the White House – one day it would all make sense, he thought. The indictments, the trials, the report from the Special Counsel, the news analyses, the honesty, the lack of honesty, the firings, the new hirings, resignations, replacements. Many would be *after* the next round of campaigns and the November elections. He had faith in democracy, in the system. The "checks and balances," as folks referred to them, the changes, and the ins and outs and hopefully solid underpinning of the "rule of law" – create laws, pass them, enforce them, and if they don't turn out so well, change again. Only it appeared to Stanley that the rich people were running the system more than they ought to. Perhaps it had to be that way for the sake of stability. He didn't know. But he felt empathy, sorrow, for the weak and powerless, not for the wealthy and powerful.

He got tired fast, sitting at his computer. He took his photo, with his phone, and posted it on Facebook.

"See what happens – if anything," he said out loud. "Maybe something good?"

But only a few of his friends made remarks: "Nice beard," and "What you up to these days?" "Santa Claus?"

He didn't want to reply yet. There may be more comments. He'd wait awhile. He'd tell them about the fight he'd had; they were friends from his acting days. It ought to surprise them a little.

He walked out to the patio. A "landing," really. Small. A dog was barking. He flexed his hands. Fortunately, they hadn't given way on him in his fight with that Arnold.

"Gotta get to the gym," he said once more to himself. "Soon." The rest of his body felt more or less normal. He knew luck – or rather, the Lord – had been with him. Maybe Dan was an angel. It can happen, can't it? That's what the Bible shows, doesn't it?

Morning found him refreshed and eager for a walk. But within ten minutes he felt tired. "God, not Epstein-Barr again!" he complained.

He ate at the café on Topanga Canyon and strolled back to his apartment. He fell into his chair. He'd work on the book later. But for now he rose and answered the Facebook page replies to his picture.

It didn't take long, but there was a fourth comment, now, from the previous evening, "Good pic, Stan. How's it going?"

He replied, "Thx. Not much going on except – " and he related the details of the fight. Of course there'd be more questions, but that didn't bother him. It was only that he was embarrassed having come out on the losing side of it.

The next day he took another walk feeling the same tiredness. Yep, Epstein-Barr. He picked up a few items at the liquor store – beans, beer, and bread, along with aspirin. Times would be hard while he waited for the weakness to run its crazy course. Once again, he felt disinclined to go to the doctor for B-12 injections. He knew he should, but...too tired!

He sat in his abode, wondering was the shot B-12 or B-6? And how many? Not important; the doctor would figure it out.

The next day Stanley didn't go for a walk. He did some half-sit-ups and shadow-boxed and took a glass of water and finally ate a bowl of cereal. He looked out the window. He prayed.

A knock came at the door. He said, "Okay," and when he opened it saw the unpleasant face of Arnold.

"Hi!" he about yelled, with a big grin.

"Oh, well," was the reply Stanley made.

"Sorry if I'm bugging you, man. Sorry can't cover it, I expect. But anyway..." Arnold's eyes went blank and he fell forward onto Stanley, who caught him and set his limp form down to the floor.

"Shit," Stanley muttered. He looked out his door, peering left and right, and down the stairs. Nothing but a car at a distance; nothing else.

Arnold was unconscious. He had a pulse. He failed to respond to a glassful of water splashed onto his face.

Stanley closed his door and felt around to see if there was a wound, or a gun, on Arnold. Nope. He took his wallet out. ID, credit cards, in his name.

He slapped him. He stirred. He slapped him again. More stirring. No smell of booze, though. Call 911? The guy was breathing. No signs of any bleeding.

"What are you doing here, man?" Stanley spoke the words out loud. He kicked the side of the limp body. Arnold's eyelids fluttered.

So he did call 911, paramedics arrived, and they did revive him and take him away. Fine. "He'd have to pay for the ambulance, not me," Stanley told himself. It was a mystery, though.

Police dropped by. Just one. To get his story. Had to say he knew the guy. Told about Preston and the hundred dollars. But not the fight.

The policeman asked more than once did he have any idea why Arnold showed up. Stanley had no idea.

"To borrow another hundred?" The officer made it a joke. He said Arnold was still in the hospital undergoing tests. His heartbeat was irregular. No appetite. He'd given no explanation as to his fainting, or his visit to Stanley. Said he didn't remember at all.

"Contact the father," he said to the officer as he went out the door.

Drugs? Stanley couldn't expect the police to tell him – but possibly they thought there was a connection, that Stanley might even be the supplier. So he was being watched if Arnold had illegal drugs in his system, like meth, for example.

Stanley called the old folks' home, left a message for Preston that Arnold was in the hospital. Not much of a massage because he didn't know the name of the hospital. Seemed the right thing to do, however. Preston could get the information calling the policeman – a sergeant was he? – whose name he *did* know. Sergeant Chambers, Sheriff's Department.

That might have been the end of it, except the police could be tailing him. And Chambers called a week later – Arnold snuck out during the night, and was picked up when his ex-girlfriend reported he'd hit her, demanding heroin, which she said she hasn't had for several years.

So...Stanley asked Chambers, was Arnold a "junkie"?

"It appears so."

"But I hope you don't think I was helping him. I *wasn't*," Stanley said.

"Why would he go to you, then? For what?"

"Like I said, I can't explain it. Unless he wanted more money. As if I'd give him any!"

Sergeant Chambers chuckled, "If he was strung out, he might've done anything."

"Yeah."

"Be careful. We released him."

"Oh."

"The girlfriend wouldn't press charges."

"They seldom do, I hear," Stanley replied.

"No. Take care."

"I will. You also."

So, released. Could stop by here again, then, Stanley mused.

Life, after that, plowed along as usual. He still felt tired and weak. He exercised anyway.

"Well," Stanley thought, "where there's a will, there's a way." A good motto to live by, mostly.

A new friend, he reminded himself. "Find one." He felt that would be at the gym. But for now he hadn't the energy for going to the gym.

He worked on his novel, fixing things here and there, adding more descriptions of people and places.

The a.m. The phone rang. The piano ring tone. He got up to see who was calling. A number he didn't recognize. He let it go, he went to the bathroom, he went to make coffee. He thought about Arnold. Why'd he come here in such a condition? For help, obviously. He figured softie Stanley would help him. "Which you did, softie. Ha ha ha."

He had to smile. Arnold wasn't dumb, drug addict or not. But bad, no doubt about it. Or did the drug addiction cause his bad behavior? Was he just another gentle soul on the inside, like many people? Likely, he thought. Or not.

There was no message from that phone call. Good, he thought, struck by a vague notion it could have been Arnold. Gentle soul within or not, the man was...what? Trouble, to avoid if possible.

Stanley whipped up some fried eggs and warm refried beans and toast to accompany his coffee.

Halfway through eating, he heard his downstairs neighbor arguing loudly on the phone. At least it sounded like a phone call. If not, the other person down there was not saying anything Stanley could hear.

Then, feet on the steps outside his door. He went to see who it was, and at a knock, opened the door. It was Jud.

"Well, sir, how you doing?"

"Fair," Stanley answered, trying to read the man's bland brown eyes.

"May I come in a moment?"

"Why?"

"To – to – tell a story of, uh, woe and betrayal."

Stanley laughed in spite of himself. "Formal talk, I'd say. What's it all about? Considering how you broke in here that time, I'm not, frankly, inclined to let you in."

That caused Jud to remain silent a moment.

"Uh, well, naturally," he commented then. "Only..." he took a small leather pouch from his shirt pocket. "This here is part of the woe." He shook it at Stanley. "I'd like to talk in private."

"Nope," Stanley said firmly.

Jud frowned, looked down the steps behind him, sighed a bit dramatically, and held the package out to Stanley. "Important. Take it."

Stanley did. It felt too heavy to be paper inside. He felt the contents with both hands.

Jud smiled. "Yes, sir, jewels. Mine. For now."

"Aah."

"Can't let them be found in my possession, you understand. I beg you to –"

"Oh hell," Stanley interrupted. "Why come to me? Put 'em in a bank or something."

"Well, you know, it would lead back to me, wouldn't it?"

"So what?"

"The betrayal. My friend. Ex-friend. Can't I come inside?"

"No. What about your friend?"

"She inherited them, and entrusted them into my care, but she disappeared. On purpose, I assume. So *I'd* be stuck with them."

"Stuck? What's wrong with them?" Stanley wanted to tear open the pouch to see, but resisted that inclination.

Once more Jud looked down the stairs. "Not stolen if you suspect that."

"Sure, whatever. But who betrayed you?"

"She did! I don't want them! She knew that."

Stanley now sighed in a dramatic fashion, himself.

"But – well – her aunt wants them."

Stanley shook his head. "Yes? So?"

"They live together. My friend wanted them out of the reach of her aunt."

"Valuable?"

"I'll say! Fifty thousand dollars, man."

"Why give them to me, then?"

"I have, uh, enemies, and –"

"Yes, you told me before. Will they hurt you if they know you have these? Is that the deal?"

"Certainly."

"You still owe money to them?"

"Unfortunately," Jud answered.

"Well, man! Sell this stuff and pay them!" He held the package out to Jud, who didn't take it.

"No, I don't really – I can't...."

"Yes. They ain't actually your jewels to sell." Stanley *so* wanted to see them, but once more decided not to open the leather pouch.

Jud began to back up to the stairs, and step down them, keeping his eyes on Stanley. "Only a few days. I'll find...her. She can't be too far because she left her credit cards and –"

"Wait a minute. Stop."

Jud stopped.

"I want a cut. For hanging on to these." Stanley hardly believed he was saying that. "Okay?"

"Okay." Jud turned and proceeded downstairs. As he stood in his doorway, Stanley thought, "I'm living in the Twilight Zone."

Later, he couldn't resist any longer. He'd thought of a good hiding place, a box of cookies in his kitchen cabinet – under the cookies inside. But before an hour had passed, he pulled out the small package and placed it on his table and unzipped the zipper. He looked inside, he poured the gems out. Red, green, blue, white. He touched them. Real? He didn't know, but thought so. He put them away, and sat in his chair sipping beer. He'd best count them, because Jud or someone might get in there and take a few – if they could find the hiding place.   But he'd wait for tomorrow, too tired now to count the gems, as nice as they were.

Thirteen, he found in the a.m. Not quite a fortune, but enough to kill him for. Not that Stanley cared all that much for his life. He was ready to go, if need be. He couldn't think what else to do, really. Like a fool, wait and hope this girl Jud spoke of does return and ask for the stones, and Stanley would get rid of this unlikely burden. He cared for his life just so much he'd rather live than die. His life wasn't so bad. Better than others' in respect to the poverty and starvation and wars around the world. Better than living under an oppressive government, like Russia. Or Saudi Arabia. Better than being in prison. Better than a lot of circumstances.

He moved his gun closer to his bed. It was also better to be safe than sorry. Stanley did have a few dreams left. Daytime ones, not nighttime ones. But he was so tired! He'd have to rethink that aversion to seeing doctors.

How long to wait, in suspense, for news about the jewels? A week? A month? Longer?

He meandered along. He even went to church one Sunday. He remembered that he used to be a Seventh Day Adventist many years before. Frankly, the beliefs of Sunday-going folks and Saturday-going worshipers were similar enough, aside from the Saturday service doctrine, that he didn't care which church he attended. He could pray to Christ in both.

But he worried. Were those gems somehow illegal? Maybe. God wouldn't care for him holding them, if so. Or the police either. So….

He knocked on Jud's door, who answered, wearing a black robe.

"Hi," he said. He had an expression of curiosity on his face but said no more.

"Any luck? You know, the ex-girlfriend?" Stanley asked.

"Nope. Want to come in?"

"No, thanks. Frankly, I'm kind of stressed." Stanley lowered his voice. "I want to give the stuff back."

"Understandable."

"You have no objection?"

"It's for you to decide. It puts me in jeopardy, but what the hell, you have to do as you see fit."

"Too stressful. Could even be stolen property, right?"

"Sure, could be," Jud murmured. "Bring 'em down." He glanced away, shrugging.

"Okay," Stanley replied, and went upstairs, relief coursing through his veins. He dug out the pouch, quickly looked at the contents, and returned to Jud's door, still open. But he was not there.

"Hey," Stanley said, and knocked. There was no answer from inside. He waited, unsure if it was wise to go in. "Hey!" he repeated more loudly. Then he heard a voice from the rear of the apartment.

Still he hesitated. Was Jud back there, speaking with someone, perhaps at the rear door?

So Stanley went around on the outside, to the back. Sure enough, Jud and another person, a short man in jeans and a T-shirt, were conversing. He approached them. Why not? Jud saw him first. He shook his head. The short man turned to see who Jud was looking at.

"And just what do you want?" he asked, roughly.

"Nothing much," Stanley told him. "Just to speak with Jud."

"Get out of here. This is private."

"Why so rude? I'll wait in the front," Stanley said. The man appeared displeased with Stanley's presence, so as he stepped back a bit he asked Jud, "Are you okay?"

"No," he said, simply. "But go back to the front. I'll talk to you later about our little business."

The short man stared at Stanley, who nodded and said, "Okay, but yell if this dude makes more trouble. Looks like he already has." He walked away. The men were silent until after Stanley rounded the corner of the building. He couldn't hear what they were saying, even though he stopped to listen. The jewels were burning a figurative hole in his hip pocket.

He finally approached the front, peering inside, pushing the door open further. Just a normal looking place – couch, chair, table, TV, DVD player, computer corner.

He wanted to stash the gems inside, somewhere, and tell Jud later. That dude...that dude in the rear...what was his story?

Enforcer? Collector? Or just a relative looking for a handout?

Not quite as brown-skinned as Jud….

Anyway, he waited. He was a little nervous. He heard voices again. The slam of a door. He waited more.

Nothing. He wanted to give it up, go upstairs.

"Jud!" he yelled. Nothing.

He looked but didn't see the other guy come around, or pass by, to the street, so maybe he'd taken the alley. Maybe about anything.

And then Jud appeared, *with the other guy*, from a hallway to the side of the living room. In that doorway, Jud stood smiling, the short dude behind him.

"Got the stuff?" Jud's voice sounded strained. Stanley wasn't sure what to say, so said weakly, "Within reach."

"Fred here wants them," Jud managed to say, still in a strained manner. He jerked his head back in the short guy's direction, and stepped further inside the living room.

"And so? Does that mean he gets them?" Stanley asked, not liking this.

Jud hesitated a split-second. "Yes."

"I can have them here in two minutes, but – you, who are you?"

Fred glared. "An associate."

"So...tell me what you want, precisely."

"Jewels, my friend."

"To pay a debt? To pay off a debt?"

Fred was silent, so Stanley, boldly, continued, "I feel like you are forcing this. Strong-arming Jud."

Fred laughed, mechanically. "Explain it." He prodded Jud with his finger.

"Uh...we were in business but the deal collapsed. The stones were like a deposit Fred made. And it's reckoning time."

"Odd term. All of this is odd, but I don't seem to have any choice, do I?" Stanley pulled the important pack of stones from his back pocket. He dug a finger in. He got one out, he put it in his front pocket, hoping it was a diamond. He smiled at Fred, "My fee. This is not fun, to be a middle man." He tossed the packet across the room, to Fred, and turned to walk out the door. He tried to be casual as he heard Fred catch the packet.

Over? After he shut the door, Jud reproached his companion, "Didn't need to be so stern, fellow. That guy was wanting to comply. He just didn't like the looks of it, or, I think, your manner."

"No sweat," was the reply.

Upstairs, Stanley breathed more easily. He wondered, though, should he have taken the jewel? Perhaps it was "hot," no matter those assurances Jud had given. Funny, however, neither of them had batted an eye when he took it.

A ruby, it was, he guessed, as he pulled it from his pocket. Sparkling red, and fairly large...worth...?

Easy enough to find out – go into a store which sells such items – and rings and necklaces, of course. A risk? If stolen, would a store owner be on the "lookout" for a single gem? Possibly, but not very likely.

And the ex-girlfriend – what happened to her? Did Fred and Jud plan on giving them to her?

He shadow-boxed and drank a glassful of water, still wondering, was it over? And then he lay down on his bed. He also began to wonder...had they "done away" with the ex-girlfriend? He needed to speak with Jud, but not so soon after that event downstairs. A few days, perhaps.

Later, Stanley rose and had a cup of coffee and wrote in his mystery novel. It was coming together nicely.

Jud showed up the next day. He was flushed and desperate-looking.

"Help me," he said, "Just tell her I don't have them, will you?"

Before Stanley could say "Huh?" a tall, nicely dressed black woman mounted the stairs. She turned her opaque eyes on Jud. "You pissant."

"Darling, he can tell you."

She looked at Stanley. "Okay, tell me."

"I guess you mean about the, uh, twelve items?"

"Right. Those. Wait – you say twelve?"

Stanley laughed to cover his embarrassment. "I took one as payment."

"Okay, maybe that's all right, but he says you gave them to my boyfriend."

"I suppose I did. Fred?"

"Yes, well, why?"

"Uh," Stanley stammered, "he, Jud, said to. That was wrong?"

She smacked Jud on his arm. "No, but, Fred is unpredictable."

"Yeah," Stanley responded. "Be that as it may, they were turned over to Fred, so *he*," pointing to Jud, "doesn't have 'em." Unless he does, Stanley thought, but didn't say it.

"My name is Hanah," she added, as nice as you please. "Those stones came into my hands and Jud talked me into – well, never mind. Thank you." She spun around and went down the stairs.

"Whew," Jud breathed. He put his hand to Stanley's shoulder. He smiled. "It'll be all right. Thanks."

Later, the sparkling red gem (it was a ruby, indeed) fetched three thousand at a jewelers', Frankfurt Jewelry in Woodland Hills. Stanley even told the truth – it was given to him for a service he "rendered." The old man behind the counter only nodded vaguely and wrote a check. He seemed pleased, no doubt having made a good deal, in his mind.

So, a little work on his car – a tune-up, a new fuel filter, a power-steering flush, to start with. And a new shirt, a new pair of Levis, a few pairs of socks...he was happy to have the extra money – a godsend.

The rewrite of his novel was nearly finished. He needed someone to type it up for him, in the proper format, and he'd self-publish it on Amazon.

He drank beer, watched the news, wondered what the hell was going on. Such times! Division in Congress like never before. Investigators, accusations, denials, counter-claims, references to Watergate, fake news claims, etc., etc. And Bob Woodward bringing a new book out titled *Fear*. Had he uncovered another "Deep Throat"? What did the title mean? Stanley didn't particularly feel any fear, just distress. That seemed the suitable emotion, considering the state of things.

A night's rest and Stanley felt less weak. "By God, thank God, this strange Epstein-Barr stuff is for sure dissipating," he convinced himself.

A day like previous days, but for his improving physical condition, producing a more positive mental outlook and a fuller sense of his abilities – including going to the gym soon. ("Presently," as some might word it?) He felt, too, the weird world of political affairs may have a proper, realistic, and still more perfect "change" coming, mightn't it? He believed so. "More perfect Union," the famous document says, doesn't it? Couldn't such a predictive ideal be extended to encompass the entire world? But no, Stanley actually didn't believe that. The world was loaded with sinners – only Christ's triumphant return would change it.

He ate breakfast at Denny's.

Tomorrow, he decided, he would pack his gym bag and go on over there to that gym and pay dues and change into shorts and wrap his hands and loosen up and punch around in front of the mirror – there was one there, wasn't there? – and put on bag gloves, and pick out a bag to hit and pretend he was a young man and have a nice fine workout. Yes, that's what he'd do.

This day, he walked from the coffee shop in the sunshine, rejoicing, feeling stronger, thanking God, recalling how he used to feel when he was an active boxer.

Stanley hoped there weren't going to be any more unpleasant adventures, even if they turned out okay thanks to his guardian angel or more specifically, to God, because actually, he was rather tired of adventure. He wished to carry on as a normal human being, even though obliquely.

Printed in Great Britain
by Amazon